PRAISE FOR *LI*

I read *Liberty Landing* and greatly admire Gail Vida Hamburg's prose and literary savvy. Her writing, in historical terms, follows a new line of 21st century Asian American writing and addresses globalization, or more specifically, the nuances of globality. Literary realist writers in this tradition include Amitav Ghosh, Gish Jen and Bharati Muhkherjee.

Hamburg is marching in the tradition of writers who offer a new vision, but who never stray far from literary realism, and in so doing, she reinforces a literary style that is accessible to many, while simultaneously weaving deeper philosophical and intellectual questions within the narrative.

She extols an American ideal that is rooted in an understanding of history and the turmoil of movement and migration. This work presents a vision that is both familiar to many, yet cleverly speaks to the chaos of the maligned and mythic American dream.

Her deft handling of difference, diversity, and a polycultural society show the grace and certainty of a writer who is crafting a specific vision and philosophy. This is writing that will move people to feel, but writing that also merges ideas and offers a future vision, even as it bears witness to the present.

Stephanie Han,

Swimming in Hong Kong

Also by Gail Vida Hamburg

The Edge of the World

Liberty Landing

Gail Vida Hamburg

This book is a work of fiction. Names, characters, settings and incidents are either the product of the author's imagination or used fictitiously. Any resemblance to actual events, settings or persons, living or dead, is entirely coincidental.

Other authors' quotes, and the books or articles they appear in, are cited and promoted in the acknowledgments section at the end of the book.

Printed in the United States of America

Published by Miráre Press, Boston, MA

978-0-9798275-5-6

First Edition 2018

For more information, please contact Miráre Press at
ariapr@sbcglobal.net

Gail Vida Hamburg

Gail Vida Hamburg is an award-winning American journalist, author, and museum storyist. She is the author of *The Edge of the World* (Mirare Press, 2007), a novel about the impact of American foreign policy on individual lives. A nominee for the 2008 James Fenimore Cooper Prize, it is a frequent text in undergraduate post-colonial studies, war studies, and creative writing programs. Born in Malaysia, she spent her teens and twenties in England before migrating to the United States. She holds a Master of Fine Arts in Literature and Creative Writing from Bennington Writers Seminars at Bennington College, Vermont. *Liberty Landing*, the first volume in her trilogy about the American Experience, is her love letter to the great American Experiment.

She lives in Chicago—the setting for *Liberty Landing*, a finalist for the 2016 PEN/Bellwether Prize for Socially Engaged Fiction.

For Mummy, Papa, Valliette and Jacob—in memory.

And for my son, Joshua Hamburg

& my brothers, Rodrigo Silva and Tom Silva

Gail Vida Hamburg's *Liberty Landing*

"... America is a nation not of immigrants but of refugees. Trauma, displacement and fanatical hope have marked all new Americans from the occupants of the Mayflower through every subsequent group who came to these shores, or who were brought here by force. This is the unspoken and sometimes unacknowledged fear and fact of being American. These unkind ghosts of our pasts, these specters of previous selves and previous nations that will not be dismissed so easily, always attend our daily negotiations around identity. They cause a torment that can turn us violent, hateful and self-destructive, and the uneasy grace we win is in itself a remarkable thing. The longer our stay in the United States, the fainter the ghosts get, until they are not much more than a vague unsettled feeling that itself causes even more confusion."

Chris Abani
Vu Tran's Dragonfish,
New York Times

"... a thread of a story
stitches together
a wound."

Ibtisam Barakat
Tasting the Sky

Author's Note

The words of John Dos Passos, S. Yizhar, Mahmoud Darwish, Edward Said, Kurt Vonnegut, Soren Kierkegaard, Graham Greene, Ron Chernow, and Founding Father Alexander Hamilton captured my imagination during the writing of this book, providing navigation, instruction, inspiration, and consolation at key moments. I've been moved to quote some of their lapidary sentences in this novel, and ardently promote their luminous writings.

Gail Vida Hamburg

Chicago, December 2017

Table of Contents

Chapter 1

NEO-AMERICAN

Gabe Khoury strode into the private elevator that connected his bi-level residence on the 28th and 29th floors of IBI Worldwide, his business headquartered on Azyl Square, to his office on the 27th. He held a cellphone, a blue suit jacket folded over that arm. Knuckling a button on the control panel, he touched the spread of his collar, stroked the hollows of his cheeks with a pincer grip. Black haired, dark eyed, sand skinned, he didn't quite reach six feet, but he owned his space with a taut physicality.

IBI, Inch by Inch, was a hustler's comeuppance. Its food division wholesaled all manner of groceries—staples to upscale ethnic, humane Halal to kind Kosher, goat to ostrich meat—to brokers and retail chains across North America. Its lifestyle division distributed apparel and top line electronics; its health division sold experimental health supplements and regenerative cosmetics from Korea and Japan.

Over the previous decade, Gabe turned bullish on real estate. Unlike buyers looking for quick 3x and 4x return, he didn't flip. He bought to hold. IBI owned a third of the commercial and housing stock in Azyl Park.

Three years earlier, on the eve of his thirty-fifth birthday, Gabe signed a deal with Pequod Corporation, the ubiquitous global cafe chain, to be sole supplier for its new "Luxe " coffee menu. At $4000 a kilogram, the wet-hulled Irena Puella beans expelled by Asian fairy blue birds, velvety with a long chocolate and raspberry finish, put him on the cover of Inc. and Businessweek.

Gabe was nineteen, splintered, raging, illegal, when a bus disgorged him in Azyl Park. The town was thirty minutes north of the Midwestern city. Population 97,000, Latitude 42° North, Longitude 87° West. *In the heartland, on a slice of the continent, in a set of laws, in the speech of a people.* Its eastern edges hugged a great lake. It lay between Roseland, a working class village of second and third generation Catholics—Irish, Italian, Polish, Lebanese; and Idyllwild, a leafy, bucolic northern suburb. Azyl Square extended ten blocks along Shoreland Drive, the busy artery that split from Route 66, traced the curve of the lake, sliced through the Square, and tapered into a two-lane road leading to Idyllwild and American Pastoral.

Gabe stepped through a gap in the ridge of hoar frost lining the outer edges of the sidewalk. The strip was only slightly higher than the newer snowfall that blanketed the pavement. The low tread sneakers he was wearing were wrong for the weather. Granules of snow leaked through the eyelets and tongue and seeped through the thin nylon socks his mother had pulled over his feet just days before, as she knelt in front of him. Gabe kicked his feet roughly to loosen her grip, kicked her in the stomach. "*Tawaquf ean dhlk.* Stop it," he scolded. His mother wailed.

His aunt, Zulima, gripped her by the shoulders and urged her to her feet. "This is his chance. Bless him and let him go." And then, harshly, "Let him go. Stop it!"

Gabe adjusted the duffle bag on his shoulder, shifting the overstuffed pouch diagonally across his back to redistribute its weight. He walked fast to avoid sinking into the snow. His breath condensed in front of him into misty fog. His feet felt heavy like frozen meat, numb in the arches and heels. His toes burned with pain each time they pressed the ground. He felt he had been cold forever. He felt plane wrecked, lost, vulnerable, incomprehensible even to himself. Don't die here, he muttered as he buried his chin into the collar of his parka. Not a petition to God—don't let me die here—but a command, an order to himself. The words seeded into a cloud in front of him, into an embodied intention.

The Square was a densely packed mix of restaurants, grocery stores, butcher shops with Halal and Kosher emblems on windows, beauty and nail salons, clothing stores, a hammam, a hookah bar, immigration lawyers, and realtors. Mehta & Sons sold groceries from asafetida to zatar, and dosa makers to tortilla warmers. Whole World Style traded budget clothing and knock off designer goods—Levy Jeans, Lewie Wooten bags, Tuffany watches—that recent immigrants purchased for themselves, or to send home to relatives to signal their prosperity. Globe Silk Emporium, "purveyor of luxury looms and precious gems," also supplied uniforms to the local cricket and bicycle polo clubs. Acres of Diamonds sold furniture on hire purchase to new arrivals with nesting instincts but no credit or FICO scores; and prayer beads, statues of gods, and electronic hadiths to bolster their faith. Asian Nights Video trumpeted the arrival of the latest releases in pink and blue chalk on its windows: Finally here! Khabi Khushi Kabhie Gham!!; Just arrived in DVD! Season of Guavas; All Waiting Is Rewarded, Just In!! Chala Murari Hero Banne. A *souk*, Gabe thought.

The Square had far too many restaurants—eateries ranging from two-table dives to restaurants with pink napkin swans on plates. Many were last ditch attempts at solvency by immigrants who had failed at everything else. The owners could be easily identified by the stricken look on their faces, a controlled hysteria in the set of the mouth, eyes puffy with worry, as they gazed at empty tables, counted their wait staff of illegal Mexicans whom they loved like family, tallied pedestrians on the busy sidewalks, calculated how to keep the lights on, and tried to divine lottery numbers from 1 to 52 to wager on God while cursing him. *Tamē kādava dēva chō, Ti sibog blata, Du mi ts'yekh astvats*. You're a mud god, God, you bastard.

Gabe ducked into Acres of Diamonds to escape the bitter cold. A saleswoman attending to a customer looked at him. Handsome boy, ugly clothes, no kind of style—refugee, she decided. The diamond stud in her nose flashed. He raised a hand in acknowledgment and scanned the shop floor for a chair. If he could just sit down in a corner and peel off the sneakers and socks to rub his feet and thaw them. He walked slowly, striking the pose of a shopper with more capital than the dirt on his neck and the stink on his breath. He brushed his hand against furniture and checked price tags as he scoped the peripheries of the room for a chair, a stool, an ottoman. A four-poster king bed dominated the right side of the back wall, centered against the corner joint. A fold of white organza dropped from a canopy, parting like a bridal veil. Four layers of pillows in shades of white, some embroidered, some shiny, some twilled, some pebbly, crowned the bed. A gold damask panel trimmed a lustrous white quilt. The dark wood of the four posts gleamed with oil, the finials of each post, a winged *deva*. It was the most beautiful thing Gabe had ever seen in his life. He circled the bed clockwise and in reverse. A bed to take a good—*khallas*, he rebuked himself, the syllables hollow. *Takhlus minh.* Get over it. He sat down on the bed, his knees angled towards the headboard, and studied the ornate carvings on the poster. He eased his feet out of the sneakers, using the toe boxes of each like shoe horns. He bent down and tore the socks off his feet, wincing from the pain.

The saleswoman drew near; Gabe heard the swish of her embroidered sari as she walked towards the bed.

"You understand first class quality." She wrapped an arm around the post opposite Gabe. "The four posters are temple carvings from the marriage of Shiva and Parvathi. All the divinities and celestial beings are in them. Vishnu and Lakshmi are on the one near you. Brahma is here officiating the wedding," she traced a finger over an engraving on the post near her. "You should buy it."

Gabe pressed the sole of one foot over the slope of the other, then a heel across toes. Nothing helped. "I need other things first," Gabe said, looking at the diamond in her nose.

"So why are you sitting on my bed, you?" She set her hands on her hips. "What the hell, boy?"

"I'm sorry." He wanted to transport himself back to where he'd left the other half of his body, the other sagittal and coronal planes that his mother was likely clutching still. It had to be the right half of his body he'd left behind, since he could feel the petrified stone beating in his chest. "Very sorry," Gabe rose from the bed, yelped, and sat down again.

Lakshmi circled the bed. "What's wrong with you?"

"My feet," he said. He wanted to cry but inhaled to plug his tear ducts with his will.

"Lift them up so I can see."

Gabe looked at his feet but didn't move.

"Do I look like I have time to waste, you?" Lakshmi said, knowing full well she had all the time in the world to waste since she expected no customers that day on account of the weather.

Gabe clutched a foot by the ankle and lifted it. Lakshmi squinted and twitched her mouth as Gabe lifted the other foot.

"*Are baap re*. Frostbite *yaar*," she made some clucking sounds, ish, chee, tsk, that seemed oddly familiar, like the sounds his mother and aunts made when they were trying to solve problems.

Lakshmi walked to the counter and returned with a brown sandwich bag. “I’m thinking cold dosha needs hot for balance.” She fished out a banana, peeled it, and gave him the fruit.

“What am I to do with it?”

“Eat it, stupid.”

She stooped down, cuffed her hand around his left ankle and lifted it. “You’ll lose your toes if you don’t take care of it,” she said, as she brushed the banana peel against the pads of his toes. “This will defrost them.”

He gritted his teeth from her touch. His mother was everywhere.

“I’ll warm some oil with cayenne, turmeric, ginger. Then we’ll wrap your legs in plastic.” “Sleep on the bed, you’ll be comfortable.” She’d boot him out the door if he had the temerity to accept the bed, help him if he declined.

“I’ll use that one,” he pointed at a black futon, most of it hidden behind a row of gray metal filing cabinets. “I’ll leave in a few days,” he walked towards it. By accepting her charity on his terms, he drew a green line and an unbreachable zone of privacy around him. “I need a job. I’ll look tomorrow.”

“Then you will buy this bed?” she searched his face.

“Yes.” Yes, he said to himself.

“I can help you, bhai. I know all the merchants. Best day to interview is Tuesday, day after tomorrow, when things are slow. Until then, take rest.”

Gabe’s first interview on the Square was at Globe Silk Emporium. Tarun Advani, the owner, was looking for someone to manage his luxury line of gemstones and textiles—*Tarun’s Splendor Collection*.

"Lakshmi sent him," a sales clerk ushered Gabe into Mr. Advani's office.

"Yes, yes, I know all that," Mr. Advani waved the clerk away.

Gabe held the job classifieds page from the neighborhood weekly in one hand, the tabloid shrunk to a trifold, five jobs circled with a red marker after Lakshmi had filtered out the thugs: Don't go there, he's a cheater. That guy, he will sell his own mother. If you see a snake and that fellow, shoot him first. That bastard owes me money.

Gabe did not take the seat Mr. Advani offered him, choosing instead to stand by the door. Best to be upfront. "I don't have a green card."

No green card was a big problem. In Gabe's favor, he looked strong enough to lift and haul the shipping boxes and pallets that arrived at the store daily. "Why should I hire you?"

"I learn fast. I'll do what you need. I'm honest." He tapped the newspaper against his thigh keeping four four time.

Mr. Advani drummed his desk with his nails at a galloping tempo. "Can you lift seventy five pounds?"

"I lift double that without sweating."

Mr. Advani didn't want to lose Gabe to other merchants on the Square who would gladly pay him minimum wage. "I'll pay you eight dollars an hour in cash. I'll try you out month to month. If you're still here in six months I'll give you more."

"I'm worth fifteen. And I need a month upfront." He needed that number to get away from Lakshmi and into a sublet.

"You're illegal." Very arrogant for someone with no papers, needs to learn humility, Mr. Advani thought.

"I need to make that number." Gabe placed a hand on the door knob and stared at swatches of fabrics pinned to a corkboard behind Mr. Advani.

"Fair enough." Mr. Advani stood up. "Come with me." Gabe followed Mr. Advani out of his office to the shop floor. A dozen salesmen and women stood behind showcases, attending to customers. Some looked at him with curiosity. A couple smiled.

"You don't need to mind any of their business," Mr. Advani said as he led Gabe to the storeroom.

"Something wrong with you," Mr. Advani's sister, one of the salespeople, shouted across the room in Sindhi. "You know nothing about him. He'll rob you blind." Mr. Advani pinched two fingers across his lips and turned an imaginary key. Zip it. Lock it.

"Your main job is to take care of my collection," Mr. Advani told Gabe. "Nobody sells it but my good self. After I decide that a customer is worthy to buy from my line, I will instruct you over walkie-talkie to bring items from the vault. You will kindly write down my requests on a requisition form and bring the items with the form to the parlor in the back office. You will await further instructions from me just outside the door. You will also be in charge of shipping and receiving for the line. You follow?"

Gabe broke the news to Lakshmi while she was ringing up a customer at the cash register. He didn't want a scene.

"Which one?" she said, noting that he had his bag over his shoulder.

"Globe Silk."

"Advani is a good guy."

He lifted a hand, then dropped it. He didn't know the right thing to say. He dipped his chin and nodded.

"Come back for the bed," she said, and turned back to her customer.

Each morning as Gabe entered the store, Mr. Advani looked up from his morning ritual of tea by the front cash register. Lucky boy, another day free, one step ahead of ICE and deportation. He'd acknowledge Gabe and check his watch. Even before Gabe shed his coat or reached the counter, Mr. Advani would start reeling off instructions about incoming shipments, outgoing special orders, replenishments, and other tasks to be completed that day. The directives were succinct and synoptic. Uncertain in English in those days, Gabe latched onto the jargon: cut ins, cycle counts, gondola, J hook, NOP, OOS, reorder point, reverse logistics, SOQ, shipping manifest, surge, Telzon. Words stripped of emotion, rich with executive efficiency. Mr. Advani always reverted to Sindhi to conclude his morning encounters with Gabe. *Theek Aahe*—okay.

Gabe would walk past the store's employees and Mr. Advani's sister already stationed behind their counters, men in white dress shirts and black trousers, women in salwars and saris, to the storeroom in the rear. Only he and Mr. Advani had the four-digit code for the vault's electronic deadbolt.

Steel shelves, rising from the floor and scraping the rim of the popcorn ceiling, lined all four walls of the windowless room. And on the shelves, fabrics and textiles of every feel, color, and hue. Rolls of vicuna spun with diamond fragments, cashmere woven with chinchilla, and bolts of mulberry, muga, and spider silks stood at vertical attention on the shelves, each roll, bolt, and bale, alphanumeric tagged. In the center of the room, a glass showcase held open squares and rectangles of antique laces and embroidered silk floss too delicate to fold.

The human eye can discern ten million colors, a thousand variations of light and dark, a hundred levels of red, green, yellow and blue. Neon and fluorescent fabrics made Gabe's eyes teary; pink and lemon made him nauseous, green, red, black and white made his heart ache.

Next to the showcase, a seven-foot tall safe with a combination lock held the store's inventory of precious gems. A trove of Alexandrite, Fire Opal, Jadeite, Musgravite, Red Beryl, Serendibite, and Taaffeite sat in drawers, each stone resting in its own cushioned compartment. Gabe wore clean nitrile gloves before handling the stones. The tenderness and indifference they demanded made him afraid. Alexandrite cost $12,000 a carat, Jadeite, $20,000 a carat. The eggs he routinely held in his hands had the power to alter his life, the lives of his family. His father would have pocketed a few, maybe even swallowed a couple to evacuate later, wash clean, and fence. He could take one the size of a sparrow's egg and disappear; he'd be set for life. But he hated himself when he thought of his father. I am not him. He is not me.

Working in the vault quelled the tempest inside him. The mundane, mechanical nature of the work, unboxing, boxing, unfolding, folding, retrieving, storing, subdued him, lulled him, appeased him into a state of ineludible acceptance. You can get over anything. You can get over everything. Between nine and ten in the morning, when there were few shoppers on the Square and Globe Silk was quiet, he spent his time tearing open corrugated shipping boxes that had arrived, and preparing the contents for storage. He kept the fabrics in their original packaging or repackaged them, before labeling, coding, cataloging, and arranging them on the shelves. He lifted gems from their bubble wraps, examined each one for flaws and scratches, placed them in individual sheer silk habotai pouches, and organized them in the drawer compartments in the jewel safe. During the course of a day, Gabe hardly spoke at all. The vault was his safe haven. There, he had control over everything. He found he could expand and contract time, control its tempo and pace and duration. If he disregarded the clock, dismissed his conscious self, and surrendered awareness, he could dive into a day and swim through it, cut and knife through seconds and minutes, butterfly, backstroke, breaststroke, and glide through the hours. He didn't have to think of the past or the future, just float. You can get over anything. You can get over everything.

Gabe's direct engagement with people was limited to conversations with Mr. Advani and instructions he received over the intercom and 2-way radio throughout the day. Bring me Angora blue and Arrasene ruby, Baldachin and Cambresine in mikado and xanadu, Charmuese and Matelasse in amaranth and Falu in orchid. Mr. Advani relayed his requests for gems in five digit numeral codes. Gabe was meticulous about transcribing the codes with accuracy. After a month, he knew the codes fluently: 27758—Musgravite, 13314—Serendibite, 33258—Alexandrite. Gabe would place the requested items in a cart and roll it to the shop floor. He'd make a loop around the counter and steer the cart to the parlor in the back office. He'd set the merchandise in front of Mr. Advani and return to stand at the door, half his body in the back office, the other half on the shop floor. He didn't engage with customers; his job was to blend into the woodwork and make himself invisible until he was spoken to. If he had to fetch more merchandise, he'd return to the vault. If he didn't, he'd still his body to watch the activity on the sales floor. He'd hear American English, broken English, Sindhi, Hindi, and other languages he couldn't identify. Multicultural trading was a contact sport. Though all prices were fixed, customers still tried to bargain and make a deal. "I'll pay you cash less the tax." The staff would have none of it. "You want to put us in jail?"

One evening just before closing, Gabe picked up a tray of gems from Mr. Advani's desk to return to the vault. He checked the gems in the slots against the requisition form. A postcard lying on Mr. Advani's desk caught Gabe's attention. It was not the size of an ordinary postcard, it was larger than a book. Everything was jumbo in this place he was now a part of—postcards, cars, food portions, houses, people. The handwriting seemed familiar to Gabe; though written in English, it retained the ornamental flourishes of Arabic script. A Sindhi changes his colors according to the lay of the land, it read.

Mr. Advani was at the front door bidding farewell to a wealthy customer who had bought a two carat Red Beryl. He locked the door, flipped the "Open" sign, and walked towards the back office. It would take him two hours to close out his register, tally the sales, reconcile the amounts from the other ten cash registers in the shop, and reset them with the required starting floats. If there were shortfalls in any of the floor registers, he would record them and submit a request for reimbursement from the responsible cashier who had overseen the register. Usually, the discrepancies never amounted to more than a dollar. But still, Mr. Advani insisted on being reimbursed.

"You like it?" Mr. Advani asked Gabe, as he rotated a dimmer switch on the wall to brighten the lights in the room. He proceeded to his desk and adjusted the articulated arm of a task light.

Gabe shrugged, embarrassed to have been caught reading private mail.

"My brother in the jungle sent it."

"Jungle?" Gabe stared at Mr. Advani blankly.

Mr. Advani reached for the card, turned it over, and tapped the image—a verdant rainforest, one electric blue Nosy Be panther chameleon on a horizontal bark in the foreground. "Amazon rainforest. He sells duty-free electronics on the border of Brazil and Bolivia. Anywhere in the world, you'll find us Sindhis selling."

"Where you come from?" Gabe held the gem tray with one hand, its base slotted at his hip.

"Sindh. We lost it in 1947 after Partition gave it to Pakistan."

"You get it back?" Gabe picked up the postcard. The color of the lizard reminded him of the Fire Opal, iridescent blue with glimpses of magenta and gold.

"No." Mr. Advani said.

"You're still fighting." Gabe understood long wars.

Mr. Advani shook his head. "We chose not to fight. We chose to carry our homes and our country on our backs. Like turtles."

"That's crazy." The men he knew would die for country or go mad. Death or Insanity. Insanity or Death. The primal rage of the dispossessed to claim what was rightfully theirs was an either or proposition.

"We believed we were enterprising enough to rebuild anywhere. Make home anywhere."

"Makes no sense," Gabe said.

"It will one day. Now, kindly collect and bring me all the cash tills."

A year later, after a busy week running in and out of the vault for Diwali shoppers, Gabe lingered in front of Mr. Advani's counter on the shop floor. Mr. Advani stood behind the glass showcase, a phone clamped in the crook of his neck as he completed an order form. Yes I can, he said, and placed the receiver in its cradle. "Tokhe chha khape?" he asked Gabe.

Gabe placed his walkie talkie on the counter. "It needs batteries."

Mr. Advani found it extraordinary that Gabe absorbed language not his own and always guessed the right response "So get them." He looked down to complete the tax and shipping amounts on the form.

"I want to leave here and try something else." He had been rehearsing the conversation in his head for weeks. He was losing his mind in the vault, from the riot of colors, from the colors as words and stones as numbers. At night, when Gabe let himself into the studio he'd sublet from Vijay, a waiter who decided to change lanes and become a long haul truck driver, he was grateful for the blank white walls that relieved retina burn like eye wash. In every iteration of his rehearsed speech, Mr. Advani had persuaded him to postpone his decision. But he was restless. Vijay was driving through time zones, moving strawberries from California to New York and Mexican avocados from Texas to Maine, clocking five hundred miles and more on the road each day, and he was stuck in a box, all day every day. It's not that he lusted for movement, he just wanted to break out of those four walls, get more. He sensed opportunity.

"You're not ready, son," Mr. Advani ran a pen under the final tally on the sheet and underlined the number twice. He didn't want to lose Gabe. He had so much to teach him still.

Gabe wanted to hurl the walkie talkie against the mirror behind Mr. Advani. Instead, he gripped its center and spun it like a top. "When will I be ready?"

"Trust me, Gabe. Be patient," Mr. Advani reached for the device.

"I don't owe you anything." Gabe knew he was being rude and possibly ungrateful, but he couldn't bear another day in the vault.

Surprised and stung by the rebuke, Mr. Advani fumbled with the device to open the battery compartment."*Theek aahe, theek aahe.* Then go." When Gabe didn't move, he said. "Go. What are you waiting for?"

Rejecting fidelity to a single employer, Gabe hired himself out as a freelance jack-of-all-trades to other merchants on the Square. He was their courier, driver, mover, runner, and bodyguard. They handed him manila envelopes and bulging mail pouches with precise instructions. Give it only to Shan. Don't ask for a signature. He cleared shipments of imported goods through customs and delivered them to various drop off points. He helped load black money, under-the-table counted stacks, into safe rooms and modular vaults in industrial park offices in the outer boroughs. He drove merchants who had never learned to drive to their meetings and dalliances.

Bring a baseball bat. Wait fifteen minutes and honk. It will be quick and dirty. She's a slut.

He managed their businesses and served as their witness and protector. When accompanying the merchants to meetings, he hung back like a shadow, never drawing attention to himself, but alert to run interference if the situation warranted it. Though he served dozens of merchants on the Square on contract, many competing against each other, he never divulged confidences or traded information.

"So what is that money hungry bastard up to these days?" one would ask about another.

"What's that gangster banking on now?"

Gabe would cast an impenetrable look at the enquirer. Neutral, opaque, anodyne. Gabe was a walking non-disclosure agreement. The merchants grew to value his discretion, his reserve, his spurning of fraternity, his rejection of communal inclinations. They trusted him with combinations to their safes and numbers to their bank accounts, their secrets and their swindles, their trysts and their transactions. He never stole from them. In return, they surprised him with frequent bonuses.

A year later, Gabe gave notice to his steady clients that he was retracting his services.

"But why Gabe?" asked Mr. Mehta of Mehta & Sons—a state-certified denial of his five daughters and lack of sons. He stepped down from his perch near the entrance of the store—a standing desk stationed on a dais that elevated him three feet off the ground. The high post afforded Mr. Mehta an aerial view of the establishment, allowing him to offer his customers assistance, navigation, aphorisms, and spun philosophies. On the left. Over there. Money in the hand is honey in the lap. Sons make a millionaire.

"All crackpot nonsenses," he'd comment as he watched CNN on a small TV suspended from a wall mount near his desk. Mr. Mehta had a peculiar relationship with the English language. In his mouth, it was a twice born language. He made it do what he wanted it to do. He reinvented it. Nonsenses was not mere nonsense, it was a scaled up mega level of balderdash, baloney, bilge. He held on with white-knuckled ferocity to rules of grammar. To teenagers loafing inside his store with more hair gel than money, he yelled, "Move your asses." He insisted on plurality when it came to more than one ass.

Mr. Mehta felt a special obligation to flatter women who entered his store. The plainer the woman, the harder he worked, the more embroidered his compliments. You are a vision, my God. Don't run away from me. In the next life. As they strolled through the aisles for papads and pickles and whatever, he sang his favorite song from *Fanaa* in a yearning falsetto. *Mere haath mein tera haath ho, saari jannatein mere saath ho, tu jo paas ho phir kya yeh jahaan, tere pyaar mein ho jaayuun fanaa.* When my hand is in yours, all of paradise is mine, when you're with me what use have I for the world? May your love annihilate me.

By offering himself in this way, he saw himself no longer as rotund, stocky, short, and bald, but as the Bollywood prince of his fantasy. Arjun Rampal had nothing on him. But this wasn't merely about his needs. He viewed his profuse compliments, so intoxicating to the recipients, as his *dharma*. They were his virtuous duty to ensure the natural, moral, and sacrificial equilibrium of the world. A mighty fine fellow who is upholding the Rta, I am.

You're my Aamir Khan, more than one woman whispered as she paid for her purchases. And you're my Kajol, he'd say, one hand over his heart, the other over his big belly. The women never shopped anywhere else.

When he wasn't attending to his customers, Mr. Mehta plotted mind maps and Venn diagrams in his head on all the ways he would encourage each of his daughters to elope. Money in the hand is honey in the lap. A thousand dollars just to rent a white horse from a farmer in Wisconsin for baraat procession. *Are baap re*! Dowry, smowry! Not one dime.

"But Gabe why?" he asked, as if rearranging the words in the question would yield a different answer. Only a year and already talking about departure. He didn't understand Gabe at all, at all. A damn botheration!

Gabe, his back to Mr. Mehta, looked up at the metal shelves that reached the ceiling and hemmed the back wall of the store. He turned around to examine a new shipment of small appliances stacked in twin towers on the counter, and swept a gaze over the span of shelves. He checked the model numbers of the boxes and looked up at a grid of shelves. His cross-referenced filing and index system was a meticulous enterprise—one hundred and fifty thousand dollars of SKUs organized, color-coded, and catalogued on the shelves, documented on an electronic spreadsheet, and stored on an online portal.

"Have I not treated you like my own?" Mr. Mehta had grown fond of the boy. He'd even called him *Beta* once. But Gabe rejected the endearment; he was nobody's son. "Gabe will do thanks."

"Why now? Why the hurry?" Mr. Mehta liked having him around. Gabe's quietude was a pleasant respite from his own compulsive verbosity.

"It's the right time." Gabe walked to the edge of the room to a ladder anchored on metal tracks. He slid it in front of a grid dedicated to mid-priced electronics.

"My wife and I have big plans for you," Mr. Mehta said to Gabe's back. Gabe didn't turn round.

At least acknowledge me when I'm talking to you, Mr. Mehta wanted to say but bit his tongue. He regretted that he hadn't corrected Gabe's habit of looking away when he was being spoken to, of not responding when he was being addressed, earlier in their relationship. There'd been plenty of opportunities to counsel him on manners and etiquette. But Gabe had been industrious and indispensable, formal but never rude, and Mr. Mehta hadn't wished to offend him over what he'd then considered to be small lapses in courtesy. "We agreed on giving you a pick of our daughters. Each can please you in a different way," Mr. Mehta said. What he wouldn't do to get his girls married with no money down.

Gabe worked methodically, carrying several boxes in the sling of his arm as he climbed the ladder to arrange them on the shelves. He behaved like a Brahmin, Mr. Mehta thought. It took something close to arrogance for someone to refuse intimacy offered by a superior. Who the hell did he think he was? But still, no harm trying. "If you want pure sweetness inside and out, Rekha is the one," Mr. Mehta moved towards the counter and spread his arms wide, his inflated stomach jutting over the glass case. "If you want a Bollywood beauty with the IQ of a laddoo, take Mala," he slapped his belly like a drum, tharp, tharp. "The others also have their qualities. Just stay away from Priya, she's a ball buster." Still no response. He watched as Gabe finished the task of sorting and arranging the stock, as he repositioned the ladder, sliding it back to the edge of the room. "If it's a matter of money, I can double your take."

Gabe made a loop around the counter, placed his hands on his hips, and scanned the shelves to verify that the merchandise had been stacked in the right compartments.

"I can triple it in six months even. This will not be an issue."

Gabe turned to face Mr. Mehta. He pulled a ring of keys out of his trouser pocket, twisted several off the chain and handed them to

Mr. Mehta. "You'll be fine," he nodded. "I'm leaving everything in order. Instructions on your desk."

Mr. Mehta's eyes turned dewy. "Just like this you leave me, Gabe?"

"You'll be fine." Gabe looked past Mr. Mehta at the store window, his jaw tightened. People need to learn how to let go. They want too much.

Immigrants are like that, what can you do, Mr. Mehta consoled himself as Gabe walked out of the store. Cold-blooded, capricious, self-centered, self-absorbed, without regard for others.

Gabe tried his luck with several businesses on the Square. First, he took over a video store whose owner had taped a hand scrawled note on the door: "Failed. Fucking off to Alaska. Call landlord." Gabe called the number.

Rae Oberoi had seen Gabe on the Square many times, as they both went about their business. One day, Gabe would be hoisting rolled up carpets over his shoulder to load into a truck for delivery. Another, he'd be opening the back door of a sedan for a merchant like a trained chauffeur, or unloading boxes onto a dolly. Other times, Rae would see Gabe, dressed in a dark suit, climbing into the back of a car with the merchant, somebody else at the wheel. He'd see Gabe sitting alone in fast food joints and diners, flipping the pages of business magazines while eating. That's a human doing, Rae observed.

"How many jobs do you have?" Rae had asked him once as they both stood in line at the bank.

"I have several dozen clients." Gabe filled out a deposit slip, a rolled up magazine serving as a clipboard.

"Why so many?" Gabe reminded Rae nothing of himself.

"You were born to be a royal," Rae's wife, Nila, had once remarked on his lack of ambition. "We're going to have to fix that," she'd said, and pushed him quietly to pursue a career in business. She did it in so subtle a way, his memory of his work was wiped clean of her influence, of her answers posed as questions that led him to his career. Soon he found himself enjoying the intellectual challenge of creating an enterprise. He owned Raj Cabs, a fast growing taxi company with a fleet of seven hundred sedans and vans. The cabs displayed signature grill ornaments of a turbaned head in profile, reminiscent of Air India's Maharajah, and the legend *Ride Like a Royal* emblazoned on signboards perched on the roofs. Nila had kicked his butt.

"I like to keep moving." Gabe said.

"Quit them all and come work for me. It'll be more interesting than anything you're doing now."

"I'm okay on my own thanks." He pulled a cellphone out of his shirt pocket and scrolled messages.

"Call me if you change your mind." There was no wobble in his trajectory. He'll either crash and burn or rise to the top, Rae decided.

"I'm good," Gabe replied.

Rae agreed to let Gabe see out the remainder of the lease. "I'll apply the security deposit to your rent for two months. Give it a shot and if you want to stick with it, I'll give you a deal to renew."

Gabe handed the keys back to Rae after the free rent ran out. "There's no margin in this."

He tried a foreclosed laundromat that gave him a healthy return. He sold it after ninety days because he found counting the daily return in quarters demeaning. He assumed ownership of a struggling carpet store, held a flash sale of *kilims* and remnants that he'd tagged as prayer rugs, and made his money back. He shuttered the store, swore off retail, and turned his attention to wholesale. He found his calling in distribution, in sourcing and moving consumer goods to suppliers and brokers around the world. The business suited his nature. He didn't need to talk to people in any meaningful way. He just had to move product up and down the supply chain. How much do you need? When do you need it? I'll get you a quote. Wire me my money. Where's my money? I need my money. Send me my money.

Chapter 2

ANOTHER DAY

Gabe heard raucous laughter as the elevator doors opened. After years of working in close proximity to his employees in open plan offices on the floors below, he decided after the Pequod deal to remove himself from the clamor and nerve center of his operations. While each of the floors below accommodated fifty people comfortably, only he, Nadia—his personal assistant, and David Cohen—his lead broker, occupied the twenty-seventh. He walked past two public elevators that serviced the building from the basement to the executive wing. The airy loft with cloud white walls and vaulted ceilings was filled with light streaming in through tall windows. A large twisted metal sculpture separated the reception area in the front from Nadia and David's workspace, Gabe's private office, and a row of conference rooms in the back. Nadia and David were at their desks. When Gabe had first asked Nadia to move to the new space, she had demurred. But what about David? What about David? He makes me laugh. And this is relevant to me how? I work better when I'm happy."

"Hey boss, wassup?" David paused a call in mid-dial and replaced the phone on its cradle. He was a soft, doughy man, the only child of needy parents who, instead of moving to a retirement home in the suburbs, had bought the townhouse next to his on the beach side of Anemone Street. His parents were from a long line of centenarians. David believed that he had a better shot of ending up a lonely octogenarian without a family of his own than of being an orphan. He wished them dead every day. He seldom smiled, his face set like number three on the pain measurement scale—between hurts little bit and hurts little more. After he began to go prematurely bald a few years earlier, he settled on a buzz cut that did nothing to harden his cherubic features. He wore a kippah on days he thought there might be a G-d. That day, his head was uncovered.

"I should be asking you. Where are you with the Ridge lease?" Gabe looked over his shoulder at David as he stood in front of Nadia's desk.

"Working on it. I'm checking the capital stack, seeing if the lease is bondable."

"You're taking too long. Get it done." He took a sheaf of mail bound with rubber bands from Nadia.

"I'm working as hard as I can."

"Try thinking harder." Gabe leafed through the envelopes, lifting one with a Par Avion emblem out of the pack to study the back and front.

Even when Gabe was pressuring David, he did it with a light enough touch that had kept the broker in a job he had meant to leave a decade ago. A work environment that was free of drama made dealing with his second career, indentured laborer to narcissistic parents who hollowed him out with their demands, bearable. *Mah nishtanah, ha- laylah ha-zeh, mi-kol ha-leylot.*

"A reporter is looking for you," Nadia held up a message slip. The blue paper matched the hijab that she was wearing, coordinated with dark wash jeans, a mauve and blue top, and purple cowboy boots. A headset snaked from her right ear to her left, its silver-tipped microphone hovering below a cheek.

"I'm done with media for a while. I need to focus," Gabe said, though he didn't know what exactly he needed to focus on. He'd caught the big fish in industries that interested him. His work had settled into a predictable, metrical hum that pulsed and throbbed frequently enough to stave off boredom. He didn't know what his next big project would be, what he should get excited about. But he wouldn't break a sweat.

He would take the measure of things, seek counsel from no one, act decisively, or retreat to live another day. Let the world exhaust itself. He wouldn't get involved. He'd tread lightly and he would take possession. Sindhis had taught him.

"She said it's urgent." Nadia thrust the slip at him.

"I'm not available," Gabe ignored the proffered note and walked towards his office.

"It's Angeline Lalande from WBYN!" Nadia scooted from behind her desk, waving the message slip in the air.

"I don't want to talk to her," he said, a hand on the doorknob.

"She's important! Her book on abolitionists was major." Nadia said. "She's big time." Big, she raised a spread of fingers. B I G.

"I know who she is," Gabe stepped into his office and closed the door behind him.

"Pwwrrr!" Nadia breathed like a horse. "He's so difficult," she complained, spinning around, clicking her boots in a flamenco stomp.

"He's alright," David said.

"I guess." Nadia chewed her lip.

Nadia was serious around David except when he told her jokes. Before Gabe had walked in that morning, David had told her a joke he'd written for a comedy workshop he was taking at the local repertory. The class was a new addition to his weekly schedule of preemptive strikes against his parents' attempts to hijack his evenings. The Thursday class was a relief, after Monday and Wednesday sessions with a Jungian and a Freudian that wrung him out.

"Did you dream, David?" the Jungian began every session.

"I have no dreams. I have dream killers."

"Let's take your mother," the Freudian had said.

"You take her."

His parents didn't know when to stop, and he didn't want to end up in a rubber room, ergo he never missed a session.

"Nadia, want to hear a joke?" David had watched her apply the first of many daily rounds of lip gloss.

"Come here." She pressed her lips together to spread the glaze around and screwed the applicator back into its tube.

"No, you come here," he said, standing up from his desk.

Nadia walked over to a horizontal file cabinet near him, leaned against it, and folded her arms in the manner of reality show judges. David stood with his back towards his desk, a few feet in front of Nadia, his hands in his trouser pockets. He rocked back and forth on the balls of his feet and told her the joke. He nailed the punch line. He was pleased because she was a tough audience.

Nadia flopped back against the wall, her legs ungainly splayed, her head back, her eyes narrow. Her laughter was a raw, wondrous, bawdy thing. It began with a low snicker, broke into a giggle that took off like a winged creature, grew louder into a cracking chortle, and crested with a big roar before it subsided.

She stood up, laughing still, and adjusted her scarf. She pulled a tissue out of her jeans pocket and traced it across the mascara smudges from under her eyes. "You're insane."

"You're making it worse. Give me it." He cupped her jaw and cleaned the smudges with the balled up wipe. He could feel the warm steam of her exhale, the release of a cord of anxiety as she relaxed. He trained his eyes on the smears under her eyes, sweeping a clean tip of tissue under the bottom lashes. "You."

"Masha'Allah," she said, an uncatchable Mona Lisa smile on her lips.

Gabe sat down at his desk and powered up his computer on a side console. He began to open the airmail still in his hand, thought better of it, and slid it under the blotting pad on his desk. Work is always good, he thought. What else was there? It gave his life meaning in a way no relationship could. It was now March and he'd already dated and broken up with nine women since the New Year. Though he liked the anticipation of a new, wanting, yielding body, it was usually accompanied by the recognition that whatever was to be discovered, taken, tasted, was bound to be a disappointment after the first bite. As one of the city's most eligible bachelors, he'd been relieved from the necessity of pursuit. He was the catch. They chased him and if he liked them well enough, he allowed himself to be caught for low-risk, low-ROI interludes that withered quickly. If it was a Friday night when he couldn't face going back to his empty quarters and if he found the woman tolerable, he'd try to end the night at the Dorset Hotel in Idyllwild. He usually regretted the act after he'd finished, when there was an obligation to talk. Several of them had declared "I love you" after sex, to which he could only respond, "Thank you." He had promised them nothing; his conscience was clear. Sometimes, they'd wait for a different response. Hearing none, they'd disappear into the bathroom, and he'd know it was time to get dressed and leave. He never stayed till morning. Some of them would give him a second chance, they'd email or call or text. If he was bored or had no other plans, he'd go on a second date. But the last one had been a mistake.

“You’re my first Arab,” she’d smiled widely. Hair like corn silk, skin of peach confectionery, agile as a contortionist, dim as a 15-watt pygmy bulb.

Gabe rolled off her and flipped onto his back. He stared at the ceiling, waiting for his heart rate to settle, thinking that he should have kept walking when she’d made a pass, instead of stooping to the floor to pick up spare change.

“Hello, where are you?” she propped herself on an elbow and placed an open palm on his chest.

“I ran out of words.” He needed to get the hell out of there. But his heart was thumping against the wall of his chest and he found the idea of getting up somehow beyond his ability.

“Aren’t you Arab?” she nuzzled his neck.

Gabe pushed her away and sprung out of bed. He picked his clothes up from the tufted ottoman at the foot of the bed and dressed quickly.

“What did I do?” she sat up, hugged herself. “What?!” Teary eyed.

He bolted out the door. He didn’t want her cornering him while he waited for the elevator. He pushed open a door to the fire escape. He ran down the stairs two steps at a time. The perforated metal warped to accommodate his weight, creaked from his effort. He was livid with himself for his lack of judgment, for his carelessness.

When he touched ground, he exhaled. Farah! He clenched his fists, dipped a knee, lunged forward. He would outrun the thought.

By ten, Gabe had cleared his email inbox with short replies, five lines or less, crisp declarative statements with no fat on the written body. He found this a way to clarify thinking and direct people. He used single and double arrows and bold font and asterisks to emphasize urgency and highlight important matters. When something was extremely important, he used the subject line, “Orange Alert,” although the TSA had eliminated the color code system after the Bush years. Gabe wrapped up phone calls inside four minutes. He counted on Nadia to interrupt his meetings after eight minutes so that he could wind them down safely in ten.

His business units were managed by division heads he trusted who worked in open plan offices on the floors below him. They reported to his CFO and COO, who reported directly to him. Herschel Weinstein and Henry Wong were two sides of the same coin. Herschel’s father was Jewish and his mother, Chinese; Henry’s father was Chinese and his mother, Jewish.

“We’re very much alike which is why we’re going to get along,” Herschel had said after meeting Henry a dozen years ago.

“Yeah, self-doubt and superiority bred into us in two accents,” Henry agreed.

“Don’t forget the guilt,” Herschel offered.

“Or the gefilte,” Henry said.

Gabe was composing an email to his trade lawyer about a shipment of cancer remission elixirs stuck in Customs, when Nadia poked her head through the door without knocking first. He raised his eyebrows and stared at her. She walked towards him with small steps, at kimono-wearing geisha pace, the phone in her hand extended like an offertory. “Reporter,” she mouthed the word as she pressed the phone into his hand.

Impossible to fire her for insubordination since she kept Gabe organized and running. He was forced to overlook her occasional tendency to go rogue as she held the institutional memory of IBI inside her hijab-wearing head. Nadia backed out of the room with her hands held in a *namaste* followed by a reverent bow, to cover her bases just in case she’d gone too far this time.

Gabe swiveled his chair towards the north-facing wall of steel framed factory windows. Pain in the ass reporters, what a way to make a living, he thought. He stretched his legs, hooked his wingtips to the pulls on a low file credenza, and tilted back in his chair. He could see Azyl Park stretching northward to the town limits before it disappeared and Idyllwild began. Gabe stood up, the phone in his hand, the call still on hold, and walked towards the high range telescope on the far side of the room near the printer. His designer had extolled its virtues: only one of four cast in Florence to mark the fourth centennial of Galileo's skygazing, a statement piece that complemented the antique Armillary Sphere already resting on the credenza. The polished white body rested on a heavy black metal tripod. It was a terrestrial telescope with a zoom magnification of sixty—so powerful that Gabe could train it at the shops below and read the amounts rung up on cash registers. Sweeping the telescope from east to west, he could see the lake, the turrets, gables, and towers of gracious old Victorians, the low-pitched roofs of bungalows, and the clean lines and overhanging eaves of Prairie homes. Azyl Landing and Azyl Crescent, on the East of Shoreland Drive by the lake, consisted of detached homes and rows of town houses. To the west of the Drive, apartment buildings that decreased in rental price with increased distance from the lake julienned the north south grid. Gabe, Rae Oberoi, Tina Trang, Bruce Halliday, and Maja and Ivan Novic together owned the majority of Azyl Park's real estate. As members of the Elders Council, they could steer the town in any direction they chose. By melding his hunger and fury into a serrated blade, Gabe had managed to cut and claim things from the world, from its coppices and groves and thickets. It had not been easy, but he was young, naked with want, and had nothing to lose.

He stepped away from the telescope and released the hold button on the phone.

"Gabe Khoury here."

"Gabriel! It's Angeline Lalande at WBYN. Thank you for taking my call."

He felt a worm slide down his mouth, slip into the lacuna of his throat, and take root in the middle lobe of his left lung. Nobody but his dead mother had called him by that name.

Saba Khoury had been a devout Christian with a special devotion to the archangel. She had called him Jibril, the Arabic way, until a famous American photographer visited Dbayeh, the refugee camp in Lebanon, run by the United Nations Relief and Works Agency, where they had lived. Hoda, the manager of the camp, announced the visit a few days before the American's arrival. After Father Karam offered the concluding rites to sunset mass in the camp chapel and retreated to the vestry, Hoda sprang up from the front pew waving a copy of Life magazine. I have big news! Don't leave!

She told the congregation that the photographer's images of Nelson Mandela and the accompanying interview with him had catapulted his independence movement onto the world stage. She told them of her hope—that their testimonies together with the photographs taken at Dbayeh would help publicize their struggle. "Please choose your words carefully. They must be words that start a fire."

The American arrived in a convoy of white and blue UN jeeps, one dedicated solely to the transport of her photographic equipment, escorted by a dozen UNRWA officials and accompanied by four assistants. Though she was not beautiful, Gabe was struck by her confidence and ease. Unlike the female residents of the camp who were swathed in impractical long skirts and somber robes, she was dressed intentionally—for that morning, for that work—in a white cotton shirt with rolled up sleeves, olive khaki pants, and brown leather work boots. The fine blonde hairs on her arms glistened in the sun. Her blue eyes were greedy, restless, wandering, taking in everything. Gabe watched how she used her two instruments, her body and her camera. She dropped to the mud on one knee, the other leg bent with an elbow resting on it to serve as a tripod for the camera. Her pants and shirt were soiled, but she looked clean, queenly. It was he who felt dirty. He looked around the camp. All the residents looked grimy, ugly. He felt deeply ashamed.

She peppered her subjects with questions as she worked to capture them, as she calculated the sun, fixed light, fought shadow, erased glare. She asked the camp residents about their lives, about their families, about what home and place meant. Hoda and another UNRWA official, Salim, acted as interpreters.

"There I grew olives and figs. Here I'm given ration cards."

"This place has nothing to do with me."

"My feet are lacerated, homelessness has exhausted me."

"I want only what is mine."

"We want the world to be fair with us."

Her assistants recorded the interviews on tape, and transcribed them in a ledger that looked like a holy book.

Hoda and Salim stood near the entourage and spoke to each other.

"What language are you speaking there?" the photographer asked. An assistant held a battered leather case open for her. She ran her fingers down a row of lenses. "Slow speed," she said firmly. "It's not Arabic," she turned to the interpreters.

"Aramaic," Salim said.

"The language of Maronite prayers, the Kaddish, and the Talmud," Hoda said.

"And Jesus?" She handed the camera to her assistant to change the lens. "Let's try a round with the Leica."

Salim and Hoda nodded.

“There’s a phrase he uttered,” she squinted from the harsh sun, her blue eyes absorbing light rays so the irises bloomed. She made a canopy with both hands to shade her eyes. “When he raised Jairus’ daughter.”

“Little girl I say to you arise,” Hoda offered.

“Yes. Talitha Cumi,” she said. “It makes him real somehow. You know?”

The interpreters and entourage looked at her, baffled.

She waved her hands and shook her head in a retraction. “Never mind! The Middle East makes me crazy.”

The group nodded in understanding. She took the camera from the assistant, looked through the viewfinder, and found him. “What’s your name?” she lowered the camera to her side.

“Tell her your name,” Saba nudged him.

“Jibril,” he squeaked.

“Jibril?” she looked at Saba. “Like Gabriel?”

“Like Gabriel? ” Hoda asked.

Saba smiled. “Yes, for the archangel.”

“Yes, for the archangel,” Hoda translated.

“It’s a splendid name. How old are you?”

“Five,” he held up ten fingers.

“Let’s take a picture of handsome Gabriel and his beautiful mother.”

Saba loved the sound of it. Three vowels instead of two, a held note at the end that gave it a musical flourish, different from the amputated original. She began to call her son, Gabriel.

“Sure. What can I do for you?” Gabe said, as he walked towards his desk.

"I've been working on a Fourth of July special about our multicultural city," Angeline said.

Who cares, Gabe thought, sitting down.

"The Mayor's Office is championing it. Azyl Park is of course the definitive multicultural neighborhood, the most diverse township in the US. It could even be the world. I don't think there are a hundred languages spoken in one town anywhere else on the planet."

Her voice was full of lilt—expressive, euphonious, liquid, lyrical—trained in the art of broadcasting to have just the effect it was having on him then. He held the phone closer to his ear. He had both elbows on his desk. He pressed a finger against his other ear so that her voice was contained, held, walled, territorialized, colonized, inside his head.

"You're probably right. There isn't another place where you'd find the Lost Boys of Sudan and Bosnians living on the same block," Gabe said.

"It's quite amazing," she agreed.

"Listen," she said quickly when he didn't respond. "The series is in the chute, my part is done. I tried to schedule an interview with you but Nadia told me you were unavailable."

"I was traveling." A lie.

"Yes. She arranged for me to speak to Rae Oberoi and Tina Trang."

"How did that go?"

"They had great stories. But that's not why I'm calling. I received some documents from the archivist at the North Shore Historical Society. It's too late for the show and my producer doesn't think it's relevant. But I think you'll find it interesting."

Gabe closed his eyes. Her voice made him think of early rain falling over the lake when it was at its calmest, the first surprise of drops that stippled the water.

"Hello? Are you there?" she asked.

"Yes." Gabe opened his eyes.

"I'm not sure how this remained buried without anyone finding it."

"This is the most boring place in America. Nothing happens here. Our vice is work. Everything is sacrificed to it. We count our money, grow it, keep to ourselves. So I can't imagine that it's big news. And if it's not, why would you care?"

"It's information you especially will want to have. Being the town elder and all."

"Elder makes me sound so old." He had disliked the name from the beginning, but Rae, Tina, and Maja had overruled him and the name stuck.

"Well, you are. The town elder I mean, not the old part," she said.

Radio silence.

"It could be major, scandal worthy. Not anything I'm planning to touch though," she said.

You especially? What information could she have that was so important? And why hadn't she called Rae or Tina? Gabe clicked through his mental rolodex to check if he had unwittingly crossed anyone—in business, in his sex life—that could be the source of a scandal. The contortionist didn't have the brains to harm him. Confident that he'd always been a standup guy, a careful person, who'd done nothing to anyone, he decided to indulge her. "I have two minutes before I go into a meeting. What have you got?"

"It's a long story. I'd like to discuss it with you in person," she said.

Chapter 3

THE APPOINTMENT

Nadia held up a hand like a traffic cop to stop David in mid-sentence. "It's her," she whispered, breaking away from him as Angeline stepped out of the elevator. Nadia walked briskly towards her. The clicking sound of her heels bounced from the floor to the exposed ceiling ducts and pipes, to reverberate and ricochet around the room.

"Ms. Lalande, I'm so excited to meet you!"

"Nadia?" Angeline smiled.

"I'm reading your book," Nadia thrust her hand out to shake Angeline's. "Will you sign my copy?"

"Of course," Angeline bowed her head. Readers were royalty. They had to be given their due.

"Great. Gabe is going to be a few minutes," Nadia led Angeline to a seat. "Can I get you something to drink?"

"I'm fine." She stared at the mangled metal sculpture embedded with gems. "Is this turquoise?" Angeline drew closer to it. "It's not a color I've seen before."

"Eilat stone."

"Eilat?" she looked at Nadia. "In Israel?" she looked back at the sculpture.

"Yes. Or King Solomon stone."

Angeline studied the stones and traced her fingers over them. "So many layers and veins. So much complexity."

Nadia didn't understand. It's just stones, she thought. "We can do the book signing now. I'll be right back. So exciting!"

Angeline chuckled as she sat down on the sofa.

Nadia reappeared with a copy of *Code Noir to the 13th Amendment.*

Angeline's book about key figures in the abolitionist movement had won a history prize after its release. She hadn't anticipated the commercial success. She'd thought it would be a small book, saved from total obscurity only by kind academics adding it to Black Studies reading lists. But an imprimatur from the reigning diva of daytime television changed everything. It had shocked Angeline to see people reading about America's original sin on trains and buses, in restaurants and cafes, at airport gates and on planes.

She'd watch them. They read with their bodies. Some fell into the book, their shoulders rounded over it in a protective cocoon, greedy for the story. Others kept it at arms length, full of attitude and entitlement. Go on, dazzle me. Some suffered while reading painful information, others were stoic. Most were curious, attentive, and brave. But there were those who did battle with the book. They'd read the early pages, start to fidget, flip through the book, and search for Angeline's author photo to gauge her motives. Angeline would see a glimmer of something: irritation, anger, rage—red hot, ready to combust. She didn't blame them. It was easier to read the sports pages or plug in earbuds to stanch the flow of history, than to receive the memory of it, acknowledge the ugliness of it, engrave on the soul the barbaric nature of it. Once you learn a true thing, how can you unlearn it? It stays with you all your life, under your skin, held wisdom, garrisoned knowledge, like a balsam tree holding its seeds tightly in green pods, until its truth is ready to explode. History doesn't keep you safe. It eviscerates you.

Nadia extended the book open at the flyleaf, a pen lodged in its gutter. Angeline stood up, took the book, held it so it touched her sternum and the dip of her breasts as it gave way to bone. She tapped the pen against her cheek as she studied Nadia.

Nadia smiled shyly.

Angeline nodded from the dawning of a realization and scratched the paper with the felt tip pen. When she finished, she presented the open book to Nadia with both hands.

Nadia trailed her eyes across the inscription. Blushed. Understood. "Thank you. I'll tell Gabe you're here." She walked to the reception desk, one arm wrapped around the book held close to her heart.

Gabe rose from his desk and crossed the floor to greet her. When Angeline had joined WBYN a couple of years earlier, she had been all over the news. It was a major coup for the local affiliate to sign a network correspondent, an award-winning journalist, a distinguished prize-winning chronicler of history. The station mounted a celebratory media campaign with the recurring legend, "She's Here" emblazoned across the ads. Gabe had seen her towering mega visage, arms folded or in Wonder Woman stance, cosmeticized, polished, photoshopped to perfection, on highway billboards, on the sides of tall buildings, buses, and trains. Now in front of him, Angeline's living, breathing, human scale, dainty compared to the enormous billboards, felt to him like an enchantment. Wild curly hair tumbled to her shoulders. Her neck, thin and long, rose from a pronounced clavicle. Her upper lip was defined by a deep tubercle, a plunging v that gave her a childlike tenderness. He knew gemstones. He thought the color of her skin could rightfully be described as carnelian, a deep honey gold, and her eyes, axinite—clove brown. Angeline was austere in her dress. She wore a long sleeved white tailored shirt with flared black pants, a thin necklace of rice pearls the only embellishment. She reminded Gabe of the photographer from his childhood.

"Hold my calls," Gabe told Nadia.

Gabe studied the business card Angeline handed him. "Is it Angeline Lalande?" Gabe pronounced her name in French.

"Yes. But not for American TV."

"You're from?"

"Louisiana," Angeline said. "Via Nevis."

"Nevis. I don't know where that is." He gestured to a seat in front of his desk.

"West Indies?" she offered, a wry smile playing on her lips.

Gabe made a mental note to look it up online.

"Do you know how your town got the name Azyl?" Angeline sat down, unzipped the tote on her lap.

Bullshit waste of a question. Gabe took the chair at his desk. "I'm pretty sure it's a variation on azaleas. You can see them everywhere. I'm pretty sure it's the town flower,"

"Unfortunately this is in no way true." Angeline pulled out a notepad and folder from the bag. "May I share my research with you?"

"Please." Serious woman. All business.

She leaned forward, pen poised above the notepad she placed on Gabe's desk. "So," she looked directly at him as if he was the camera and she was beginning a broadcast. Her eyes cycled from dark brown to hazel as the light adjusted in the room. "In the late 1800s, the Czechs, Poles, Greeks, Irish, and Italians began arriving here."

"Old Europe," Gabe sat back in his chair. Unusual woman. A pleasant way to spend ten minutes.

"Right. Slumlords called it South of Eden as a joke and that's what it was called for a long while. Between 1939 and '45, Bosnians and Latvians started coming, then Lithuanians and Mexicans. Then Jews after World War 2. In '48 and '67, the Palestinians. Ripples and waves of broken people. That's when it was named Azyl Park,"

"This isn't breaking news." All the same, he hoped Nadia would break his rule and not interrupt them.

"It didn't stop with them. Torture victims from everywhere found a home here. It explains the Kolbe Center." She flipped the page of the spiral pad. "Kolbe House," she corrected herself.

"Kolbe House is not a place we talk about," Gabe said sharply, leaning forward.

"Why not?"

"People are hiding there from every dirty war and every murdering dictator. And you're blowing its cover. What are you, stupid?"

"Of course not. I merely mentioned it to you," Angeline was surprised by his rudeness. "I'm not a moron."

"I hope not." Tilting back in his chair, he swept her business card to the edge of the desk. Half the card lay on the surface, the other half hung precariously over the edge.

"Wow." She stared at the card, expecting him to send it flying across the room.

"Reporters charge through doors thinking they're Woodward and Bernstein, blissfully ignorant of consequences." He knew the harshness was unwarranted, over the top, but he couldn't stop himself.

"I won't argue with that. Treating every story as if it's Watergate is a requirement in journalism. We're awful. I get it." Out of control rich jerk.

"Why are you digging into this anyway? What's your beat?" he switched gears. He straightened the chair, leaned forward again, swept the card towards him in an arc.

"Mostly human and civil rights."

"Why this story?" he pressed.

"I also cover immigration." Angeline was unaccustomed to being on the receiving end of questions and started to shift in her seat. "Umm, so," she drummed the desk with her pen.

He wheeled his chair further into the arch below his desk. "What's the information you dug up?"

She flipped a page of her notebook. "The words azyl, asil, and asilo mean asylum. The town fathers didn't like the new arrivals, loathed them in fact. Thought they were lunatics. During a drunken night at the tavern they decided to christen what was then loosely called north side as Azyl Park."

Gabe turned to the windows. He could see the white lighthouse at the end of the pier, its lantern room topped by a cupola of lapis blue, its deck enclosed in grill metal of blue and white, its widow's walk etched in black. "Asylum has other meanings," he said. "There's haven, harbor, refuge. Protection, sanctuary, shelter. There are more I'm sure."

"The correspondence between them suggests otherwise. There's a thread of letters between Warren Smith, the biggest landowner then, and Thomas Wilkinson, the councilman. Quite a racist rant even for that era. I have copies for you." She handed him a document from the folder.

Gabe held himself with reserve as he turned the pages, except for an economical rotation of his wrist. No wasted movement, not relaxed, not tense, but coiled, controlled, alert, capable of springing and striking if he needed to.

Angeline who had a restless body that acted up whenever she had to sit still to read or write found his composure, so soon after the display of pique, worthy of admiration. She had to work hard to control her reflexive movements on camera when she had to read from script or teleprompter.

"Stop! Is there an earthquake? Why the fuck are your shoulders shaking?" a voice would bark into her earpiece from the control room. "Cut it out!"

She'd grip her knees to stop them from their rapid-fire wiggle.

But in the privacy of her own home, when she was immersed in reading or writing, she jiggled and clapped her legs, chewed her lips, bit her nails, cracked her knuckles, ran her fingers across her brows and down her lashes, ironed her curls into straight ribbons, sucked on the tips of her hair, and played with her jewelry as if praying a rosary.

Gabe hardly stirred. He blinked after long intervals like a child. As they'd say back in Nevis, all cassava got same skin but all nah taste same way, Angeline thought.

He looked up after turning the last page. "I hate history."

Angeline flinched as if he had struck her. "That's nuts! How can you hate history?" Her voice wavered. She drew a hand to her throat.

"It's bullshit," he said.

"History shapes us. Makes us," she said kindly, the way she would speak to a very small child.

Nadia opened the door after a triple knock. Out of respect for Angeline, she had given her thirty minutes instead of the customary eight. "Excuse me, Gabe, you have another meeting across town and you're running late."

"I rescheduled that this morning." Gabe said, surprising himself.

This was news to Nadia. She looked at Angeline who was looking at Gabe, and then at Gabe, and then at Angeline, as if watching tennis at Wimbledon. "I see," she closed the door. "Some shit is going down," Nadia said in a low voice.

"Huh?" David looked up from his laptop.

"Nothing," Nadia waved her hands and shook her head.

"Don't drive me nuts. What!?"

Nadia reached for lip gloss. "It's hot in there," she glazed her lips.

"It's hot in here," David murmured. He had Nadia pegged. An ascetic and a sensualist, a fundamentalist and a libertarian, a prude and a hedonist, many Nadias contained in one body, living in tension with each other, fragmented. His early diagnosis: DID—Dissociative Identity Disorder. He knew his psych. He owned several books on mental illness that he consulted frequently to understand himself, and others. His two favorites were *Diagnostic and Statistical Manual of Mental Disorders* and *Clinical Handbook of Psychological Disorders.* He was still on the fence about his father; he couldn't decide if the man was a psychopath or a sociopath.

One of David's recurring childhood memories was from the time he was eight years old. He was a pudgy kid that year in second grade, plumped up by pizza delivery, junk food, and all you could eat school lunches. His cheeks were inflated like balloons and he had a big belly. His classmates were cruel. They called him Bubble Eye, and when it came time for team sports, both teams would howl in protest when he was assigned to their group. "Awww. Noooo. We've got Lard Ass." There was no mercy for him.

After a particularly brutal day at school, David was relieved when he came home and found no one there. Usually, his mother would be home by then, after working half days at the symphony as a phone fundraiser. David threw his backpack against a wall of his bedroom and brought a lamp crashing to the floor. He walked over to his desk, ripped the phone from its jack, and threw it against a window. The double pane cracked but didn't shatter. He picked up a hardback dictionary, a wire basket, and a metal tray and hurled them against the wall. He screamed profanities and curses at his tormentors. #% @*&%!!@#$@%#%$##@@#$$%$#@#$$#%$#@#$%#%@$#$ @$&&&%&@&$#%$##%&&&@&!!#%@*&%!!@#$@%#%$# #@@#$$%$#@#$$#%$#@#$%#%@$#$@$&&&%&@&$#%$# #%&&&@&!! And he sobbed.

He closed the blinds to hide the cracked window and swept the broken lamp under the bed with his feet. He wiped his tears and snot with his sleeves and went to the kitchen to make himself a snack. He pulled out a box of leftover pizza, a stick of pepperoni, and wedges of colby and cheddar from the refrigerator. He latticed the pie carefully with a layer of pepperoni and cheese, stood back to admire the yellow and pink lacework before setting it in the microwave. He set a woven placemat on the breakfast bar before placing the dish on the counter. The pie was too hot to bite into but he couldn't wait. He sat on a barstool, bent his head back, and held a triangle of pizza above his mouth and blew the tip. The cheese slipped off the pie and into his mouth. He rolled the glob of hot cheese around his mouth with his tongue.

His father entered the kitchen through the back door, home early from work. Where's your mother?

I don't know, David bit into the slice.

You're going to turn into a fat pig eating that shit. I'm going to put a lock on that fucking refrigerator, fat pig.

"Sometimes I don't understand people at all," Nadia said.

"They're not that hard to figure out." Psychopath, David decided.

Gabe was in a fighting mood and sorry about the impression he was making on Angeline. His father's letters had a way of stirring him. That morning, he'd lifted the leather pad on his desk to retrieve the envelope he'd slipped under it the day before. He sliced it with his finger and quickly regretted it when he saw blood flower crimson on the web between his thumb and index finger. His father's thick Arabic scrawl cut deeply into the paper like Braille. No salutation, no loving prelude, no queries of his well being, no expression of longing to see his only child, no articulation of hopes for a reunion. It was a rambling five-page manifesto and treatise on the Occupation, replete with redundancies. It also elucidated his full and final rejection of nonviolent resistance.

I have at last been cured of the delusion of a just peace through nonviolence since the latest invasion of our territory. I categorically reject biblical, theological and moral precepts, and am interested now only in what is rightfully ours. I will fight to my last breath for the total withdrawal of the occupiers from all our lands. I call you now to join me in the fight for our land. Others have a spare country because our fathers ran like cowards instead of staying and fighting. We have to fight until we have the only country that is ours. Leave everything. Take your place next to me.

When the odds and the Gods are against you, is intransigence the best statecraft? Gabe thought.

His father ended the letter in a blazing finale, with an attack full of vitriol and bile, a castrating screed. *If your new country has made you soft and turned you into a coward, let us real men do the fighting for you. We will take it as our duty to fight for our women, you included. You may even be useful to the movement as a coward and a woman. Send us money for the resistance. We need everything. A brother will come to you with wire instructions. Freedom for Palestine. From the river to the sea.*

Gabe was grateful for the distance between them, for deliverance from the psychosis that had created him, for the life he had made for himself in a new country, guided by wise, avuncular men. Mr. Advani had taught him how to start with the shell on his back, how to endure a profound separateness and loneliness, how to find his way out of trauma and pain through work. Gabe skated the letter under the blotter and pressed a tissue against the blood rising in the wedge of his fingers.

"History guides us. It's our map!" Angeline snapped.

"I'm not lost," Gabe pressed down the flap of torn skin with a thumb.

Angeline felt a change in her body, a heat rising from her like a cloud. If she were placed in front of a thermal imaging camera, she thought the whole area from her neck to her chest would glow red with anger. She stood up. "I think you are." She gathered her folder and notebook and hooked her bag over her shoulder.

"Have a nice day," she said, her face set in stony judgment, looking not at Gabe but at the window behind him.

Gabe swiveled his chair turning his back on her. He cupped a hand around his jaw feeling bone and molar as he waited for the door to click shut behind him. He felt his breath warm and moist against his hand; he ran his tongue lightly against the cut.

Outside, the sun tinted the rooftops and facades of buildings. It licked metal pipes, windowpanes, and shop canopies an effervescent lemon. Gabe's buildings glowed, radiating light rays. The laced dome of the Baha'i temple, on the north end of the beach before Shoreland Drive curved into Idyllwild, disappeared behind a pearly haze of morning gleam.

Gabe angled the telescope at the Square and looked through the eyepiece. Angeline was on the sidewalk, walking at a fast clip towards the pedestrian crossing at Shoreland and Hyacinth. He clicked the auto zoom several times until he could see the grain on her leather tote. She stopped before reaching the crosswalk and turned to face traffic heading north. Gabe adjusted the focuser to zoom in on her face. He clicked the zoom button again and brought her so close, he could see the vermillion border of her lips. He could have traced the dip of her cupid's bow with a finger. He couldn't name what roiled her.

Chapter 4

GATHER

The Elders usually convened at Lucky's, a woebegone place run by Sophie and Cris Costas, a somber Greek couple with leathery suntans from Januaries in Puerto Vallarta, cracked voices from too many Gitanes, and sclera and fingernails tinged yellow. The bar stools at Lucky's were patched together with silver duct tape that pinched buttocks and thighs. The ambient music included the saloonaire's favorite French balladeers. Sophie, who told anyone who reminded her of the dangers of smoking that she lit up for medical reasons, loved Damia, the chanteuse who died a painful death from a three-pack-a-day habit, after imploring in Le Goeland: *Ne tuez pas le goéland.* Do not kill the gulls.

The Elders always occupied the corner booth near the arched doorway that separated the bar and lounge from the game room and restrooms in the back. Patrons usually clustered at the bar, around the high tops, near the pool table and television, and by the arcade games Cris had bought from an Armenian restaurant across the street that had gone belly up. The booth, cordoned off with stanchions and red rope, was deemed a private area. When not occupied by the Elders, it served as the Costas' parlor where they held meetings with vendors and entertained friends.

Despite its sorry state, Lucky's was more popular than the bistro across the street owned by the brothers Zalinsky—Mark, the dentist,

Andrew, the building contractor—who had grown up in Azyl Park. Oasis reeked of taste that you felt obliged to dress up for: original art on the walls, glazed tin ceiling, zinc bar, epic wine and microbrew list, tapas. But it was usually empty. Tapas lacked the density immigrants needed to fill substrates of hunger and palliate unpicked grief. Worse still, the pall that hung like clouds inside the joint. Mark was a bitter, bristling man, ill suited to hospitality, who thought his establishment superior to its patrons. "People here don't belong. This bar should be in Idyllwild," he'd bemoan his tribulation.

Lucky's regulars who had ventured there for chic and glam voted with their feet. They eased themselves back onto their familiar buttocks and thigh-pinching stools. Neither Sophie nor Cris mentioned their unceremonious decampment or their prodigal return.

The corner booth had upholstered red leather seating and a resin mahogany U-shaped table. Gabe, Trang, Ivan, and Rae, compact people, usually sat in the middle. Bruce and Maja sat at each end, since they were, let it be said, ample of girth. Bruce was a burly presence, all shoulders and chest. His torso yielded to no one. Trang, a diminutive figure, always found a lull during the meetings to tease him.

"Bruce, you're wasting away," or "When's the baby due?"

In response, Bruce would pat his belly and tease her back. "Go on, you know you want to rub it."

"Oh go away," she'd roll her eyes.

Bruce Halliday had been a master brewer at a brewpub in Geelong, Australia when the philistines of American television, bankrupt after two decades of formulaic Japanese and British tripe and desperate for new programming, went Down Under.

"I could make you the next superstar," Zach Goldsmith, the producer responsible for half the mind-numbing, IQ-detonating fare on American television, told Bruce when he saw him drawing pints at Calhoun's.

"You look like a rugby player. I'm digging the look," Goldsmith appraised him like a slave buyer at an auction. He didn't need to see Bruce on all fours to know that the blonde Aussie brew master had stratospheric Q-rating magic up the wazoo.

Bruce was a tall man with a rugby player's body it was true, but he had none of the skill. When he saw a ball flying towards him, its lift and drag coefficients in some mysterious dance of aerodynamics and velocity, his reaction was to double over. He attributed his indifference to sports to having been raised by women—his mother, Janice, his grandmother, Rhonda, and his aunt, Nin. They were much-married women with three misbehaving, drunken, battering, loser husbands a piece.

A week after Bruce's seventh birthday, just before dawn on Anzac Day, Janice drove her station wagon into town, with Bruce and his sister, Glory wedged in the seat next to her. Where are we going? Bruce asked, as they whizzed by the cross on top of the church belfry. At dawn the whole town would be at church, at memorial services for the fallen soldiers of World War 1 at Gallipoli. His friends would be there. Glory didn't care. Her friends had turned into scrubbers, all they could think and talk about was boys and sex. Glory only wanted peace, escape from the madman her mother had married. She gripped Bruce's hand and squeezed. Sshhh, she whispered, looking straight ahead.

"No other way." Janice said. "He's a thug."

"Shoulda done it sooner." Glory said.

Janice pulled into the empty parking lot behind the supermarket. An unmarked white campervan drew up in the spot next to theirs a few minutes later.

"That's Grandma," Janice said. "Get in the van calm as you please. Glory, help him with his things."

"Where're we going?" Bruce asked as Glory opened the door. All his friends, the whole town, would be at church.

"We're going to disappear," Janice said.

Bruce remembered Amazing Arturo, the magician at his birthday party who had pulled a white bunny out of his top hat and made it vanish. "Like magic."

"That's right darl," Janice said as she retracted the key from the lock cylinder.

"Nin!" Bruce exclaimed, as Glory lifted him into the passenger row of the van. His aunt, Nin was seated behind his grandmother who was in the driver's seat. Glory climbed in after Bruce and slid the door shut. Nin took the children's backpacks and Janice's rucksack and placed them in an overhead compartment. The rear of the van held a galley kitchen and bathroom. The middle of the camper was arranged as a living and dining room. The bench seats would convert into twin cots, the table would fold out into a double bed.

"We have everything?" Janice asked as she scooted in the front seat next to her mother.

"Yep," Nin said. "Camping gear, food and water for a week. Water catchers, matches, pots." Nin settled back into her seat.

"Satellite phone, flares, first aid kit, fly nets?" Janice asked.

"Check."

"What if we break down?" Janice asked.

"All set. On the rack," Nin pointed and dipped a finger at the roof.

"That's that then. Seatbelts everybody. Glory, help Bruce." Janice turned to her mother. "Are we sure about this, Mum?"

"Never surer," Rhonda adjusted the rearview mirror. Her arms and face were deeply tanned and studded with freckles. "I'm done with the bastard."

"Let me see," Janice said.

Rhonda turned her face towards Janice.

"Mum!" Janice raised her hand to Rhonda's cheek.

"Leave it," Rhonda pushed her daughter's hand away. "I'll come back and kill him soon enough," she put the van in reverse and pulled out of the lot.

"I'll come with you. I want to finish mine off," said Nin.

"I want to shoot mine through the asshole," Janice said.

"You'll need a long rifle for that," Rhonda said gravely.

Janice and Nin laughed. Rhonda gritted her teeth. If she so much as smiled, her torn lower lip would split wide open.

They drove through the Outback, through ghost mining towns, through the Bush, through endless stretches of red brown dirt. They took wrong turns and ended up on earth that led to nowhere. They cut through desert and thought they saw UFOs. They saw 95 million year old footprints of a dinosaur stampede. Late at night, after the women passed out from driving fatigue and too much beer, Bruce and Glory lay in bed, their puffy shared pillow wedged in the bow of the open window, their foreheads and eyes tilted back so they could look at the sky. They whispered to each other, what they saw. Star clusters and constellations. The Southern Cross and the False Cross. And formations only they could see. Bruce saw rabbits, wolves, dogs, horses, horsemen. Glory saw doves, winged angels, God as a woman. Because the bed was narrow, Bruce learned to lie on his side and tuck his body into his sister's contours as she lay on her back. She made extra room for him by extending an arm so that he could drape his face against her side. He would listen to her heart beating against his cheek, and try to sync his breathing with hers as he fell into sleep.

During the day, the women took turns to drive, sometimes they'd fall silent for hours, listening to the radio, turning the dial to find better songs. The desolate outback stretched forever in front of them, a blank canvas for quiet introspection. Now and then, Janice would slide a hand behind her seat and graze Bruce's bare leg, or turn round and lean over to stroke his cheek and say, "You're such a good boy," or "Give us a kiss then." The women talked about everything, except the lives they had left behind. They talked about what was immediate, what they encountered on the road—the man at the motel who walked like a platypus, the woman at the farm who was as wide as a bus, the family of camels, the clan of emus, kangaroo mothers, the dingoes who ate babies, impossible velvet carpets of purple and red wildflowers, the flies, the mosquitoes. When they ran out of conversation, they stopped at roadhouses and inns to talk to strangers and tell them nothing. What we need is a roadhouse of our own, Janice ventured one day after they'd stopped at a trading post to stock up on provisions.

No one questioned the squatters as they claimed the abandoned saloon somewhere north of south, between Coober Pedy and Katherine. People don't come back to the scene of their failure, Rhonda said. She made the beer and tended bar while Janice and Nin cooked and served the food. When Bruce and Glory were old enough, they began working as bar backs and bar hops: cleaning glassware, turning tables, stocking the bar, mopping floors, polishing the wood fixtures to an oily luster, and operating the fryer in the kitchen.

When Bruce turned thirteen, a miner, covered in soot and sweet on his mother, gave him a guitar. "Made it from a felled acacia. A beaut ain't it?" he beamed at Bruce.

It was far from a beaut. It was a pig's arse. Ugly, a double bagger. It had a crudely cut body that looked like the obese figure of a fertility goddess, its thick stem and strings were made of catgut. It hadn't been sanded down, there were tiny splinters up and down the neck, bouts, and rosette.

Bruce set to work. He used several sizes of chisels, rasps, planes, and gauges to carve, shape, and whittle the wood into a proper guitar. He used steel wool to gently grind down the splinters. He cadged a pumice stone from Glory's shower caddy and worked it across the surface in soft circular motions. The grain of the wood revealed swirls and streaks of deeper colors—coffee, whiskey, muscovado. He filled its hairline cracks with a granular paste and primed and sealed it with a lacquer that dried to a high gloss. He was pleased with the metamorphosis, proud that over the course of a hot season he had teased and unsheathed from a raw thing worthy of rejection, something beautiful and true. Bruce stood in front of the long mirror in Glory's room and held the guitar. It felt natural, like a part of his body.

He taught himself how to play the instrument, first strumming it, then learning basic chords and how to bar the chords. He played them at different places up and down the neck. His fingers burned and bled at first from the strings, but once the cuts were covered with calluses he felt no pain. He felt vibration and pulse, hum and throb, whisper and murmur, course through his fingers and radiate through his body. He couldn't feel the sting, couldn't remember the pain. Before the year was over, he began singing at the bar. Hank Williams and Johnny Cash, Merle Haggard and Waylon Jennings, Jimmie Rodgers and George Jones. The patrons heckled him, yelled for him to sing Down Under and For The Working Class Man. But he would only sing American songs.

Bruce's family were all dead by the time he turned twenty—first his grandmother of lung cancer on his eighteenth birthday; then Nin of breast cancer the following Christmas. Then his mother. She was hanging out the wash in the back yard, admiring how white the sheets looked after a final rinse in borax. Bruce was swaying in a large hammock he'd strung between two boab trees on the edge of their property, just before the carpet of red desert pea and yellow andamooka lilies gave way to orange and sienna outback dirt. He was plucking out chords from memory to a song he'd heard on the radio. The blasts from a hunting rifle scattered a covey of tweeting, chirping finches, lorikeets, and budgerigards, before uniting them into a billowing, shuddering mass of beating wings. He heard his mother's scream, No!!!, rise and ride over the flapping wings. An old lover from a previous season who wanted his mother back. A country song.

A month later, he found Glory at the back of the restaurant. In the meat cooler, flanked by several sides of beef, four vertically sliced cow carcasses carved clean of their innards, a dozen racks of sheep, and two pig cadavers, their skin still on them, suspended by their snouts. She was hanging from a rope trussed to a meat hook, swinging gently, her eyes open, eyeballs protruding, mouth open, tongue out, her hands holding the rope choking her neck, her body heavy with regret. For the rest of his life, Bruce would remember how his sister, whom he called Lil, for Lilliput, because she was so tiny and light, had felt so leaden, so dense, so packed and weighted like iron, when he had cut the rope and brought her down, hung over his shoulder like the meat he readied for the barbie. She was frozen to the bone from hanging in the freezer for two days.

Their deaths left him with a hole in his heart so immense he could dive into it, a murky black pool in the soft epicenter of his being. Numb from booze, cocaine, heroin, meth, pills, patches, he'd stay there for weeks at a time without hitting bottom or touching sides. A dead baby floating in amniotic fluid still tethered to its cord. He'd stay sober for a week and then go on twenty-one day benders holed up in the coach house behind the bar. Curtains drawn, lights out, television at full volume so he'd never forget the sound of human voices. When he woke up next, he'd be lying on the bathroom floor, or by the water well behind the kitchen, or in Glory's bed. His customers migrated to other watering holes in other towns until he hung a sign indicating he was once more open for business.

One Sunday, he'd shaken himself awake in Glory's bed when he felt his cheek burning. A thin shaft of sunlight had cut through the window at an angle and torched the right side of his face. A gentle wind made the lace curtains on the window rustle and billow up like a woman's skirt. He stared at the window expecting to see his dead but he could only see the four boab trees in the backyard. Their swollen bottle-shaped trunks made them look like people. He stared at them until he was able to project and imagine the faces of his family on the top of each tree. "Ma. Lil, Nin, Gram." They didn't answer. But when he swung his legs off the bed, he felt an interior locution, a voice that worked its way like a caterpillar through the whorls and volutions of his brain, and spilled out of his right ear. Keep moving, it said.

All that was left of his dead, after Bruce had sold the outback saloon to finance a thirty percent stake in Calhoun's, was an envelope of photographs that he kept in a box under his bed. Bruce was grateful that his excessive drinking and drug use had erased most of his long-term memory. He learned how much effort it took to hold a mind together and how little it took to let it fall apart. His family had faded into the shadows and margins, rims and peripheries, edges and borders—vaporous beings stripped of blood and bone, marrow and essence, heart and soul. He could hardly remember that he had once belonged to others, that he had been accountable and answerable to them, that he had been owned, loved, deeply, completely, without limit. Where are you going, lad? Down to the river, Ma. When will you be home? Soon. When? Later, Nin. Don't give me lip, laddie. Gram! When Gram and Ma are gone, will you look out for me? Yes, Lilliput. You're our boy, aren't you? Yes, Ma, yes, Gram. We're alright, aren't we? Yes Nin.

In that dimly lit bar saturated in brown—cordovan, chestnut, mahogany, palmetto—Zach, in his bleached white linen suit with his glowing orange face, shining blonde hair, and glinting white teeth, looked like a heavenly apparition. Bruce had yet to see the video of Jon Stewart calling Zach Goldsmith the man who will make you, your children, and your parents stupid, and the one where Stephen Colbert had called him a knuckle dragging troglodyte and carbuncle in the buttocks of American culture.

"You're the real deal, a rugged alpha male Australian master brewer," Zach said, as he appraised Bruce: blond hair down to his shoulders, a neatly trimmed Van Dyke, gray eyes with death secrets in them, and a tattoo on his right bicep—an upright guitar with the letter "L" inked in cursive under the saddle and bridge. Zach found fault only with the slender, graceful, double-jointed fingers, feminine fingers, guitar playing fingers—an anomaly on a body so unconditionally male.

"I'm feeling Paul Newman in those eyes," said Chip, the co-producer, a bespectacled man wearing three tones of denim.

Bruce placed Zach's and Chip's drinks in front of them. He rubbed the toke sitting in the bridge of his earflap that he was keen to light up.

"And the exotic appeal of Crocodile Dundee," Zach said. "Can you say, "That's not a knife. That's a knife?"

"You just did, mate," Bruce replied. His regulars were eyeing him with equal parts pride, jealousy, and contempt. They'd have strung him alive and hung him by his knackers if he had demeaned himself, his countrymen, or his country to a bunch of foreigners.

"A magic ratio of good looks, sex appeal, strength, and vulnerability," Chip said, nodding like a bobble head dog.

More than the flattery, Zach and Chip lobbed money at him, more zeros than he'd ever thought he'd earn in his lifetime. During an early discussion over lunch at a high top near the jukebox, they offered him a sum that he thought must have been a telephone number. He sat in a Buddha trance to ride out heartburn from the greasy Calhoun's Cardiac Arrest burger, the house special he had just eaten and chased down with a pint. Zach mistook Bruce's indigestion for hardball negotiation and upped the offer to a number that looked like an international dialing instruction.

There were many things about America that were familiar to Bruce. There were places where the country songs he loved took him to, that he had visited in his reveries—Amarillo, Arizona, Carolina, Cheyenne, Georgia, Galveston, Luckenbach, Memphis, Wichita. He loved the sound of them, more lyrical than Australian places that he felt could never be written into songs: Boing Boing, Burrombuttock, Chinamen's Knob, Cock Wash, Mount Buggery, Pimpinbudgie, Titty Bong. He wanted to taste American women, the kind who wore bikini tops, low riding short shorts that showed the gentle curve of fanny, cowboy boots, and danced to Mustang Sally or Susie Q like in Apocalypse Now.

It had taken Bruce five years to put the shards and fragments of his life back together, to forget the warmth of the matrilineal skein that had held and consoled him, and to consign the past to where it belonged—in that box under his bed. He tried to make a tolerable life for himself, though his relationships with women had been nothing but folly. They hadn't understood his black moods, his drunken and drugged stupors, his silence.

"What's wrong with you?"

"Do you feel anything?"

"Are you made of stone?"

"You gutless, selfish bastard."

How to explain that he was a dead man walking? That feeling anything would unlock battened down memory and require him to count his losses. That he wanted nothing, that he had nothing to give. That he'd wonder while cutting lemons at the bar to garnish drinks, what it would feel like to plunge the knife into his neck. That his heart thumped when he went into the walk-in freezer to retrieve shrimp for the barbie. That he was afraid that the tendinous chords that held the muscles and valves of his heart together would snap from the weight of his grief. That when he was on top of a woman, he wanted to choke her until her eyes bulged with fear, to punish her for the crime of waking up each day to an ordinary world.

America was the place everybody he knew wanted to visit—it's on my bucket list, mate. He had won the bucket and he could off himself there just as well as he could in Geelong if he felt the urge to. At the rate he was going he figured he'd be dead in a year, from a bad needle, a liver that gave out, or a gun in his mouth. A perverse, willful part of him wanted to live, wanted to rise above the ashes and bones of his dead.

"We have a problem," Gabe said, as he seated himself at the table between Bruce and Trang.

"What? Worldwide shortage of bird poop?" Trang, who believed that she was a savvy businesswoman with a finger on the pulse of American consumer tastes and how to make money off their fickleness, was smarting still from the fact that she'd known about bird coffee long before Gabe had discovered it. How the hell did an Arab discover it when I'm from Vietnam where we've known about dung beans forever? She scolded herself for her stupidity and failure and tripled her subscriptions to business forecasting magazines and trend reports.

"Actually, the less beans the better for my bottom line," Gabe said.

"Jerk," she dug an elbow into his side.

"I know you mean that in a loving way. Feel better?"

"No," she whined.

Gabe told the group about Angeline's discovery.

"I don't see anything wrong with it. Many immigrants are nut jobs so it fits," Ivan said.

"What are we talking about? Who's a nut job?" Cris set drinks in front of each of the Elders, and an appetizer tray in the center.

"Immigrants. A lot of us are psycho," Ivan explained.

"Speak for yourself," Rae set his phone on vibrate and placed it on the table. Maja snickered and looked at Rae as if to declare herself independent from Ivan's opinion. Ivan glowered at her. He had been tethered to her for so long he'd forgotten what it felt like to be supported by anyone.

"Cris, what's the word in Greek for asylum?" Trang asked.

"Asyl," Cris replied.

"Our town means loony bin? This is terrible," Trang spooned goat cheese dip onto small plates for the men. Rae offered his to Maja.

"No, that can't be right," Sophie said from behind the bar. The Elders and Cris turned to look at her. "It's named after flowers. There's azyl for azalea, anemone, iris, lily, lavender, hyacinth, and trillium."

"Angeline confirmed otherwise," Gabe said.

"As a realtor, I have to say we have no choice but to rebrand." Trang bit into a carrot.

"Soho, Noho, and Tribeca were not always high rent," Rae said. "Name is everything."

"Chop up a name and join vowels to gentrify," Trang agreed.

"Call it AzPa," Bruce spread his hands to stretch out the word on an invisible marquee.

"Be serious," Trang scolded.

"What? You think I'm taking the piss, taking the mickey, do you?"

"Speak properly. We do not understand what you are saying," Ivan said.

"Bruce is being ironic," Tina explained.

"Say what you mean. Mean what you say. This is too much to ask?" Ivan scolded Bruce.

"Sorry," Bruce said.

Of all the Elders, Ivan was the least knowable, the most secretive. He was a brooding presence with shifty eyes that wouldn't fix on people but skirted around their edges. There were people in Azyl Park who referred to Ivan as the war criminal. But nobody knew the source of the allegation. Since he was one of the Elders, people were inclined to give him a wide berth. But still, there was something about him that was more wrong than right.

"I like the idea. The simple shortening retains our heritage and erases the problem in one stroke," Rae said.

"Sounds too much like Ass Park," Trang said.

"I agree," Gabe said.

"We need something catchy to bring in Millennials and Bohos," Rae said.

"No hobos please," Maja said.

Trang who was sipping a glass of wine snorted and had to set the glass down to wipe wine bubbles trickling down her nose.

"Tina, explain the meaning of Bohos to Maja," Rae said, finding himself once again assuming responsibility as forger of group solidarity. If he didn't dull the sharp knives of the two women, the meeting would grind to a halt.

"Please. I need nothing from this woman." Maja inserted a cigarette into a holder and said something to Ivan in Serbian.

"This is America, speak English. It's in the bylaws of the Council," Trang said. "Seriously, Holly Golightly?"

"That's low, Tina." Rae scolded, even though Maja wouldn't have understood the film reference.

"Here's some English. You have the loyalty of a snake." Maja shot back, her jaw set, thin lips disappearing as she sucked on her cigarette, ready to fight.

The feud began during the waning days of the Bush administration when Iraqis were moved to throw shoes upside the President's head. But still Maja had not recovered from her loss.

Mrs. Sach, the last of the pioneers of Azyl Park and sole occupant of 1 Azyl Crescent had died that year. Her grown children from the northern suburbs, who had worked hard to scrub themselves clean of their Azyl Park pedigree, listed the house on the market soon after placing their mother in the ground.

Maja and Ivan already owned and lived in 2 Azyl Crescent with their thirteen-year-old twins, Alek and Sonja. The house was so large Maja had smart TV screens installed in every room, the better to Instant Message her children that pizza had been delivered. Still, Maja wanted more space. Her only option was Mrs. Sach's house as the couple to the right of her, the Robinsons at 3 Azyl Crescent, had already declined two of her offers.

"You're new to my country," Mrs. Robinson told Maja. "Have some respect."

Maja dreamed of knocking down the interior walls she shared with Mrs. Sach, thus doubling the capacity of her existing rooms. She had confided her dream over the years to Trang and Rae.

Trang owned 4, 5, and 6 Azyl Crescent. She rented No. 4 to Dr. Richard Langley, a plastic surgeon, and his wife, Caroline—a woman, perpetually startled as a result of her husband's aggressive scalpel wielding largesse. Whenever Trang saw Caroline, Neil Diamond's song immediately popped in her mind. *Pulled Caroline, Good times never seemed so good.* Niall Carson, a silver haired octogenarian who had served in diplomatic missions in the Far East under President Reagan and still cut a dashing figure, occupied No. 5. Tina lived in No. 6 with her husband, Roger. No. 7 was owned and occupied by the Oberoi family. No. 8, owned by Gabe, had been vacant since he bought it nine years ago.

Gabe had hired Andrew Zalinsky soon after the closing to tear down the house to its studs and rebuild it from the ground up. "I want it built to last. Don't cut corners, even on things I can't see."

Despite the luxury renovation, the house remained a beautiful shell except for a baby grand piano in the living room, a leather sofa angled near the French doors that opened out to a balcony overlooking the lake, a glass coffee table, and a wool rug in front of an electric fireplace that dominated the south facing wall.

"You've spared no expense, why not go all the way and furnish it?" Andrew had asked, as he gave Gabe a final walkthrough of the renovated but empty upper floor. "Why not live in it?"

"One day," Gabe replied, face expressionless, circling the room and looking up at the vaulted ceiling.

"I don't get it," Andrew said. Foreigners were shadowy figures. They took too much effort to figure out. Andrew liked homegrown ordinariness and neuroses, things he could understand. Have a nice day and sports fever, July Fourth and Thanksgiving, screwed up kids and disappointed spouses, regrets and the one that got away, right wing left wing madness, Black White whatever, home decorating fixation, stainless steel appliances and granite countertops, 110 inch HDTV screens, wine, cocktails, yoga, porn, botox, money, sex, car, house, summer house, swimming pool, yacht, plane, anxiety, depression, anti-depressants, opioids, ennui, angst, rage. We used to be alright, what happened?

Gabe visited the house once a month after Yankee Maids, staffed by Polish, Irish, and Russian women with sketchy visas, had finished polishing the uninhabited aerie to a high glow. Gabe walked through the house with its cathedral ceilings, admired the sheen of the ebony wood floors, tinkled the keys on the piano though he didn't know how to make it yield music, ran the water in the jetted tubs in the bathrooms, and peered at the lake from each window.

Trang didn't need or want Mrs. Sach's house, but something in her refused to allow Maja the satisfaction of realizing a dream. A ping-pong bidding war for the house ensued. Each time Maja raised her offer, Trang raised hers until it exceeded the original asking price by two hundred thousand dollars. Maja loved the house but was ruled by practicality. She could not imagine buying a house for more than its appraised value.

"Gentle ladies, please," Rae said. "We should skew upscale, aim for high net worth, set a quota for others."

"You want to get sued? I can't afford to lose my reputation," Trang said, looking at Gabe, Bruce, and Ivan for support.

"You lost your reputation long time ago," Maja spat.

"Nobody is going to get sued, everybody at this table will make money. We need a new name. I don't know how we lasted this long with this one hanging around our necks," Gabe said.

"What do you think?" Bruce asked Ivan who had been silent while taking drags on a cigarette and sipping vodka.

Ivan shrugged.

"We need a consultant. Somebody who knows about a lot of things, like signs and symbols and meanings," Trang said.

"I know someone," Gabe said.

Chapter 5

OBSESSIONS

Gabe shook Angeline's hand and kissed her on both cheeks. She had been stewing since their last meeting and was surprised when he'd called her a week later. Not a text or an email but a call.

"Angeline, Gabe Khoury here. Forgive me for what I said. I need to see you."

Though she was impressed by his call—most people she knew hid behind email firewalls and suffered from phone phobia, even timing voicemail messages after hours to avoid actual conversation—she concluded that it had nothing to do with reflection and remorse and everything to do with wanting to be viewed as a good person. She was certain his mea culpa was for PR reasons. She was a journalist after all, capable of a hatchet job that could cause him embarrassment at the very least.

"You smell wonderful. What are you wearing?" He wore a deep navy suit; he wore it extremely well. His recently shaved face had an appealing high glow. But was he ever going to release her hand?

She hesitated before replying, "Royaume des songes. Kingdom of dreams."

He took her hand and raised her wrist to his nose. "Jasmine, vanilla." He drew it even closer, his nose and lips pressed against her pulse, his eyes closed. "Frangipani." She felt his breath on the river of veinous green that marked her wrist, a spectral breeze washed over her, warmed her first then made her shiver. "Patchouli, ylang ylang, cinnamon. And something I can't place," he said as he opened his eyes.

"Let me guess. You've cornered the fragrance market as well," Angeline reclaimed her hand.

"I distribute a line from Spain. I had to do competitive analysis so I learned everything I needed to know about perfumes. I went on a perfume factory tour of France and Italy."

There was a promiscuity to his endeavors that appalled Angeline. Unlike a Renaissance Man who pursued intellectual curiosity, everything Gabriel Khoury did was to line his own pockets. Gems, perfumes, coffee, distribution. Prior to her meeting with Rae Oberoi and Tina Trang, while running a LexisNexis search on Azyl Park, Angeline had learned about Gabriel's insatiable appetite for new ventures. The enterprise that disturbed her most, that told her everything she needed to know about him, was his recent acquisition of two acres of vacant land on the southern tip of Idyllwild. A decade earlier, archaeologists had conducted a virtual dig on the tract using ground radar. Fourteen feet below a sand mound, they saw a formation of black and white spots and squiggles on the radar. A protracted investigation confirmed that the series of blobs were log tombs of the Pottawatomie, Chippewa and Ottawa Indians dating back two millennia. Idyllwild's town council, eager to replenish its coffers after a misguided casino project and greedy for upscale shops and condos for the horsey set, invited bids to purchase the land. Gabriel submitted a winning proposal for a mixed use development with luxury residential and retail. Morally reprehensible, contemptibly vile, Angeline had thought as she read the article. But here he was and she felt tentative, unable to muster the outrage to match her initial indignation.

"You love everything you do?" she stared at him.

“I don’t know about love but I try to be good at what I do.” She probed too much. Asked too many questions. Couldn’t leave things alone.

“One day I’d like to hear what drives you,” Angeline said, as she sat down. “Other than money that is.”

“One day.” Too difficult. Too intense. He took the seat behind his desk. Too much work.

He conducted himself like no one she knew. She had dropped by the station the day before and endured an hour of American frat boy culture of joshing, profanity, scatology, high fives, sports talk, and inanity to fill silence as if silence were a sin. She had never minded the banter and ribbing before. But Gabriel’s reserve and restraint made them seem undisciplined and excessive. What must it be like to be so contained, she wondered. You devolve into a solipsist, she decided.

“So, why did you want to see me, Gabriel?” She leaned forward and hitched her elbows on the table.

“Tell me what you said about history,” Gabe said.

“You tell me what you mean about history,” Angeline challenged him.

Gabe traced a finger down a cheek, pressed down on muscle, touched skeleton. He looked out the window, ran a palm down his neck. He stared at the glistening white quartz of the Baha’i temple set near the water’s edge. He let his eyes roam over the arabesque panels, across the lacework. He scissored and crimped his tie between his fingers. “I come from history’s biggest losers.” In the circles he moved in, he’d kept this part of his life under wraps.

Talk to me about slavery and then dare tell me that, Angeline thought the thought but swallowed her words.

“I’m Palestinian.” He’d never thrown that about lightly. If people asked where he was from, he responded with a casual, here where else and changed the subject. And before that? New York. DC. LA. But he felt he could be serious with a woman who took things seriously.

"I didn't know that," she sat back in her chair. She'd give him a pass. "Where in Palestine?"

"Galilee."

"Where Jesus walked," she moved her head in a slow sweep.

"Can you see what history would mean to someone like me?" If she could, it would mean something.

"I would imagine a lot." Angeline reached for the small Newton's Cradle sitting between them. She lifted one metal orb and released it. The ball struck the second in the series and came to a dead stop. The fifth ball swung up.

"I hate it. I want nothing to do with it." He stopped the motion of the pendulum with an open palm.

"So you don't believe in identity and culture?" Angeline lifted two orbs and released them.

Gabe slid his chair back, gripping the armrest. "I believe in shedding skin."

"We are human beings Gabriel, not snakes."

"I trained myself to forget." Gabe stood up and walked towards the framed metal grid of windows. He could see tiny figures at the pier, urban fishermen casting their rods for smelt, pumpkinseed, walleye, goby, muskellunge. He admired the smallness of their ambition, the ease with which they invested their time, only to return their catch to the water. He had set his sights on only one thing—possession. Inch by inch. Brick by brick. He had learned how the Sindhi merchants on the Square had replaced the longing for place and home with work. They had taught him how to chisel a new self out of the detritus of his life. "Get over it and get yours, that's the Sindhi motto. Forget the bullshit about homeland," Mr. Advani had counseled him. Gabe listened. He made the decision to discard what was useless, bury the refugee from Dbayeh, kill the longing for roots, and chisel what remained. In those early days, his body had held his fear like a reliquary. He had an incessant twitch under his right eye, twin wings of anxiety about his future that beat against his temples, and a thickening shame that coursed through his blood. He was terrified of his past and his future, that his biography would cripple him, that his future would fail him because of his past. The obligation to succeed clung to the walls of his chest like tar. It urged him forward, drove him to make a mark, for his own sense of pride, for his grandfather who had been unmanned by the Nakba, for his father who had been swallowed whole by rage.

Gabe had built an American life through revision and reinvention. Even the name by which she called him now, a name rendered numinous by her voice, was an invention. During the naturalization oath ceremony formalizing his arduous path to American citizenship, a clerk had told him to fill out a form. "What you put down is what will appear on the citizenship certificate so make sure it's spelled right. If you want to change your name this is the time to do it. No need to go to court to make it legal, just start using it." Gabe changed his name from Jibril to Gabriel with the glide of a pen, one more stratagem to eliminate the foreign, the alien, the other in him. He was now unquestionably himself—a man without origins.

"That's such a glib way to live, Gabriel. The only way I know to face the future is with my past," Angeline walked over to stand near him.

"It will kill you," Gabe looked at the dome of the lighthouse.

"We can't sever our past. Our stories are what makes us who we are," Angeline said.

"Palestinians have been living inside a story, a nightmare, for sixty seven years. Look where it's got them." He was irritated with the conversation, angry at himself for taking it there in the first place. He rejected stories. He believed in ownership, in titles, in deeds, in things real and concrete. Unlike his grandfather and his longing for a place, remembered in exile. "*Mount Carmel is in me, and on my eyelashes the grass of Galilee.*"

The sun was glistening over the water in a particular way. The light didn't look like light at all but like silver butterflies hovering over the water. Angeline gravitated to a shaft of sunlight piercing through the window and turned towards him.

"One day, when America sees it can no longer be on the wrong side of history, it will be because of memory keeping."

"Dream on," Gabe said.

"Sea change takes time, but when it happens, it happens quickly. Look at slavery and civil rights. And apartheid. And it can't happen without people remembering," she said.

Her dulcet voice exuded confidence and trust that made him want to believe her. "I don't have faith in the past or an attachment to what's failed. I guess I'm confounded by your passion for it," he said.

"We have to keep rolling the stone of history in front of us, Gabriel. It's the only way."

"What's your story?" Gabe looked at her with curiosity. Her eyes had a freakish quality, gold streaks lit her irises. He moved to the edge of his desk and leaned against it, his arms folded, his legs stretched to full length, crossed at the ankles. "Where did Louisiana come in?" He didn't care about history but he wanted to extend the conversation so he could have more time with her.

Angeline leaned against the credenza near Gabe's desk. She cupped the elbow of her right hand with her left, her fingers stroking the beads of her necklace. Dressed in her monastic white and black, all of her receded into the background while her neck and face and hair were thrown into high relief.

“In the 1700s, Louisiana’s founder, Pierre d’lberville, decided to drive the English out of Nevis and to stop pirate attacks on French ships. He promised his men a bounty if they would fight—the right to capture slaves and sell them in Martinique. The English fled as soon as the French attacked, but the slaves who remained to fight, three thousand in all, were captured. Most were sold in Martinique. Seven of them were shipped to Louisiana, the first Africans to arrive there.”

Angeline stood up and walked towards Gabe’s desk and the Newton’s Cradle.

“I’m the descendent of one of them, bought by a man named Lalande,” she lifted the whole rack of orbs high, to give the drop energy, force, momentum.

“Your memory is too long, the trace of it too deep,” he closed his hand over hers.

“We can’t all find consolation in money so I try to keep the stories alive.” Angeline said.

Gabe withdrew his hand as if from a fire. “You judge me too harshly,”

“Perhaps. It’s just that you have so much, but it’s never enough. How much is enough?” Angeline asked.

“So much for fair and balanced. You don’t even know me.” He could feel a cloud of anger rising inside him, a tension headache coming on, a stiffness in his neck. He straightened up, straightened his tie.

“I’m sorry Gabriel, you’re right. Forgive me,” she walked back to her seat and gathered her coat and bag. “Why did you want to see me?” She put on her coat and looked down as she buttoned up.

He finally remembered the point of the meeting. He'd promised the Elders he'd secure Angeline's assistance.

"I need help renaming our town. We want to get rid of the word Azyl. It's no small thing," he said, circling the corner of his desk to stand in front of her. "We'd need city approval, the bureaucracy is going to be maddening. It's going to be onerous and expensive. We'd have to change not just the street names but also the schools, the clubs, the sports teams, and dozens of businesses. With one sweep, we need to change it all. But the name has to be the right one. I need a wordsmith and researcher."

"I'm very busy." She looked up at him, both hands in her coat pockets. "I have no time."

"Come on. Nobody is that busy."

Angeline checked her watch. "Oh! This is bad, Gabriel. I'm going to be very late. I'm on air in half an hour. Can we talk about this later?" She seemed jittery and panicked.

"Where's your car?" At that hour, it would take twenty minutes to get downtown; he didn't see the problem.

"I took a cab. Oh, this is bad," she placed both hands against her temples. "Excuse me while I have a meltdown."

"I'll drive you," he said calmly.

They were silent as Gabe pulled his Audi out of the IBI parking lot, drove south on the Square, which was fairly deserted at that hour, and onto Shoreland Drive. He was an impatient driver. He drove too fast and kept changing lanes incessantly. The privilege of driving while not black, Angeline thought. Once on the freeway, the green-blue of the lake, the ripples of sun on the water, and the whisper of German luxury engineering relaxed Angeline.

"Thank you. It's nice of you to do this."

Gabe didn't respond.

"You giving me the silent treatment?"

"You make me crazy." He stared at the road ahead.

"Why do I make you crazy?" Angeline turned her head to look at Gabe.

"You undo me with all your talk."

"I don't know what to say." She studied his profile, saw a faint pulse, a tremor on his cheek. If he lost control, she imagined he could hurt people.

"You don't stop. You're a jack hammer," he said.

"I'm sorry. I'm a bit manic maybe."

"There's much to be said for unuttered thoughts."

"You're talking to a writer. We don't believe in unuttered thoughts."

"Silence is an art. Try it."

Major anger problem, Angeline decided.

Gabe extended his hand over her to reach the glove compartment, his eyes on the road, grazing her thighs. She held her breath. He retrieved a pair of sunglasses and put them on. "Make it up to me with the renaming," he looked at her.

Skyscrapers came into view. Axis mundi ambition cast in metal, concrete, and glass, covered in skins of varying hue and temper: icy blue and commanding, smoky gray and morose, cool pewter and serene, granite and irrepressibly grim. New architecture—undulating forms and silky lines evocative of waves and Mobius swirls—punctuated the bar graph skyline of towers, spires, and needles. Above the built world, clouds made Rorschach impressions on the lateral planes and facades of buildings. They lumbered like giant white seals treading water, or floated like nymphs in billowing robes across the mirrored panes, or hovered like sopranos pregnant with fermata.

"I wish I could, Gabriel. But I need another project like I need a hole in the head."

"What are you working on that keeps you so busy?" he glanced at her.

"I'm writing a book about Alexander Hamilton. It's taken over my life. I asked the station to downgrade me to correspondent so that I can finish it."

Gabe steered the car around a serpentine. "Everybody's writing about him now. Why not Madison or Jay? We know too little about them," Gabe reclined his seat.

"When I began the research, he was only capitalism's golden boy. I was interested in him because he was from Nevis, our one famous son. But then he became immigration's poster child, star of a Broadway musical. A rapper no less."

"Nothing is ever original. Ideas are like a virus."

"Synthesis is original."

"Synthesis is only as original as the intellect and emotion that shape it," Gabe said.

"That's the struggle," she sighed.

Angeline wasn't sure exactly when her interest in Alexander Hamilton had become a consuming fixation. During grade school history lessons in New Orleans, she remembered being pleased to hear that one of America's Founding Fathers hailed from the West Indies. And not just any West Indian island but from Nevis, the land of her ancestors.

After graduating from Tulane with a double major in journalism and African Diaspora studies, Angeline had won a scholarship from the Harriett Tubman Institute to research the African diaspora in Nevis, St. Croix and St. Kitts. While researching the Middle Passage, Angeline found traces of Alexander Hamilton's life in library vaults and index card drawers, in church and medical records, at the historical and conservation societies on the three islands, and in his birthplace in Charlestown. In St. Croix, she found records of his mother, Rachel's incarceration in the notorious Christiansted jail.

She had been a spirited woman by all accounts, and the only woman who had ever been imprisoned there. Alexander's stepfather had manipulated the legal system to toss his wife in jail for the crime of behavior unfitting of a wife. In St. Kitts, Angeline found Alexander Hamilton's father's employment record as a lightman or a linesman—the inky words had blurred with time and the middle letters were illegible. In the troves of papers, she found a young life of suffering and subtraction, punished by illegitimacy, poverty, betrayal, and intense grief.

After she returned from the islands, she kept reading and what she discovered felt like a found object. Think continentally, he had written. While other Founding Fathers had identified their states as their countries—Thomas Jefferson and James Monroe referred to Virginia as their country, John Adams called New England his country—Alexander Hamilton—a foreigner, an alien without native roots—declared, before anyone else had, that he was an American.

During her first winter at her lake house she began to read about Alexander Hamilton in earnest. She spent a month from morning to evening reading the Federalist Papers. The sheer volume of words, the volley of original thoughts, the considered jurisprudence, made her dizzy. This was no arriviste or poser or pseudo intellectual, this was pure, unadulterated genius. Since her Hamilton obsession began, she started to pay special attention to currency. Whenever she received a ten dollar bill from a cashier or proffered a ten dollar bill for a purchase, she felt compelled to gaze at Alexander Hamilton's portrait to acknowledge him. On the new ten dollar bill, his visage had been reimagined so that he looked nothing like any of his paintings. His delicate, almost feminine, oval chin had been redrawn into a square jaw. His bright, playful, intelligent eyes had been transformed into an aristocratic stare, lacking the humor and irony evident in the paintings. His thin, tender lips had been given American heft.

She'd told no one about her growing obsession. She went for an extended weekend to New York to visit his grave on Wall Street, to take a tour of the Grange, his home in Harlem, and to root through historical documents at the New York Public Library. When she returned, she began a reading marathon of his biographies and letters. After she finished all six volumes, she started on the biographies of George Washington, John Adams, Thomas Jefferson, James Madison, James Monroe, and others to discern their relationships with Hamilton.

All the while, there seemed to be a new and growing interest in the West Indian. Alexander Hamilton was having his moment. When the Treasury debated removing him from the ten dollar bill, a Twitter fight ensued. Leave him the f*$# alone @USTreasury. Take that slave owner Jackson off the twenty, jackasses @ USTreasury. Clickbait blog titles like Why Hamilton was an epic badass and Hamilton was gangsta appeared frequently in her online searches.

"Hang right, it's one block on the left. Don't get out. I'm running in," she said as they reached a cross street off Shoreland.

Gabe eased the car into a spot outside the front door of the station. "Will you help me anyway?" Gabe said, taking of his shades.

"I can't. Sorry," she stepped out of the car.

"Make time for me Angeline," he craned his neck towards the window by the passenger seat.

He was a man who made no pretense of what he wanted and he wasted no time. He cut to the chase as if time was too valuable to squander on preludes and overtures. Time is money. Yet he disarmed her with the way he demanded her attention, with the way he both revealed and withheld essential parts of his story. You don't even know me.

She bent low, her head level with his, her hands on the roof of the car. "Alright Gabriel. I'll help you."

Chapter 6

HISTOIRE

Nevis Peak was an immovable hulking giant. A cauldron of primordial volcanic soup simmering in the center of the island. It was horizon, landscape, panorama, topography, vista. It was excessive, voracious, commanding, commandeering. It controlled all experience and usurped everyone's imagination. It offered no relief, no reprieve, no rest for the eyes. For those with hyper vision, it was blinding.

If he looked at Nevis Peak with his back to the sea, without tilting his head upwards, he'd see dry forest turn slowly into humid jungle, thirsty matte leaves giving way to lush shiny foliage, sun rays bouncing off bark and soil and trees and vines and rope as old as time. If he lifted his head a little, he'd see the rainforest canopy hiding the secrets of small lives, and as he lifted his head higher still, he'd see the cloud forest. The mountain sat in biblical judgment, its presence seared into his consciousness, memorized from every slant, every incline, every perspective. The volcano hadn't been known to erupt since prehistoric times, but he felt disquiet around it. It could change at any moment. He instinctively tuned his ears to pick up rumblings from the crater, waiting, hoping not to hear a higher frequency rumble than the gurgling effervescence of the sulfur-infused hot springs. He had to be ready to flee. If the volcano spewed lava, he knew he would run into the sea. If he swam further out, he'd find it teeming with fish of all kinds. If he dove down to keep the black ash from reaching him, he'd find colorful companions—kingfish, barracuda, snapper, wahoo, dorado, tuna.

Sometimes, he would halt in the middle of a conversation and his eyes would turn towards the mountain. Was it a shriek or an imagined shriek? If real, was it of a green vervet monkey, her baby clinging to her breasts, caught in a hunter's trap? Was it a hallucination? Or was it a slave fleeing to Peak Heaven with freedom as his lodestar, only to have his throat cut by the spiked iron collar still around his neck? Or parrots learning to talk? Or mongooses killing red-necked pigeons?

He had trekked up the mountain twice. Once, as a child in the company of his brother, James and his friends; later, alone as a teenager. He entered through the thicket of wood, clearing low hanging branches with a sickle, dodging bamboo and desert palms. He saw dozens of varieties of orchids and heliconias, sprouting, blooming, flowering, on trunks of upright trees and fallen tree branches. The aroma of crushed black peppercorns, lemon grass, cerese, and balsam wafted through the air as he trampled on the potpourri. The higher up he went, the more lush and abundant the foliage and flora became. The leaves were oily and shiny, some as small as coins, others as large as cattle. The burr and hiss and chirp and shriek and howl and scream of mosquitoes and insects and birds and monkeys filled the air. Giant moths the size of clenched fists flitted about, as shy birds—rails, coots, crakes, and gallinules—hid under the dense vegetation. Caterpillars stripped the leaves off trees. Ravines and steep valleys sloped down to habitable parts of the island. Rainwater filtered through the clouds and ran down the ghauts and muddy paths. Something was terribly wrong. He felt no awe at the grandeur, he felt out of his element. He ran down the Peak.

Unlike the rock that he left alone to its dull immutability, he found the sea intriguing. It delivered the world to his narrow door—the rich and the dispossessed, the brave and the foolish, the adventurous and the desperate, the powerful and the powerless, the dreamers and the delusional. From his house, on the waterfront in Charlestown, he could see arriving French, Spanish, and English vessels. Brigs and barkentines, clippers and fluyts, battle, cargo, and passenger ships. Floating emporiums conveyed every need and luxury. Slave ships from Africa brought frightened human beings. Unmarked privateers delivered outcasts, thugs, thieves, pimps, murderers, mercenaries, and buccaneers. Fingers cocked the triggers of guns, ready to duel and die.

Walking past the courthouse, he would see manacled pirates dragged out after sentencing, hauled abroad schooners departing for St. Croix, to be hanged at Gallows Bay. As he walked past Crosses Alley or Market Shop, he'd see men with their branding irons walking with purposeful Christian dignity to the slave auction blocks. He'd see terrified, naked, emaciated, sick black men, women, and children standing in rows—the whites of their eyes so white in contrast to their ebony skin. During the inspections led by an auctioneer, a doctor, and men armed with two whips each, the slaves were ordered to jump, run in place, bend, squat, bend over, get on all fours, open their mouths, show their tongues, show their rectums, their vaginas, their penises. If they didn't move fast enough, they were whipped, either with the leather lash that marked the skin or drew blood, or with the other made of serrated wood, which ripped the flesh and broke bones with a single blow. He would hear the bloodcurdling screams of newly bought slaves branded by their owners, and the animal sound of pain of families torn from each other. The smell of burnt flesh and the sound of grief burrowed a dread in his already frightened heart.

There was no salvation, no redemption, on the rock. No deliverance from the monster. Not for his father, James A. Hamilton, the fourth son of a Scottish Laird, who had journeyed from Glasgow to St. Kitts, and then to Nevis and St Croix, to claim a better life, only to be crucified for his longing for more. Not for his mother, Rachel Faucette, driven to a fugitive life to escape her tormentors, only to die a death fit for a dog.

The sea and what lay beyond beckoned. He would go. He would leave what he knew. He would not live with the Peak as his only vision. He would not grow old with the smell of burnt human flesh on his nostrils. He would not die with the screams of slaves having their throats cut ringing in his ears. He would walk on the water. He would carry himself to a new world.

Chapter 7

THE ROOF

1996. Gabe was eighteen, living with his parents, grandfather, and aunts at Dbayeh. He was selling bottled water from the front of his family's one room zinc box. It was a thriving business since the water supply in the camp was broken and eighty percent of the water that sustained the camp was salinated. The extreme salt concentration meant stinging eyes, itchy scaly skin, and clean hair you couldn't put a comb through. You couldn't brush your teeth without wanting to retch. Most families used salt water for cleaning their food, clothes, and homes, and bottled water for drinking and bathing. Bath water was recycled. While showering, the final rinse water was caught in a tub to be reused for washing the salt out of laundered clothes. Gabe started work at six each morning. He wheeled a broken baby carriage that he had found outside the camp and converted into a sturdy crate with fortified wheels. He used it to haul bottles from the sundries shop down the hill. He bought four five-gallon bottles of water each day, loaded them into his cart, and made the trek back up to camp. He would set the bottles on their sides on a wooden bench near the mouth of the alley where he lived, and wait for customers. Most people sat outside their boxes on the alley with coffee, radios blaring next to them, and extra chairs for anybody who cared to join them. Gabe would thumb through newspapers and magazines borrowed from his neighbors and try to tune out the cacophony of broadcast sounds, laments, prayers, dirges, wailing, news, political speeches, and music that didn't move him. By eight, the first customers would arrive with their vessels. He poured water into jugs and pitchers held by hands that were dry, chapped, wrinkled, pruned, hands with knorls and warts and scabs and sores. These were his people. This was his lot.

"Can you fill this?" she'd asked, holding out an enamel pitcher. Her hands were unexpected. Caramel, dewy, set off by nails that were pearlescent.

Gabe found them pleasing. When he looked up, he was startled to find her beautiful. He stood up quickly and took the pitcher. Her head was uncovered and her auburn hair mesmerized him. She had full lips and dramatic, arching eyebrows. She was older than him, thirty at least.

He filled the pitcher from the dispenser and handed it to her.

"Ismee Farah. Ma Ismuka?" she asked.

Gabe blinked. He had no words. He forgot his name. He had to think before it came to him.

"How much shall I pay you?" she smiled, her eyebrows raised.

"It's alright," he said.

"I must pay you," she insisted.

"Next time," he told her.

She came back the next day and the next and the next. She pointed to the top of the hill. "I live with my dead grandmother and my dead mother over there," she said.

"I live with my mother, my aunts, my dead father, and my dead grandfather over here."

"Come to me tonight," she said.

Gabe could not name the force that propelled him towards her. It was so strong, so powerful, a hand on his back that pushed him forward. He walked the narrow alleys of the camp, past the political posters, the electronics repair shop, the tributes to those killed at the camp during multiple invasions by Lebanese militias. The evening was hot. He felt hotter. He took long strides to leap over puddles, walked on the edges of the alleys to avoid sewage and backed up open drains, and ducked his head under exposed electrical wires. He could hear the crackling of electricity, the loud hum of it, or perhaps it was his own body sizzling.

She opened the door and drew him in. Sshh, she lifted a finger to her lips as she took his hand and led him up the stairs of the concrete box to the roof. Her father, when he was alive, had worked for the Maronite church, which afforded him a privilege no other refugee at Dbayeh had been granted—a concrete roof. It allowed him to build an open room, a deck, with high retaining walls above the ground floor. Three window openings on the west wall gave a view of the Mediterranean, and three more on the east side gave an aerial view of the camp settlement running down the hill. Clothing, linens, and a pair of curtains hung from four lines, arranged in a square in the middle of the space. She slipped through the curtains, her fingers lacing his, leading him into the room within a room. Three tin tubs stood in the center, next to a covered red clay urn. Gabe's shirt was drenched with sweat.

"We should be clean for each other," she said.

They undressed and placed their clothes in a heap on a chair. He was sick with fever for her body. It was a woman's body, voluptuous, fully developed, so ripe, so beautiful he wanted to weep, so full of sin he wanted to run away. He felt sure it would devour him.

She stepped into the tin tub next to the urn. Gabe filled the two pitchers floating in the urn and turned to her. He held the jugs high over her head and poured. He filled the pitchers again and stepped inside the tub. She took one jug from him and poured it over his bent head. She set it in the open urn and took the other jug from Gabe. He held her hips as she poured. Gabe had to summon all his will to hold on, to hold himself in, to wait as they soaped each other. They stepped into the second tub to rinse off the lather, and into the third tub for a final rinse. She grabbed two towels from the clothesline and they dried each other. "I have thought of nothing but you," she said.

He pulled her down to the low divan near the sea-facing wall. He ran his fingers through her damp hair, over her face, across her body, the territory of her, the borders of her being. He wanted to remember everything, he wanted to impress his mind with the materiality of her, the substance of her. He wanted her to love him, wanted to love her, without blindness. "Don't close your eyes," he said.

When he placed his mouth on her breast, she moaned. When he mounted her, she buried her face into his nape, breaking the skin on his neck with her teeth. He gasped. They rode each other. They rose. They flew. Above Dbayeh. Away. Away

You give me breath.

You give me life.

A month passed. The roof was their sacred place. Gabe thought he would die if he couldn't be with her always. Without her, he did not exist. Pleasing her with his body made her say things he needed to hear. Life-giving words. Man-making words. *I have waited my whole life for you. You are the water of my life. I hear nothing but your voice. You are my language. You are my meaning. You have changed me completely. I will die without you.*

Gabe turned over all the possibilities that would allow them to marry and make a life outside the camp. They were both stateless refugees without a country, Palestinians who couldn't go back to Palestine. They couldn't apply to Jordan or Saudi Arabia or Iraq or Syria since they were Christian. The doors to Europe, America, and

Australia were hard to open; everybody he knew who had applied had been rejected. They could apply for citizenship to Lebanon. They were Maronites, Lebanon would welcome them. But his father wouldn't allow it.

"If you go somewhere else, you will be stripped of your Palestinian identity and any future right of return."

"I don't care about your politics. I care about my life." Gabe said.

"Come in," Farah said, as he stood at the door.

"I have found a way," Gabe said.

"What is it?"

"Shall we go to the roof?" Gabe asked.

"You can tell me here."

"It's about us."

"Tell me here."

"We marry and apply for citizenship here in Lebanon."

"What about US, UK, or Canada?

"Everybody is getting rejected. It's too hard."

"What about France or Germany? Or Norway?"

"We can begin something good here. In a few years we can apply to any of them. We'll stand a better chance," Gabe said.

"Jibril," she took his hands in hers. "There's a man from this camp already settled in Germany. He has asked to fiancé me. I am to give him an answer. What will you have me do?"

He was stunned. How could she say the things she'd said, you are the water of my life, you are my language, my meaning, I will die without you, and say this now?

Every corner of his life had been claimed by poverty and politics.

He couldn't find work. He eked out a living selling water from a baby carriage. He didn't have an education, he couldn't vote, he was a man without a country, trapped in a hellhole.

"What will you have me do?"

"You should go to him. He can give you a future now. I have to find my future," Gabe said.

"Stay with me one last night," she reached for him.

Gabe swiped her hand away. Whore! He wanted to be farther than the moon from her. He walked out the door. He broke into a run. The rubble heard his rage. The stones cried out.

Saba watched Gabe with concern as he slipped into a deep well of sorrow, past pain, beyond grief. "What troubles you, habibi?"

"Every day is the same. I will go mad if I stay here."

"She broke your heart," his mother said.

"Before her, my mind was empty. It was so clear. But now my mind is not clear and I am full only of her."

"First love happens only once. It shows you all of life, all the happiness, all the pain. And then it is over," Saba said.

"Who can endure it more than once?" Jena, Gabe's widowed aunt moaned in remembrance.

Saba, Jena, and Zulima huddled with Musa, the fixer, around a low table on the floor of their zinc box. Gabe's grandfather, Yahya, sat in a corner cutting a lump of coal into small chalks and smoothing the edges on the concrete floor. His father called him a traitor and stormed out of the box. Saba served tea and halwa.

Gabe sat on the floor, his back against the wall, his legs stretched out in front of him. He was so tired, so desolate. Farah had inflicted on him a near fatal wound. He needed to change his life to save it. Somewhere out there, he felt, there must be a life waiting for him.

"Where can you see yourself?" Musa asked.

Gabe shrugged.

"Europe is very hard. Nobody is getting a visa and crossing is more risky now. Eight boys from Bourj and Shatila were caught yesterday trying to cross into Turkey," Musa said.

"What happened to them?" Jena asked.

"They will be returned to the camps."

Returned. The irony was not lost on them.

"Australia is possible with more money."

"I have given you all the money we have." Saba had borrowed thousands of lira from relatives in Europe and America to pay him.

"South Africa is very easy. We can get you there, you work and save for two years. From there you apply for Europe or Australia."

"This is what I pay you for?" Saba scolded Musa. "People are running away from Africa, not going there."

"Nothing is easy," Musa said.

"My son, where will make you happy?" his mother asked.

"What one place?" Zulima asked.

Gabe drew his knees to his chest. He stared at the holes in his jeans. "Amreeka," he said.

"Issh! Impossible," Musa said.

"Russia has sent monkeys to the moon. Why is this impossible for a man named after a prophet?" Saba asked. "We will sit here until you come up with an answer. You will not leave until you have found a way."

"And don't open your mouth to catch flies," Zulima scolded.

"Only open it if you have a way for him to Amreeka," Jena added.

They sat in silence drinking tea and eating halwa. Musa drew a cigarette out of a tin, tapped it on the lid, raised the cigarette as if he had an idea, than shook his head in retraction.

Saba sat down near Gabe and made a sign of the cross on his forehead.

"Leave me alone," Gabe pushed her hand away.

They watched Musa thinking, the unlit cigarette in his mouth.

"We do it this way," Musa finally said. "He is handsome, smart, tall boy. He looks Amreekan. They will like him. We will forge an acceptance letter to a university there. The three of you will go with him to the US Embassy in Beirut. He will show the acceptance letter and his permit and apply for a two-year student visa. This will be easier than four-year visa.

"This is too much risk. I don't want him in danger," Saba said.

"It will be a small university in a small town. Not Harvard. Nobody will question it," Musa said.

Gabe remembered that period, after the decision had been made, while Musa worked to find a virtuoso counterfeiter of documents, as a time of unmooring, limned by shades of white gold promise, liquid hope, and foreboding. Once Gabe had accepted the idea, it became what he wanted most in the world. But daily, he worried that it would elude him, that some diabolical force would never allow him to have it. The same unholy providence that had taken Farah from him; that had ground down the men in his family, who stood with their fists empty, no ground beneath their feet to call their own, for so long. So long.

Chapter 8

CHRONICLER

Heartland Transformed, the five-part documentary on immigrants to the U.S. that Angeline had been working on for more than six months, was in post-production in preparation for broadcast on July 4th. Her work on the project was for the most part complete before Christmas. But her producer and sound engineer had told her to stick around during the editing process, in case scenes ended up on the cutting room floor that altered the narrative flow and she was needed for new voiceover. Angeline's plan to spend winter in Nevis to be with her family and finish her book, a sabbatical she had previously negotiated with the station, evaporated. Her producer agreed to a horse trade—Angeline could work on her book now and take a field trip to Nevis in summer if she'd deliver a roundup a week for the evening news via remote and contribute digital content to the station website.

Midwestern winters undid Angeline. She felt alone, lonely, sorry for herself, pining for her family. Like the plants on the windowsill elongating their stems towards the light, she inclined to it. She woke up each day hoping to see sunlight, following it throughout the day from room to room, dragging a chair, open laptop in her hand, to settle in a sun pool to work. She listened closely to weather reports, timing her ventures outside her apartment with temperature spikes. If it dipped into the single digits or low teens she paid premium for home grocery delivery. She remembered that January as a month of daily and often hourly crying jags. By mid-February, she weaned herself from full on tear festivals and reserved her crying to half hour bouts as she prepared and ate lunch. Thus cleansed by a vale of tears, she allowed herself to think about Nevis and its most famous son. And she read.

She received a document in the mail from the National Archives in DC, accompanied by maniacal annotations from the researcher. "This is the first extant document in which Hamilton is mentioned. Both Bancroft (George Bancroft, *History of the United States* [Boston, 1858], VII, 79) and Lodge (Henry Cabot Lodge, *Alexander Hamilton* [Boston, 1899], 283–85) refer to an earlier document dated 1766. Bancroft states: "The first written trace of Hamilton's existence is in 1766, when his name appears as witness to a legal paper executed in the Danish island of Santa Cruz." Lodge elaborates on this statement as follows: "I have carefully examined an exact tracing of this signature. The handwriting is obviously Hamilton's." This document has not been found."

"Probate court transaction no. XXIX"

The case of the deceased Rachael Lewine. James Towers, by His Royal Majesty of Denmark and Norway duly appointed administrator of estates in the Christiansted jurisdiction on the Island of St. Croix in America, and Ivar Hofman Sevel, appointed bailiff in the same jurisdiction, together with Laurence Bladwil, administrator of estates, Isaac Hartman, and Johan Henric Dietrichs, appointed town and probate court recorder in the aforesaid jurisdiction, make known that:

In the year 1768 on the 19th day of February in the evening at 10 o'clock sharp the probate court met in a house here in town belonging to Thomas Dipnal, where an hour earlier a woman, Rachael Lewine, died, in order to seal up her effects for subsequent recording. Present at this transaction were the aforesaid Thomas Dipnal and Friedrich

Wilhl Larsen as witnesses to the sealing up of a chamber containing her effects together with a trunk etc., thereafter were sealed an attic storage room and two storage rooms in the yard, after which there was nothing more to seal up, except some pots and other small things which remained unsealed for use in preparing the body for burial, among them being 6 chairs, 2 tables, and 2 wash-bowls. The transaction was then closed.

"In witness thereof

James Towers *Johan Henric Dietrichs*

As Witnesses

Thomas Dipnal *Friedrich Wilhm Larsen*

In the year 1768 on the 22 of February the probate court administered by me, James Towers, as acting administrator of estates, and by me, Johan Henric Dietrichs, duly appointed by the King as town and probate court recorder in the Christiansted jurisdiction on the Island of St. Croix in America, met in Thomas Dipnal's house here in town, where on the 19th of this month Madam Rachael Lewine died, and whose effects were forthwith sealed up, in order now to take an inventory of them for subsequent distribution among the decedent's surviving children, who are 3 sons, namely, Peter Lewine, born in the marriage of the decedent with John Michael Lewine who, later, is said for valid reasons to have obtained from the highest authorities a divorce from her (according to what the probate court has been able to ascertain), also 2 other sons, namely, James Hamilton and Alexander Hamilton, the one 15 and the other 13 years old, who are the same illegitimate children sc. born after the decedent's separation from the aforesaid Lewine. The above mentioned Peter Lewine has resided and still resides in South Carolina and according to reports is about 22 years old.

Angeline began email exchanges with the director of the Historical and Conservation Society in Nevis, and the archivist at the History Association of St. Croix, where Alexander Hamilton spent his later years. Celestine Harper, the archivist in St. Croix, rattled Angeline with her island tempo. Angeline would send her multiple emails and then be forced to cool her heels waiting for Celestine to respond. Angeline's attempts at cultural understanding and patience turned to irritation, then anxiety, then anger as she waited weeks without a reply. Just when she thought she'd boil over, a flurry of emails would arrive from Celestine with precise subject lines: Alexander Hamilton's Mother's First Marriage, Alexander Hamilton's Brother's Bio, Alexander Hamilton's Father's Final Days. Angeline would print the attachments and read and re-read them as if divining the runes.

Rachel Lavien, Hamilton's mother, was the daughter of John Faucett, a doctor and planter, and his wife Mary, both of the English island Nevis. Either in 1745 or somewhat earlier, Rachel Faucett went to St. Croix where she married the merchant John (Johann) Michael Lavien. In 1746, Peter Lavien was born. The marriage was not a happy one, and in 1750 Rachel left her son, Peter, and her husband and ran away from the island. In 1759, Lavien obtained a divorce from Rachel. Shortly after leaving her husband, Rachel Lavien had met James Hamilton, who was the fourth son of Alexander Hamilton, Laird of Grange in Stevenston Parish in Ayrshire, Scotland. Unmarried, they lived together on St. Kitts as man and wife and had two sons, James and Alexander. In 1765, James Hamilton moved his family to St. Croix. Soon after, he returned to St. Kitts, leaving his family on St. Croix. He never saw them again. In February, 1768, Rachel Lavien was taken ill with a fever and died shortly afterwards. Peter Lavien, Hamilton's half brother, was the sole heir of his father. In 1764, he went to South Carolina and was living there at the time of his mother's death. After his mother's death, Hamilton's brother, James was apprenticed to a carpenter on the island of St. Croix. Nothing is definitely known concerning the remainder of his life. According to Ramsing, he died in 1786.

Angeline learned to adjust her pace to island time when talking to the researchers and scholars and archive keepers.

"Every day is a fishing day but every day is not a catching day," the archivist in Nevis wrote, after Angeline had asked her one too many times for Alexander Hamilton's church attendance records.

Angeline wrote to Celestine asking for Hamilton's surviving diaries and letters and anything that could shed light on his astonishing future success. Celestine wrote ten days later: It takes time to find the ant's belly.

Angeline alternated between two poles: telling herself to calm down and stop being a hot-headed American with the attention span of a three-year-old who needed instant gratification right now, at light speed, baby; and convincing herself that Celestine was a sadist who got her kicks playing with Angeline in order to drive her nuts like Charles Boyer drove Ingrid Bergman stark raving mad in Gaslight.

Angeline stared at Hamilton's portraits for hours. He was a chameleon; he looked different in every painting. In the earliest portrait taken of him at age seventeen after he had just arrived in New York, he looked impoverished, malnourished, etiolated, of no account or consequence. In his eyes were written the biography of bad luck and tragedy. Later, in a painting of him taken just six years after the first, he exuded the air of someone who had claimed his rightful place in the grand scheme. His shoulders and chest open, head and chin tilted back, the beginning of a smile or the discipline of one playing about his mouth. His lips had a hint of humor and sensuality about them. He radiated amusement in his liquid blue eyes. He'd torn the American fabric, woven himself into the skein, and sewn the cloth into a seamless whole. How America changes a man, Angeline thought.

Chapter 9

Runes

Colonel Hamilton,

As the perusal of the political papers under the signature of Publius has afforded me great satisfaction, I shall certainly consider them as claiming a most distinguished place in my Library. I have read every performance which has been printed on one side and the other of the great question lately agitated (so far as I have been able to obtain them) and, without an unmeaning compliment, I will say, that I have seen no other so well calculated (in my judgment) to produce conviction on an unbiased Mind, as the Production of your triumvirate. When the transient circumstances and fugitive performances which attended this Crisis shall have disappeared, That Work will merit the Notice of Posterity; because in it are candidly and ably discussed the principles of freedom and the topics of government, which will be always interesting to mankind so long as they shall be connected in Civil Society.

Yours – George Washington

I consider Napoleon, Fox, and Hamilton the three greatest men of our epoch, and if I were forced to decide between the three, I would give without hesitation the first place to Hamilton. He divined Europe.

– Charles Maurice de Talleyrand

Hamilton was indeed a singular character. Of acute understanding, disinterested, honest, and honorable in all private transactions, amiable in society, and duly valuing virtue in private life, yet so bewitched & perverted by the British example, as to be under thoro' conviction that corruption was essential to the government of a nation.

– Thomas Jefferson

Vice, folly, and villainy are not to be forgotten because the guilty wretch repented in his dying moments. Hamilton is an intrigant—the greatest intrigant in the world—a man devoid of every moral principle—a bastard and as much a foreigner as Gallatin.

– John Adams

He was the greatest statesman in the western world, perhaps the greatest man of our age ... he has left none like him—no second, no third, nobody to put us in mind of him.

– Rev. John M Mason.

He made your government. He made your bank. I sat up all night with him to help him do it. Jefferson thought we ought not to have a bank and President Washington thought so. But my husband said, "We must have a bank." I sat up all night, copied out his writing, and the next morning, he carried it to President Washington and we had a bank.

– Elizabeth Schuyler Hamilton

That bastard brat of a Scottish peddler! His ambition, his restlessness, and all his grandiose schemes come, I'm convinced, from a superabundance of secretions, which he couldn't find enough whores to absorb them.

– John Adams

He was the most brilliant American statesman that ever lived, possessing the loftiest and keenest intellect of all time.

– Theodore Roosevelt

His ambition, pride, and overbearing temper destines him to be the evil genius of this country.

– Noah Webster

One cannot note the disappearance of this brilliant figure, to Europeans the most interesting in the early history of the Republic, without the remark that his countrymen seem to have never, either in his lifetime or afterwards, duly recognized his splendid gifts.

– Lord Bryce

... I pray you to present my best wishes, in which Mrs. Washington joins me, to Mrs. Hamilton and the family, and that you would be persuaded that with every sentiment of the highest regard, I remain your sincere friend and affectionate honorable servant.

– George Washington

To John Jay.

From Alexander Hamilton

Col. Laurens is on his way to South Carolina, on a project, which I think, in the present situation of affairs there, is a very good one and deserves every kind of support and encouragement. This is to raise two three or four battalions of negroes; with the assistance of the government of that state, by contributions from the owners in proportion to the number they possess ... I have not the least doubt, that the negroes will make very excellent soldiers, with proper management ... I frequently hear it objected to the scheme of embodying negroes that they are too stupid to make soldiers. This is so far from appearing to me a valid objection that I think their want of cultivation (for their natural faculties are probably as good as ours) joined to their habit of subordination which they acquire from a life of servitude, will make them sooner become soldiers than our White inhabitants. ... I foresee that this project will have to combat much opposition from prejudice and self-interest. The contempt we have been taught to entertain for the blacks, makes us fancy many things that are founded neither in reason nor experience; and an unwillingness to part with property of so valuable a kind will furnish a thousand arguments to show the impracticability or pernicious tendency of a scheme which requires such a sacrifice ... An essential part of the plan is to give them their freedom with their muskets. This will secure their fidelity, animate their courage, and I believe will have a good influence upon those who remain, by opening a door to their emancipation. This circumstance, I confess, has no small weight in inducing me to wish the success of the project; for the dictates of humanity and true policy equally interest me in favour of this unfortunate class of men.

– Alexander Hamilton

... Mine is an odd destiny. Perhaps no man in the UStates has sacrificed or done more for the present Constitution than myself—and contrary to all my anticipations of its fate, as you know from the very beginning, I am still laboring to prop the frail and worthless fabric. Yet I have the murmurs of its friends no less than the curses of its foes for my rewards, What can I do better than withdraw from the scene? Every day proves to me more and more that this American world was not made for me ...

– Alexander Hamilton

He embodied an enduring archetype: the obscure immigrant who comes to America, recreates himself, and succeeds despite a lack of proper birth and breeding. He was the messenger from a future we now inhabit. Today, we are indisputably the heirs to Hamilton's America, and to repudiate his legacy is, in many ways to repudiate the modern world.

– Ron Chernow

Chapter 10

NINETY SIX NAMES FOR LOVE

Rae Oberoi had been sitting at the kitchen table drinking coffee, biting into toast, scrolling emails on his laptop and listening to sports radio. He was dressed for work in a navy blue blazer, crisp white shirt open at the collar, dark denim jeans, and black loafers.

His wife, Nila, ambled into the kitchen. She was still in her robe, a short blue satin kimono with an embroidered iridescent peacock set on the back, its wingspan folding over her breasts and hips. She walked towards the coffee machine, sliding a white scrunchie off her wrist and holding it between her teeth. She lifted her waist length hair with both hands and twisted it into a rope. She slid the waffled band to the roots of the hair, wound the hair into a coil, and tucked the end into the clasp.

"Why aren't you dressed?" Rae looked at his watch and then at his wife's thighs. "You're going to be late."

"I called in sick." She reached into a cabinet for a mug, pulled a drawer open for a teaspoon, took out creamer from the fridge, and poured the last of the coffee in the carafe.

"Wish I could do the same, but I've got a full day of meetings," he looked back at the open laptop.

She turned her back to the kitchen sink, holding the mug in the bowl of her hands.

"Are you going to sit or hover?" Rae asked.

Nila walked over to the table and sat down facing him. He continued to stroke the scroll button. Rae used to be a different person before his business empire swallowed him up. She remembered a time when he would linger, dally, tarry.

Nila had no right to complain. It was she who had drawn out his ambition, helped him focus it like a laser, inspired him with confidence in the early days when he couldn't catch a break, when he suffered rejection after rejection. "I don't think I'm cut out for this," he'd say after failing to close a deal or find financing for his ventures. She fortified him, made him stand up and try again when he was in danger of giving up. "You're so close, don't give up yet. Give it another six months. I believe in you," she'd say, even as she worried about his ability to pull it off. She encouraged him to keep trying, and finally the success he neither lusted after nor wanted in any profound way came to him. She was surprised to find herself the wife of an exceedingly wealthy man. Raj Cabs had grown into a fleet operating in four states, and Rae owned a major stake in real estate in Azyl Park.

"Can we afford for me to quit?" she'd asked over the years. She was an admissions counselor at the private school her children attended. She had begun working there when Hari had started kindergarten and Zara, first grade.

He encouraged her to keep working. "Yes, but I don't want you turning into a bored housewife having affairs with the cable guy. Your mind is too active. Do something that makes you happy."

"Look at me, Raja," Nila said now.

Rae looked up, half his mind on her, half on the meetings with his accountant and lawyer and banker that morning.

"I don't like my job. I want to make a change."

Rae closed the laptop. "How long have you felt like this?"

"At least six months now in a serious way. I've grown to hate it."

"So, quit your bellyaching and do something else."

"What should I do?" Nila asked.

"Figure out what makes you want to wake up in the morning or what you do exceptionally well."

"Like what?"

Nila dressed like no one Rae knew. "You're a clothes horse. You have great taste and fashion sense. Open a boutique. I'll set you up."

It was true that Nila loved beautiful, feminine clothes. She was thirty-five and old fashioned. Seeing women hide their beauty in men's clothes and joyless colors depressed her. While other women who had lived in America a long time, including her own sixty-eight year-old mother, had traded their native clothes for trousers, yoga pants, jeans, t-shirts, sweatshirts, hoodies, and subdued colors, Nila had emphatically reclaimed her Indian roots. She felt true to herself wearing the traditional clothing of India, though she had grown up and lived in Madison, Wisconsin since the age of two, the daughter of the Dean of the Dental School and a Post Colonial scholar. Her jeans-wearing mother had accused her of exoticizing and fetishizing India.

"You've Orientalized yourself. Edward Said is rolling in his grave. You are not my American daughter," her mother scolded her.

"How can you have vagina monologues wearing pants?" Nila defended herself.

Nila wore soft silks, palazzo pants, long tunics, brocaded vests, and saris, like women who lunched at the Hermitage Club back in Goa. She loved the riotous colors of Indian textiles and the degrees of discernment: not simply red but iridescent ruby, jeweled paprika, and deep garnet; not simply green but matte chutney, shimmering mint, and creamy sea foam. She loved dressing in these colors, an anomaly in a sea of executive gray, black, and navy blue. She had made some accommodations of course. In winter she wore heavyweight weaves with stylish shearling boots and richly pigmented cashmere shawls. In severe weather she donned a fur lined coat, cloche hat, cashmere scarf, and warm gloves. But she couldn't imagine dressing other people. "I don't care about it in that way," she said.

"What would you do even if you could do it for free?"

She considered Rae's question as she reached for the uneaten slice of toast on his plate. "I know what kind of partner someone needs to become fully themselves," she said biting into it.

Rae smiled. "That you do. You have a PhD in that," he said.

Rae had gone to college with Arun, Nila's older brother. Both business students at UC Berkeley, both misfits among the Desi student body of engineering majors, Poli Sci idealists, and medical school geniuses, they struck up a friendship over pints at the Albatross on San Pablo. Rae had accompanied Arun home to Madison on several breaks because he couldn't go home to Indiana. His parents had divorced during his freshman year and he hadn't figured out how to treat them as freestanding individuals instead of a yoked pair. He felt guilt that he had kept them shackled in a loveless marriage for more than two decades, that he had been the glue that held their marriage together. He didn't know where to park himself. His parents had sold the house he had grown up in and bought one-bedroom condos, his father in a golf community, his mother in a seniors complex with five award-winning chefs. They had wiped out his childhood, his history. It seemed that there was no longer a home for him, no place to drop anchor, no place for him to fold himself into.

Nila was a junior in high school when she first set eyes on Rae. He was skinny, of average height. He had cool pecan skin, long narrow eyes framed by spiky eyelashes, and black hair sprinkled with grey at the top and sides. What a freak, an old man's head on a young man's body, she'd thought. He charmed her mother with his fine manners, shared laughs with Arun and her father, but was indifferent to her.

Sometimes, as she walked up the driveway to her house after school, she'd see Rae and Arun pulling out of the garage. He'd remain silent in the passenger seat, looking straight ahead, while Arun acknowledged her. It was clear that Rae had a lot on his mind, and not a single thought revolved around her.

One day, her mother called out to Rae from the living room, as he was walking towards the front door to Arun's car.

"Is it true that you are to marry Divya?" Nila's mother asked.

Rae was taken aback by the question. "How could you have known? We haven't told anyone yet."

"Her mother and my sister are the best of friends," Nila's mother said.

Arun's impatient honking from the driveway grew louder. "Musn't keep your son waiting." Rae rounded his shoulders and walked out of the room. Nila walked beside him in the narrow hallway.

"How's school? Good?" he asked, to break the awkward silence. When she remained silent, he answered for her, "Good." Why was she following him anyway?

He opened the front door and stepped outside.

Nila stood there, her heart beating, her mouth dry. Her whole life would be defined by the moment in front of her. She could act or not act. The outcomes would be dramatically different. As Rae was halfway between the front door and Arun's car, she clutched her shoulders with crossed arms and cried out, "Bloody idiot! You should be with me." "I'm your twin flame! Wait for me to grow up, you ignoramus."

Rae turned to her, dazed. He blinked. Everything felt hazy, nebulous. Was he hallucinating? He looked around. No. Arun sitting in the car impatiently gesticulating was real, the metallic gray Saab was real, the doormat with the word, Swagatam, was real.

"Yaar, I'm growing a beard here," Arun yelled and honked again.

Rae lifted his hand and spread his fingers. Five minutes, he signaled to Arun. He turned back to Nila. "I don't believe what I'm hearing."

"Wait for me! I love you!" Tears ran down her face. "Idiot! Meet me at 6 pm tomorrow at Leona's." She slammed the door before Rae could say anything.

Rae arrived half an hour before their appointed time and stationed himself at a booth facing the front door. Nila arrived at 5.69 wearing big Jackie O glasses as if she was being trailed by paparazzi.

"I didn't think you'd have the guts to show up," she said as she sat down, dropped a backpack on the chair next to her, and took off the glasses. She wore jeans and a shimmery blue blouse with cap sleeves that accentuated her well-toned arms. She had made an effort with makeup that made her look older than she was. Her eyes were lined with kohl and a gold shadow that was too much makeup for that time of day, but somehow on her warm skin, seemed natural and not overdone. She wore a row of Indian glass bangles in shades of blue on both arms. When she moved her hands, the bangles made a soft tinkling sound.

Smart ass little girl copping an attitude. "I've been here half an hour," he said.

"I'm impressed," Nila studied the menu and signaled the waitress.

"I don't know what to make of you." Rae said after they'd placed their order.

"I'm not that complicated. I don't hold things in."

"Arun tells me you have your head in the clouds."

"It's true. But I'm not stupid. I know what I want."

"What do you want from me? I'm minding my own business."

She dipped a straw in a glass of water and stirred. Her bangles jostled. “I took Sanskrit at Madison over the summer,” she said.

Apropos of nothing, he thought. “Nice to have professor parents. You go for free, right?”

“Do you know how many names there are in Sanskrit for love?” Nila leaned forward, laid her hands on the table, palms open. “Do you?”

A kid trying to play a grownup, he decided.

“Ninety-six.” She searched his face. “Understand?”

“You must be a good student,” he said. A baby.

“In English there’s only one. But it explains everything I feel for you. I love you, idiot.”

Who behaves like this? He was an ordinary guy who had failed to elicit strong emotions in anyone including his own parents. They couldn’t care less about him, so this seemed highly irregular. “You’ve been watching too many Bollywood romances.”

“Oh, I love romantic films! Not just Bollywood. English, French, Middle Eastern, Japanese. I watch them all. People should love like that in real life.”

Such a silly girl. “You’re what, sixteen? How can you talk like this?”

“Seventeen. I don’t care if you don’t love me back yet. I’ll make you love me. I’m crazy about you. Wait for me to grow up.”

Rae had never considered himself lucky. When he was a kid, he’d squirm when games of chance and draw contests were announced at birthday parties. His fingers would grow clammy as lots were drawn and kids he knew to be cruel by nature won the prizes with ease. He never won. He’d plaster a fake smile on his lips and sit silently until his father or mother arrived to pick him up. The experiences were testaments to the arbitrary nature of things, the inequality and unfairness of the world, that he added to his articles of faith. It had left him with a view of himself in the universe, average, always wanting, never quite having. Nila made him feel lucky.

"You have no fire in you. I will be your fire. I'll adore you, make you feel like a Raja, so you can go out and conquer the world," she said.

"You sound like you're thirty instead of seventeen," Rae said.

"I'm bossy and opinionated. Full of myself. I know how to motivate people. I'm a good manager," she said.

"What do you want to do yourself?" Rae asked. She was something else.

"I don't like routine or answering to people. I've got a brain but I don't want to suffer using it. I want to follow my own interests wherever they may lead me. I will help you so we can afford this," she said.

Rae admired how sure she was of herself and her future. Unlike her, he hadn't made plans so much as fallen into life. He was indifferent to taking action. He left it to whatever organizing intelligence was out there keeping the world turning, the earth orbiting the sun, the tides washing in and out to an ancient clock over the world's shorelines, to locate him somewhere pleasant. "Do you like kids?" he asked.

"I want two. A boy and a girl. And if that doesn't happen, I want to try for a third," Nila said.

"You have it all worked out. You're so good," he made the mistake of telling her.

"No I'm not!" she said. "If I ever catch you with another woman, I'm warning you now, you won't live to regret it."

Divya had no such emotion. She was a cold, clinical person—a pathologist. What did he expect from somebody cutting up the dead? Joie de vivre dissecting a cirrhotic liver? La bella vida sawing up a cancerous lung? La vida loca storing rectal tissue in formaldehyde?

Nila on the other hand. "Listen to me," she reached across the table for his hands. "You make me tremble."

"Don't play with me," he would have told her if she was someone else. But her heart was tender and pure and good. She was someone who would live without regret. He wanted to be with someone who was reckless and grabbed love without hesitation, who was greedy to give love, who chose him. She was the bravest person he had ever met. She would be his fire. She had him at bloody idiot. He waited for her.

"I feel I'd be a good matchmaker. I know what people need. I know how they lie to themselves and fool themselves and hurt themselves choosing the wrong mate, and living in bad faith," Nila said.

"But technology has taken over. All the websites, match.com, e-harmony, ok cupid, desimatch. It's all about algorithms now. The competition is fierce. You'd be like an independent bookstore against Amazon," Rae said.

"Then why is every single person I know having a hard time finding someone? Complaining about the terrible Internet dating scene? Jeanie told me she's giving a bounty to anyone who finds her a partner. $25,000. I know exactly who she should be with. I told her she better not renege on the reward," she said.

"Give it a shot then," he said finally. "Now come here."

She set her mug down on the table, walked towards him, and slid into the triangle of his legs.

He put his arms around her and looked up at her, his face in the valley of her breasts. "Why didn't you tell me earlier? I could have spared you misery."

"You know how impulsive I am. I wanted to be sure."

"Always tell me what you need to make you happy," he said.

"You're the best husband ever." She pulled him to his feet. "I want to have my way with you right now. Come upstairs. I want to ride you like a polo pony."

"Nila, I have to go to work. Back to back to back meetings." He released her hands and picked up his phone from the table. "I have to go."

She unfastened the belt on her robe, slid it off her shoulders, and let it fall from her naked body into a pool around her feet. "Right now."

He text messaged his secretary on the way up the stairs: Cncl mtgs down w/ high fever.

That afternoon, Rae took Nila to lunch at a new French-Indian fusion restaurant on the Square. Afterwards, they walked, his hand around her shoulders, hers circling his waist, to a building they owned three blocks south of the restaurant. It stood between a sari emporium and a hookah bar. The vacant ground floor unit had a City Realty "For Rent" sign with Tina Trang's photo and contact information.

"You'll have a captive audience of both men and women," Rae said, as his property manager opened the door to let them in. "Eduardo, come back in fifteen to lock up. Nos vemos, pronto."

Nila walked the length and breadth of the empty space. "It's prime location. I hate to see you losing rent on account of me."

"I was expecting you to make it up to me in other ways," Rae narrowed his eyes.

Nila giggled. "What's the rent we get for this normally?" she asked, as she tried to visualize the space with furniture.

"Ten K a month."

Nila whistled. "I better get cracking and learn some new moves to write that off."

"I want a new position from Vatsyayana every time. Morning and night."

"You just wait," she said, drawing her hands over her eyes like an Odissi dancer. Nila consulted Rae about choosing a name for her company. Make it easy to remember, he told her. Sit with it and think about it.

"How about Twin Flames Matchmaker?" she asked Rae a few days later.

Their naked bodies were parked. They were looking up at the slow spin of the ceiling fan as it churned the air in the room.

"I know it's what you told me and it's beautiful. But does it have a meaning beyond what you have bestowed on it?" Rae turned on his side to look at her.

"I found out it's from Greek mythology," She twined a leg around his hip.

"I already have issues buying into the Gita. Can't handle anymore fairy tales," he said.

"The gods felt threatened by humans and their great strength. So Zeus, the father of Gods and Men, split humans in half as punishment for their pride. These split humans were so broken and miserable they would starve to death. So, Zeus's son Apollo, the god of healing, sewed them back together and reconstituted their bodies," Nila said.

"I'm a rational man, Nila. I don't buy any of this," Rae said.

"They believed that when the two halves found each other, there would be an unspoken understanding of one another. That they would feel unified and would lay with each other, and would know no greater joy than that. They believed that when you met your twin soul, your twin flame, you would be forced to face your self."

"This I believe. Forced is right. Knocked down. Dragged kicking and screaming."

"Do you regret it? I stole you from Divya. She would have given you a different life."

"Very different. But I don't regret any day with you."

Chapter 11

REMAINS

Irina was still in her robe, her hair damp, her skin wet from her ritual morning swim in the lake. She was lighting her first cigarette of the day from the pilot light on the stove when she heard the closing of a car door on the street below. Her apartment was on the second floor but she was sure she heard the click click of automated locks. She was three weeks late with her rent. She was sure Ivan had grown tired of the string of promises she had left him on his office voicemail, always after hours when she knew he would have left for the day. Irina was surprised that he had waited this long. She stepped into the folds of the cheap curtains at the kitchen window. Her long blonde hair and pale skin, and the yellow satin of her ten dollar kimono from Whole World Style, blended into the buttercream panels. She saw Ivan leaning against the side of his car, talking on his cellphone and stroking the bald spot on his crown.

Ivan had risen further in America than anyone from the old country could have imagined. Back in the village he was five foot three with a broken nose that tipped to one side, teeth that sloped towards each other, and no assets but a wheelbarrow and a bicycle. Ivan's nose was inspired now, like Michelangelo's Brutus. His teeth were sculpted from titanium, each one a monument to his dramatic rise from penniless immigrant to Lexus driving land baron. He wore supple black leather jackets, black shirts with bold vertical stripes, tapered black trousers without cuffs or pleats, elevated alligator shoes, and a haircut that began high above the ears—a black tuft that stood up two inches above his head, stiff with gel and the shock of prosperity. The clever sartorial and cosmetic tricks all added up centimeter by centimeter to make him appear taller than he really was. Ivan and his wife, Maja owned dozens of apartment buildings in Azyl Park occupied by tenants of every nationality but Serbs. Maja had set her policies in stone: Don't rent to our people, they are thieves. Always check references and credit. Insist on three months security. For Irina, Ivan had bent all the rules.

The knock when it came was a quick, impatient thrice-repeated rap. Irina retied the belt on her robe, slid her fingers through her hair from scalp to tips, and walked slowly to the door. Her dead mother's photograph, a black and white portrait larger than life, hung on the wall above the television. Her mother looked weary in the photograph, crushed by widowhood, poverty, and the devastation of war. But it was all Irina had of her mother and she was comforted by it.

During the day, Irina sat at a desk at the east-facing window—sunlight mottling her face and hands if she was lucky—and sewed beads, precious stones, and bird feathers onto evening gowns for Zang Xin, a local dressmaker. In the evenings, Irina sat cross-legged on the bed, facing her mother's photograph and the television, and did what she called monkey work—stuffing envelopes, folding tri-panel brochures and menus, squeezing Free Tibet. Free Kashmir, Free Kosovo, Free Aceh, Free Palestine, and Free Iraq shirts into cardboard tubes, and any other piecework that came along. While working, Irina kept the television on CNN, studying the anchors mouths and listening to their pronunciation to open her ear to English. But she switched back to her own language to talk to her mother in the picture. Irina felt her mother respond silently, through inner locutions, from a place located deep in the back of her heart, a place that could neither be pointed at nor touched.

"Mama, remember Fadil Fejzic and the milk?"

Irina loved this story. Her mother unspooled it for her, and for the other women and children who needed comfort, repeatedly, after the war came to Gorazde. It was during the heavy fighting, as Irina's father, two brothers, twin uncles, and Luka whom she loved and hoped to marry, were taken away, one by one. Her father, younger brother, and Luka—who alone among them was Muslim—were taken by their own Serb militias. Her older brother and uncles were taken by Bosnian Muslim police. Their arrests made no sense to Irina, her mother, and the other women in the village. Who is the enemy? Everyone. Who is the friend? Nobody. Who do we trust? Only women. Everywhere in Gorazde, men were taken away never to return. Killed by the enemy. Eaten by their own. The women were not so lucky. They were taken to the rape camps.

After the men and young women disappeared, and the fighters had left for other villages to exterminate the enemy, the few remaining women of Gorazde, both Serbs and Muslims, and their remaining children, came out of hiding. They gathered in each other's houses in the evenings and sat in the dark without electricity, gas, water, or food. They meant to stay alive by enumerating their blessings and testifying their losses.

"We were four."

"We used to be seven."

"I was the mother of five."

"I had three sons."

"My husband loved me."

"Mine was a hungry man, even on Sundays."

They held their infants and toddlers, consoled their older children with raw potatoes and dandelion leaves picked from the fields, and saved the last of the good provisions for their youngest. Of their own hunger, they said nothing. Sometimes they sat paralyzed, wondering if they should flee to other towns and cities where no one knew their names, or if they should stay and forage for food like the rats and dogs now roaming the streets.

In 1992, when Gorazde was broken and in pieces, nobody at the nightly gatherings could remember a time when anything was ever good. Nobody could remember anything but pain and heartache and evil and death.

"We are cursed," one would say, and the others would not argue.

"It is God's punishment for our sins, that we wash our hands with the blood of our men," an old woman said.

Irina's mother would not, could not, accept this ugly idea of God. Even if God did not exist, she needed to believe in the godly to make sense of their suffering. She told them the story about the Soraks, a Serb family who lived on the other side of the river.

Rosa and Drago Sorak had lost two sons, one by Bosnian Muslim police, another run over by a car. The first son's widow gave birth to a girl, but she was unable to nurse her. Rosa and Drago gave the baby tea because they had nothing else to give her. After five days without milk, the baby was ready to die.

On the eastern edge of Gorazde, Fadil Fejzic, a Bosnian Muslim farmer, kept his cow hidden in a secluded part of a mountain bluff. To protect his cow and himself from enemy soldiers and snipers, he milked the cow only at night. Just before dawn on the fifth day, Fadil Fejzic knocked on the Soraks' door. He handed Drago a pail with half a liter of milk. He didn't say a word and he refused their money. He returned the next morning, and the next, and the next. All told, he gave the baby half a liter of milk every day for 442 days, 221 liters in all. "For free, when the going rate of salt was $80 a kilo," Irina's mother shook her head in wonder. "Don't forget," Irina's mother would say each time she came to the end of the story. Irina never forgot. She carried the story with her to America.

But this day, as Irina prepared to open the door to Ivan, she was angry with her mother for believing in fairy tales, in human decency beyond the particular kindness of Fadil Fejzic. Her rent was eight hundred dollars a month. She had less than two hundred dollars and she needed half of that for food. What would she need to do for seven hundred dollars? She thought that if she drew the blinds and directed her gaze inward, she could make herself believe that Ivan was Luka.

It was Ivan who turned her mother's picture to face the wall. He walked towards Irina's desk and placed his phone, keys, sunglasses, and wallet on the blotter. When he turned around he stared at the butterflies on the bodice of her kimono. Irina pulled the flaps tighter around her.

"You think I need to do this?" he said, his eyes hard, a look of boredom as he unbuckled his belt.

Irina folded her hands across her body and shook her head. "No," she looked down, grateful for the veil of hair to hide under. What would she need to do for seven hundred dollars? As long as he didn't hurt her, didn't rip out her insides, didn't sodomize her, she would survive. The last time, he shred her skin with his bites.

You try building a life from scratch with just your bare hands, she told her mother facing the wall.

Chapter 12

GOLDEN CAGE

A year after landing in Hollywood, Bruce become the star and king maker of "The Beer Meister," a reality elimination show for aspiring brewers. Potential brew masters were installed in a house in Glendale. The house, glinting in the California sun, looked luxurious to the contestants—nineteen men and five women who had won the right to expose themselves on national television, after answering casting calls posted in restrooms of bars and taverns all over the land. The California Mission style house had a low-pitched roof of red tiles, stucco walls of yellow gold, and a parapet rising above the arched entryway trimmed with red slate. A series of arcaded, arched openings with patios in the foreground and narrow doors in the background led to various rooms in the bungalow. The house was too small to house twenty-four adults comfortably but Zach Goldsmith liked it that way. He knew from experience that strangers thrown together in a place that afforded them no privacy, none, nada, zilch, increased the likelihood of incendiary television—friction, flaring tempers, raging meltdowns, tears, sex, sex, sex, erection, ejaculation, betrayal, jealousy, coup d'état, violence, psychological breakdowns, rejection, ejection, escape. Hostage situations, he knew, made for television gold.

The house was a short commute to the brewery set—a foreclosed microbrewery that the Goldsmiths had purchased and repurposed for the show. *Hops and Barley* was in good condition when Zach acquired it. Five rows of beer barrels, double walled casks, fermentation tanks, beer aging vats, and holding tanks—all in stainless steel—endowed the ancient craft of beer with clinical, industrial, high-tech, near scientific qualities. Chip, the set design team, and the broker had stood at the edges of the room while Zach wandered through the brewery in silence, stopping to look at the equipment, turn on taps, press knobs, jiggle thingamajigs, stroke whatchamacallits, palm doodads. After the inspection, he turned to his retinue and spread his hands out like Vitruvian Man. "Some men see things as they are and ask why. I dream things that never were and ask why not." He proclaimed that the focal point of his field of dreams would be a Star Trek style Captain's Deck.

The command center had an elevated throne for Bruce "The Hammer" Halliday that made him seem godlike, and three low seats for his guest judges: a succession of sitcom Dads, athletes rehabilitating dented public images, and bit actors from police procedurals. Behind the throne, The Hammer's Wenches, a quartet of beautiful women in corsets and short shorts squealed, bumped, grinded, and twerked for their leader, not a Lieutenant Uhura among them.

The cameras followed each crop of brewers for three months. They'd be seen performing their meister work—adjusting valves, dipping tasting sticks into vats, and rhapsodizing about the forthcoming nectar that would catapult them from reality show stardom to beer company licensing deals, or back into obscurity and shame. At home, they'd be filmed bickering, bitching, boozing, bedding, bonking, and bailing. In the final segment, the contenders would stand in a row in front of "The Hammer" and the trio of judges. The panel would taste each contestant's beer as an ominous soundtrack played in the background. The set was equipped with a rating system of life-size plywood cutouts: realistic looking kangaroos and dingoes that snapped up from a supine position. The brewer of the most flavorful beer received a golden kangaroo pop-up and Bruce's praise, "Fair Dinkum, Mate" or "Good Onya," or "That's grouse." The worst alchemist received a black dingo and Bruce's verdict: "Kangaroo's piss filtered through farts, you bludger," and the like, and a lecture on the divinity of beer.

Bruce's promotional trailers promising beer, boats and Sheila to one lucky Brew Meister, and his sign off "G'day Mate," became fodder for comics from Adelaide to Wagga Wagga. Bruce knew he could never set foot in Australia again after reducing his country and its culture to a set of offensive stereotypes. But the money was rolling in and American women went wagga wagga for the unusual aggregation of him—a lusty, loud, ironic, rakish elephant with hooves of grace. And that accent, oh that accent.

"It doesn't get better than this mate, you've struck major chord, you lucky bastard," Bruce reminded himself, after reading hate email from Australia that called him among other things, a whoring wanker and a pimping wombat. Robert De Niro's Jimmy Doyle in *New York, New York* was one of Bruce's favorite philosophers. While Bruce hadn't met any one woman who grooved him or whom he wanted to groove with, he thought everything in his life had worked out perfectly. He had everything he could possibly want: a revolving harem of sexually adventurous women from the show who thought two a lonely number, work that allowed him to be the high priest of beer, and more money than he knew what to do with.

He spent it on guitars: a 1965 Fender Composite Stratocaster played by blues legend, Stevie Ray Vaughn for $700,000; a 1939 acoustic Martin for $750,000; a 1964 electric Gibson gently used by Eric Clapton for $900,000; and a Fender Stratocaster signed by Mick Jagger, Keith Richards, Eric Clapton, Brian May, Jimmy Page, Pete Townsend, Jeff Beck, and Ronnie Wood for a cool $2 million. Bruce drove Keith Urban to near insanity by outbidding him on Waylon Jennings' Fender Telecaster, a black and white hand tooled leather beauty that Urban considered the Holy Grail. He had created the riff that started off *Georgia Woods* on that guitar.

Bruce loaned several to the Grammy Museum but kept the Jennings on a stand near his bed. He played it on nights he didn't have two, more, or his entire quartet lying next to him.

One night, in the middle of hiatus after the fifth season of Beer Meister, Bruce, sleeping on his back in a nest of hair, arms, and legs, bolted upright with a shudder, gasping. He shook his head from side to side, his long mane fanning out like a cone, to rid himself of sleep. He'd dreamt he was falling. It was sweet capitulation at first, sinking into a cloud of soft pillow; his dreamer smiling at the sublime pleasure his dreamt self was feeling. But then, as both dreamer and dreamed united in a single frequency of consciousness, the dreamt world revealed itself—a vertical cave alive with deformed, furry creatures wedged in its nooks and crannies, some hidden only their eyes visible, others cowering in the dark ledges.

He untangled himself from the jigsaw of limbs and groped his way in the dark to the closet for a pair of shorts and t-shirt. He stepped onto the balcony and eased himself into a swing, a hanging transparent shell that faced the balcony wall of seamless tempered glass. He pushed the swing back and forth in a slow rocking motion. The black sea and sky, thick and living, moved too so that Bruce, his heart, and the waves fell into rhythm, slow clapping time together. The darkness of the vista matched the color that was residing inside him. It dawned on him that he had been treading through a murky black pool, no demarcation between the one inside him and the one outside of him, the whole of last season. This thought surprised him. In his reveries, after he'd signed the contract with the Goldsmiths and before he had reached LA, the color he envisioned of his future city was a canvas of bold and lurid, the palette broken only by swimming pool blue and palm tree green and oily green grass. But California's drought had turned grass brown, an unnatural tint, cheap fantasies of grass.

Rocking on the swing, he felt something old but familiar return to him—raw grief. He wanted to sleep but the thought of diving back into the phalanx of women disgusted him. He lay down on the cool tiled floor by the balcony wall, pressed an open palm to the glass, and counted the laps of waves rolling to shore. Something has to change or I'll blow my fucking brains out. The thought, a declaration of intent, a line drawn in the sand, felt like a thunderbolt strike to his forehead.

"Oh my god, oh my god, oh my god, he's dead," Jackie, Bruce's born-again assistant, squalled when she found him sprawled, arms out like Christ on the cross, on the balcony floor the next day. She shrieked as she dialed Zach's number while looking down at the mastodon corpse. "Zach, the Hammer is dead! Facing Australia!"

"Get a damn ambulance over there now and start CPR. I'll be right there," Zach screamed.

Jackie had seen such events play out on television so many times, the scene in front of her assumed the quality of a palpable television event—the inciting incident for a full throttle media orgy. She imagined herself on the news, walking behind the paramedics as they wheeled him out on a stretcher, his body covered with a sheet. She wondered what she'd say when the newshounds stuck their microphones in front of her. The words she uttered would go around the world, turn viral, keep getting played and replayed, return to her like a boomerang. She tossed around some profound and memorable things she might say, as she knelt on the floor beside him. She checked her bag for her cosmetics purse. She reminded herself to lose the shine on her nose for the cameras. "Bruce! Are you dead? Wake up if you're not. Bruce?"

"Huh?" Bruce roused himself, drool running down the sides of his mouth, eyes blinking, first together, then separately, squinting at ten o'clock sun.

"You Lazarus!" she hugged him.

Zach and Chip panicked. Bruce acting up was Code Blue—cardiac arrest for the Goldsmiths as the show hauled in $8 million a week in advertising.

"There's something wrong with his fucking head." said Zach.

"So let's talk to him. Tell him to turn down the crazy," Chip said.

"We need an intervention."

Chip recruited a team of interventionists to help Bruce find his way back to the light—away from a twenty-first century crisis of the soul to the religion of show business whoredom.

"Let's do this thing," Zach, immaculate in Armani Collezioni white, rallied the interventionists the next day on Bruce's driveway. "We have to bring him back up," he told the group: a personal trainer, a yogi, a nutritionist, and a massage therapist/reiki healer. Chip and the team followed Zach up the stairs to Bruce's bedroom.

"Are you ready to do the deal, Bruce?" Zach hollered like a motivational speaker strung out on joy pills as he entered the room.

Bruce, propped up on two pillows, one hand curved around the neck of the Jennings, the other near the pick guard, stared at them. He was alone. He had tired of the quartet and had sent them away. "What do you want?"

"You gotta do the deal," Chip mumbled.

"Do the deal you will," the personal trainer said. The others nodded in agreement.

This is worse than the worst Hollywood movie, Bruce thought. He tried to rank the worst Hollywood movies ever. The worst sell-out, the worst pimp, the worst prostitute, the worst performing chimp, the worst Aussie minstrel ever. That would be me.

"Don't try. Do," said the yogi in t-shirt, swim briefs with aggressive stitching around the genitals, and water shoes.

This is where I go mental, Bruce thought, as he rose from the bed.

The clean, svelte California congregation gasped at the sight of Bruce, naked, an aggressive paunch declaring itself, greasy hair untied from its signature ponytail, van Dyke full of menace.

"What do you say, Bruce "The Hammer" Halliday?" Zach bellowed in song, pumping his fist in the air.

"What do I say?" asked Bruce as he looked at the team. He stabbed Zach in the chest, "I say that you should get on your knees and smile like a donut."

"What does that mean?" Zach blushed.

"And you," Bruce pointed at Chip. "I hope your chooks turn into emus and kick your dunny down."

Chip tapped his phone to plug chukes doney in Google search.

"And the rest of you can bloody bugger off," Bruce yelled so loudly, his face turned crimson from the blood rush to his head. "Get out!" he screamed and went to the bathroom to relieve himself. When he came back, they were gone.

He felt great, like he was finally touching shore after wading in molasses for five seasons. He called his agent and left him a voicemail. "I'm going walkabout. Get me out of the contract with those fuckwit drongos."

Bruce slipped into jeans and a polo shirt and stuffed a large duffle bag he found in the closet with clothes. He worked quickly. He took his music pod and charger off the bureau but left his phone still plugged into the wall. He flipped through a thin deck of credit and bankcards in the drawer and slipped them into his wallet. He placed the Jennings in its leather and lambskin guitar case, slung it over his shoulder, picked up the duffle bag from the bed, and walked to the front door. He figured that the Pagani Zonda and the Reventon, sex magnets on wheels given to him by the Goldsmiths during the first and second season, like the gold and diamond encased cellphone he'd left behind, were probably equipped with tracking devices to keep tabs on their Aussie investment.

When Bruce opened the front door, he saw Roberto tending to the garden. He grinned at his own luck. Exactly what he would have asked for if there was a God and Bruce had him on speed dial—a landscape gardener with a pickup truck.

"My man, Roberto," Bruce waved as he walked across the lawn dodging sprinklers. "Por favor, can you give me a ride to Hertz car rental?"

"Bruce?" Roberto smiled through his irritation at the blight on his lawn.

"Roberto," he shook his hand and gave him a robust thump on his back. "Ayúdame a sacar la mierda de aquí."

"Si," Roberto knew all about getting the hell out of somewhere. He walked towards the truck. "Not so clean at the back. Put your things up front."

"Thanks." Bruce placed the bag under his feet and wedged the guitar between his legs.

As Roberto merged from the ramp onto the highway, he looked at the directions he had retrieved on his phone. "Exit in eleven minutes," he read out loud and relaxed a little. "Where are you going?" Roberto rested his elbow on the open window and held the roof of the cab.

"I wish I knew," Bruce said. He looked at road signs: A man running, leading a running woman and child, the child holding the women's hand, dragged, powered by the woman's energy more than her own.

"Why are you going?"

"I'm not sure," Bruce said.

"You take free advice?"

"Sure, why not?"

"You are rich and famous but also kinda stupid," Roberto said.

"Not kinda. Very stupid," said Bruce.

"Si."

"El Stupido. That's me."

"So you take vacation. Heal the stupid mente. Come back. All good." Roberto had it all worked out.

"All good except for one thing. I burned the fucking house down."

"Then," Roberto said, stretching out the word two extra beats on the vowel, "it is not so simple."

They drove in silence, resigned sitting Buddhas, moving in inches, crawling through rush hour LA traffic. "With music is better," Roberto said.

"With music is always better," Bruce agreed.

Roberto fished in the door compartment and pulled out a black vinyl CD case. He placed it on his thigh and flipped through the sleeves, lingering at some, ignoring others, until he settled on one midway through the álbum. "This one," he tapped it. "Mehico Blues. La jaula de Oro. The Golden Cage," Roberto said. "Listen," he ejected a CD still in the console and inserted his new selection in the deck.

De que me sirve el dinero, si estoy como prisionero, dentro desta gran nacion, cuando me acuerdo hasta lloro, aunque la jaula sea de oro, no deja de ser prision,

"It sounds hopeless." Bruce drew the visor down to block the sunlight, as the song repeated a refrain.

"He's saying, What's money good for if I live like a prisoner in this great nation. When I'm reminded of this, I cry. Although this cage is made of gold. It's still a prison. La jaula de oro. Comprender?"

Bruce looked straight ahead. "Si yo comprendo, mate."

"No se olvide."

"I won't forget," Bruce reassured him.

Roberto pulled into a parking space at the rental car lot, stepped out of the cab, and stood by the truck's tailgate.

"That's everything," Bruce said as he slipped the guitar strap over his shoulder. "Well, mate, this is where I walk into the sunset without looking back," he looked at Roberto.

"Si, never look back," Roberto said.

"You're a good man," Bruce nodded and began walking towards the red brick buidling.

"Bruce un momento," Roberto called out.

Bruce turned around. Roberto lifted a chain from around his neck and over his head as he walked towards him. He thrust it into Bruce's palm.

"What's this, mate?" Bruce studied the nickel medal.

"La Patrona de America y Mexico. She's good luck," Roberto said.

"Thank you, brother," Bruce said.

"Hasta siempre, Amigo." Roberto said and turned towards his truck.

"Wait Roberto. What's siempre? I don't know that word."

"What my mother told me before handing me to the coyotes to bring me here," Roberto said as he opened the door of the truck. "Until forever."

"But you saw her again obviously." Bruce asked, concerned.

"By the time I was ready, I was too late." Roberto started the engine and eased out of the spot.

Chapter 13

VISITATIONS

All the talk of history with Angeline creaked open a shoe tip width of door in Gabe's deliberately constructed edifice. A few days after her visit, while Gabe was halfway through his customary dawn swim, in the two-lane lap pool that ran the length of the rooftop solarium above his penthouse, the door flung open. Gabe was knifing the water, eyeing the developing orange and pink sky through his swim goggles. His ears were plugged with silicon buds that buried sounds with a counter sound, a meta noise of peace. He saw an apparition hovering at the end of the pool in front of him. Obviously a trick of the eye and light, a reverse mirage, a refraction of light on a uniform medium. Or an extension of the garden statues next to the topiary and water fountain. As he swam closer, the figure, a male, came into sharp focus. He was dressed in white qamis and wore a black and white keffiyeh on his head secured with a braided black agal. Gabe's heart lurched from disbelief but he kept swimming, because he knew it was a hallucination, and because he liked to complete fifty lengths without breaking the circuit. As he kept slicing water and moved closer to the figure, he recognized his grandfather, Yahya. In the split second of his understanding, he gasped and choked on water. He stood up, heart racing, chest deep in the pool, and tore off his goggles. He blinked the water out of his eyes and stared at the spot where his grandfather had stood. He saw only the life size marble triptych of the Horae, standing like sentinels against the far ivy covered wall, their faces turned slightly towards the tipped urn water fountain that stood near them.

Nemi Khoury, Gabe's great-grandfather, had been born in Kafr Birim, a Christian village in northern Galilee. Since Nemi had three older brothers who stood to inherit the family's homestead and farm in succession, he knew he had to leave his village to secure his future. He moved to Iqrit, a neighboring Christian village of five hundred people who lived in a cluster of eighty homes made of stone. The villagers drew their water from two springs and from numerous rainwater storage wells in courtyards and orchards that dotted the village. The community had an elementary school, two olive presses, and two granaries. Standing guard over all Iqrit was the white-robed, life-sized statue of the Madonna atop the Church of Our Lady, next to the belfry.

Iqrit stood on a steep hill. From its highest point, you could see Lebanon: men walking donkeys laden with wares for the market, women grinding spices with pestles in stone mortars, children carrying younger siblings on their backs. Nemi found a home in the homely shape of Abrar. Her widowed mother had promised Nemi cultivatable land and a house that stood at the far edge of her property if he would marry Abrar. "I will give you two dunums for every pock mark on her face." Nemi received forty dunums. He was hard pressed to find a single blemish on his wife's cratered face.

The couple had six children, a gaggle of boys named after the first apostles – Butros (Peter), Yahya (John), Marta (Matthew), Luqa (Luke) and two girls—Illsaba, after the mother of John the Baptist, and Mariam, after the Mother of Jesus. The family grew olives, figs, pomegranates, and grapes, and set aside half the land for grazing their small flock of sheep.

Because Yahya was frail in health, his father steered him away from manual labor, charging him instead with the sale of the farm's surplus to villagers. His favorite trading spot was under the shade of a fig tree at the mouth of the village. He was also sacristan of the church. He maintained the priest's vestments and chalices and made sure there were flowers and candles for Mass. He arranged the altar according to the liturgical calendar and tabbed the Bible's pages with ribbons to mark the appropriate gospel and readings. He decorated the church according to the Maronite calendar, made communion wafers on an ancient waffle machine that he'd designed and forged in iron, and kept careful inventory of the wine that he made from the first fruits of the family's yield. Yahya married a distant cousin, with the blessing of both their parents, and raised three children. The fourth, Gabe's father, Jairus, would be born in the Dbayeh camp in Lebanon.

In 1948, the Israeli military swept through Galilee to expel Palestinians from their villages during Operation Hiram, Prime Minister David Ben Gurion's plan to occupy Galilee and create a northern border free of Arabs. The first caravan of refugees from the village of Khirbet Khizeh, speechless men leading their livestock and wailing women carrying bundles and crying children, walked past Iqrit and Kafr Birim, the last of the villages still standing, on their way to forced exile in Lebanon.

"Please rest awhile. Eat with us," the villagers invited the refugees.

"You have nothing yourselves."

"Then we will have nothing together."

The people of Khirbet Khizeh spoke of the Haganah's visit to their village, how the soldiers had sprayed bullets from machine guns and rifles at women and children, at old men and the mentally ill. They shot us even as we held up white veils in surrender. We never believed they were capable of such things.

One man, Afreen, the village storyteller of Khirbet Khizeh, the memory keeper, who had seen the events unfold, gave an account of the taking of his village.

The Haganah rode into the village in a convoy of six jeeps. Seeing the caterpillar wind up the lane, the villagers stopped what they were doing and hurried indoors. I hid inside the granary to watch them. They were dressed in khaki uniforms and wide bowl helmets. Six held guns at the ready, the barrels pointed to the ground. The others held cameras and surveying instruments. One soldier untied a donkey standing under the thick bough of a terebinth tree, and beat its rump with the stock of his gun. The donkey brayed in distress and galloped away. He put a green tarp on the ground and the surveyors placed their equipment on it. The cameramen walked the length and breadth of our village. They took photographs of every house, every tree, every well. They talked with their arms outstretched, pointing at the church, the fig orchards, a stone wall, the small stream behind it. The surveyors measured every inch of the village. How many dunums? one asked. Thousands and thousands, another replied. The argued among themselves about the estimates. They wrote things down in a big book.

The bravest of our men, two of them, went to meet them in front of the church. What is it you seek? Can we help you? God is good.

Several of them sniggered.

God is great, the man who looked like their leader said.

We will prepare a meal, the elder of our men replied. We were a hospitable people.

There's no time for that. The army is doing security work here and you must all leave, for your own protection, the leader shot a spitball near our elder's feet.

But our homes.

We will protect your homes. Take what you need for two days. Keep walking.

When our men did not move, the soldiers pointed their guns at them.

We were a gullible people. Stupid beyond redemption. We did as we were told. It made no sense to us then why they were moved to shoot us.

The Israel Defense Force entered Iqrit on October 31st of 1948. The villagers offered no resistance. They hoisted a white flag on the belfry of the church and remained in their homes. The priest greeted the IDF with a bible, salt, and bread. A week later, an army commander asked the villagers to vacate their homes while the army carried out training and military activities. The villagers were told that they could return in two weeks. Fifty of the villagers, including Yahya, remained to watch over the houses. The rest of the villagers were advised by the army leader to take only food and water with them, and taken by army trucks to a village half an hour away. When they tried to return to their homes two weeks later, officers of the IDF told them that Iqrit had been declared a restricted military area. Those who remained, including Yahya, were driven out of the village in a truck and dumped at the border crossing to Lebanon. Yahya and his family were processed and sent to Dbayeh, seven miles east of Beirut. One of a dozen eventual UNRWA camps for Palestinian refugees in Lebanon, Dbayeh housed Christians driven out of Galilee. Both Gabe's parents were born in the camp in 1953, five years after their own parents' expulsion from Iqrit. Gabe was a second-generation Dbayeh refugee.

In 1951, while in exile in Lebanon, the leaders of Iqrit took their case to the Israel High Court of Justice and won the right to return to their homes. But on Christmas Eve of that year, the Israeli Army placed explosives under all the houses in Iqrit and detonated them. Only the church and the cemetery remained standing. Two years later, the State of Israel seized Iqrit's lands under the Expropriation for Public Purposes Law for defense, agriculture, and Jewish settlements.

The first UNRWA issue tents at Dbayeh had to be tied with ropes to pegs staked in the ground. In strong winds, the tents blew away. While later camp dwellers lived only in zinc boxes, and then concrete boxes, Gabe remembered living in a tent with his parents, Yahya, and his two widowed aunts, when he was fourteen. The alley outside his family's zinc box had flooded with sewage and the area became infested with rats, mice, worms, and maggots. The smell was intolerable and UNRWA deemed the area a health hazard. The agency directed the zinc box dwellers to pitch tents higher up the hill. Gabe was tall by then, he had grown almost to his full height. He remembered having to stand inside the tent with his back curved, his neck hunched into his shoulders, his knees unlocked and bent. They were assigned a concrete box after that, a one room with a toilet wedged in a corner that became their permanent address in the camp. The room was so small, he knew when his mother and aunts had their periods. He could smell their menstrual blood, his grandfather's flatulence, his father's arak flamed halitosis, everyone's feces. His mother strung a clothesline across a corner of the room and hung a sheet over it, held in place with a dozen wooden clothes pegs, so that the family didn't have to undress in front of each other.

"Listen Jibril, I believe in a tomorrow. I believe in the struggle. I have faith in olive trees," Yahya said every day for years until he forgot the words.

Gabe cut short his swim and climbed out of the pool. He dried himself with a towel as he looked at the spot of the apparition with a combination of anxiety and anger. His time was strictly subscribed from the moment he woke up to the moment he fell asleep. He had learned to motivate himself and stave off useless emotions with a grueling schedule, so that he was never at a loss for activity or vulnerable to extended reflection. Leave me alone, he thought as he put on a robe. He took the elevator down to the penthouse and went to the kitchen. Though Gabriel did not cook, the refrigerator and cupboards were well stocked by his personal chef, Joaquin, who had earned his stripes at several fine restaurants on the Square. Gabe hired him after a month's trial because he was impressed with Joaquin's Excel spreadsheets with columns for days of the week, clear descriptions of daily menu choices, calorie counts, and nutritional values. That kind of obsessive compulsion, Gabe knew, was an indicator of want and ambition.

Joaquin visited several times a week with a refrigerated cart filled with meat and produce that he prepared in Gabe's otherwise unused kitchen. Joaquin washed, prepared, cooked, and artfully arranged his gourmet creations in blue and white Spode dishes fitted with cut glass covers, and elegant freezer-to-oven tableware, and organized them in the fridge and freezer. He replenished the pantry with dry foods and left detailed reheating instructions for the dishes and the following week's menu in the drawer next to the cutlery.

Gabe drew a bowl of mixed fruit from the refrigerator and a fork from the utensils drawer, and sat at a barstool at the kitchen counter. His eyes settled on the design magazine setting of his loft. The teardrop lamps hanging from barely discernible wires looked like they were suspended in air. The sun, diffused through gauzy white drapes and gathered in a pool of light on the hardwood floor, gave the room a golden glow. In the living room, his art collection was shown to advantage as if in a gallery at MoMA. He was surrounded by beauty and luxury unimaginable to him half a life ago.

Gabe knew what it took to grind a beating heart to dust. Locate it in squalor, in places absent of trees, flowers, birds. Enforce it in an ugliness that violates the soul's code of beauty. Surround it in concrete to erase the memory of soil, roots, home, land, olive, fig, and lemon trees. Give it a tent to live in. Let it smell sewage while it eats, drinks, sleeps, loves. If it works hard enough, let it graduate to a zinc box. And if it works harder still, give it a concrete box with a zinc roof—to prevent it from building, growing, staking a claim, ever forgetting it is a refugee.

There were things that came to Gabe even now, when his mind was fixed on nothing before drifting off to sleep in Lakshmi's canopy bed, or when he was swimming. No music, no color, no hope anywhere but on American television at the community center, where nobody stood with their backs curved, or their necks hunched into their shoulders, or their knees unlocked and bent.

Gabe shivered as he thought about his grandfather on the roof. In Lebanon, in the camp, Yahya retreated into himself. He drank, and he drew maps on the floor and walls and ceiling of their one room. He drew precise physical maps with every house, fig tree, and pomegranate shrub in Iqrit accounted for. He drew the eighty homes of the village as he remembered them, each one exactly as it stood, before the Israelis blew them up. He drew the Church of Our Lady, its steeple a larger than life guardian that towered over the rest of Iqrit. He drew topographic maps showing the whole of Northern Galilee and Iqrit and Kafr Birim, and Khirbet Khizeh. Yahya lived a temporary existence for sixty years, trapped in his madness. "I have sat on my suitcase for sixty years waiting to go home," he said, before he gave up his spirit inside a concrete box, on a hot July Fourth, far from his American grandson.

Chapter 14

THE ESCAPE ARTIST

Bruce stood in line at the car rental desk, behind a pear-shaped family dressed in khaki shorts and tank tops. Father, mother, teenage son, and daughter looked at their phones. They grunted at each other occasionally. A young couple stood in the next line, the man's hands around the woman's waist, his fingers hooked in a loop of her jeans. She pulled out a cellphone from her handbag and scrolled through messages. He let his hand fall from the loop and pulled out his own cellphone from his jacket and began to text. "There's no more love in this world," Bruce thought.

He remembered a time when love could be found on trains, on buses, sitting at a café, walking down the street. Hi. Hi. What's your name? Leah. You? Bruce. That's a nice name. Yeah? Yeah. Where're you from? Over there. You? From here. What're you doing here? Passing through. Grab a cup of coffee? Sure. What's up? You know. Yeah. You? I'm not sure. I'm searching. Me too. Do you ever feel that you did everything all wrong? Yes. That you fucked up your life? All the time. You? All the time.

Tell me something true. I'm lonely. Tell me something true. I'm alone. Have you ever fallen in love? I've never been lucky. You? I don't know what love is. Stand in your truth. I'm lost. Own it. I want to kill myself. I want to make love to you. I want to feel you inside me. I want to rock you till tomorrow. I want to ride you till you beg me to stop. Make me cry. Save me.

As the family in front of him inched up the line, Bruce slid his duffle bag across the expanse of red tile with his feet. The Jennings remained hitched over his right shoulder.

"I'll take an SUV silver or black. No red," he told the woman at the counter.

"What's wrong with raid!? Raid is da bomb," she said.

"I don't think so."

"Hey, you that guy!" she said, handing him a printed agreement to sign.

"No, I'm not," he said, signing the form.

"Don't be rusing me," she said. "I didn't fall off no turnip truck."

"Okay, I'm his twin brother,"

"Okay," she said, "I'll buy that."

Bruce drove out of the lot to a liquor store. Five cases of beer, six bottles of vodka, a cooler with ice, two large steel thermos cups. At a dispensary on Ventura Boulevard, he sprang for eight ounces of indica and sanjay gupta kush. No sense going over the limit and getting pulled over by CHP. He figured he'd stop along the four hundred mile route for refills.

Pacific Coast Highway from Los Angeles to San Francisco, Highway 1, ran parallel to unremitting ocean for miles. On the other side, where the sea spilled over the rim of the earth, his dead, his loves. And here, woven into his heart tendons, melted in the collagen, they coursed through his veins. How do I live with this pain? Why not just die?

He drove past elephant seals, otters, and sea lions; past waterfalls and over bridges; through fog and smog; near giant cliffs and jagged boulders the size of men; on curving roads and changing elevations. In a beer, vodka, and marijuana stupor, he drove through Santa Barbara, Santa Maria, Pismo Beach, San Luis Obispo.

"It's time for the Man," he said as he killed the vapid noise on satellite radio and docked his I-Pod in the console. Bruce sang along with Waylon Jennings about pain songs and train songs and Luckenbach,Texas where nobody felt any pain.

The songs took Bruce through Big Sur, Monterey, Santa Cruz, San Jose, Half Moon Bay, and San Francisco. He drove across the Bay Bridge for ten miles and found himself in Emeryville. He pulled into the parking lot of the first motel he saw.

"How many nights, please?" the Vietnamese woman behind the counter asked.

"Maybe a day, maybe a month."

"I give you best room," she handed him two key cards.

"I just need one. Where's the dining room?"

"No dining. Food delivery menu in room."

"I need a haircut. Where's the nearest barber?"

"My uncle is barber."

"Send him to my room," Bruce said.

Bruce walked out of the elevator and down the corridor to his tier. The carpet's design of hot orange and neon green sprung a throb at his temples. It smelled heavily of deodorizer and made him want to retch. He slid the key card in the door. The fixtures and furnishings were cheap and ugly, but the room was clean. The rose petals scattered on the crisp white bed covers touched him. Two stars with an extra star for Zen grace. He drew open the curtains and cracked open the windows. The room overlooked a desolate train station with an empty train yard and no trains. He sat on the bed and heard the first rumblings of hunger. He realized he hadn't eaten since breakfast and that the only fluids he had ingested since leaving LA were beer and vodka. He ordered pizza, lay down on the bed, and turned on the television.

He passed out, awaking only because of the loud banging on the door.

"Food delivery," a male voice said.

Bruce opened the door to a grinning man with a gold tooth. He gave the man a twenty-dollar bill from his wallet, took the box, and began to shut the door.

"You don't want haircut shave?"

"Yes."

"I have to come in for that," the man smiled, holding up a black bag that looked pretty impressive.

"You deliver pizza and cut hair?" What kind of a racket was this?

"I'm the barber. I just brought the pizza up."

"Okay, sit while I finish eating," Bruce said.

"No worry," said Dao.

Bruce set the pizza box on the table, and sat down. "You want some?"

Dao shook his head, no, and placed his bag on the bed, on top of the rose petals. He took out a rolled towel from the bag, unfolded it, and laid it at the foot of the bed. From the bag, he pulled out various objects that he placed on the towel: a newspaper, large scissors, small scissors, long comb, short comb, clippers, electric buzzer, bowl, shaving brush, electric shaver, spray bottle. He looked around the room to scout a favorable location, and dragged a chair to the window. He carpeted a small area with the newspaper and placed the chair in the center of the square facing the window. He went to the bathroom with a spray bottle. He returned with the bottle filled with water and a pile of towels. He went back to the bathroom and returned holding a wastebasket.

"Where did you train to be a barber?" Bruce asked, as he bit into another slice.

"Vietnam." Dao placed the wastebasket next to the chair.

"Where in Vietnam?" Bruce cooled the bites of cheese and crust in his mouth before swallowing.

"It's not important."

"Sorry," Bruce said. Who knew where this man had been? He could have been a barber in a death camp, hair stylist to the Viet Cong, shaving the throats of murderers. Everywhere in America, there were people from faraway places with unspeakable pasts. Avoid small talk asshole, he reminded himself.

"What style do you want?" Dao clicked the scissors open and shut.

"Give me a full shave and a cut above the collar," said Bruce, as he wiped his mouth on his sleeve and took the chair by the window.

"All off?" he clicked the scissors in a question.

"Everything off."

Dao worked methodically. He placed towels around Bruce's shoulders, lap, and chest. He doused his hair with sharp spritzes of water that dripped into Bruce's ears. He combed the hair, clipped it in sections, and used the big scissors to take away the heft and the bulk of the hair. Then he picked up the small scissors to do the finer detailing. When he finished the head, he moved to the beard.

"You look like somebody else," Dao said standing back to admire his work.

"You think so?" Bruce stood up and walked to the mirror above the bureau. He stroked the skin across his cheeks. He didn't recognize himself.

"You are tourist?" Dao rolled up the paper mat on the floor and stuffed it into the wastebasket.

"Sure. Why not?" Bruce peered into the mirror. He turned his face from side to side and studied his mien.

"Where are you going?" Dao started folding the towels.

"I'm not sure," he walked over to the window and looked at the empty train yard. "Is that a working train station?"

"Yes. One train a day."

"Where does it go?" Bruce ran his fingers through his hair. He felt twenty pounds lighter.

"All the way to the middle. Arizona, Nevada, Utah, Colorado, Nebraska, Iowa, Indiana,Illinois, Midwest," said Dao. "Heartland."

"Heartland," Bruce blinked. "I like that."

The next day, Bruce shouldered his guitar case and duffle bag and stood at reception to check out.

"One day only," the woman shook her head sadly.

"Yes."

"You want bao and coffee?" the woman asked, extending a bag from the bakery next door.

"Isn't that yours?"

"You take please."

Bruce opened his wallet but she waved it away. "No, you take please."

Bruce gave her a hundred dollar bill and the keys to the SUV. "Please take care of this for me."

"No worry. I ask my uncle."

Bruce thanked her, walked from the motel to the train station and bought a one-way ticket on the California Zephyr. Emeryville to the end of the line, fifty-two hours and thirty minutes to the Heartland.

A steward, dressed in a blue blazer with yellow epaulets and blue slacks, welcomed him as he got on board. Cyril showed him to his cabin. Bruce had booked a Superliner Bedroom: six feet by seven feet, a sofa that converted to a bed, a reclining easy chair, and a sink-shower-toilet combo impossibly wedged into a nook. Bruce stroked his chin as he took a measure of the nook and reckoned he would need to enter it sideways.

"It's a nice idea, but most people end up using the common bathrooms at the end of the car," Cyril said. "I'll turn down your bed at night and I'll bring you newspapers and beverages. Anything you need, just ask."

Bruce thanked him, stowed his duffle in the storage locker by the sliding door, and sat down in the seat by the window. He lifted the armrest between the seats, and shifted and settled his body across both seats. Crossing the shallow tidal estuary of San Pablo Bay and Carquinez Strait, Bruce felt a giant fear descend on him, an eight-legged creature that gripped his heart. He had been given two choices—stay and die or leave and still die—and he had made the wrong choice. What were you thinking? That's just it, derro, you don't know how to think.

When he entered the dining car for lunch, the attendant looked him over and stared at his tattoo. "I'm gonna mix it up and put you with some respectable people."

He ushered Bruce to a table for four occupied by a couple, Bob and his wife, Robin.

"I hope I'm not in the way," Bruce apologized.

"Of course not," Robin said. She had striking gray hair down to her shoulders. She wore a blue blouse and jeans and a thin denim jacket with an Aztec design around the bib. When she smiled, the loose skin around her eyes made a triptych of horizontal stripes.

He ordered two cocktails and downed them before the salad was placed in front of him. The drinks made Bruce relax a little. It opened a door and primed his lips to talk. Bob sipped his coke while eyeing Bruce's drinks.

"Where are you headed?" she asked.

"End of the line," he said. "How about you?"

"Bob and I volunteer at Indian reservations around the country. We're headed to a Shoshone reservation in Nevada," she said.

"What kind of work?"

"We work with alcoholics at a rehab center."

"Oh," Bruce said.

"I'm always thinking, see?" the attendant smiled as he placed Bruce's sandwich plate in front of him.

"Last year, we worked with the Lakota people at Pine Ridge. It's a toxic combination of pathologies: domestic violence, sexual assault, alcohol, drugs, and unemployment. Half the population lives below the poverty line. It's the second poorest place in the country," Robin said.

"The population is about 40,000 but they buy 13,000 cans of beer a day. They're twice as likely to die in their twenties than any other race," Bob said.

"All kinds of reasons why people drink," Bruce said.

"I disagree. There's only ever one reason. It's the same one every damn time." Bob lifted his glass to his lips. "You know what I'm talking about."

Bruce placed a hand over his glass and turned it like a knob. "Yeah, well."

"You should hop off the train with us. We need volunteers," Robin said. A month on the reservation with nothing to see but bad ends would set him straight.

"I'm useless to anyone right now including myself," Bruce said.

"I know all about that," said Bob, raising his glass. "Ten years sober."

Bruce returned to his cabin, sat down in the armchair, and looked out the window. He wanted to jump off the train and disappear into the blur, wipe himself clean from the human race. He'd be doing the planet a favor. Hinged to no one, responsible for no one, accountable to no one, he was by any definition, a statistical waste of space. Too spent to pull down the bed, he reclined the seat and fell asleep.

Bruce stirred awake as the train pulled into Martinez. "We're pulling into the birthplace of the late, the great, Joe DiMaggio," a male voice, smoother than smooth jazz intoned. Where have you gone, Joe DiMaggio, Bruce thought.

As the train pushed through the Great Central Valley, slicing through the Sacramento and San Joaquin sides, Bruce began to see the rice fields of Yolo Basin. The voice, who Bruce imagined was a cross between Barry White and Teddy Pendergrass, followed the crackle of the intercom. "Those waves of yellow and pale gold you're seeing now, that's the amber waves of grain right there." Bruce had an urge to pull out his guitar and sing. What did he want to sing? Not *America The Beautiful*. Bob Dylan. About gambling and losing and leaving and running without turning back and praying for a future.

But he was so tired. So wasted. He could only surrender to the train's motion. It wasn't comforting, it wasn't rocking him. It felt like he was being tumbled at fast speed in a giant dryer, his bones aching from the repetitive, lurching *chug chug* that sent his torso pummeling back and forth into the metal under the upholstery. This is going to be hell, he thought. I'm going to blow my brains out. The train stopped for fifteen minutes in Sacramento. Bruce got out with the other passengers to walk around and undo the stiffness in his legs. It was dusk when the Zephyr crossed Interstate 80, leaving the California Trail to cut through Emigrant Gap, the portal to the California Gold Rush back in 1848, into Sierra Nevada.

He ate dinner in the club car with a family of German tourists. He ordered eight bottles of American beer and drank it under the judgmental gaze of his dining companions. The man shook his head sadly. "I don't understand American beer." The liquor put him in a stoical, philosophical state of mind, so that when he returned to his sleeper car, he felt reconciled to his fate and life in general. He peered out the window thinking of the show and how easily he had sold himself to the Goldsmiths. He laughed like a hyena when he thought of the financial calamity he had caused Zach and Chip. "You talentless money hungry bastards," he shouted and howled like a wolf, as the train pulled into Reno at nightfall. Ah-woo-ooo-ooo! Ah-woo-ooo-ooo!

When Bruce awoke the next morning, the train was parked in the middle of a ghost town and the passengers were milling about outside. "Where the hell is this?" Bruce yelled, as he stepped off the train.

"Thistle," said a man with a thick moustache as he spat tobacco juice. He was wearing faded blue jeans, a belt buckle the size of a cellphone, cowboy boots, and a tan cowboy hat. He looked like Robert Redford in Butch Cassidy and the Sundance Kid. Bruce wanted to be that man; he felt like a loser in his dark blue designer jeans. He immediately wanted a pair of stone washed Levis and a cowboy hat, and to learn to chew tobacco.

The Zephyr crossed the Utah-Colorado state line by lunchtime. Bruce felt himself pushing through time, pressing closer to the center after living for so long on the edges of things. He remembered that journey through the Outback with his family. Stripped of everything but each other, somehow they had made it through to the other side. This time he carried nothing but himself, a cowardly, unloved, unlovable, drunk derelict. The train speared through Grand Junction, past canyons, mesas, and blue mountains, through peach orchards, old mining towns and ghost towns. When they rode through De Beque, a whole herd of magnificent wild horses ran alongside the train. There must have been fifty of them—blacks, sorrels, grays, and bays. Bruce spotted several palominos, white mustangs, and buckskins. There was one cremello in the herd. The smoky voice over the PA system pointed her out. "Sadie is the resident slut. She's run around with Bill and Bob and who knows who. She's been with nineteen of them stallions, always putting out, our Sadie. And that's her three youngest behind her. She's got her evil ways, know what I'm saying." Bruce chuckled.

"In a short while we'll be pulling into Glenwood Springs," the voice said. "On the right, you'll see Glenwood Caverns. This is where Doc Holliday, the legend of the Wild West from the gunfight at the OK Corral, spent the final months of his life." Bruce went into the scenic car and claimed a seat to look at the American West he had known up to then only from songs. It was a canvas of canyons, mountains, rivers, waterfalls, and trees. The car was as quiet as church. Families stood together holding hands, arms around each other, dumbstruck by the majestic, magisterial sweep of it. He wanted to weep.

The Zephyr entered Plainview at midnight. Bruce was in his sleeper car and could see the lights of Denver, fifteen hundred feet below. When the train turned the next bend, he could see the Rockies come into view. This is where we sing the songs, Bruce said as he drew his guitar from its case. He strapped it across his chest and edged forward, rocking from side to side, moving in motion with the train, as he headed towards the scenic car.

“Hey Bruce,” Cecil greeted him. “What you got there? That’s a helluva guitar.”

“Yep. What we need is some singing and some drinking around here,” Bruce said.

“What kind of songs?”

“Country, mate,” Bruce said.

“Country? Damn! Black people don’t do country,” Cecil said. “Except for Charlie Pride.”

“You’re wrong, mate. There’s Cleve Francis, Huddie William Ledbetter, Mississippi John Hurt,” Bruce said.

“Yeah?”

“Yeah.”

“Play me one,” Cecil challenged him.

Bruce started the riff to *I’ve Been Everywhere.*

The train hurtled through the Colorado-Nebraska state line as the sun cracked through the sky. The Zephyr rushed past Hastings, Lincoln, and Platte River and reached Omaha by lunchtime. By evening, it had left Nebraska behind and pushed into the flatlands of Iowa. The Midwest—the Heartland—stretched in front of them as they rode along the Missouri River. Crossing the Big Muddy, the train made stops at Council Bluff and Osceola, and Ottumwa and Burlington, before crossing the Mississippi River into Illinois. Bruce could see the lights from farmsteads, like lone stars illuminating a night sky, as the train raced through Monmouth and Galesburg, Galva and Kewanee, Princeton and Aurora and Naperville, before touching down at its final destination.

Chapter 15

TWIN FLAMES MATCHMAKER

Each morning, Nila stands at the front stoop of the house on the Crescent and watches her children, Zara and Hari, board the school bus. Hari sits in the front row and Zara way in the back. They're older now and she no longer waves or blows them a kiss, but she stands there until the bus disappears from her view. It matters to her that they know she's watching them. At that hour, Rae will already be at his office on the Square. Nila retreats into the house and goes into the kitchen. She loads the used breakfast dishes and mugs into the dishwasher, wipes the counter with a sponge, and puts away the placemats from the dining table. After she casts a last glance at the room, she climbs the stairs to the bedroom suite and into the walk in closet. She traces her hand over the row of saris hanging from bi-level hangers, matching blouses folded over the lower rungs, and picks one that matches her mood. She lays the ensemble on the bed, before going into the bathroom. After showering, drying, and moisturizing her face and body, she walks back into the bedroom, naked, and sits at the dressing table. She coils her dry hair into a French chignon, the top of which she anchors with a mother of pearl comb. She applies cream on her face and powders it, shapes her eyes with black kohl, glosses her lips, and sprays herself with scent. She dresses, and sets the sari off with wrist cuffs of coordinating glass bangles. She chooses matching shoes, boots, or sandals. She dives into the day always in this way, slowly.

When she enters Twin Flames, after silencing the alarm that Rae had insisted on installing to give him peace of mind, she enjoys casting her eyes around the space. She decorated it like a living room, with two sofas facing each other, accent chairs, and a coffee table. A rosewood console stands against the wall with a painting hanging above it—a scene with a man and a woman with their backs to the viewer.

Twin Flames is a one-person operation because Nila doesn't know anyone else who has her gift. She believes that one cannot recognize love, or the potential of love, without intuition. She is deeply intuitive, an intelligence she cannot explain that has served her since childhood. She can clarify people's motives, see them for who they really are, without deep knowledge or experience or familiarity. There seems to be a vibration around people that she can hear, an aura around people that she can see, if she remains in silence. She is acutely sensitive about her husband and children. She has premonitions about them. She values this important knowledge about the three people on this planet she loves without limit.

When Hari was in kindergarten, a classmate kept inviting him to sleepovers. Nila didn't want her five year old under someone else's roof and told Hari he couldn't go. Even when the boy's mother pressed Nila directly, she politely declined. But Hari wanted to go. He fell to the living room floor, writhing and screaming as if someone was pulling his nails out. "I want to go. I want to go." Rae came home from work to find Nila in the kitchen calmly chopping scallions, and Hari wailing like a professional mourner. Rae stood at the entrance between the kitchen and living room. "What's his problem?" His children were a mystery to him. While he found their developing minds interesting, he left the parenting of them to Nila. He'd never woken up in the middle of the night to feed them as infants or changed their diapers. He'd never given them baths or read them bedtime stories. He himself had grown up in a home with formal parents who gave him little attention and no emotion, and a succession of nannies. He only cared about Nila. The children were the price he had to pay to be with the woman he loved madly, completely.

"Hi Raja," she looked up and smiled. "No problem. We're working things out." She started dicing peppers.

"Mommy won't let me sleep over at Jason's." More wailing. All Rae wanted to do was fix himself a martini, sit on the deck, and talk to his wife.

"Any reason why he can't?" Rae walked into the kitchen.

Nila lifted the lid off a slow cooker. "He's not ready," she pierced a piece of meat with a fork. "Maybe in a couple of years," she lifted the chopping board and scraped the onions and peppers into the pot.

"You'll turn him into a Mama's boy," Rae said.

"I don't feel good about it. I'm not okay with it."

He walked over and stood behind her. Her hair was swept over one shoulder. He traced a finger down her nape. She leaned her head back against his chest and sighed. "You know what that does to me."

"I can't take the crying and the whining. Let him go, babe."

She relented. She called Jason's mother and agreed to drop Hari off in Idyllwild after dinner that Friday. Hari sat in the backseat on the drive north, his backpack stuffed with transformers and a change of clothes.

"Thank you, Mommy." "You're welcome, son."

Slowing down on the street Jason's mother had texted her, Nila saw Jason standing on the front porch of his house, smiling, waving, jumping up in the air. Hari squealed, clapped his hands spasmodically, kicked the back of her seat with excitement. Gestalt talking, Nila thought. Her gaze settled on the yard sign in front of Jason near the curb. WE DON"T CALL THE POLICE. The snarl stretched across the picture of a gun. "Oh no, we don't," Nila said and stepped on the pedal.

"That's him! That's their house," Hari shouted.

"Shut up!" Nila screamed.

Hari burst into tears.

She gripped the steering wheel, drove the car very fast to the end of the street, made a left onto the adjacent street, and onto Shoreland. Hari screamed in the back seat, kicking her repeatedly with both feet through the leather frame, his anger all the force he needed to give her whiplash.

As Zara and Hari entered their teen years and questioned her, fought with her, opposed her, tried to beat her down with teenage attitude, she was serene in her responses. "I'm not here to be your buddy. This is not a democracy. You live in a benevolent dictatorship."

"You suck, Mom." Good.

"You're not cool, Mom." Excellent.

"I hate you." I love you.

"I hate my life." It's a beautiful life.

Nila's first client was Jeanie O'Hara, a bookkeeper who served several of the businesses in the Square. She was offering a bounty of $25,000 for a husband.

"It's easy money because I'm setting a very low bar," she had told Nila. "He needs to have all his limbs, have an average IQ, own a business, own a car, and own his own home. My non-negotiables, I never want to see him sitting on the couch with his hands down his pants watching sports. Never!" Jeanie said.

Non-negotiables. The business of love. Nila wondered what question she would need to ask prospects to acquire this information. Do you ever sit on the couch like a vegetable watching non-vegetables while playing with your cucumber?

“He should like going out to try different things. He should be delighted with children and animals. If he had an unhappy childhood and is still talking about it, he should keep walking,” Jeanie said.

“That is easy to find out,” Nila said as she scribbled notes on a pad.

“And if he has a wandering eye, he should not cross my path if he wishes to keep his genitals.”

“You are a very angry person,” Nila said.

“I am pissed off. I know there’s a right man out there for me but I can’t find him. There are what, hundred million adult males in the US? Why is it so hard to find somebody decent?”

“You scare people with your anger. You’re scaring me,” Nila said.

Jeanie looked ashamed. “I’m so burnt, you know. From all the men I’ve invested energy in, who took so much from me and gave me so little back. And the worst thing is I put up with it,” Jeanie looked out the window, her eyes turning glassy with tears.

“Can you believe in the idea of being lovable and loving?”

“It will take a lot of work to change my feelings. I’m angry, bitter.”

“It’s not an option, you have to do it,” Nila said. “Also, is this how you normally dress?”

“Yes. What’s wrong with it?” Jeanie looked down at the heavy weave black wool jacket and pants she felt especially powerful in.

“You look like a undertaker. We’re going to take you shopping so you look like a woman.”

“I haven’t worn a dress since high school.”

"Men like women looking like women. Also, you need your hair styled and some makeup. Some color on your lips and cheeks, some shadow on the eyes, and get your brows tweezed to open them up. Bangs, you'd look pretty with bangs."

Jeanie erupted into tears.

"Oy, he bhagavana," Nila said handing her a box of tissues. "This is all very doable. Let's have some chocolate. It will improve the situation."

Nila emerged from the kitchen with a purple box of truffles. She slit the cling film with an envelope opener. "These will set you straight. Mayo Clinic says it has a similar effect to marijuana." Jeanie smiled through her tears and blew her nose, emitting a trumpet sound. Nila and Jeanie studied the chocolates with all the seriousness they deserved. "The Oaxaca is amazing for curing weeping. Chilies, pumpkin seeds, Tanzanian chocolate and paprika. The Black Pearl clears sinuses. Ginger wasabi, black sesame seeds and dark chocolate. And Red Fire heals ennui. Ancho chilies, Ceylon cinnamon, and Venezuelan chocolate," Nila said pointing to each one.

They bit into the truffles in silence, Jeanie's sniffles receding as she savored the chocolates.

"Okay. Let's keep working. What else are you looking for?" Nila said as she wiped the corners of her mouth with a tissue.

"He should not smoke or drink and he should believe in God," Jeanie said.

"You want an Irish man who doesn't drink?"

"Yes."

"None of this would be a problem if you'd consider a foreigner," Nila said. "Give me a month to work on this. And start studying the Baha'i faith. You will find great consolation in it."

"What is Baha'i?"

"A hundred year old religion that believes in the oneness of God, the oneness of religion, and the oneness of the human family."

"Is Baha'i your religion?"

"No, my family is my religion," Nila corrected her. "But I dabble in it. If there's a perfect faith about unity, Baha'i is it. It believes in the earth as one country and mankind as its citizens. You should try to understand it. It will cure you of your anger and make you a better person."

"I don't care about religion," Jeanie said.

"The man I have in mind for you is Baha'i. Start praying. Go to the temple. It's down the street before you hit the curve to Idyllwild."

People were cowards when it came to love, Nila believed. They had to be forced to confront the idea of love. And it was usually the woman who had to force the issue. Men, if left to their own devices, didn't mind being left to their own devices. They lived only for the present. Women, Nila thought, were acutely aware of their bodies and mortality, and peered into the years and decades ahead. Giving birth and caring for new life, taking care of aging and dying parents and relatives, seemed to make them more aware of how fleeting life was. She thought this explained why they wanted to reach into the future, to not disappear completely from the planet, but to leave something of themselves behind. For Nila, her life beyond her death mattered. She thought of her children and her children's children carrying her cell material in their bodies. It warmed her heart to know that she would touch the future. Her descendants would be her graffiti on the wall, writ large in psychedelic neon with bold black outlines burning on Main Street: **Nila Waz 'Ere Yo!**.

"Jehan, have you considered a bookkeeper?" Nila launched the opening salvo to win the bounty and a husband for Jeanie at Whole

World Style. She felt that some subterfuge was justifiable as Jehan had never expressed a desire for a mate, and even if he had, he would have insisted on someone who belonged to the temple.

"Why do I need a bookkeeper? I have Quicken." Jehan said.

"She'll make you run better, dream bigger. Trust me on this."

"I don't need the expense. Quicken is $19.95 a month."

During her next visit to Whole World Style, she tried another approach.

"You really need this bookkeeper. Can I give her your number?"

"Like I said, I'm all set with Quicken."

"Yes, but can Quicken put its hand down your shirt and rest its chin on your shoulder, and breathe on your neck while you're tallying numbers?"

"I'm not into that right now," Jehan said.

"Jehan, you're going to die. Worms will eat you up and leave only your bones. Be into everything right now. Don't be lazy."

Nila got the bounty.

Nila's second client was Roger Jensen. Roger, a gray-eyed Buddhist originally from Des Moines, was as gentle as the swaying corn in an Iowa breeze. To question three on Nila's questionnaire, what are you seeking in a wife? Roger had answered, "A spiritual soul mate with simple pleasures, a love of children (at least four), and an utter devotion to the Buddha within."

"The person you're looking for is looking for you also," Nila said.

"Do you really believe that?" Roger asked. He needed so badly to believe that his soul mate had been yearning for him as desperately as he had been yearning for her. He had looked for her for so many years. He had been to every Tibetan temple in the Midwest, every

Buddhist conference from coast to coast, every Buddhist gathering place, casting his eyes around auditoriums, galleries, bookshops, panels, plenary sessions, looking for her. He was certain he'd recognize her immediately. But after fifteen years of looking for her, he was disillusioned.

"Yes, I really do. Love is logical. I don't say that love is all happiness. It is about growth, and growth involves pain."

"I don't know if I like the sound of that," he said.

She reviewed the application form and asked him questions about his family.

"I don't have any," he said.

"Whatever do you mean?" Nila said.

"I haven't seen my father and mother in twenty years."

"Are they alive?"

"Last I heard."

"But why?" Nila couldn't fathom it.

"We just grew apart. Different values. They're good people. Farmers, church goers, rural folk."

"This is stupid. In life we're given a handful of people to love. Why would you throw them away like that?"

"We don't have anything in common."

"Did they abuse you? Torture you?"

No, he shrugged. "They clothed and fed and cared for me until I left for college, and then I didn't want to speak to them. They're not educated, not spiritually enlightened. They got the message and stopped calling after a few years."

"Not spiritually enlightened. I see. And what do you do at Thanksgiving?"

"I go to the temple."

"Terrible! Just terrible! This is not the way to live." Nila slapped the folder shut and placed it on the table next to her.

"That's why I want to make my own family."

"What for? So that your children can walk away without turning back? This is crazy!" she said. "I'm very sorry. But I cannot work with somebody who thinks family is disposable," Nila stood up. "Thank you for coming," she said, and walked towards the door to hold it open for him.

Six months later, Roger pressed his face against the window of Twin Flames, holding his hands around his face like a scuba mask to scope her out. He tried the door but it was locked.

Nila was seated at a desk tucked behind the couch studying the profiles she had assembled of Samuel, a plain, dull banker and Rachel, a dull, plain dentist. The match held an internal logic to Nila but it was proving to be a very difficult case. She had seen elegance in the uninspiring union, a morphing of twin flames. Yet neither of them viewed themselves as either plain or dull. He wanted a woman with a figure like Pamela Anderson or Kim Kardashian, a mind like Rachel Maddow, a glamorous career, and no sassy talk. She wanted a man who looked like Richard Gere or Keanu Reeves, gave her flowers, surprised her with foreign travel, French kissed her when they woke up in the morning, and talked but didn't fart in her company.

"I have news for you," Nila told Rachel. "Halitosis will kill you both if you French kiss when you wake up. And the embargo on farts is lifted after four months," she said holding up four fingers with the thumb folded in like a Boy Scout's salute. "And it is a bilateral situation, either side can end the moratorium."

Nila looked up from the folders, shaking her head at the complexity of the assignment and the absurdity of Samuel and Rachel's requirements. She saw Roger with his face pressed against the glass, his hands lifted to his face. She swiveled her chair to turn her back on him. He rapped the glass with an incessant knock. She lifted her hand in a gesture. Go away, it said.

She called Rae. "Hi Raja."

Rae had left Nila, not more than two hours ago. "You alright? What's going on?"

"Nothing. I called just because."

"No you didn't."

Azyl Park was one of the safest neighborhoods in the city. Even in the cold months, a citizen corps of seniors sat on benches everywhere in the Square shooting the breeze, waiting to pick up their grandchildren from the school on Anemone, or for their adult children and spouses to come home. Nevertheless, Rae had a security company install their most advanced surveillance system in the shop, including a webcam that showed the front of the shop. Every now and then, Rae logged on to the server to see what Nila was up to, to see what she was like when she was not with him. She worked with executive efficiency, she didn't daydream or go into reveries. When she was on the phone interviewing clients, she acted like a clinician. She rarely smiled or laughed. She listened to symptoms and considered a diagnosis and treatment. She was serious about her work, and when her energy began to fade, she would close the shop and take a walk on the Square.

"Why are you calling me?" Rae asked. He had a busy day and Nila was high maintenance. The week before, she had called him on his cell as he was walking from the bank to his office on the Square.

"Can you come home?" she'd asked.

"Why? What's wrong?"

"It's an emergency."

Rae's mind raced. A fire, a flood, what.

"I'm on fire. Bring your hose."

Nila told him about Roger standing outside the door and how she was ignoring him.

"Let him in, Nila. People change," Rae said.

Nila returned the phone to its cradle and pressed the buzzer under her desk to admit Roger. He walked in with a serious look on his face, chewing his lip.

"Would you like tea?" Nila said, a forced smile on her face. "Yes. Thank you," Roger said.

He sat on the sofa and looked around the room as Nila went to a back room. She reappeared with a tray bearing a cloisonné teapot, two cups on saucers, and a plate of halva. She placed the tray on the coffee table and sat down on the edge of the sofa across from where he was sitting. She offered him a cup with milk already in it before he could say lemon.

"So you are here," Nila said, taking a nibble of the sweet between sips of tea.

"Yes." Roger said

"I hope you don't expect me to change my mind. I have my articles of faith. I won't budge," she said.

"I reached out to my parents soon after you booted me out of here," he placed the cup and saucer on the table He leaned forward, his arms on his thighs, his hands clasped. "It killed me to make the first call."

"That's the psychic cost of making amends," Nila said. "How did they respond?"

"My mother was polite but brief. I asked her how she and my father were, she said "peachy keen." I know it was my fault so I sucked it up. I went to see them Thanksgiving."

"That's great. How did it go?" Nila was suddenly interested.

"My father has Alzheimer's. It has made a once intimidating man almost childlike. He was this larger than life figure once, and to see him so small, so helpless, felt weird. My mother didn't want me to explain anything. She just said, you were loved. When you disowned us, we were ashamed. We didn't know how to be with each other or what to say to each other."

Every mother lived in fear of losing her children to some unfathomable force out of her control. Nila thought about Hari and Zara and touched her heart.

"I tried to apologize to them but they didn't want to hear it. My father said, Let's move on. It's the Iowa way. To be practical. My mother said she wanted us to forget the last ten years. I don't know how people can forgive like that." Roger shook his head in disbelief.

"And you're the Buddhist," Nila said.

"Will you work with me now?"

"How do I know you're not lying?" Nila said, piercing him with a stare. "You could be making the whole thing up for all I know."

"I have pictures. They're date stamped." Roger pulled out his phone from his trouser pocket, slid his hand across the screen, and retrieved an album. He handed the phone to Nila. "That's my Dad and his dog, Charlie. The next one is me and my Mom at the soup kitchen where we volunteered Thanksgiving morning. The next one is of the three of us in the backyard."

Nila talked to everyone in Azyl Square about eligible Buddhist women. At Saigon Nails, she explained her search in confidential tones to Min Phung, her manicurist and one of the daughters of the owner. Min broadcast Nila's request in spirited diphthong-laden monologue at full volume to her mother and three sisters, as if she were a CNN embedded correspondent filing a report from the frontlines, who needed to be heard over the mortar shelling. The Phungs fanned out in front of Nila and conversed among themselves in a quarrelsome tone, looking at Nila for clarification. She didn't understand a word they were saying, but nodded in agreement each time one of them spoke or gave her a questioning look.

Bạn đang nói chuyện rác!

Bạn có nhiều hơn một con trâu ngu ngốc!

Finally, Mrs. Phung waved a nail file in the air and brought the squawking to a halt. *Tôi biết người phụ nữ hoàn hảo.* I know the perfect woman.

The girl was famous in her community. She had been the youngest passenger on the second last Chinook that lifted off the roof of the US Embassy during the fall of Saigon. There were sixty people already on board the CH-46 Sea Knight, call sign Lady Ace 09, including US Ambassador to South Vietnam, Graham Martin. She was nine months old, bundled in pants, tunic, and a heavy coat. Her mother thrust her into the hands of one of the young Marines who stood guard at the door of the helicopter. Before the mother could climb in herself, a clutch of men overtook her, scrambling past her into the vehicle. The Chinook began to lift off the roof. The mother wailed, an animal pain, *con tôi, con gái tôi, cô ấy là tất cả tôi có* – my baby, my daughter. She held on to one of the external hooks on the belly of the helicopter, as the Jolly Green Giant tilted from side to side, weighed down by its human cargo, and lifted itself higher and higher. The tamarind trees on the Embassy grounds that had been cut down to give the Chinooks a chance to land lay on the grass like corpses. She released her grip. The Chinook swayed as it flew to the USS Blue Ridge docked at the South China Sea. As the remaining Marines lifted off the roof on the last helicopter, they saw charred and blackened embassy documents floating in the wind like phoenix birds, the US currency they had been ordered to burn flitting about like black butterflies, and one twisted, broken body lying on the concrete roof, dead as dead could be. The child was raised in the home of her mother's older brother, who remained guilty for the rest of his life. He stewed in a particular kind of sorrow and guilt that leeched into his bones, for failing to attend to his sister during that mad scramble to survive.

Nila flew to Minneapolis to meet the uncle and niece.

The living room in the tiny apartment had a rollaway bed that served as a sofa. A large cardboard box, television packaging covered haphazardly with a cotton sheet and topped with a mirror, served as a wobbly coffee table. Two dining room chairs were arranged opposite the makeshift sofa and in front of the coffee table to form a conversation pit. A television stood in the corner of the room, its base covered in lace, its top decorated with a tin of joss sticks and a statue of the Laughing Buddha.

Trang was beautiful and silent. She was five years younger than Nila but had the figure of a young girl—very thin, small boned, thin waisted, flat chested, angular. Her straight black hair, parted in the middle, fell to her waist. The uncle, wearing a wife-beater and pajama pants, smoked a cigarette,

"She is obedient, good cook, loves children," the uncle said.

"Do you wish to marry?" Nila asked the girl.

"I am poor. She will marry," the uncle said quickly.

"This is America. Slavery is over. I need to speak to your niece alone." Nila said.

The uncle rose. He spoke to the girl in Vietnamese, his voice rising in agitation. "No choice," he told Nila.

"I know what he wants. But what do you want?" Nila asked.

"I want to leave this place. If I stay here and work hard at dry cleaner, maybe they make me counter girl. Maybe I am lucky and find job in nail salon to shave dirty feet and wax vagina."

"And you want to get married?"

"I am very practical. If he is not ugly person, if he can support me for short time, I can do something with my life."

"What about love?" Nila asked.

"If he is not ugly person I can try to love him."

"What do you mean ugly person? You mean to look at?"

"No. His heart must be good, kind, clean. If it's ugly dirty heart, I cannot be with him."

"This man has a good heart. He is Buddhist, a beginner who is learning to be a good soul. He is gentle and I think you will not find another man more kind," Nila said.

"You have his picture?"

Nila extended a four-leaf photo binder with the Twin Flames insignia embossed in gold leaf on the white leather.

Trang flipped through the book. There were photographs of Roger as a teenager in high school, a mop of blonde hair falling over his eyes; sporting a crew cut and a Letterman jacket in college; various photos of him in his late twenties and thirties in lumberjack shirts and sweatshirts and jeans and chunky boots. She traced her finger across the picture of him from a decade ago. "He has nice eyes. His eyes light up when he smiles. They make him seem very honest."

"Yes, he is an honest man."

Trang smiled for the first time. "I will go to him."

Nila called Roger from the cab on the way home to Azyl Park.

Chapter 16

FOUND

Roger stood near the baggage carousel at the airport with a hand-lettered sign announcing her name, Nguyen Thi Hong Trang. She walked uncertainly towards him, wearing a pink *ao di* with slim black pants. She clutched a stiff handbag under her arm; it was designed to look like a folded magazine, an Oui! cover laminated in clear plastic.

There is a moment in life, after an extended period of loneliness, when one thinks, "Isn't there even one person on this planet of seven billion just for me? Send me my love." Roger thought at that moment that this woman was the manifestation of his yearning and dreaming, that he had been able to conjure her up with his prayers and intention.

"Nguyen?" He smiled and feasted his eyes on her quiet loveliness.

"Chang," she said.

"You're not Nguyen?" he asked, puzzled, studying the sign and her, first separately, then together.

"Yes."

"Yes, you are Nguyen? Yes, you're not Nguyen?"

She blinked and made a harrumphing sound as if she was dealing with the stupidest person in the world. She directed her gaze at the bags gliding down the carousel to collect herself, before looking at him again. This time, she gave him a piercing look. Listen carefully idiot, the look suggested. "Nguyen family name. Thi connecting name that means poem. Hong middle name, which means pink rose. Chang first name which means loyal."

Roger pointed at the sign. "But it's spelled T R A N G."

"Yes. T RANG pronounced Chang," she looked past his shoulder as if she had explained this to Roger countless times, and what was he? A simpleton?

"I see," he said, and then, "Mine's Roger Jensen." When it didn't elicit so much as a blink, he said, "It doesn't mean anything as far as I know."

Trang slackened her jaw to make the raw sound but he heard it only as Wahjer.

They were incompatible from the start. He wanted a quiet life that revolved around activities at the Buddhist temple in Azyl Park. She wanted to take a large bite out of America's big, round, apple ass. She wanted to hear the crunch, and feel the thin, sweet liquid dribble down the sides of her mouth, and masticate on its fruity yield until it turned into a soft mealy paste, and spit out the tiny seeds in an arc that touched a rainbow.

She placed her *ao dis* in vacuum-sealed bags and stored them in a plastic bin in the basement. She bought a professional wardrobe of grays, blacks, blues, and whites. She cut her hair and wore it in a blunt cut that dropped to her shoulders with bangs that touched her eyebrows. Two months after her arrival, she enrolled in college—first for English classes, then an Associate's degree in business, a Bachelor's two years later, and finally an MBA. But her career took off only after she earned a real estate license and changed her name to Tina Trang, pronounced as it is spelled. Working long hours at the largest real estate brokerage firm in the city, leaving the house before Roger awoke and coming home after he retired, she made her money on commission alone. After she made her first big commission, she began purchasing properties in Azyl Park and the Crescent.

Roger should have been happy, but he resented the changes in her. He had longed for a woman as sensitive and gentle as he was, a meditation partner in the Way of the Buddha, a soul partner—a far cry from the newly minted American before him. He couldn't embrace the four kinds of happiness that came from wealth that the Buddha had talked about. The Anguttaranikaya could not persuade him. He believed in the Reclining Buddha school of Buddhism, not the Laughing Buddha that his wife had placed in their own home, and in the houses she tried to sell. "For good luck," she'd say as she rubbed the Laughing Buddha's belly with an Alexander Hamilton.

Roger's heart was a soft thing that he felt sure was known deeply by his God, but wildly misunderstood by his wife. He withdrew himself from the marriage and took early retirement from his job as a high school art teacher. He pulled up the drawbridge, retired to his fort, and set up an artist's studio in the living room overlooking the lake. From this vantage point, he could see the lake change every day like a woman trying on new dresses. He began to think that though he couldn't understand his wife, he understood deeply the secrets of water and tides and waves. He painted what he saw, imitations of Monet's seascapes.

Before mornings in his studio, Roger would select five furled prayer flags from a vessel in the foyer. He would carry the colorful rectangles of cloth printed with scriptures and mantras that hung vertically from long flagpoles, to the beach. He would wade into the lake in his bare feet until the water reached his knees, and plant the prayer flags in the water. When snow and ice covered the lake, Roger would plant the flags on the beach, using a shovel to make holes in the ground and drive the poles deep into the earth.

After several hours of painting in the studio, Roger would go down to the basement to sit in the meditation room he had built a month before Trang had entered his life. He had carved the enclosed room out of a corner of the East wall and paneled the walls with blonde maple veneer plywood. He hung light-diffusing rice paper screens to break up the wood, and lay mint green tatami mats on the floor. He placed a long three-tiered rosewood altar against the wall and hung a tapestry of the Shakyamuni Buddha, the Enlightened Buddha, above it. From the second level on each side of the Buddha, he hung texts from the Heart Sutra. On the lowest tier, he placed thirteen lotus shaped votive candle and incense holders.

It confounded him that his wife found her redemption in work.

When Trang returned from her real estate agency on Azyl Square, she would make a point of seeking him out in his studio and complimenting his work. She did this to assuage her guilt, for she forgot far too often that if not for him, she'd be clipping toenails and waxing pubes in Minnesota, and still under the thumb of her uncle. "I like the light that is in this picture," or "The sea looks like glass in that one," she would say to Roger.

But behind his back she told a different story. She mocked him in front of the women at Saigon Nails.

"Typical spoilt lazy ass. Painting his watercolors that nobody is crazy enough to buy," she said, looking alternately in the mirror at Min, the Phung sister plucking her brows, and at Diep, the manicurist sitting by her side, massaging her nails with cuticle cream.

"He is artist," Diep offered.

"Artist, my butt. Each one looks exactly the same as the last one. He stands there mixing his colors, studying the sky and the lake, his forehead crunched like he is doing brain operation."

"Oi Troi ơi—Oh my God. Like the monks," Min exclaimed.

"Then he squeezes different types of blue out of tubes and mixes them in a palette. He looks through a pair of binoculars over and over again to check for the accuracy of his observation, and finally he paints his landscape. Same scene, every day. He won't even try to sell the crap."

Though they sniggered, the women at the nail salon were amazed that a grown American man had elected to reject the affairs of the world. "He is like the Buddha," Diep said with reverence.

"Buddha, my ass," Trang said.

Chapter 17

KOLBE HOUSE

Gabe alighted the elevator in a pensive mood. As long as he was in control of his emotions with women and wasn't moved by them, he felt he was in equilibrium. He could satisfy his sexual needs and leave when he wanted. He didn't have to give anything of himself away. But when it graduated to something higher, his mind, normally razor sharp, focused, and supple, leaked its finely honed ability to do mental leaps and somersaults and grew foggy. It had taken him years to get over Farah, more years than she deserved after being so careless with his heart. He needed to gather his forces. He stopped at Nadia's desk to pick up messages and mail.

Nadia was standing in front of her computer, spraying a canister of pressurized air over the keyboard. "Good morning?" she looked up at him.

Gabe nodded.

Nadia straightened her back. "Let's try it again, this time with feeling. Good morning Gabe."

"Leave me alone." Gabe picked up a stack of mail that Nadia had annotated in her inimitable style, comic strip speech balloons that offered Gabe a synopsis of the contents. Needs carnet. Wants sign off on exceptions. Authorized move. He shuffled the mail as he walked towards his office.

"She's lovely isn't she?" Nadia said to Gabe's retreating back.

"I don't know what you're talking about," he said.

"59 carat flawless pink diamond," she said.

"Nadia, stop sticking your nose in my business," Gabe turned to look at her as he opened the door to his office.

"A blind man can see you'd be good together," Nadia brushed the keyboard with a feather duster. "B L I N D," she said.

Gabe took a deep breath and sighed. "Anything else?"

"Eva Krohle invited you to lunch at Kolbe House."

"Set it up for end of week."

"Will do. And call Angeline! You have to chase her. She's not going to run after you."

Kolbe House was on Hyacinth Street, two blocks north of IBI, on the beach. A white Victorian bungalow, it did not conform to the row of red and gray brick multi-family townhomes. It faced the lake instead of the street. The facade was covered in board and batten siding. The door, windows, and gables were trimmed and decorated with fretwork, crowns, spindles, and lineals. White lattice overhangs covered in ivy framed the door. In summer, a canopy of trees, Quaking Aspen and Black Tupelo, standing like sentinels, obscured the house from view. In winter, it blended into the landscape with the naked trees serving as blank-faced totem poles.

Named after Saint Maximilian Kolbe, a Franciscan priest from Poland who had been tortured and killed in Auschwitz, the house served torture survivors from around the world. The center's executive director, fundraiser, lead therapist, and guardian of the residents was Eva Krohle, the ex-wife of Mark Zalinsky, the depressed dentist.

Before Kolbe, Eva had worked at a busy practice in Idyllwild listening to the pain of American Royalty—teenage princes and princesses born of affluent parents, who had been told since birth, first in high-pitched coos then with sung praise, that they were exceptional. They came to their weekly sessions stoned or strung out. Eva would recommend rehab to many of them, and shepherd their parents through the process of treatment. They'd fly to expensive rehab centers in sunshine states and the Caribbean, return tanned and sober, and relapse within weeks. Little shits. She decided to apply for a counselor's job at Kolbe House and leave the treatment of royal pain and suffering to others.

"They are easily startled," Ross Quinlan, the director had said. "We need somebody who is non-threatening, who can enter the silence with them, and understand their language when they're ready to speak."

Eva's gentle demeanor and multilingual skills—she was a former Peace Corps worker in Africa proficient in Arabic, Spanish, and French—secured her the position. Lacking clinical training to work with traumatized patients, she focused in the early days on the practical—to create a peaceful environment for her clients. The office occupied by her predecessor had been a ghastly place with white walls, black furniture, and photos of Freud, Skinner, James, and Adler. She told Ross that tranquil-colored walls were more appropriate for torture victims, many of whom had been subjected to sensory deprivation in ultra-bright rooms with white walls. "The photo display is ludicrous," she'd said.

Eva had the walls painted sea glass blue. A dark blue sofa and a recliner covered in a shell print formed an L. A large framed poster of children playing with a puppy hung on the opposite wall, and a misting humidifier stood under the print. She declined the water fountain Ross offered her, as water had been used as an instrument of torture with many of the residents at Kolbe. For those who could not find the words, she set out a tray of crayons, color pencils, drawing pad, and clay. A basket on the floor held rolled-up prayer shawls.

The shawls were a donation from a knitting circle—a group of women at the retirement home nearby whom Nadia had organized for the purpose. Nadia chose yarns for the shawls with a nod to color psychology and a desire for soft comforting textures that would enfold, embrace, mother, and console the clients. The knitting circle recited prayers together while they crafted the shawls:

Celtic prayer: *Deep peace of the running wave to you, deep peace of the flowing air to you, deep peace of the quiet earth to you, deep peace of the shining stars to you, deep peace of the shades of night to you.*

Blessing of the Earth: *May the earth be soft as you rest upon it.*

Druid Prayer: *Within the great circle of humankind, may you find peace.*

The residents at Kolbe held onto the shawls like children cling to security blankets; they draped them around their bodies, held them like leashes attached to invisible dogs, and slept with them.

Eva dispensed with timetables, objectives, goals, outcomes, and treatment plans. She discovered that asking a traumatized person how she was feeling was too big a question. So she began with rice grains of words.

"Where does it hurt, Isa?" she had asked a new arrival from Sierra Leone, a young woman with blue-black skin and quarter moons of sorrow under her eyes.

"Everywhere," Isa said, her chest heaving.

"Can you point to your pain?"

"Down here from what they did to me. And here in my chest."

And to Lara, a teenager still: "You don't have to say anything. We can just sit. Or you can draw or use clay. Whatever you want."

After twenty minutes of silence, as Eva thought she'd explode from the tick of the Chinese clock, the cluck of American guilt reminding her of minutes and Planck time eaten, swallowed, lost, irretrievably, irrevocably, Lara shifted in her seat and swaddled herself with her shawl. "They did all kinds of things to us. It cannot be described and I don't want to remember. It is a nightmare that cannot be talked about, or described, or understood. Sometimes I think that I will go crazy and that the nightmare will never end. I want to forget everything. I cannot live with these memories. I will go insane," she said.

Eva would sink into a depression after listening to the stories of unspeakable violence and atrocities, each one different, each one ending the same way. Her clients had been broken into a million pieces and she, who was charged with helping them, was certain she couldn't find all the pieces. She'd slip at night into long dreams about her own helplessness. In her dreams she was always lost or she couldn't find what she needed. She dreamt of being at airports without a passport or the required visa. She dreamt she couldn't close her suitcase or withdraw money she desperately needed from an ATM. When she felt incompetent, useless, and irrelevant, she'd compose a letter of resignation to hand to Ross. But always, something would make her change her mind—a client gripping her hands as if she was the only thing making them feel real and alive in this world, a moment of grace, a sliver of a story that made her heart lurch.

"What color comes to your mind when you first wake up?" Eva asked Hana, a woman who had been kept in a rape camp for five months, and hadn't spoken to anyone at Kolbe House for nearly as long. Eva had run out of ideas to draw Hana out of her silence. Nothing had worked.

"The color of the sun when it first rose from behind the Joharina Mountain." Hana twisted the tissue in her hands and shredded it into confetti. "And a small white flower that grew only on the path near the river."

At the sound of Hana's voice, Eva had felt her heart leap and do a backflip. "Where did the path lead?" Eva asked gently, so gently.

"To Emil. We were both seventeen, the first to each other. We would lie behind the hedges near an empty barn, close enough to hear the living river. I would let him touch me, kiss me, taste me. I yielded myself completely to him. I willed all of the love that was bursting from my heart to my lips and fingers and held him and rocked him when he entered me. It was the holiest thing in the world that ever happened to me," she said.

"Hold on to that memory. Don't let it go. It is your truth. It will keep you safe," Eva said.

"They killed my family in front of me," a young man from Rwanda had told her. "I cannot remember anything about them other than the way they died. What they did to my family has replaced everything about who they were. My father was a kind, gentle man who taught me how to make boats out of coconut shells and drift it down the river. He worked hard on the farm and at night he played the lyre we call inanga. My mother fed us children with her hands when we were small. We sat around her and she scooped ugali and cabbage into our mouths. She loved to sing. She sounded like a songbird and sang with my father the old songs. My brother and sister were full of jokes and laughter. I can remember none of this. I cannot remember the important things about them—who they were and what their lives were about. All I can remember is what those men did. The men who tortured them and me still have all the power."

"We will work together to give you back the good memories and bury the bad ones," Eva told him.

As a clinician, Eva quickly realized that the normal work of handing clients tissues or sympathy when they crumbled wasn't enough. She felt that an essential part of their treatment was to allow them, for whom touch had been perverted, to know the kindness of touch. Eva invited massage therapists to Kolbe House to work with the clients. Because most torture took place in bunkers below the ground, she decided to set up the therapy in the sunroom. She asked Ross for money to decorate.

"You're always rolling me over. Where will it end?" he said.

"Stop whining. Give me the money, Ross!"

The room had daffodil yellow walls, thick cream carpeting, hanging photos of new life—puppies, kittens, babies; and four massage tables in the center. It took many weeks before some of the residents would allow themselves to be touched. At first, they would shudder or freeze or curl up in a fetal position or cry or scream when they were touched. Some would relax enough to allow their scalps to be massaged or their necks rubbed. Eva fired a couple of therapists for lack of feeling. "It's soul work that needs to be done," she told one therapist.

"I do body work, not soul work, whatever that is," the woman replied.

"Get the hell out. Don't let me see your face here again."

That was half a life ago. Kolbe Center under Eva, who had assumed stewardship of the center after Ross's retirement, had grown and gained recognition in the field as an exemplar in torture rehabilitation.

When Eva had first invited Gabe to Kolbe House, soon after the Pequod deal, he braced himself for a feisty conversation with a tenant with legitimate grievances. He was aware that he had neglected his duties as a landlord. Kolbe House needed a new roof and the boiler was more than ten years old. He took his foreman and his electrician with him to show his commitment to making good on the repairs. Gabe had a large property management crew to handle his affairs, but he felt Eva warranted special attention. She was a rising star in her field, and he'd known her since he'd first arrived in Azyl Park. Though she was married to Mark, Gabe had never seen her with her husband. Always alone. Once she'd walked into Lucky's and planted herself on the barstool next to him. Sophie, standing in the well, polishing a row of copper cups used for Moscow Mules, stiffened in surprise.

"Alright?" Gabe had asked, as he looked at her in the mirror behind the bar.

Cris placed a cocktail in a martini glass in front of her. "On the house, Eva."

"I'm in over my head every which way."

"A therapist needs a bartender," Cris said. "Talk to me," he placed an unlit cigarette in his mouth and offered her one.

"I don't smoke," she said.

"Don't light it."

Gabe stood up, gulped his drink, and raised a hand. "I'll leave you to it."

"That's right Gabe. Always run away when it gets to heart talk," Cris said, giving a thumbs up.

Sophie came out of the well and sat down on the stool vacated by Gabe. They listened to her story, in slices of three or five minutes, making her wait when they needed to attend to other patrons who entered the bar. Eva waited patiently as they tended to their customers, sipping her drink, dangling the unlit cigarette from her mouth. Sophie and Cris picked up the conversation exactly where they had left off.

"I don't know what to do," Eva said.

"You know exactly what to do." Sophie patted her hand.

"They need you Eva. You know what to do," Cris poured her another drink.

"Eva. I know I've been tardy, but I promise you, you'll have your new boiler and your roof fixed asap," Gabe said, as soon as he saw her at the door.

"Come in, come in," she smiled. She was wearing a yellow knit dress with navy blue birds appliqued at the neckline that highlighted her blonde hair and the blue in her eyes. A prayer shawl fell over her shoulders.

Gabe followed Eva into her office after giving his crew instructions. The room had several large plants, fresh flowers in vases, a humidifier misting in a reassuring hiss, and her cats.

Caravaggio was an attention seeker; he stood up on the armrest of the couch to brush his face against Gabe's hand. Eva would have taken Caravaggio alone, but the shelter's counselor had said a young cat needed a playmate. Cleo, a two year old watched from a corner. All her paws were heavily wrapped in bandages—she had been fully declawed by a sadistic owner. Though the shelter pressed other cats on her, Eva took Cleo. She reminded Eva of all the clients at Kolbe: four-paw declawed, broken, torn, frightened, and struggling to survive.

"You're still living here," Gabe said, as he stroked Caravaggio under the chin. Cleo was wedged between the wall and the sofa, a secure fortress too narrow for others to invade.

"You doing okay?" Gabe knew that her divorce had been Mark's fault. Everyone had known about Mark's affair with Caroline Langley, the plastic surgeon's wife. Mark had been brazen about it. Lying on top of her on the beach, feeling up her pneumatic breasts, kissing her augmented lips behind the bar at Oasis, visiting her at her home on the Crescent.

"Don't you want to settle in your own home? You can't live here forever. David has lots of listings, it's a good time to buy."
"No. This feels right for now," Eva said.

Eva's divorce from Mark had been a surgically clean amputation. It happened at light speed. Eva had been in the kitchen folding parchment paper around chicken breasts, her face set in concentration as she crimped the paper into a pouch with diamond cut edges. Her I Pad was leaning on its triangle with a recipe for poulet with shallots, garlic and white wine.

Mark could have kept the affair going and Eva wouldn't have known. But he'd had a bad day, immigrants with bad dental work in need of deep scaling and a restaurant with more wait staff than customers, and he was depressed. He wanted to see what a happy, well-adjusted, religiously inclined, self-reliant person would do if he pulled the ground from under her. He told her about Caroline.

A guttural sound Eva had never heard before rose from her throat. She pushed the ceramic dish off the counter. It crashed on the floor and broke into four large pieces. She hurled at Mark a phone, a frying pan, and as he began backing out of the door with his hands covering his face in a featherweight defense, a bottle of St. Julien Beychevelle. It missed him by an inch and exploded into a red waterfall against the pristine white cabinetry.

"I'm glad you're doing well, Eva." Gabe walked towards the door. "Make a list of what needs doing and give it to my crew. Alright?"

"Listen, Gabe. I need your help. Will you sit with me a minute please?"

What now? Gabe thought.

"Please."

Gabe sat down on the couch, next to Caravaggio. The pleasant hum of the humidifier and Caravaggio's attention had a tranquilizing effect on him. "What's going on?"

Eva leaned forward in the recliner, her hands laced neatly on her lap. "Kolbe House is in a money hole. I can screw around for the next year wasting time I should be spending with my clients, wining and dining small donors, or, and it's a big or, you can give me the money."

"Eva," Gabe was embarrassed for her, for himself. "You put me in an awkward position." After the Pequod deal had made the news, fundraisers from everywhere began calling. He charged Nadia as his gatekeeper and told her to admit no one.

"I need three million dollars to keep Kolbe House running for the next five years."

"There are dozens of causes in front of me, Eva. Naming rights to a B School, the new wing of a museum, endowing an art collection. I'll have to pass," Gabe said.

"I pass on your pass," she said angrily.

"What does that mean?"

"I reject your pass."

"You're being unreasonable."

"When you die, this is the thing you can be proud of. Not selling poop coffee or supporting a museum or having your name on a B School."

"Are we done?" Gabe stood up.

"I'm sorry, Gabe. Forget it. Let's have tea." Eva stood up and extended a hand to him.

How do you turn down a nothing request from a secular saint? No big deal to give her five minutes. Gabe took her hand.

She gently led him through a maze of corridors to the kitchen, one hand in the crook of his arm.

Six of the residents were seated at the dining table. A woman stood with her back against the wall, her hands stretched out, as she inched towards the door. Eva walked with Gabe towards the kitchen counter. He leaned against the counter next to the dishwasher; she stood near the double sink. She took two teabags from a box, placed them in mugs, and belatedly said, "Orange pekoe?" Gabe shrugged and stared at the mugs, trying mightily to avoid looking at the residents and the woman against the wall.

Eva poured hot water from a carafe into the mugs. "Sugar?"

He was angry with Eva for manipulating him.

"Let's sit outside," she motioned to a patio table beyond the sliding glass doors.

Gabe wanted distance between them and chose the seat furthest from Eva.

Eva held the cup under her chin with both hands. "I know you hear stories all the time. But let me tell you two. It will be good for you to hear them."

Gabe wanted to be somewhere else. He didn't touch the tea. People liked dumping their problems on him because he was a community leader, because he was financially well off, and because he was a good listener. To his credit, he found he could absorb other people's troubles without letting them ruin his own sense of wellbeing.

"That woman enacting Christ in there, she was hung upside down by her ankles and electro-shocked in her genitals."

Gabe cupped his hand over his mouth and pulled his phone out of his pocket. He'd give her sixty seconds.

"And take a look at the bird feeder over there?" Eva ballooned her cheeks to blow into the mug to cool the drink.

An elderly man was sitting on a parsons chair in the back yard. He was covered in breadcrumbs and birdseeds and dozens of birds were nipping at him, his hair, his arms, his face, his lips. The whirr of the birds, as they flapped their wings and pecked at him, cut the air with chip and whoosh sounds.

"They killed his entire family."

"Eva, stop. I don't want to hear anymore." Gabe stood up and rushed to the sliding door, derailing it from its tracks as he pulled.

"How nice it must be to feel nothing and still get full credit for being alive," Eva said. She regretted the words the minute they issued from her mouth, but she felt she had the moral high ground. Why couldn't he just do the right thing without her having to shame him?

"Tell my crew to fix this," he said coldly, as he walked towards the kitchen door. The woman by the wall yowled as he walked past her.

Gabe took long strides to reach the front door. He ran down the stairs and broke into a fast clip as he turned onto Hyacinth from the beach. He began to run, his heart racing, to his office on the Square.

The rest of the day was ruined, he thought as he switched elevators to ride to his penthouse on the 29th. He stripped off his clothes and bounded naked down the spiral staircase into his exercise room on the floor below. He put on shorts and t-shirt, socks and sneakers. He took a pair of red gloves hanging on a hook and went ten rounds with the punching bag. When the strikes landed on the bag, he felt his shoulders cramp and his ears ring. He threw the gloves onto the floor and climbed on the threadmill at the other end of the room. He set it on a deep incline and ran eight miles, increasing the speed at intervals until he felt pain in his legs, and grew breathless and winded from his heart pounding the wall of his chest. When he finished, he reset the button for three more miles. How nice it must be to feel nothing and still get full credit for being alive—she was merciless.

Eva sent him emails, at the rate of two a day, for weeks after their meeting. The subject lines compelled him to read her missives: Gabe, you're meant to …, Gabe, you'll feel…, Gabe, give so ..... He could have ignored the messages but he felt an obligation to read them:

… do repair, … the morality of love, … it doesn't hurt... She sent reports, links, victim testimonies, white papers, truth commission transcripts. He couldn't turn away. After reading one of Eva's reports, When Heaven and Hell Traded Places: Survivor Testimonies, Gabe leaned back in his chair from the weariness he felt. Sooner or later one must choose a side if one is to remain human.

He summoned Herschel and Henry to his office and told them about Kolbe House. "I want to guarantee Kolbe House's survival."

"What's your motive?" Herschel asked.

"Eva Krohle. A pain in the ass who won't leave me alone."

"We need a better reason to sign off on that," Herschel said.

"I want to sleep at night," Gabe said.

"Ambien or Lunesta is cheaper," said Henry.

"Why not the B-School? It would be sexier," Herschel suggested.

"I'd recommend it go to one of the museums. You'd get a lot of PR," Henry said.

"She's doing work none of us would. There's so much need. There are a hundred and fifty countries that torture. I'm not going to do it. It's cheaper to fund Eva. Set up an endowment. Help her through the formalities and structure it. Make it low liquidity, just enough to cover operations, and divert the rest to an aggressive growth fund. I'd like you both to manage it. Also make her sign an NDA. I want to remain anonymous," Gabe said

"Are you sure?" Herschel asked.

"Get it done."

After an appointment with Herschel and Henry, Eva stopped by Gabe's office. She held a pastry box of baklava that she'd picked up at Gupta's, and a sealed envelope with a note and a medal of St. Maximillian Kolbe.

"Is he in?" she asked Nadia. She was dressed in yoga pants and a tunic, and had one of Nadia's prayer shawls wrapped around her shoulders, the ends left to hang in front of her.

"I knew this was the one that would call your name," Nadia smiled and fingered the shawl.

"I love it so," Eva smiled and hugged Nadia.

"Let me find out if he's available," Nadia said before disappearing into Gabe's office. Eva stood by the stone sculpture wondering its meaning.

Nadia emerged from Gabe's office. "Umh, so, he says he's really, really busy."

"Oh!" Eva said. "Shall I wait?"

"I think it's going to be a very long while," Nadia said kindly.

"Oh. Okay. I didn't realize," Eva said. "Will you give this to him?" Eva handed Nadia the box and envelope.

Nadia placed the items on the reception desk and walked Eva to the elevator. She pressed the button. "I've got the seniors casting off a few more. Silk, kid mohair, and baby alpaca. Green, the color of hope. I'll drop them off this weekend."

"Did I offend him? I know I'm a barbarian about Kolbe House. I think I went too far."

"No, Eva," Nadia said. "You know how he is. Doesn't like drama, likes to keep things on the down low."

"What he's done is so incredible. I wanted to tell him about all the lives he's touched." Eva grew teary-eyed.

"That's exactly what he doesn't want to hear." Nadia kissed Eva on both cheeks and blew her a kiss as the elevator doors closed.

She tapped Gabe's door and entered. "From Eva," she placed the box and envelope on his desk.

"Yes, thanks," Gabe said, his back to her, opening a screen on his computer.

"Gabe, you did a beautiful thing. Why wouldn't you let Eva thank you properly?"

"Did you bind those reports I asked you to?" He flipped through a sheaf of stapled papers and stared at the document on the screen.

"Gabe, what would have been the harm?"

"I need those reports," he said, sliding the headset wrapped around his neck over his crown.

"Yes, Gabe. I'll get them for you now."

In the evening, after turning off his computer, Gabe leaned back in his chair and stared at the box. He reached for the envelope and slit it open with his finger.

"Gabe, Only gratitude, Eva."

He slipped the card face down under the pad on his desk. He set the medal in a well in the desk drawer, next to the paperclips. He lifted a square of candy from the box and bit into the caramelized paste of honey and nuts. A lachrymal haze blurred his vision.

Chapter 18

SONGBIRDS

It was March in the cold city and Bruce was without a coat. He hailed a cab that had a turbaned head on the grill and a sign on the roof that promised, *Ride Like A Royal*. "I need a coat and a place to live," Bruce said, as he closed the door.

The driver turned to look at him and stared at his disheveled appearance. "You have money?"

Bruce stuck forty dollars in the payment slot in the glass partition. "I'll give you the rest when we get there."

"Where is there?"

"I don't know, mate. Recommend a place."

The driver gave him an Indian head bob and pulled out of the cab corral.

As the cab entered Shoreland Drive, heading north, Bruce saw the city on the left and the lake on the right. A large flock of birds flew in V formation above the shoreline. Bruce estimated at least a thousand birds. They flew with precision, exploiting aerodynamics, each one, except for the leader of the formation, equidistant from those in front, behind, and at each side. He had read once that birds time their wing beats perfectly to save energy. Each bird helped its immediate companions conserve energy by timing its own wing beats to its neighbors. This allowed each bird to glide and ride the tail winds from the efforts of its companions. A bird alone would never survive a journey.

"What kind of birds are those?"

"It's songbird season. They're flying to South America," the cab driver said.

Twice a year, from April to May and late August to November, the lights in many of the skyscrapers in the city go dim from midnight to sunrise—a courtesy to the seven million birds traversing the avian flyways to their nesting grounds in the north and their winter retreats in South America. More than three hundred species: songbirds enough to orchestrate a symphony, blackbirds and cranes, flickers and gulls, juncos and kinglets, meadowlarks and nighthawks, orioles and phoebes, swallows and tanagers, warblers and vireos. They journey three thousand miles and more, soaring to fly in a giant shifting, changing, morphing lariat, riding and gliding on the thermal winds, eluding predators and planes, swooping down for food, and sheltering from extreme weather. Vigilant about their place in the echelon, they readjust positions each time the flock thins, and revise their wing beats for the fractured, reconstituted skein. Eventually they arrive in the Great American City. The glare and glow of incandescent, fluorescent, and halogen lights from buildings that remain lit disorient the passerines, steering them off course from the shoreline of Lake M, a reliable avian compass since ancient times. They fly around the buildings all night—in circles, in a panic—before touching down on city sidewalks at daybreak, hungry and exhausted. Others, blinded by the lights, seduced by artificial gardens in building atriums and lobbies, crash against the windows and plummet to the concrete in a death spiral. Baffled eyes stare at the sky, the futility of striving and migration branded on bloodied beaks and broken wings like stigmata; hungry hearts, dead as dead can be, with the song still inside them.

Bruce watched the birds until they flew higher and out of view.

The cab came to a stop in front of Whole World Style. "They have a good selection of coats and hats. One block down, City Realty has apartment rentals. You owe me ten dollars."

"Keep the change and pop the trunk." Bruce passed a twenty through the open partition. "What's this area called?"

"The town is Azyl Park. This is Azyl Square. Beach side is Azyl Crescent. Good luck in America," the cabbie said, before driving off.

Bruce stood outside Whole World Style and looked up and down the street. He was a long way from Geelong and Gheringhap Street.

"I need a coat," Bruce said to the man behind the counter. At a showcase near him, an Indian woman wearing a red sari embroidered with white flowers, white gardenias in her chignon, kohl lined eyes, and a diamond nose ring, was admiring a shawl.

"I don't think we have anything in your size on the floor," said the man.

"Can you check in the back then?"

"I'll see," the man parted a beaded curtain behind him that opened into a storage room, and rummaged through cardboard boxes stacked on shelves.

"You look like a princess in a fairy tale," Bruce told the woman.

"You say that to every girl I'm sure," she smiled.

"Only to princesses," he grinned.

The woman folded the shawl, all six feet of it, and placed it in a box no larger than a matchbox.

"How did you do that?"

"It's gossamer strands of nothing," she said.

The shop clerk parted the curtains again holding a pile of coats in the crook of his arm. “A couple of these may work,” he placed them on the counter.

“I’ll take this Jehan,” the woman said.

Jehan completed the transaction, wrapped the box in tissue paper, and placed it in a shopping bag. She took the bag and glanced at the stack of coats on the counter. “Forgive me,” she looked up at Bruce. “Those red coats against your skin are going to make you look like a giant rhubarb or a fire hydrant. Take the blue. It will bring out your eyes and cool your skin.”

“Better listen to her,” Jehan said.

“Thank you,” Bruce smiled at the woman.

“You’re welcome.” And to Jehan, “Give my regards to your lovely wife.”

“I will,” he smiled and pressed his hands together, palm to palm, fingers against fingers, thumbs arched to his chest

“Who was that? The Maharani of Jaipur? All that was missing was the elephant escort,” said Bruce.

“Exactly right,” Jehan said. “Nila Oberoi, wife of Rae Oberoi who owns all the cabs in this city. Raj Cabs, Ride Like A Royal, that’s her husband.”

Bruce laughed. The whole world is tied with one string.

“Like she said, this will look good on you,” Jehan said, holding up the checked blue and black lumberjack jacket. “It’s quilt lined and padded, wool outer, zip and stud front placket fastening, faux fur collar trim. It’s a quality coat. Try it on.”

Bruce took off his sweatshirt and put on the coat. He looked around and saw a mirror on a far wall. He walked over to it and looked at himself. He was looking less and less familiar to himself everyday, like he was being whittled and hewn down to his raw essence. "I'll take it. I'll keep it on," he said.

"Where's the nearest hotel?" he asked, as he took his credit card back from Jehan.

"No hotels here, but there's a B&B. Three blocks down, make a right on Iris Street. Beach side. Number 19. I'll check if they have rooms."

Jehan dialed a number and spoke in a language Bruce didn't understand.

"You're set. They're waiting for you now."

"Thanks. Where are you from?" Bruce asked as he stuffed the hoodie into the duffle bag.

"From here. Born and raised."

"But you were from somewhere else before that."

Jehan shrugged. "Who isn't?"

Bruce marveled at the ease with which Jehan straddled language and culture and identity. Neither this nor that. Both this and that. It was a gentle way to live in the world, to have no concrete shoes to place your feet into, to belong to a place in a light and fictional way and yet feel natural, grounded, and safe.

"And City Realty is on the next block?"

"Yes. Ask for the owner, Tina Trang."

Laden with guitar and bag, Bruce walked north towards the apartment rental agency. America is a nation of shopkeepers and shoppers, he thought as he walked past stores selling everything from bread to baubles, and people holding multiple bags in both hands. "Out Showing," declared a sign on the door of City Realty. He sighed and made his way towards the B&B.

The room in the attic of the Tudor style bungalow was small. It had a twin bed too short for Bruce and a slanted wall with a skylight that further diminished the size of the room. When he sat at the foot of the bed to untie his shoes, his head was less than a foot below the angled ceiling. The attached bathroom had a shower stall and a sink that reminded him of the Zephyr.

He fell asleep, lying on his side, his thighs pulled up in a ledge below his stomach, and had a series of dreams. Some, where he was a boy, others where he was his real age. Lil and Roberto waving to him as he stood gripping the rails of a passenger ship that was leaving port. While he was seeing Lil and Roberto in the dream, a thought passed through his dreamer's mind. "How would Lil and Roberto have known each other?" He'd never been on a ship. He dreamed that his mother squeezed iodine from a dropper onto a cut on his knee. He remembered the iodine but not the cut. He dreamt of Nin comforting him through a bout of hiccups with her cure: Grip my thumbs and look into my eyes and think a loving thought. Gram in her coffin looking like she would wake up at any moment. Glory in the freezer looking like she would never wake up. Bruce as clown and chimp on The Beer Meister. Waylon Jennings sitting at a barstool at Calhoun's, Luckenback, Texas playing on the jukebox.

"Why do you want to live on the Square?" Trang asked the next day, looking at him perplexed. "Too much life going on, too many people, too much noise. Don't you want somewhere quiet?"

"What's wrong with life and noise?"

"You have money and great credit," she said looking at the application form and the three credit reports she had pulled. "I can show you some nice houses near the Crescent, on the beach or with a lake view. Very quiet."

"No, I want something on this street. Above a restaurant or a bar, so cooking smells curl my nose, and paper-thin walls so I can hear people yelling and fighting and beating each other up, and passing out drunk before they kill each other. And having sex." Bruce said.

"Are you a nut job?"

"Maybe."

"What did you do? What are you running from?"

"I'm not running. It's the opposite. I want to rejoin the human race," he said.

Trang told him about the apartment above Lucky's.

Sophie and Cris had vacated it to move to a lakefront house ten years ago, but they'd left behind the cheap furniture they'd acquired over the years living there, so that they could use the place to shower, sleep, and rest when they needed a respite from the bar. Sophie was attached to it—their first real home in America. She placed fresh cut flowers in a crystal cut vase each week. In the kitchen, the pots, pans, dishes and cups that she had bought from Gupta's with her first paycheck, were arranged neatly in the drawers. The cupboards and refrigerator were stocked with basics to rustle up a quick meal – olive oil, jars of olives, anchovies, crackers, dried sausages, canned and dried vegetables and fruit.

"I'd like to see it."

"It's not on the market. He wants it rented, she's emotional about it. It requires some finesse and marriage counseling. Why don't you go have an early lunch? I'll call you when I have the keys. It may take an hour," Trang said.

"I don't have a phone."

"You don't have a cellphone?" Trang found the situation extremely disturbing. "What if you want to call somebody?" She herself was attached to her phone as if it were a heart monitor. "This is so wrong."

"I don't have anyone to call."

"Bullshit. And what if somebody wants to call you?" Trang was beside herself. The belligerence of the act, of rejecting a commonly accepted rule of engagement, unsettled her.

"I don't want anyone calling me."

"This is crazy!"

"Where's a good place to eat?"

"Try Oasis," Trang said. "Come back in one hour." Psycho guy, full on mental case, she thought. No cell phone, what a loser.

Once Bruce sat down at the table the hostess guided him to, he regretted its location. Though the busboy had filled his water glass and brought a breadbasket and olive oil cruet to his table, he decided to move to a booth in the back of the room. He held his water glass and napkin wrapped silverware in one hand and the basket and cruet in the other and established himself in his new dining position. A man standing behind the counter looked at him, ruddy faced, lips set in a bitter curl. When Bruce raised his hand and nodded at him, the man turned away. The dining room was empty except for a couple at a nook diagonally behind him, a woman wearing a veil seated across from a man wearing a kippah. They were together in a strange way, each reading and eating in silence, but glancing at each other as if to affirm themselves to each other. They spooned food into each other's mouths, like parents feeding their infants. So many ways of loving, Bruce thought.

Near the window, an Indian teenager sat alone with his laptop opened. Bruce's Maharani tapped the glass pane in front of the boy. She walked to the door of the restaurant and entered. The young man didn't get up. Nila Oberoi hugged and kissed him on his head. She talked animatedly to the boy. His expression was set to dopey teenage angst. The delight she took in the young man, the whole force of her concentration focused on him like a tractor beam, the look of pure unadulterated love in her eyes, moved Bruce. His mother had looked at him that way. It had been different from the look she gave Glory, or the look she gave the succession of men who rolled into the bar. I love you best, she'd tell him when he was little. When I'm gone, I won't really be gone, I'll be with you.

Don't go there, Bruce admonished himself. That's how you stop a memory, you don't permit the notion of it to bloom to full sorrow. On the Zephyr, he had allowed free rein to his thoughts, picking the scabs off old wounds and grief, to try to understand why he was self-destructive, why he had blown things up with the Goldsmiths. He had let the thoughts unfurl and rise up like smoke out of his brain and consciousness, unrestrained like the wild horses running alongside the Zephyr in De Beque, until he was empty. The purge had made him no wiser. He was a drunk and an addict because he had lost everyone he loved. He was self-destructive because he had nobody to keep himself alive for.

Bruce picked at his lunch, finished a wheat beer, and ordered a second. He realized that it had been four days since he had woken up to Zach and Chip and the wellness team and the guy in bulging trunks spewing lines from Star Wars. He recalled what Roberto had told him about golden cages. He suddenly remembered the medal Roberto had given him, which he'd placed in his wallet in one of the card slots. He took the wallet out of his jeans pocket and tried to fish it out with his fingers. When the leather wouldn't stretch to accommodate his fingers, he took the butter knife and slid it into the slot. The medal and the chain fell on the plate in front of him with a ting. "La Patrona de America y Mexico. She's good luck," Roberto had said. Bruce studied the medal and the chain. The chain was 3-millimeter gauge stainless steel, 24 inches long, substantial and designed for a man. The medal had been designed for a woman, a small woman. Made of oxidized steel, it was oval in shape, as large as the nail on his smallest finger. At the edge of the medal, in a banded arc matching the oval shape and ringing the oval, it read: Nuestra Senora de Guadalupe on the top half, and *Proteger a mi hijo*—protect my son, on the lower half. In the middle was a figure of a woman stamped into the metal, a woman wearing a long veil that reached her ankles, holding her hands together in prayer, surrounded by a halo. Bruce was surprised by the tears that welled up in his eyes. They fell down his cheeks, for him first of all for not knowing how to live, for being reckless and turning gold to shit, for his mother, for all his dead, for Roberto's mother who had to etch her faith in cheap metal and deliver her son to the coyotes, and for Roberto who had been ready but too late to see her again. Hasta Siempre. Until Forever.

"I see you went with my recommendation," Nila appeared beside him, eyeing the coat draped over the back of the chair next to Bruce.

Bruce brushed his closed eyes with the fleshy pads of his palms. "Yes, thanks," he said, wiping his cheek on his sleeve.

"Are you alright?"

"Yeah. Damn allergies," he said looking down.

"It's not allergy season," she said.

He lifted the glass of beer to his lips.

"My daughter, Zara, is a reality show addict. She watches everything. She was filling me in yesterday on the latest news on TMZ. Stories about an Australian reality show star. According to reports, he had a mental breakdown and caused a lot of trouble," Nila said.

"Though he may want his head examined, I don't think he had a mental breakdown," Bruce said, placing the glass in front of him, circling its rim with his finger, looking past her. He felt amorphous, pervious, like he was leaking grief, and he didn't want her pushing him over the edge.

"He's come to the right place. We need a pioneer from Australia." There were all kinds of people who washed up in Azyl Park, this one was a rare bird. He looked like he'd flown through a fire, alive, but covered in soot.

"What's a melting pot without an Aussie," he looked up.

"A fusion chamber," she corrected.

"Is there a difference?" He couldn't get over her attire, the colors made his eyes swim.

"We change ourselves, we change those around us, and we fuse into a singular new thing." She believed in this. She insisted on this. Or else what is America for?

She waved to her son. "Tarry awhile. You'll be okay here."

Bruce walked back to City Realty at the appointed time. Trang was on the phone but smiled at him. She drew a pair of keys from her desk and dipped it up and down like a yoyo, smiling.

"I had to do shuttle diplomacy between Cris who is all for it and Sophie who cannot see a stranger living there," she said, as she returned the receiver to its cradle. "You have to be on your best behavior. No weird stuff." She lifted her coat from a chair and put it on, a big puffy poufy diamond quilted black number that reached to her ankles.

"Why is everyone walking around wearing blankets?"

"Because we're bracing for 50 below zero."

"Great. I've come to Paradise." He fell in step with her on the street.

"Let's cross here," she said, pulling him by his arm.

"The cars are speeding, there's no stop sign."

"You have to have faith in people, Bruce. They'll always stop."

My realtor, the philosopher, Bruce thought.

Tina dragged him by the sleeve across the street as buses, cars, bicycles and motorcycles came to a stop cartoon-style.

"I brought Bruce," Trang said, not just to Sophie and Cris, but to everyone at the bar.

It was an old fashioned pub that reminded Bruce of Calhoun's. Dark mahogany bar, glass and mirror etched with gold and copper leaf decorations, round pedestal tables, poseur tables, tub chairs, booths with tufted vinyl seats, bar stools striped with silver duct tape that looked like they'd pinch buttocks and thighs. Sophie was dressed in a black turtleneck and jeans, her dark brown hair, a short bowl cut. She was smoking a red cocktail cigarette. Cris had an unlit cigarette dangling from the corner of his lips while he mixed a drink for a patron.

At the end of the bar, two men sat with their drinks, cellphones next to their glasses. Ivan Novic was silent and morose, his visage a perfect visual for the melancholy French song playing over the speakers. To his right, Rae Oberoi sat on a stool drinking beer. Rae was a handsome man in his mid-thirties, of medium build and average height, with a widow's peak and a striking head of salt and pepper hair. He wore a green shirt of the palest pastel mint and a brown and green tweed jacket. A smile played on his lips as he checked an incoming text message.

"You will take care of my home?" Sophie asked, one hand on a hip, the other holding the cigarette near her lips.

"Absolutely."

"Sophie, we have a beautiful house now but only half of you is there," Cris said. "It's time to let this go."

"I'll show Bruce the place," Trang said, guiding Bruce through a side door and up the stairs.

The front door opened into a living room with two distressed leather sofas and an embossed wooden table. A canted bay window overlooked the Square. A shelf below it held a sizeable collection of travel books about the Greek Islands—Kos, Paros, Samos, Chios, Corfu, Crete, Skiathos, Rhodes, Santorini. To the right, a hallway led to a bedroom and bathroom. A short corridor on the left flowed into a kitchenette with a single sink, a slim refrigerator, a microwave, and no dishwasher, and into a sunroom and dining area at the rear. A door opened from the sunroom to a stairwell leading to the yard that had a shed, patches of grass, and a lone crab apple tree.

"I like the vibe. I'll take it." Bruce looked around, sized things up. Nothing like the villa and nothing like Geringhap Street, but still.

"It's a good place to set broken bones," Trang said.

"Who said anything about broken bones?"

"I know everything about you," Trang said.

"I hope not," Bruce said.

"We're all wretched refuse."

"I'm flattered." He bowed and raised his hand like one of the three tenors.

"You'll be fine, Bruce. When do you want to move in?"

"Right away." He had no idea what would become of him. The slate was clean.

"That can work. Let's talk to Sophie and Cris and I'll write up the contract."

Chapter 19

RISING

Bruce moved to the apartment above Lucky's with his guitar and duffle bag. In the months that followed, he slept either twelve hours a day or two hours a night depending on booze and memory. Some days, he stayed in bed until he needed to relieve himself or relieve his thirst. What did he think about as he lay there staring at the ceiling? Nothing and everything. What a fuck up he was. What a sick joke life was. What a waste of space he was. That if there was a higher power, he couldn't wait to get to that plane and knee that higher power in the groin for taking so much of the ground beneath him, leaving him only the span of his feet to build his life on, and for taking away everyone he had loved.

His earliest memories were of being passed from one set of arms to another, from his grandmother to Nin, from Nin to Lil, from Lil to his mother. "That's the most loved boy in the world," he remembered a nurse at the clinic say, as he was comforted by his family of women after receiving a round of vaccinations. If he'd just had ten more years with them, if they'd just waited for him to make good, he could have taken care of them. He would have kept the Beer Meister gig. Brought them all to California. They would have enjoyed the house in Malibu and the luxuries he could have given them after a lifetime of scarcity. They would have been in on the joke of exploiting the stupidity of the American television viewer. They would have been practical. Ride the jeep till the wheels fall off, they would have told him.

He stayed away from Lucky's because he didn't want his landlords to know he was on an extended bender. He did most of his drinking at Oasis and took his meals at Two Tables, a dive around the corner that served pizza and falafel sandwiches, or at some of the eateries on the side streets that looked like they were ready to go under. A couple of times he ran into Tina.

"You look like shit," Tina said when she walked into Two Tables one lunchtime to collect a takeout and spotted him hunched over at a corner table, his back against the wall, staring into space.

"You don't like the way I look?"

"Seriously you look terrible."

"I'm doing okay."

"It's all over the Square, that you wake up at the crack of noon and get shitfaced. That is not doing okay, you lazy ass."

"Leave me alone," Bruce said.

"You're a coward, Bruce."

Nila was more forthright.

"Hello Maharani," Bruce had greeted Nila as he passed her on the street, in front of her shop on the Square.

"Bruce," Nila smiled as she appraised him. He had a gray pallor to his skin, his face hadn't seen a razor in a long while, and his hair was uncombed and ratty. "How are you?"

"Some days I think everything is humming along, and other days I don't want to get out of bed."

"That's normal."

"Twin Flames," Bruce eyed the sign on the window. "What do you do exactly?"

"I'm a matchmaker."

"You mean of people?"

"Of course of people," she said, as she opened the door and pointed a remote at the security console to silence it. "Come in."

He walked into the store and took stock of the room. "I get it. You've going for domestic serenity."

Nila looked around the room. "It's all I know." She adjusted the *paloo* of her sari—magenta and black and a matching choli with black brocade around the scooped neck and sleeve cuffs. "Sit down. I'll make tea," she said.

"You like a lot of color," Bruce said, moving from the magenta of her sari to the deep colors of the room.

"I don't like to limit myself. I like change and possibilities," Nila said, walking towards the kitchen.

"Gray black and blue are enough for most people," he said.

"Life is for living, no?" she turned to him.

Nila returned from the kitchen and set a mug of cardamom tea on the table in front of Bruce. She sat down and wrapped the *paloo* around her like a shawl.

Bruce lifted the mug to his mouth and drew a sip. "This is good," he said.

Nila watched him.

"So you arrange marriages?" he looked around the room again. "How quaint."

"People are lonely. They don't know where to find love. I help them. I take the stress out of looking for them."

"For a fee."

"Yes. A very high fee, because unlike my clients who don't have a clue about who is good for them, I have impeccable tastes."

"You have someone for me?"

"Please. I wouldn't trust a dog to you right now."

"That hurts Maharani."

"Bruce, I want to give you advice. Do you want to hear it?"

"Is it free?"

"Yes. Do you want it?"

"Yes, Maharani."

Nila stood up and turned her back to him as if to fortify her humors. Then she turned around. "Listen to me. I'm very sorry to be using bad words but you have to wake up. Wake the fuck up, you fucking fuck up. Put whatever is hurting you in a paper bag and bury it, and start doing something with your life. Do you hear me?"

"If only it were that easy," he said.

"You think you're the only one bad things happened to? Go to Kolbe House and see what real suffering is. Stop being a self-pitying, drunken fuckup."

Bruce's face collapsed at the vicious blow. He felt his cheek muscles twitch from hurt and his eyes grow watery. "Thank you," he set the mug on the table and rose.

"Bruce!" Nila raised her hand to her mouth. "I have wounded you. I'm so sorry. I have no business talking to you like that. Forgive me, please. I'm so sorry."

"Think nothing of it, Maharani," he said, walking fast to the door. If he didn't leave, his chest would explode from the pain.

Bruce wasn't sure if it was Nila's words—acid etched in glass with expletives that must have taken a lot out of her royal highness—that roused him from his stupor, but he woke up the next day with no desire to reach for the bottle. Without asking Sophie or Cris, Bruce ripped the "Barback Wanted" sign off the window at Lucky's.

"What are you doing?" Sophie asked.

"Meet your new barback."

He cleared empty glasses and small plates from the bar and tables, loaded them into the dishwasher, and returned them clean to the racks under and behind the bar. He arranged rows of blue cheese, garlic, jalapeno, and anchovy olives on trays, cut lemons and limes into wedges, trimmed stems off cherries and mint, and stocked the refrigerators under the bar with mixers. He restocked liquor, filled the ice bins, replaced the kegs, and made sure there were enough coasters and napkins in the well. He cleaned the bar, polished the furniture before opening, and mopped the floors each night after closing.

"I should pay you," Cris offered several times.

"I don't need money," Bruce said.

"Let me take it off your rent."

"I have money. I don't need money."

He enjoyed the mindlessness of the job, the specificity of his tasks. He didn't have to tax his brain, he didn't have to talk, he didn't have to remember. Only the small things mattered. How many lemons and limes to cut. How many olives to buy. How many bags of ice to haul up from the basement. The tasks were clarifying, crystallizing, categorical, conclusive.

But Damia was killing him. One morning before opening, Sophie was arranging the float in the cash register: $50 in ones, $20 in fives, $50 in tens, $100 in twenties, $20 in quarters, $5 in dimes, $4 in nickels, and $1 in pennies.

Bruce looked in the refrigerator under the bar to do a count of garnishes.

"We're out of the habanero cheese," Sophie said.

"I ordered them," Bruce said. "Asked them to toss in a fire extinguisher."

"Heh?"

"Harbanero, fire, put out the fire?" Bruce said.

"Oh," Sophie lit a cigarette.

"Sophie, why do you smoke?"

"Bruce, why do you drink?"

"Fair point," Bruce raised his hands in surrender. Damia was killing him.

"Sophie, will you allow me control of the music deck?"

"Why? Something wrong with my music?"

"Customers want to slit their wrists after Damia. I want to slit my wrists after Damia." Bruce spritzed lemon oil on the bar and polished the wood with a cloth. The smell of citrus rose from the wood.

"I love her songs." She tilted her head to blow smoke.

"Sophie, you may love it. But they hate it. It's for suffering. Please let me make some playlists. I beg you, before there's a tragedy."

"What are we talking about?" Cris lifted the hatch on the side of the bar and entered the well. What tragedy?"

"Bruce thinks my music is depressing," Sophie said.

"He's right. The only reason we still have customers is because Oasis is run by a psycho. I've told you for years to play something else." Cris said.

"Like what?"

"Smooth jazz, or something bubbly, or opera. Mario Lanza," Cris said.

"Oh God. No, Cris," Bruce said "Please just leave it to me."

Bruce curated the playlists like his life depended on it. Lucky's was open from 11 am to 2 am. Bruce needed to find soundtracks for everybody at Lucky's. He decided that he'd start by softening Sophie up to get her used to the idea of change. He made a playlist with contemporary French female artists. Coeur de Pirate's *Pilgrims on a Long Journey* and *Last Kiss,* Zaz's *Eblouie Par La Nuit, Le Long's De La Route,* Carla Bruni's *J'Arrive A Toi.* He progressed to French shake your booty songs by Shy'm and Ben L'Oncle Soul's *Petite Soeur* and *Elle Me Dit*. To these tracks, he added surround sound of global beats from Brit New Wave and Swedish pop, to Bhangra and Reggae, to homegrown Blues, Pop, Soul, and Country. Lucky's patrons thanked him, bought him drinks, tipped him double the bar tab, gave him their numbers, grabbed his ass in gratitude. Some patrons started dancing near the arcade game machines. When the bump and grind got too raunchy, Bruce came out from behind the bar and issued dictas. "I want to see at least this much room between you for the Holy Spirit," he'd say holding his thumb and forefinger an inch apart, or "I want a coaster width between the short and curlies."

One afternoon, Cris stood behind the bar watching Bruce as he replaced the bags in the tonic, soda, and ginger ale dispensers. "I need to talk to you," he said.

Bruce's heart sank. He was working for free. He'd have to be the biggest screwup of all time to get fired. "You're firing me!?"

"What? Heh heh. No, nothing like that." Cris giggled. He bent his head over the bar and scanned the perimeter of the arcade in the rear like a meerkat.

"What're you doing?"

"Sophie's got eyes in the back of her head."

"Yes she does." Bruce closed the tops of the dispensers. "Listen, I want you to make sure *Eblouie Par La Nuit* is the last song

Sophie hears every night before we leave the bar. Put it on repeat ten minutes before we lock up."

"Why's that?" Bruce asked, squinting, testing the soda guns.

"That song drives her crazy," Cris whispered. "Be a brother. Take care of it."

"For real?" Bruce pulled the trigger on the guns and spritzed the liquid into the dispenser's overflow well.

"I don't know how it happened. We stopped having sex ten years ago, like we both just ran out of batteries. Now she hears it and can't get enough." Cris began to sing and sway like a demented Charles Aznavour. "*Éblouie par la nuit à coups de lumières mortelles. Faut-il aimer la vie ou la regarder juste passer? De nos nuits de fumettes, il ne reste presque rien. Que des cendres au matin.*"

"Damn, mate," Bruce gave him a high five.

One night, near closing time, the bar was quieter than usual. An Arctic blast had kept most of Lucky's regular patrons at home. Sophie had gone home early, leaving Cris in charge. Bruce sat at one end of the bar drinking tonic water. Rae and Ivan straddled seats in the center of the bar, two empty stools between them. A couple of stragglers in the bar, a man and a woman, were on the edge of their seats watching "Who's yo Daddy, Where's yo Mama." In the show, childless and infertile American couples spent a television season in a luxury resort in Seychelles, where they squared off against each other to win the right to adopt orphans from sub-Saharan Africa. Every now and then, Bruce's eyes settled on the big plasma screen against the wall near the game room.

"Fucking lunatics," Bruce muttered in disgust. The show was the latest brainchild of the Goldsmiths.

Cris, who was standing behind the bar, looked at Bruce and then at Ivan and Rae who were sitting in front of him, and shrugged.

"Barbarians from the fucking gates of hell," Bruce raised his voice louder.

"You have something on your mind Bruce?" Cris asked. His lips clamped an unlit cigarette.

"He has problem?" Ivan asked.

"Bruce hates American television. He's just getting started. Wait for the full rant," Cris said.

"I don't understand," Ivan said.

"Greedy soulless fucking pieces of human excrement," Bruce yelled and dropped his fists like hammers on the bar. "Please turn up the music before I lose my mind."

Cris dialed the volume up on Bruce's drinking songs playlist.

"I have a cure for how you're feeling Bruce," Cris said, rolling his hips and shaking his butt to John Lee Hooker's *One Bourbon One Scotch One Beer*.

"There's no cure for how I'm feeling."

"I'm telling you, I created a new drink. It makes you see things differently. I could make millions bottling it. I want you three amigos to try it."

"I'm trying to stay on the wagon instead of under it?" Bruce said.

"I'll make yours a small pour. Don't worry," said Cris.

Bruce, Ivan, and Rae watched as Cris drew a martini shaker from the fridge under the bar top. He poured liquor from four different bottles and mixed it with great fanfare. He poured a sample into a shot glass to taste it, then added small spikes of liqueurs to the mix, and sampled the new formula. Satisfied with the taste, he grinned, and poured the dirty brown-red concoction into four highball glasses.

"It's dynamite for the brain," he said as he set the glasses down in front of the men.

"What's in it?" Bruce took a sip of what definitely was not a small pour.

"Vodka, whiskey, tequila, rum, lime, with a dash of cayenne pepper and tabasco," Cris said, lighting his cigarette and taking a big gulp of his brew.

The men raised their glasses to sniff, smell, and sip the drink. "What do you think?" Cris asked, eyeing each of the men. "Be frank."

"It hits home for sure, mate," Bruce said as the liquid snaked down his throat and warmed his pipes. This was bad, he'd be under the table, flat out, paralytically wasted in no time.

"Very aggressive drink," Rae said.

"You don't like it?" Cris asked.

"I like it is the problem. I'll lose all my money if I make a habit of this," Rae said.

"What do you think?" Cris asked Ivan.

"It is very dangerous. The fire goes from the brain to the toes," Ivan replied as he took a big draught of it.

"Did I call it?" Cris grinned.

They sat in a meditative state, moving in and out of timelessness. Cris topped up their glasses.

"Bruce, my wife says she's worried about you. She says you're lost and in need of direction," Rae said.

"She's right that I don't know where the fuck I'm going or what the fuck I'm doing," Bruce said.

"What brought you to Azyl Park of all places?" Rae asked.

"Why does anybody end up in any place? By accident obviously."

"I don't buy that," Rae said.

"Why not?" Bruce said.

"There's an internal logic to things. Why we end up in one place and not another, why we meet the people we do, why we fall in love with one woman and not another, its like there's some intelligent force driving us, willing us towards our lives." Rae said.

"I reject that. I think everything is random. Anything can happen to anyone at anytime." Bruce said.

"What about you Cris? And you Ivan? How did you end up here?" Rae asked.

"I was young and Greece was ancient. There were two options, Australia and America." Cris said.

"That's what I mean, you could have had this life in Australia," Bruce said.

"I don't think so. I wanted to be in a young country which had an idea about itself."

"Australia is a young country. I'm sure it has an idea about itself." Rae said.

"Maybe. But it seemed alien. Here, I could see myself. I was ready for America and America was ready for me," Cris said.

"What about you Ivan?" Bruce asked.

"I wanted to go to Argentina or Venezuela but I couldn't get a visa."

"Bruce, do you have a plan for your life?" Rae asked.

"Yes I do, Rae," Bruce declared with confidence. "I plan to wash dishes and glasses, and clean the bar and sweep the floor. I plan to make sure we have enough olives lemons and cherries. I'm going to be the best dish and glass washer I can be, the best cleaner and sweeper, the best olive lemon and cherry stocker. And—"

"And he won't let me pay him," Cris interrupted.

"Umm," Rae pondered Bruce's position, shaking his head slowly.

The men turned quiet.

"What's the opposite of manufacture?" Rae finally broke the long silence, his brain and jaw slack from the drink.

"Don't manufacture?" Cris said, the cigarette in his mouth moving up and down like a symphony conductor's baton.

"What's the opposite of artificial?" Rae persisted.

"Natural, organic." Ivan offered.

"And what is God not making anymore of?" Rae asked.

"Water. Air. We are very drunk. I may have overdone the vodka whiskey rum tequila combo," Cris said.

"You're not following. God is not making anymore of blank. What, Bruce?" Bruce! Come on. Think!" Rae shouted with frustration. "You two shut up," he ordered Cris and Ivan. "I'm talking to Bruce."

Bruce looked at Rae, his eyes half closed, weaving in and out of lucidity, and suddenly the answer came to him. It felt to him like he had been on a dark stage that suddenly burst into high wattage brightness with hundreds of floodlights. He smiled and pounded the bar with his fist. "Real fucking estate, mate," Bruce hollered with confidence, a beatific smile on his face.

"That's where you want to put your money. You follow?" Rae said.

The words had taken so much out of Bruce, he lay his arm on the counter and rested his head on it.

"I called it," Cris said to no one. "My work here is done. Now, everybody go home."

Ivan staggered to the door, the couple who had been watching television close behind him. Rae walked to the coat stand in the corner of the room near Bruce.

"How long since you had a home cooked meal?" Rae asked as he put on his coat and adjusted his collar.

"I can't remember."

"Come to dinner Saturday night. Number seven on the Crescent."

"Hello mate," Bruce said when Hari opened the door.

"Ma!!!" Hari turned his head and yelled.

"Is that the way to greet people?" Nila said, coming out of the kitchen. "Say hello to Bruce properly."

Hari raised his hand stiffly. "Hi Bruce."

"Hi mate," Bruce gave him a fist bump.

"Hello Maharani," Bruce said as he stepped inside. For you, he handed her a bouquet of Gerbera daisies and a bottle of wine in a bag.

"Ruby reds are my favorites. Thank you. Glad you came." "Hari, take Bruce to the deck, I'll be right there."

"The deck? It's minus ridiculous outside." Bruce said.

"It's weatherized," said Nila.

Bruce followed Hari to the living room and through French doors that opened into a glass enclosed deck perched above the lake. Rae and Tina Trang were seated on opposite ends of a long L shaped sofa on the left of the deck. A low brick pit with a dancing fire squatted in the middle of the L, its edges wide enough to place drinks and food. On the other side of the outdoor room, a dining table, already set, was framed on three sides by a bar, a trellis of orchids, and a barbeque grill.

"Grab a beer and come join us," Rae said.

"So Bruce had an epiphany this week as we were sitting at Lucky's," Rae told Tina, as he sipped wine.

"Was there alcohol involved?" she asked.

"Don't tell Nila," Rae craned his neck to make sure they were alone, "but I was lucky I found my way home instead of falling in a ditch or getting hit by a car."

"Cris should be locked up for that drink," Bruce agreed.

Nila set down a tray of appetizers on the ledge and dropped down next to Rae, her body clicked into his like a plug into a socket.

"You're sitting too far away. Come sit next to me," Trang said to Bruce, patting the seat next to her.

"Yes, do. Come closer," said Nila.

Bruce moved his drink and sat next to Trang.

"Where are the kids?" Trang asked.

"They'll have a meltdown if they have to have a normal conversation or sit down without their phones or games. I'll call them when we're ready to eat," Nila said.

"I hate cell phones," Bruce said.

"Don't start. I'm still trying to figure out how a grown man can function without one," Trang said.

"You should get one Bruce. If you're going to work your real estate plan, Tina will want to reach you. And so will I."

"Me too. I'd want to call you," said Nila.

"Why would you call me?" Bruce looked at Nila.

"To shoot the breeze. To make a dinner date. To ask you how your day is going. To see if you're alright. To ask you to take Hari to pick up cleats, or take Zara to soccer practice."

"What are cleats?" Bruce asked, his forehead furrowed.

"Foreigners," Trang shook her head and explained.

"You want to start the grill, Raja?" Nila turned to Rae.

Rae stood up. So did Nila.

"You can start bringing out the sides," Rae patted her butt and walked over to the barbeque. He pulled out a tray of meat and fish from a small refrigerator under the counter.

Nila went indoors and returned shortly after with the children, all of them bearing bowls of salads and prepared vegetables which they set down on the table.

"It's a dream how perfect they are together," Tina said softly.

"Indeed," Bruce said.

The meal was slow, the conversation, a six player ping pong match with countless permutations of strike and response. Rae to Nila, Nila to Bruce, Bruce to Tina, Tina to Hari, Bruce to Zara, Nila to Hari, Tina to Rae and on and on. Bruce was moved by the sound of human voices communing, making effort, taking time to belong to each other. He had wanted to call Rae and Nila earlier in the day to say that he wouldn't be coming to dinner after all. He felt put upon, irritated with Rae for forcing him into company. But now that he was there, he felt a bittersweet emotion well up inside him. He wanted to remember more of what he couldn't have, what he had forgotten.

Chapter 20

NAMES OF THINGS

Nadia entered Gabe's office waving a black binder. "We have it."

"We have what?" Gabe asked.

"Angeline's dossier on names."

"Is she outside?"

"She messengered it, said it's complete and self-explanatory."

"I was hoping to discuss it with her in person." Gabe was disappointed. He knew a woman like that needed to be pursued and attended to if he was to have a chance with her, but something held him back, even as she was beginning to get under his skin. He found himself scrolling the web to find images, news clips, videos, and stories of her. He knew a lot about her, how old she was, her birthday, where she'd gone to school, her books and awards. But there was no mention of her private life, no husband, boyfriend, children. In every photograph, she was alone. In the videos, she was authoritative and solemn, striking the appropriate note for the kinds of stories she was reporting. She rarely smiled, which Gabe realized was her natural disposition. What must it be like to be with her, he wondered.

"Mayor's Office called. They want an update on the name change," Nadia said.

"Set up a call for this week." Gabe flipped through the binder.

"Okay boss."

"Stop calling me boss." Gabe lingered on a page with rendered logos of the new names. "Anything else?"

"Sorry. The Dot Heads are outside wanting a meeting with you."

"Rae and Tina banned them from using that name months ago," Gabe said.

"I'm pretty sure they said, 'Yo, we're the Dot Heads and we're looking for the main man cos yo, we're in our crib and thinking we need the big dawg president, yo,'" Nadia said, her words choreographed to jerky hand signs.

"Did they say what they want?" Gabe asked as he flipped through Angeline's binder.

"They said they have a big idea," Nadia said.

"The Dot Heads have an idea?"

"Apparently they have the next Facebook, only bigger."

"Everybody is Mark Zuckerberg. Show them in. Leave the door open. Interrupt me in ten minutes."

"Right you are, big dawg," Nadia said, and fetched the group.

"IBI Worldwide. Executive Wing, can I help you?" Nadia adjusted the mouthpiece on her headset after she ushered the Dot Heads into Gabe's office. "Mrs. Cohen! How are you? This is Nadia. David? He may be at his desk," she walked towards David's desk. "You in?" she mouthed to David. No, he said bug-eyed, his hands waving like a manic air traffic controller. "Ah, he's out showing listings. Can I take a message? No he hasn't been here this morning. An emergency! I'll try to reach him. What shall I tell him? You need soy sauce right now? Ah, okay." Nadia looked at David who had his head buried in his hands. "Low salt or regular? Regular? Okay will do." "Alright, I'll be sure to tell him you have a soy sauce emergency. I definitely will. Yes, I assure you I will." She clicked the button to end the call.

"Your mother wants you to drop everything right now and hurry home with soy sauce." David rolled his eyes in disgust, his nostrils flared in a sneer, and reached for headphones. "David? Are you listening to me?"

"I don't want to hear that shit."

"They have lunch ready but no soy sauce. You have to go, David."

"No I won't. They'll do without soy sauce. Or call the takeout or walk a block to Gupta's."

"Not the same is it? It's not given from the hand of their loving son."

"Nadia, don't drive me loony tunes as well." He slipped the metal cups over his ears.

The Dot Heads knew the power of names. Their gang sign had been a matter of long deliberation among the boys. It was a declarative "up yours" response to racist teenagers who lived in Roseland, a no kind of place for White people who were still reeling from the fact that the country was run by a Black man and minorities were the majority. He's not American, he was born in Hawaii, I want the long form birth certificate, I want the short form birth certificate, water melon, monkey, banana, fried chicken, lazy, stole the election, he doesn't love you, he doesn't love America, he is ghetto. The case of which half of President Obama, White Kansan or Nigerian, was a monkey and liked watermelon, banana, fried chicken was never fully litigated. What Bush hanging butterfly chad? Supreme Court shoo-in? No WMD? heh heh, oopsie Bush, best beer drinking buddy, Sarah Palin genius like me, Donald Trump is God. Bill O'Reilly for Veep, Sean Hannity for Secretary of State. We're number one, world's biggest, richest, China does not own my ass, woo hoo, beatch. Dude, what happened to my country? The Roseland teens had concocted a litany of names for the people of Azyl Park that they hurled like volleys from car windows as they drove past Shoreland Drive and the Square.

"Hey sand niggers, stop fucking your sisters," they would yell at the boys, screaming their curses over broken mufflers.

As women walked to the shops on the Square wearing their colorful saris and their tilaks, Roseland's racists would yell out: "Hey dot heads, go back to fucking Calcutta,"

And to the boys: "Eat some beef you losers! Instead of praying to cows."

"We're not Hindu! We go to White Castle, you dago." Vin, the Vietnamese representation in the Azyl teen gang yelled back.

"Yeah paddy," Phan yelled.

Tina Trang and Rae Oberoi called the gang to account on behalf of the Elders Council.

"Over there," Sophie pointed the congregation of falling down pants, sideways pointing caps, and baggy sweatshirts big enough to set up as tents, to the Elders booth. Anil wheeled a Radio Flyer Wagon, which held a pair of audio speakers on its bed.

"We've had complaints about you boys that are very troubling," Rae said. "Is it true, gentlemen, that you have been identifying yourselves as the Dot Heads?"

"Yeah, Dot Heads. That's us. What's the prob?" Malik, the apparent leader of the group said.

"The prob," Trang made air quotes "is it is very demeaning to call yourself by a name that others use to insult you."

"You are revealing your self-hatred with this name. Do you think Gandhi and Martin Luther King and Nelson Mandela went around calling themselves wogs and nig-nogs?" Rae said. "Do you know nothing of self-respect and dignity?"

“Yo, Mr. O, you going to let us represent and defend or bend our ear with your wicked judgment?” asked Kumar, the group’s second in command.

“Very well, what is your defense?” Rae asked.

“Hit it,” Kumar instructed his brother. Anil bent down to plug his I-Pod into the speaker socket while holding his pants up with his free hand.

Ridiculous The Rapper bleated his philosophy through the speakers, a litany of the dreaded N word, ejaculated over migraine-inducing thumps and drums, each followed by a lunatic verb that didn’t rhyme or reason. Tina looked stricken as if repressing Edward Munch’s scream. Rae pulled his ear lobes repeatedly as he suffered through the aural assault

“That’s enough. What’s your point?” Rae said.

“Fair is fair, Mr. O. We want to submit our evidence,” Malik said.

“Yeah, evidence,” the others nodded in agreement, dancing to the beat as best they could, with one emoting hand a piece, the other strategically placed near their falling down pants.

When the rap reached its completion, Kumar signaled Anil to turn the sound off. “See, he is turning the whole insult thing into a celebration of his own identity by co-opting it. A preemptive strike against humiliation,” said Malik.

“Yeah that’s right,” Kumar said. “A preemptive strike yeah,” Anil agreed.

Trang looked at Rae, shaking her head, grateful that she didn’t have children of her own.

“Who are your parents?” Rae asked.

“We’re defending our parents. Our mothers. They wear dots and those Roseland boys insult them,” Kumar said.

"We're asking you to cease and desist from using the name Dot Heads forthwith," Rae said. Forthwith sounded authoritative, no wishy-washy weakness there, the only way to deal with American teenage werewolves.

"You are not the boss of us," Malik said.

"Yes, I am!" Rae said sharply.

The gang looked shocked, wide-eyed.

"You stop using that name now or else," Rae said at full volume, an affect that went against his nature. "Do you understand? Do I have your promise that you will not use this demeaning name ever again? Or any other demeaning name?"

Frightened, the boys looked to Malik for guidance. "Whatever," said Malik rolling his eyes.

Surprised by his powers of persuasion, Rae decided to make another demand.

"Submit a list of five appropriate names for your group and we'll take them into consideration. Understood?"

"Yeah, whatever," Kumar grunted.

"Excellent. Now go home and do your homework. All of you. I mean it."

The gang, led by Malik and Kumar, trooped out of the room, Anil wheeling out the Radio Flyer.

"And one more thing," Rae shouted, which made the boys spin around. "Pull up your pants. You look like idiots," he boomed.

"Gentlemen," Gabe said to the constellation of sideways and backwards pitched hats Nadia had ushered into his office.

Kumar raised his clenched fist.

"Fist bumps don't fly with me. Shake my hand like a professional," Gabe said. "That's too weak, put strength into it." He proceeded to shake their hands one by one, one hand on the shoulder, while he pumped their hands. Don't curl you fingers, stretch them out.

"How old are you?"

"Anil is 13, the rest are 15. I'm 16," Malik said.

"Take a seat, gentlemen," Gabe said as he eased into his chair. "What have you got?"

"We building this thing and it's da bomb," Kumar said.

"It's like we didn't count on it, 'cos we were working on something else," Chung Ho said.

"What was that?" Gabe was serious, even stern with them. He found American teenagers a mysterious tribe, a secretive cult, full of fright and flight.

The boys eyed each other, weighing whether they could trust him. "Excuse us. We need to deliberate," Kumar said. He and Malik went to the other side of the room and whispered. They eyed Gabe and then returned to talking to each other.

"Okay," Malik said as they both returned to their seats. "We were working on a game layer over the world," he said.

"Game layer? You mean gaming?"

"Bigger. Games, networked over the earth," Kumar said.

"That's right," Anil said. The other boys nodded. "Yeah. That's right."

"But that's not what you're working on now?" Gabe asked.

"No this is big," Malik said, leaning forward in his chair, stretching his arms wide.

"Give me your pitch?"

"You tell him," Malik said.

"No, you," said Kumar.

"Okay, bros," he told his accomplices, before turning to Gabe. "We are working on a program that will eat spam email before it even gets into your inbox. All those emails from Nigeria and Indonesia promising you money, all that shit promising you Russian brides, all those Mr Lid emails, penis enhancement, balding cures, diet cures, fountain of youth cures."

"HVAC Training, Viagra, Icelandic lotteries," Kumar offered.

"Groopanda, BrightTalk, Online Doctorate, Reverse Your Diabetes, Herpes Symptoms," Chung Ho said.

"Colonics, Do You Poop Enough," Anil said.

"Chee, chee idiot. Shut up," Kumar whacked his brother on the back of his head.

"How do you do that?" Gabe asked leaning back in his chair.

"We catch it in a net," Chung Ho said.

"A bit like the game layer over the world, only upside down?" Gabe asked.

"Yeah," the boys nodded. "Yeah, that's right."

"What do you need from me?"

"We need a space to work. We're working in Malik's room but his mother is watching her Egyptian soap opera shit and his father is praying the Surats, And we go to my house and my mom is cooking all the time and trying to force feed us," Kumar said. "Her pakoras and bhajis are pretty gross but she tears up when we don't eat so we do and it's making us all fatties," Anil said, blowing his cheeks into a balloon.

"Our grandfather has PTSD from the war and thinks we're spying on him," Vin said nodding at his cousin.

"What's your goal?" Gabe asked.

"We don't know shit about goals. We need advisors, resources," Malik said.

"We want a safe house to go to after school and figure what we're doing. And we want somebody who can take care of us 'cos we don't know how to be fierce," Kumar said.

"Yeah. And you're the man," Vin said.

"Have you talked to anyone else?" Gabe asked.

"Not yet." Malik and Kumar said together.

"Don't talk to anyone else. I think you guys are interesting. I like the way you think," Gabe said. "I'll help you. Come back tomorrow same time." Gabe said as he stood up. He shook hands with each of them again. "I want you guys to dress properly. Go to Whole World Style now. Jehan will set you up with business attire. It's the first money I'll invest in you. Alright?"

Gabe walked the Dotheads out of his office to the elevator.

"Where's Nadia? I need her," Gabe asked David, as he walked back towards his office.

"I'm not sure."

Two hours later, Nadia returned with shopping bags.

"What do you call this?" David said sternly.

She lifted a white plastic bag. "Lunch?"

"You've been gone two hours Nadia," David said.

"I just had an important thing to do," she said as she went to the alcove to dish food onto a plate.

"What?"

"Soy sauce delivery," she said.

"You didn't! Tell me you didn't!" David stood up and followed her into the alcove. "You're an enabler. You've ruined them for life. And me!"

"They're old. I felt sorry for them," she said, spooning carrot pudding into a bowl.

"They're vampires. My father is a psychopath. My mother is a narcissist. Stay away from them. They'll suck your blood and marrow out of your bones and you won't have a life."

"They're nice," she said, walking towards him, her face solemn.

David had seen Nadia's face turn expressive, laughing, giggling, when cooing at babies ever since her biological clock had begun blaring like a foghorn since her thirtieth birthday two years ago. "Where am I going to find an oddball like me?" he'd overheard her say to friends she consulted about everything to do with her life. David had no friends and couldn't fathom why Nadia needed to take polls on the best thread count for sheets, or the best hydrating cream for thick hair, or how to cast off a crochet project. He wondered why she didn't just Google or You Tube. Why talk about it when you could learn whatever you want by tapping a few keys? But no, she loved to engage in long conversations with her friends during the afternoon lull, midway between lunch and closing when she brought out tea and sweets—lokum, rugalach, baklava, ladoo, halwa, jalebi.

She held the saucer under his chin now and lifted a spoon of the halwa to his mouth.

"You're a sucker," he bit down on it.

"Maybe," she said.

Should he tell her that she was the one neon-lit bright spot in his otherwise colorless life? That he felt comforted, consoled, assured, when he was with her. That he. That he. That he.

Should she tell him that she loved the long hours she shared with him each day. That she hated the weekends and loved the weeks. That she felt cared for, solaced, soothed. That she. That she. That she.

Where am I going to find an oddball, a freak, like me?

I'm right here. Find me.

Gabe called Angeline as soon as the boys left. He hoped to talk to her for at least ten minutes so that he could fix his mind on her, absorb the essence of her, and carry her voice in his head through the day. But he couldn't reach her. He tried several times during the course of the day and was irritated that she wasn't available to him. He sent her an email and she responded immediately. "You're more than welcome. I hope you'll honor Alexander Hamilton. I'm inside my book but let's touch base soon."

He felt disregarded, of no account.

Chapter 21

GREAT EXPECTATIONS

Rae was confounded by his children. He had given Hari and Zara every opportunity to succeed—private schools, tutors, test prep coaches, everything they needed to vault and scale the walls of the Ivy League—and still they had failed.

Hari had been stoned on purple kush sour diesel since the Bush Presidency. It had been his Rip Van Winkle slumber—consciousness swaddled tightly in a marijuana haze that was pierced occasionally by bullets of new knowledge: Curveball lied, no mushroom cloud, no WMD oopsie, and Operation Desert Thrust, which Hari remembered vividly because of what he wasn't doing with Kamala, his girlfriend at the time, who wouldn't put out, no way, no how, talk to the hand, Mister, I'm headed to medical school. Hari went off to college in Boston, which allowed Rae to maintain a fiction without lying outright. "Yes, nothing like being in Cambridge," leaving out the essential truth of what Hari was doing in Cambridge—attending community college. Hari dropped out at the end of the year to return home, "to figure my shit out," he told his father.

Not to be outdone by her brother, Zara dropped out of San Jose State to work as a Genius at the nearby Apple Store.

"My offspring are in a mad race to the bottom," Rae said.

"Don't be cruel. They're my babies," Nila said.

"She's a genius. Have you heard of such a thing?"

"She's figuring things out," Nila said.

Nila's unconditional love for her children had no bounds and Rae thought it a mistake. "Will you stand by her if she commits a crime?"

"Yes," Nila said.

"I would disown her," said Rae.

A month after Hari's return to Azyl Park, Zara called home crying, screaming in pain like a gunned down animal. "I'm a useless, good for nothing, piece of shit loser."

"Oh, sweetheart. What happened?" Nila asked.

What happened was that Steve Jobs had paid a surprise visit to the Apple Store in Westfield Mall. He stood near the Genius Bar watching the geniuses earning $20 an hour working hard in the service of his bank accounts, found this to be Zen and Bauhaus in the best sense, and stroked his beard philosophically. Alden, the store manager, all but genuflecting, flitted about near him. Zara was helping a patron who had confessed, after much prodding about a suspiciously waterlogged I Pad, that heh heh, LOL, LMFAO, ROFL, yes, he had indeed fallen asleep in the bathtub with his device.

"Unfortunately," Zara began, shaking her head sadly, and next thing she knew, she was pulled off Genius duty.

"Mr. Jobs loathes, despises, detests, abhors, the word unfortunately," Alden said. His head was tilted at an angle as if weighed down by his lopsided haircut, the gravitational pull of lunatic corporate logic, and the wisdom of Koalemos. "We gave you a whole training session on words not to use during orientation," he said.

"Come home, baby," Nila said, before Rae could object.

After several months of observing Hari and Zara lying around watching reality shows on television, waking up in the morning to find them passed out on couches, and hearing them having a merry old time in the basement game room—Non, je ne regrette rien like Sophie's song —Rae was forced to consider discipline, immigrant style.

"This has to stop." Rae told Nila one evening after he walked in through the front door. A few minutes earlier, he had followed the stone walkway at the end of the Crescent to the beach. After a long day of looking at computer screens, he found it meditative to look into ungrudging distance. He saw Hari and Zara on the water's edge, squealing like little children, jostling each other, trying to push each other into the water. "They're regressing into infants," he said.

"I'm enjoying having my babies around," Nila said as she skewered lamb, peppers, and onions to cook on the outdoor grill.

"Nila, they're an embarrassment. I can't bear to look at them. This cannot go on. I mean it."

"They won't be with us forever, Rae. They're young still. They fell. They just need a chance to regroup, get their heads in order, figure out how to rejoin the world." She spooned yogurt and mint marinade over the skewers and covered the plate with film.

"They've been home four months and I see no plans, no strategy, just pizza and video games. Three-toed sloths."

"Don't be mean."

"They're bums."

"I think they're depressed." Nila stirred saffron threads and chopped parsley in the rice cooker.

"There's a great cure for depression. It's called work," Rae said.

"You have a plan for them?" Nila asked.

"I'm working on it," Rae told her.

Rae called Tina Trang the next day to withdraw a listing for two of his vacant adjoining storefronts on the Square that had been previously leased by a travel agency. Circle Travel had once been a thriving business with a loyal following—an airfare consolidator selling Aeroflot and Air India fares at affordable prices. But the customers gradually turned pugnacious. They'd come in wielding I-Phones and I-Pads with quotes from Kayak, Orbitz, Travelocity, Expedia, Hipmunk.

"Why should I buy from you? They're quoting $25 less. I'll go with you if you can do better," they'd mouth off to Boris, the owner.

Instead of embracing the philosophy of the customer always being right and fighting to win their business, Boris would flatten his expensive toupee over his forehead like a blintz. "A cheap man pays twice," he'd sniff, or "You're cheap," or "Cheap people should stay home," or "Take your metal detector and go look for pennies." It was inevitable that he would go the way of the Dodo bird.

"They're near prime location. I have showings today for a café and a juice bar," Tina said.

"I want them off the market," Rae said.

"You going to tell me why?"

"I'll tell you later," Rae hung up.

Rae took his residential property crew off another job to renovate the lots to his specifications. He instructed his assistant to place orders for furniture, shelving, and equipment. "I want the stores to look like this," Rae told him, pointing to some images on his laptop. "Get the place wired. Choose mega-quantum broadband."

He checked on the progress of the renovations during the following weeks, whenever he was on the Square for banking, or meetings, or on his way to Lucky's, or to meet Nila for lunch. When the units were fully renovated to his satisfaction, he took her to lunch at Oasis and told her of his plan to launch their ne'er do well in the trades.

"Rae! what will our families say?" Nila raised her hands to her mouth. "My father, oh my God! And Arun and Leela. They're so proud of Usha and Sunil at Harvard and Stanford. What do I say to them?"

"Tell them we're teaching our children the noble art of business."

"Everybody will be passing the shops. Do we have to be so public about it?" Nila said.

"Tell them the shops are pilots for nationwide franchises. That they'll be bigger than Starbucks and Kinko's," Rae said.

At home, after dinner, Rae walked into the den to find his children playing a game on their PS4. "You two. Meet me at the breakfast table tomorrow morning at eight o'clock sharp," he said.

"Tomorrow is Saturday, Dad," Hari said, his eyes focused on the screen, holding a game controller on his thighs, clicking clicking.

"What difference does it make to you? Every day for you is Saturday."

"That's a snarky thing to say," Zara said, then cheered as if she had scored a World Cup goal when her brother crashed in a blaze.

"Snarky means what?" His children had no brains at all, no manners at all, no social graces at all, Rae thought.

"Snide, critical, cutting which is what you're being right now," Zara said.

"Don't make me wait. Eight o'clock sharp," Rae said tersely and walked out of the room.

"What's his problem copping an attitude like that?" Zara asked, when Nila looked in on them before retiring to bed.

"Your father wants the both of you to grow up," Nila said.

Rae woke up the next morning with his children on his mind. He untangled himself from Nila to get ready. Dressed in sweatpants, hoodie, and sneakers, he walked downstairs. On his way to the front door, he looked into the living room. Zara and Hari were sleeping with their heads on the armrests on each end of the sectional. The television and lights were on. Rae picked up the remote from the floor and switched off the television before turning the lights off.

Rae was an orderly man who lived by routines and systems. He started his days with long walks. He walked past the houses on the Crescent, down the weathered stone stairway to the beach, to the southernmost tip, where sand ran out to give way to boulders and rocks. Like a runner breasting tape, he always touched a boulder before turning around and walking north on the water's edge.

Rae had no recollection of a love of water as a child. His family had come from inland Goa—Majorda—where they had owned a coconut palm and cashew fruit plantation. He knew that Goa was idolized by Westerners for its beaches, perhaps even as early as 1498 when Vasco da Gama landed near Goa, and possibly by 1510 when Alfonso de Albuquerque conquered it. But Rae only remembered a childhood of dry land, wet earth, and time standing still; of lush green trees licked with rain; frogs, water buffaloes, and crocodiles swimming in the swollen river near his house; snails that retracted into their shells when he tortured them with salt; cockroaches as large as cherry tomatoes; lizards that fell with a thump on his head while he was reading or in a reverie that would make him scream and jump; and mosquitoes plump with human blood. This part of his life was so far and deep in his past, he couldn't remember a time when he felt anything but American.

He walked along the shoreline until he reached a pier that ended at a lighthouse. He walked as far as the lighthouse and then turned back and veered right to the sand dunes. Designed as a landing strip for migratory birds, the dunes hosted a wide variety of flowering plants, berry shrubs, and grasses. As Rae picked his way carefully through the dunes, he passed colorful red, pink, white, and yellow clusters of hairy puccoon, beach pea, horsemint, prickly pear, smooth rose, bearberry, and sand cherry. Gradually as he reached the front of the dunes, there were large clumps and trusses, almost a forest, of marram—American beach grass. It was Rae's favorite plant—a survivor that could outlive the most hostile of conditions. Its fibrous, matted roots held the dunes together.

Rae tried not to think of anything during his walks, for what he saw, the living earth around him seemed to require a holy silence. From the dunes, he walked all the way to the northern point of Azyl Park before sand surrendered to gravel, stones, and boulders and the curve of Shoreland Drive to the suburbs.

At five minutes to eight, Rae strolled into the kitchen. Nila was sitting at the head of the table reading a Twin Flames folder. Zara and Hari were finishing breakfast. "Good morning," he said, surprised to find his children there.

Zara gobbled toast and nodded. Hari raised a coffee mug. Evolution takes times, Rae was grateful for small changes.

"Shall I come?" Nila looked up from her folder.

"There's no need," Rae said, and to his children, "Let's go."

Rae walked at a fast clip, irritated with Hari and Zara for dawdling. He stood outside his building and waited until they turned the corner to the Square. They were laughing and happy, which annoyed Rae.

"You've both run out of excuses, I want you to make a go of this," Rae said as he inserted a key into the door.

The main door opened into a small vestibule with swing doors leading to each unit. The spaces smelled of new paint. The walls in the store on the left were painted yellow. Rows of shelves and wire baskets hanging on white metal grids dominated the rear wall. A customer service counter, black base with yellow granite top, ran the length of the left wall. Against the right and back wall, a long L shaped counter held two dozen computers, bucket chairs in front of them. The other store was similarly furnished, except for a gray blue color scheme and industrial steel fixtures. Rae saw opportunity in pay-by-the-hour cyber cafes for immigrants who couldn't afford computers or Internet.

"I incorporated two companies, Silicon Curry and Geek Patel. You can choose which of them you wish to run. I'll bankroll you for six months," Rae said.

"I like Silicon Curry," said Zara.

"Am I to do this forever?" Hari asked, walking into Geek Patel.

"That's entirely up to you," Rae said.

"But I don't know what to do," Hari said.

"I know some stuff but I don't know where to start," Zara said.

"I'll have my IT guys give you a week of orientation next week, and Bruce has agreed to come onsite to coach you both and help you set up your systems." Rae said, handing his children sets of keys to the building.

"What about after that?" Hari said.

"Figure it out," Rae said as he headed out the door.

"Papa, do you have any advise?" Zara asked.

"Building a business is art and science. Lean on Bruce so you don't make mistakes you can't recover from."

"Why Bruce? Why not you?"

"It's best that we don't mix roles. Listen to Bruce."

Bruce spent the next three weeks tutoring Zara and Hari together, and then separately. Zara was a quick study, smart as a whip, excited about the business, and ready to work. She loved everything about the shop.

"You like business?"

"I like being dictator of my very own country," she said.

"You'll go far, young lady," Bruce said.

"Bruce, how do I merge a list?"

"Let me show you," Bruce rolled his task chair towards her.

Hari was another matter. His attention drifted towards life on the sidewalk, towards the girls in the Square, to his phone. He found it difficult to follow basic instructions.

"Do you get that?" Bruce asked, after showing him an automated invoicing setup.

"No, I can't do it," Hari said.

"Which part can't you do?"

"All of it. I can't do any of it."

"Hari, level with me. Are you high right now?"

"Yeah," Hari said.

"Here's what we're going to do. I'm going to help Zara finish setting up her books and then you and I are going for coffee," Bruce said.

Bruce took Hari to Two Tables. Hari flopped onto a seat as Bruce went to the counter to order. He set down two glasses of carrot juice and a plate of hummus and pita, and sat down.

"What about the coffee?"

"We need super fuel." Bruce tore the sleeves off two straws. "What's going on with you?" He planted the straws in the glasses.

"Bruce! You lost your Australian accent!"

"Don't try to change the subject."

"You really did. You lost it. And you don't say mate anymore. I liked the way you used to say that."

"It sounded stupid."

"My Mom loved hearing it. She likes you a lot."

"Your Mom's the best."

They sipped their drinks and tore the pita to scoop hummus.

"My Dad's an asshole though."

"He's not."

"You don't know him. I hate him."

"Why do you hate him?"

"He has no soul. He makes me do things I don't want to do. I just hate him."

"He cares about what happens to you, Hari. He's worried that you have no direction. Do you know what you want to do? Other than get high?"

"Some days I wake up and I'm fine, but other days I just want to put a gun right here, between my eyes, and blow my brains out."

"What would that do? You'd miss out on life and you'd shatter your family."

"I hate my life."

"Hate is a very strong word. Think about what you really feel. Maybe it's more like you're bored with your life and want it to change."

"What's it all for though? Look at my Dad. He's a slave, all he does is work to make money."

"Your Dad holds a lot of this economy together. If he stopped, there'd be a lot of people out of work. What he does is important."

"I don't know what I want."

"That's a lot different from hate. It's an improvement."

"But this shop has nothing to do with me. It's Zara's thing."

"Look, it's been what, three weeks? I think you should give the business a chance. You'll learn some important stuff. You'll make money. Meet girls. You like girls?"

"Yeah," Hari laughed.

"So get laid, it will make you feel better. Don't overdo it. You don't want your pecker to fall off. You want to keep that as long as you can."

Hari snickered.

"What else makes you happy?"

"Music."

"Medicine for the head," Bruce said.

"Yeahhhhhh!" Hari said. "You know about that?"

"All about it," Bruce said. "Are you ready to go back to work?"

Chapter 22

ALIGNMENT

It was seven on a Friday night. Gabe looked up from his desk and realized that he'd been so deep in financial spreads and his positions—everything was money, money was everything—he'd lost all sense of time. He looked out of the glass wall and saw blurry motion. He looked through the telescope. A parade of women in colorful *kameez* and *lahenga* walked in groups to the community center. A group of men in white and beige tunics and vests walked in front of them. People were entering and leaving restaurants. The sidewalks were bustling with shoppers and pedestrians, and Shoreland Drive was thick with commuter traffic to the suburbs. David and Nadia had left. Gabe was alone. He had no plans for the night. He had stopped taking calls from women. He picked up the phone to dial a number, but then tapped the receiver against his forehead, mulling over the act he was about to undertake. As an MBA, he couldn't help but run a SWOT analysis in his mind. Strengths, weaknesses, opportunities, threats—it was the perfect method to crystallize problems, assess information, data, situational knowledge, and reality-based outcomes. He thrived on quantitative data like this. When he tallied the columns of his ruminations, instead of clarity, there was only confusion. He hammered his forehead with the phone, hard enough that it hurt, and dialed.

"Gabriel!" Angeline picked up on the second ring.

"Hi, Angeline. I was just thinking about you."

"Oh yeah?"

"Yeah. How are things going?"

"I haven't talked to another human being today. Just sat in front of the computer."

"Me too."

"It's not normal. It's how people slowly go insane," Angeline said.

"How about dinner like normal people so we don't crack up."

"I'd love to, Gabriel."

Gabe walked to the elevator to go upstairs to shower and change. He was eager to see her. Since their last meeting, he'd found himself thinking about her nearly all the time—at first when his mind was at rest and not preoccupied with anything, and then when he was engrossed in work. He had been writing a contract that morning and all he could think about was the way she had called him by his name in that astounding voice that he could not hold in his mind without also thinking of new rain. Later as he was reading emails, he imagined tracing the lines around her lips with his index finger, pausing at the v of her cupid's bow, and then pressing his finger against her lower lip. It felt like a kiss.

He was filled with something close to hunger, to know her, to be known by her. Gabe thought the reason he felt drawn to her was because, like him, she too moved and lived between cultures, as a foreigner, as a racial other. He wanted to be with someone who could limn the contours and essence of him. Gabe felt sure she wouldn't call him her first Arab. He liked the quality of her. He thought her the kind of woman who would understand an exilic heart, divine the tepid stone afflicted with arrhythmia.

Gabe dressed carefully for Angeline. He wore an ink blue shirt open at the collar, black wool pants, and wing tips. He fixed the buttons on his cuffs as he announced himself to the doorman at Angeline's building. "You're on the list. Sixteenth floor, A," the man said, before turning back to a television.

Gabe alighted the elevator, walked down a short hallway, and pressed the bell. He could hear music from inside and Angeline's voice looming closer to the door.

"I love you too," she said. "You're my heart," she cooed.

Gabe felt a chill. There had to be an explanation, he reassured himself. He'd vetted her online.

Angeline opened the door, motioned him soto voice, and let him in. "Okay baby," she said. She kissed Gabe on both cheeks, smiling, delighted to see him, the phone still pressed against her ear. "Okay baby, I gotta go," she said.

She was wearing a clingy black jersey dress with ruched sleeves pushed up to her elbows; the wide scooped neck accentuated her chin and showed off the width of her collarbone. She had diamond studs in her ears and a delicate two-tier necklace of tiny seed pearls.

"You look lovely," he said.

"So do you Gabriel," she smiled. "Will you give me a minute to gather my things?" she said, and went into her bedroom.

"There's a new place around the corner I've wanted to try. Chef from Andalusia." Gabe called out as he took a measure of her place.

"Seville! Me too."

The room was textured in hues of cream, jasmine, almond, magnolia, and barley. The sectional sofa was a natural calico, the carpet was a gold-flecked berber. On the rosewood coffee table, there were several art books—Kara Walker, Basquiat, and the Impressionists. Gabe smiled at the juxtaposition. Ron Chernow's biography of Alexander Hamilton, thickened with hundreds of colorful adhesive arrows that flagged nearly every page, lay next to a volume of Alexander Hamilton's writings. A hard cover book lay spread eagled, face down—Marguerite Yourcenar's "The Memoirs of Hadrian." He took a business card out of his wallet, placed it between the separated pages, closed the book, and set it on its back. Gabe walked to an antique white console by the wall. A mirror in a heavy silver and wood frame hung above the console. Four silver filigree picture frames of different shapes leaned on the console; three candles and a pewter vase holding a lilac silk orchid stood next to them. Angeline was holding a baby in the oval frame, who became a toddler in the square one, a chubby ten year old in the next, and a teenager taller than her in the last rectangle frame. He picked up the last photograph and stared at it.

"That's my baby," Angeline said. "Andre."

"Where is he?"

"With his father in Nevis."

"He has custody?"

"No, but my adorable little boy grew into a black teenager and I found myself fearing for his life here."

"What happened?" Gabe stared at the photograph.

"We'd just moved from New Orleans to Manhattan so I could take the anchor job with NBC. Best paid job I ever had, I thought our ship had come in. But I was so oblivious to his needs. I didn't realize that the Big Apple was no place for a young black male. He was stopped and frisked more than thirty times by police while going about his life; going to school, coming back from basketball practice, clarinet lessons. My response was to drive him crazy with my fear. Don't ever be late for anything, ever, because I don't want you to run. You know what the police do to black men who run. Don't look at anybody on the street. Don't ever wear a hoodie because somebody could gun you down and say it was your fault. I was suffocating him with my fear—that he would walk out the door one day and never come back. So I sent him to Nevis. He lives with his father and his stepmother and their three-year-old. It's the best thing for him," Angeline said.

"How old is he?"

"Thirteen."

"It must be hard on you," Gabe said.

"It was harder to parent Andre fearing that I couldn't keep him safe. He's thriving now. He's doing well in school. He helps his Dad run an eco lodge for tourists. A Black male outside America is like an asthmatic on an inhaler for the first time. He takes full breaths of air after half breathing all his life," Angeline said.

"Wow."

"Yes. Wow." She was disappointed in his response.

"Will he come back for college?"

"I won't allow it. I covered both the Trayvon Martin and Oscar Grant cases for NBC and that sealed my decision. If it's open season on black men, I don't want him to set foot on American soil," she said.

Gabriel felt so far out of his depth he frowned. He didn't know what to say to help her.

"I've bored you enough with my stories," Angeline said after a beat too long of waiting for Gabe to say something meaningful.

"It's not that at all. It's that I've given up talking about race in America." Gabe said.

"It's great that race doesn't interfere with your life. The rest of us have it thrust in our face everyday," she said.

"It's too loaded and complex to talk about. Look at us now," Gabe said.

Angeline was tired. She missed Andre. She was still grappling with her book. She decided to lay her intellectual sword down in favor of a pleasant, mindless dinner with a good-looking airhead mercenary. It will take my mind off things, she thought. I'll talk about the quality of the wine and food, and admire his handsome face, and listen to expert analysis on real estate, and maybe ask him advise about refinancing. "Let's go," she said walking towards the door. The restaurant was a block from the building and they walked hurriedly in the cold, their breaths turning to clouds.

"It's good to see you, Angeline," Gabe said, after they were seated at their table. She had maintained a puckered silence during the short walk from her apartment to the restaurant. He didn't want the evening to go downhill so soon.

"Likewise," she said, studying the menu. "But why is one of the most eligible bachelors of this city alone on a Friday night?" she looked up.

"I'm not. I'm with a beautiful woman I hope to know," he said.

"Touché," she smiled. "So, how's the renaming going?"

"It's an elaborate production because the Council has to agree. But we're working through it."

"You know which name I'm rooting for," she said.

"I'm not sure it's a good fit."

"What could be a better fit? An immigrant neighborhood named after America's most essential immigrant Founding Father?"

"We'll see," he glanced at the menu. "Do you know what you'd like?"

"Yes, I'm ready."

"Is the special finished?" Gabe asked after the waiter had taken their order.

"It's in post-production. My part is done hopefully, unless they need me for voiceover after cutting room edits," Angeline said.

"What did you find out?"

"There's a gender dimension to immigrant happiness. Women in exile are more practical than their male counterparts. They're willing to do whatever it takes to gain a foothold, they're good hustlers. They seem to genuinely love their new lives here. But the men are a different story. Except for the super achievers, men like you and Rae Oberoi, most of them feel they've lost an essential part of themselves. Most were privileged in their own countries by sheer virtue of being men. They seem to be in shock that they've lost power, over their own lives, over their women, their children," she said.

"They're going through the stages of grief. They'll get over it," Gabe said.

"Hmm. That's an interesting notion. Denial, anger, what's the third one," she asks.

" Bargaining," Gabe said.

"Right. Then depression, and acceptance. That's a good theory. What would you know about grief?" she asked.

He was determined not to go down this road where she inevitably drew him. "Not one thing. How's Alexander Hamilton treating you?" he asked, as the waiter set the food on the table and flashed a large peppershaker.

"Everywhere please," Angeline said.

"He keeps me up at nights. He mystifies me. I've been working on this for so long. I've read everything about him. I try to raise the tent but it collapses. He's bewildering, impossible to explain. Elusive, enigmatic, mercurial, unknowable, exasperating." Her shoulders slumped into an acknowledgment of defeat.

"He left a lot of writing behind, didn't he? Just the Federalist Papers alone are worth their weight in gold, I'd imagine," Gabe said.

"He was a manic writer. Sixty thousand words in two weeks. He was writing four or five essays each week. Incredible! I'm lucky if I can write five hundred words a day." she said.

"He must have written lots of letters if he was that prolific," Gabe said, placing his fork down to top up her wine glass.

"He did, and there are a few that reveal something about his psychology, but he's a hard nut to crack. An orphan with nothing, absolutely nothing in his favor, who came from Nevis at seventeen, and in six years became second in command to George Washington. I mean, come on now. Who succeeds like that? What drove him? He's this slippery subject beyond my intelligence to deconstruct."

"I think people are driven to avenge pain. If you trace that to its source, I think you can begin to know a person," Gabe said.

"What do you mean?"

"Well, let's take, well, me for instance." Gabe looked away, regretting the direction he was leading the conversation, but somehow unable to reel his thoughts back in. He couldn't help it. She compelled him to narrate his story to her, to explain himself, to tell the story that was inside him. He found himself entering his own story more and more. She resided in language. It was her country. If he was to mean anything at all to her, he had to give her his life wrapped in words and phrases, sentences and story. His story. "The reason I work so hard to claim things is because I come from a dispossessed people."

"What happened to Iqrit?" Angeline asked.

"What happened to all Palestine," Gabe said. "The Israeli Army entered the village in 1948 and drove them out. Temporary evacuation to carry out a military operation, the IDF said. But when the villagers tried to return, they were refused entry. They took their case to the Supreme Court, who ruled the evacuation illegal and upheld the villagers right to return. But on Christmas Eve, the army placed explosives under all the houses and blew up the village. Nothing remained but the church and the cemetery."

"What a Christmas present. Did the villagers go back to court?"

"Yes, but a new ruling rejected the villagers right to return. Iqrit was claimed as military land and for settlements. My people are allowed to return once a month to pray or bury their dead," he said.

"Gabriel!"

"You see why I hate history. It seeps into your bones and thickens your blood."

"How do you deal with it?" Angeline asked, skating her finger around the rim of her wine glass.

"I reject it. I don't want anything to do with it. Which explains the jerk you think I am."

"I'm ashamed that I've been so judgmental. I think it's because I'm American. Complexity irritates me. I'm so sorry."

Gabe fell silent, sipped his wine, and looked around the room. Dredging up the past caused him psychic damage that made him unable to function. "Thinking is hard work. But America not thinking at all has been the cause of a brutal occupation for sixty seven years."

"Journalists report simple narratives with no complexity or psychological baggage or meta meaning," Angeline said.

Exactly, Gabe thought. He could have eviscerated her position and talked all night about how unbridled power and occupation of a people and their land changes the occupied forever. How a father humiliated in front of his children will grow violent. How occupation spawns enraged men bent on murderous revenge. How the stories of young children woken up in the middle of the night, and arrested and renditioned to jails far from home, curdle the blood of even the most tolerant. How dropping one ton bombs on civilians can create madness in a race. But this was a slippery slope. If he let go and tumbled all the way down to memory and remembering, to anger, to revenge, to want the occupiers to suffer as much as his people, his family, had suffered, what would stop him from following in his father's footsteps? This line of thought would kill him.

"Maybe that's why you're grappling with Hamilton," he said instead. "I don't think somebody like him would be anything but complex. What's the most essential thing about him?" Gabe redirected the conversation to its proper course.

"You're always turning the conversation back to me. It's a clever tactic to evade talking about yourself."

"Give me time."

"Leave the door wedged open a bit so I can find my way to you, Gabriel."

It was going to be a dance, a slow dance, a long dance.

"What's the most essential thing about Hamilton?"

"The most essential thing? That's a great question. Let me think," she said as she sipped her wine.

Gabe loved the way she looked away, and then ran her fingers across her lips. He loved the way she held her throat, and fingered the length of the pearl string around her neck, as she formulated her thoughts. He loved the way she felt so comfortable thinking in front of him, without a measure of awkwardness about the silence.

"He wanted to rewrite his own tragic life and redeem his own history," Angeline said. "He wanted to be reborn."

"That's the classic immigrant story. Through no fault of your own, just by virtue of being born in the wrong place at the wrong time you realize you were handed shit on a stick for a life. And you leave because you're dispossessed and you want to prove that life is fair to the innocent and the good, and you work to create a new self," Gabe said.

"He discovered, once he got here, that sacrificing himself to a larger cause gave his life rich meaning," she said.

"The country was birthing. It needed brilliant people like him. He was a man for that moment," Gabe said.

"Yes, for exactly that moment when hope and history rhymed. Do you know Seamus Heaney?"

He didn't. She lived by ideas and philosophy and poetry, while he lived by plans and actions. He didn't see how this could work, but he wanted to risk his heart. He felt that if he did, he would unearth forgotten fragments of himself. "Did Hamilton own slaves?" he asked.

"He was one of the few who didn't. In fact, he was an abolitionist. He was the head of the Manumission Society in New York. It made sense. He was the immigrant among them, he had to believe in meritocracy. And growing up in Nevis and St. Croix, where he had seen first hand, the injustices and cruelty of slavery, and also seeing the humanity of the slaves he knew, made him abhor it. At the height of the Revolutionary War, he advocated for slaves to be admitted into the army in return for their freedom," she said.

"Few people know that about him," Gabe said.

"Right. He's the lone Founding Father who never received his proper due. Jefferson, the biggest hypocrite of all, receives all the attention," she said. "I'm not sure how he managed to separate his conscience from his actions, when he wrote all those beautiful words. He owned more than two hundred slaves. He only set two of them free after his death, his children by Sally Hemmings. He didn't free her even after his death," Angeline said.

"How many sitting Presidents owned slaves?" said Gabe.

"The rogues gallery? George Washington, at the time of his death had owned slaves for more than fifty years. Two hundred and sixteen of them. In his will, he freed only one, his manservant, William Lee. He left it to Martha to free the rest upon her death. She freed them two years after he died. Madison and Monroe owned a hundred and seventy slaves between them. Neither of them freed their slaves. Bastards," Angeline said.

"You make my head spin Angeline," Gabe said.

"This is my neurosis. I'm obsessional," she said.

"Obsession is not a neurosis. It's a way to tread water and survive."

They had been so engrossed in each other, they hadn't realized that theirs was only one of two tables still occupied. "They're giving us the look," Angeline said scanning the room.

Gabe helped her into her coat and they walked outside. She put her gloved hand in the curve of his elbow. "It's so cold," she said. "Let's take the shortcut," she led him across the street, and turned left down an alley towards the rear of her apartment building. They walked past Camp Bark Bark, a pet boarding business.

"This is one of my favorite activities," she said, stopping at the storefront window, clutching the sleeve of his coat. In the corner of the room in a large donut bed, lay a dozen puppies, sable and white Shetland Sheepdogs curled up with their mother. "They have a puppy cam which live streams 24/7. When I can't sleep I go online to see that they're all tucked in. They're very good cuddlers. I think it helps them sleep to be warmed, skin to skin.

After watching them awhile, I feel my eyes getting heavier and ready for sleep,"

He looked at her oddly. "Why can't you sleep?"

"Don't you ever have your head full of thoughts, and they keep churning, and you go down these long tunnels, and you replay everything? It's like you live your life not once but over and over again."

"No, I don't," Gabe said with conviction.

"You're telling me you sleep like a baby?"

"Insomnia has never been my problem," Gabe said.

"What is then?" she stared at him.

"I have a very hard time persuading women from Louisiana via Nevis that I'm a nice guy, that I'm not an asshole," Gabe said.

She laughed. "I think you're alright."

"Alright or all that?" Gabe planted his arms on her hips and moved in.

"You," she said, and wrapped her arms around his neck.

They walked in quick strides to the rear entrance of her building. She punched a code to gain entry while she held his hand. As they waited for the elevator, they looked at each other. "I don't think this is a good idea," she said.

"Stop thinking."

They entered the elevator, she with arms folded across her chest, he holding his open palm against her back. She greeted an old couple with their dog and a young couple holding bags of groceries They alighted on their floor and Angeline fumbled with her keys. Gabe took them from her, opened the door, and followed her inside. She entered the room, dropped her bag on the couch, and faced him. He placed the keys on the console by the door.

"Gabriel," she said, her eyes teary. "I don't know."

"Do you want me to stay?" Gabe spread a hand on top of the console.

"I don't know," she crossed her arms.

"Do you want me to go?" he moved his hand to the door knob.

"No!" She took a step towards him. "Don't leave."

He drew close to the heat of her.

Chapter 23

BOLT

Slanted rods of morning sun pierced through the vertical blinds and awakened Angeline. When she reached for Gabe, he was not there.

"Gabriel?" she called out. She rose from the bed, unclothed. She peeked in the bathroom, then the living room and kitchen.

"Bastard," she said and walked back into the bedroom. She went into the bathroom and turned the shower on to a high heat. She was furious at herself for sleeping with him and livid with him for running away. Selfish, two-faced, emotionally stunted mercenary. She stepped out of the shower, her body raw from the heat and the scrubbing gloves she had used to scrape her skin. She dried herself, lathered herself in lotion, and wrapped her hair in a towel.

She replayed the events of the previous night. They were hungry lovers who had ravished each other, bold in their want, greedy in their claim to each other's bodies. Quiet at first, they had moaned as they feverishly, rhythmically, greedily, probed, riveted, and folded each other deeper and deeper into themselves. Love invents lovers, reshapes them, gives them back to themselves. She berated herself for falling for him.

She pulled on underclothes, yoga pants, and a long tunic, and went to the kitchen. She prepared a cup of coffee and toast and sat at the kitchen table. "What an idiot you are. You never learn," she said to herself.

After breakfast, she sat on the couch with a collection of Alexander Hamilton's letters on her lap and a composition book, pen, highlighters in three colors, and sticky flags. She read once more, the first letter in the collection that had been written by Hamilton when he was thirteen years old. He was working as a clerk for a shipping company in St. Croix, and the letter was to his best friend, Edward Stevens, who had gone to New York City to study medicine at King's College.

St.Croix, November. 11th 1769

Dear Edward

This just serves to acknowledge receipt of yours per Cap Lowndes, which was delivered me Yesterday ... As to what you say respecting your having soon the happiness of seeing us all, I wish, for an accomplishment of your hopes provided they are Concomitant with your welfare, otherwise not, tho doubt whether I shall be Present or not for to confess my weakness, Ned, my Ambition is prevalent that I contemn the grov'ling and condition of a Clerk or the like, to which my Fortune &c. condemns me and would willingly risk my life tho' not my Character to exalt my Station. Im confident, Ned that my Youth excludes me from any hopes of immediate Preferment nor do I desire it, but I mean to prepare the way for futurity. Im no Philosopher you see and may be jusly said to Build Castles in the Air. My Folly makes me ashamd and beg youll Conceal it, yet Neddy we have seen such Schemes successfull when the Projector is Constant I shall

Conclude saying I wish there was a War.

I am, Dr Edward Yours

Alex Hamilton

PS I this moment receivd yours by William Smith and am pleased to see you Give such Close Application to Study.

Angeline was struck by his words, "I wish there was a war." How could he have known when he was thirteen years old that he would need a war to engineer his life. It seemed to confirm Angeline's faith in a myth prevalent in many religions: that one comes into the world with a destiny—an image, a code, that is unique to one's soul. Plato, in Myth of Er, called it paragdima. Native American and Mormon literature, the Kabbalah and Buddhist sacred texts, and West African and Indian writings all agreed on the idea that one came into the world with an express purpose. It seemed to Angeline that Alexander Hamilton's destiny was to migrate to a country that had yet to be formed, to steward and forge its creation. He didn't have a choice. The choice had been made for him. Angeline kept reading.

New York, 1774

Men are generally too much attached to their native country to leave it, and dissolve all their connections, unless they are driven to it by necessity. The Didascalicon of Hugh of Saint Victor offers much wisdom on the matter of erasure. "It is a great source of virtue for the practiced mind to learn, bit by bit, first to change about in visible and transitory things, so that afterwards it may be possible to leave them behind altogether. The man who finds his homeland sweet is still a tender beginner; he to whom every soil is as his native one is already strong; but he is perfect to whom the entire world is as a foreign land. The tender soul has fixed his love on one spot in the world; the strong man has extended his love to all places; the perfect man has extinguished his. From boyhood I have dwelt on foreign soil and I know with what grief sometimes the mind takes leave of the narrow hearth of a peasant's hut, and I know too how frankly it afterwards disdains marble firesides and panelled halls."

- Alexander Hamilton

May the 2nd, 1797

My Dear Sir,

Some days since I received with great pleasure your letter of the 10th of March. The mark, it affords, of your kind attention, and the particular account it gives me of so many relations in Scotland are extremely gratifying to me.

You no doubt have understood that my father's affairs at a very early age went to wreck; so as to have rendered his situation during the greatest part of his life far from eligible. This state of things occasioned a separation between him and me, when I was very young, and threw me upon the bounty of my mothers relations, some of whom were then wealthy, though by vicissitudes to which human affairs are so liable, they have been since much reduced and broken up. Myself at about sixteen came to this Country. Having always had a strong propensity to literary pursuits, by a course of steady and laborious exertion, I was able, by the age of Ninteen to qualify myself for the degree of Bachelor of Arts in the College of New York, and to lay a foundation, by preparatory study for the future profession of law.

The American Revolution supervened. My principles led me to take part in it. At nineteen I entered into the American army as Captain of Artillery. Shortly after, I became by his invitation Aide De Camp to General Washington, in which station, I served till the commencement of that Campaign which ended with the siege of York, in Virginia, and the Capture of Cornwallis's Army. This Campaign I made at the head of a corps of light infantry, with which I was present at the siege of York and engaged in some interesting operations.

At the period of the peace with Great Britain, I found myself a member of Congress by appointment of the legislature of this state. After the peace, I settled in the City of New York in the practice of law; and was in a very lucrative course of practice, when the derangement of our public affairs, by the feebleness of the general confederation drew me again reluctantly into public life.

I became a member of the Convention which framed the present Constitution of the U States; and having taken part in this measure, I conceived myself to be under an obligation to lend my aid towards putting the machine in some regular motion, Hence I did not hesitate to accept the offer of President Washington to undertake the office of Secretary of the Treasury.

In that office, I met with many intrinsic difficulties, and many artificial ones proceeding from passions, not very worthy common to human nature, and which act with particular force in republics. The object, however, was effected, of establishing public credit and introducing order into the finances.

Public Office in this Country has few attractions. The pecuniary emolument is so inconsiderable as to amount to a sacrifice to any man who can employ his time with advantage in any liberal profession. The opportunity of doing good, from the jealousy of power and the spirit of faction, is too small in any station to warrant a long continuance of private sacrifices. The enterprises of party had so far succeeded as materially to weaken the necessary influence and energy of the Executive Authority.

The Union of these motives, with the reflections of prudence in relation to a growing family, determined me as soon as my plan had attained a certain maturity to withdraw from Office. This I did by resignation about two years since; when I resumed the profession of the law in the City of New York under every advantage I could desire.

It is a pleasing reflection to me that since the commencement of my connection with General Washington to the present time, I have possessed a flattering share of his confidence and friendship.

It is my intention to embrace the Opening which your letter affords me to extend intercourse with my relations in your Country, which will be a new source of satisfaction to me. Having given you a brief sketch of my political career, I proceed to some further family details. In the year 1780 I married the second daughter of General Schuyler, a Gentleman of one of the best families of this Country, of large fortune and no less personal and public consequence. It is impossible to be happier than I am in my wife and I have five Children, four sons and a daughter, the eldest a son somewhat passed fifteen, who all promise well, as far as their years permit and yield me much satisfaction. Though I have been too much in public life to be wealthy, my situation is extremely comfortable and leaves me nothing to wish but a continuance of health. With this blessing, the profits of my profession and other prospects authorize an expectation of such addition to my resources as will render the eve of life, easy and agreeable; so far as may depend on this consideration.

Alexander Hamilton

At eleven, Albert buzzed to inform her that there was a delivery for her. She opened the door to a wall of flowers and somewhere behind the foliage, a deliveryman, made obvious only by his legs. "Over the top underdeveloped idiot," she thought as she accepted them. The card read, "You're beautiful, Angeline. Thank you." You slept with a mental midget, Lalande, you fool.

A feeling of sadness, of being unloved, unlovable, ugly, hung over her as she worked through the Hamilton letters and took notes. She allowed the tears to fall. Gabriel's rejection of her sunk her own optimism about the book. What was she doing? She wondered how she was going to pull it off. She worked through the book taking notes in a legal pad and cross-referencing the pages with sticky tabs of different colors. Her heart felt so heavy, the only cure would be to talk to her child. Andre had already reminded her several times that he couldn't talk to her during the day, as he was busy with school and work at the lodge. She dialed anyway but the call went straight into voicemail. She felt bereft of everything fundamental she needed to survive—love, faith, hope, warmth. She started to weep again. She waited till lunchtime before pouring herself a glass of wine and sitting down with a sandwich. As she ate, she grew angry for giving herself to someone who refused to give even a little of himself to her.

She heard the ping of incoming email and looked at the grid of her mailbox: an email from Celestine with the subject line: The Ant's Belly. She opened it and read the message, "Alexander Hamilton was twelve in 1768." She downloaded the PDF of lined journal pages. Angeline printed the document and took it with her to the living room. She sat cross-legged on the sheepskin rug in front of the electric fireplace, her back to the hearth, and set the three pages in front of her like a spread of cards . The cursive longhand was small and spidery, written by a nervous hand, a child's hand.

St. Croix - February, 1768

By the time, Mrs. Mcdowell came, Mama was already quite ill. She had been under some duress moving the household, and us just a few weeks before the new year to No 22 Company Street. It was a few houses from No 34 where we had lived since we moved to St. Croix. She moved us back a few weeks later to 34. Father had left like a thief in the night a few months before that and she never recovered. This must have been the cause of her behavior most strange. Maybe that's why she fell sick. The fever didn't possess my brother. Somehow, John managed to escape the curse but I could feel myself going down in flames.

I shared a bed with Mama to better contain the disease. Mrs. Mcdowell did her ministrations as well as she could. Minutes turned into hours, hours into days, as Mama and I lay huddled in a delirium under the skimpy covers, our bodies scalding each other with the fever, even though we were not pressed against each other. We couldn't do anything, either of us to help ourselves. John in fear of catching the disease did not appear but we did hear him beyond the door. By the sixth day, Mrs. Mcdowell called Dr. Heering. He was clearly alarmed and began his care. He had Mrs. Mcdowell make up a tea of valerian root for Mama, to expel gas from the alimentary canal, he said. He also gave her an emetic. He gave me a purge and a bloodletting. Both Mama and I were very weak. Mama lay a few inches from me and violently convulsed. We were too weak to ask for or use the chamber pot. We soiled the bedclothes and the beds, and the disgusting odors of vomit and flatulence and feces hung in the air.

On the night, I now know to have been February 18, as I drifted in and out of consciousness, I could hear Mama breathing heavily, gasping for air, her voice like a rattle, her body raking and twitching. She held my hand and when I looked at her, she wretched. The vomit dribbled down her neck. Tears were in her eyes. She looked ashamed and frightened that I should see her that way. I was in no shape to help her or myself. I fell unconscious during that long night.

When I awoke, I felt a little better. I saw tiny particles of white float inside the beam of sunlight poring in through the window. I felt well and wanted to immediately report to Mama and John that I had ridden the fever out. When I tried to speak, my voice was hoarse and gravelly, as if it belonged to someone else. I tried again, Ma, Mam. I rolled to my side to look at her. Her back was turned away from me, her white night shirt was drenched with sweat on her back and soiled yellow and brown from feces and urine below her waist. Her black hair was coiled over her right shoulder.

I reached out to touch her hand, it was not cold but it seemed heavy like stone. I got up a little and saw that she was still and silent, she was without breath. I shook her. Ma. She didn't move. I knew she was dead but I kept shaking her. I thought I would somehow will her back to life.

"Oh my God," Angeline gasped. She read the pages for a second time. Tears ran down her cheeks, the rack of her chest heaved. Angeline rode the wave of sadness, weeping for Alexander Hamilton, and for herself.

Chapter 24

TRANSCONTINENTALS

July 2016. The birds were beginning to make their reverse path from South America. Nila stood on the deck in yoga clothes watching the passerines. She too was restless. She was a toddler when her parents arrived in the US, Rae, a teenager. They'd both lived in America for nearly four decades. They'd seen seven American Presidents elected, each Presidential inauguration embedding them deeper in the culture, hewing away their otherness and foreignness, making them identifiably, essentially, fundamentally of this place and no other. But this year was different. An immigrant-bashing, race-baiting nativist stood to be a contender for the Presidency. Everywhere on the Square, people expressed their worries.

He's set the country back two hundred years.

Two hundred and forty years.

He doesn't stand a chance.

Don't be so sure of yourself.

Nila dragged a yoga mat out of the shade and set it in a pool of light. She stepped on the springy surface to begin her daily morning ritual of Surya Namaskhar, twelve poses in two cycles to salute the sun. Rae, sitting at the breakfast bar near her composing emails and sipping coffee, watched her. She began the sequence with the Prayer pose, slowly raised her arms above her head, and arched her back into the Hastauttanasana, elongating her body from legs to fingertips.

She breathed out, bent forward at the waist, brought her hands down to the floor, and wrapped her palms around her ankles, dipping her head lower and lower until the crown of her head was touching her toes. She breathed in the air from the still morning, as she kneeled and stretched out one leg behind her, and bent her other knee close to her chest, balancing herself with both hands for the Equestrian pose. She rearranged her body into a neat stick pose before dropping to the floor for the Ashtanga Namaskara where eight parts of her body, chest, chin, both hands, feet, and knees, touched the floor. She lifted her body up in a Cobra pose, even higher to a Mountain pose, repeated the Equestrian form, hand to foot, and raised arms pose.

She was such a powerful woman, Rae thought. She had made him into a man worthy of her love. She had given him a different understanding of himself. She had forced him to mature into her idealized vision of him. So powerful.

She stood still with her hands in Namaste before letting them fall. “Let’s do India,” she turned to Rae.

“As opposed to visit India?”

“Yes. I want to show Hari and Zara where they come from. They were too young before.” She made a loop around the counter and poured herself a cup of coffee from the carafe.

“Work is very busy right now,” he shook his head.

“Work will always be busy if you let it.”

“It’s not a good time Nila.”

“When is a good time? When will it be our time?”

Rae sighed and closed his laptop. “Okay. Where do you want to go?”

“Goa where things began, and the south where the three seas meet,” she said. “By train and car so we can see everything.”

Rae had a pained expression on his face. This was going to be a nightmare. Keeping Nila sexually satisfied in equatorial heat, keeping Hari away from drug highs on Palolem Beach, keeping Zara from being pawed or worse by men in a country with a gender imbalance catastrophe, all the while keeping one step ahead of diarrhea and malaria, Avian flu and Zika, monsoons and dehydration, traffic and sweat, poverty and teeming masses of humanity, 1.2 billion people for crying out loud, fatalism and rage, sweat and suicide ideation. "Two weeks, Nila. Any longer and I'll lose my mind." Once they reached an agreement, things moved very quickly. Almost at light speed, Rae thought later. Nila told Hari and Zara about the trip.

"Goa? Is that where we come from? I thought we were from Mumbai," Hari said.

"Why did you think that, baby?" Total cultural erasure and historical forgetting took only a generation, Nila thought.

"I was sure it was Mumbai."

"India is a big place, Hari."

"Will I be able to buy weed there? If not, I can't go."

"Goa is a stoners paradise. It's where old hippies go to die."

"Cool. It will be an excellent adventure," Hari said.

Unlike NRIs who stripped whole shopping malls off merchandize and exceeded baggage restrictions to gift relatives in India, Nila told Rae they would see no relatives and do only carryon.

A month before the flight, Nila felt a strong urge to complete some things she had meant to do that she had neglected for too long. She returned five library books that were overdue by nine years. Prepared to pay thousands of dollars in penalty, she was happy to learn that the library's amnesty was still in effect. "How lucky am

I," she thought as she handed the librarian the fine in dollar bills. She stopped by her family's attorney, Saul Talith, to update and sign documents. She cleaned out her family's closets and assigned the clothes to one of three piles: for the garbage dump, for Kolbe House, for the basement. She called Bruce to tell him she had something to give him. Meet me at Oasis, she said.

"Hello Maharani," Bruce said looking up from his usual table.

"You're sitting at the same place I left you all those years ago," she smiled.

"It went by in the wink of an eye didn't it?" Bruce's eyes turned misty.

"Like that," Nila snapped her fingers.

"Do you remember telling me at Whole World Style that I'd look like a giant rhubarb?" Bruce grinned.

"Or a fire hydrant. I remember."

"And do you recall telling me to wake the fuck up fucking loser jerk asshole idiot?"

"I should be shot for abusing you like that. I'm very sorry, Bruce." Nila bowed her head in apology.

"Don't be. You were the first person who cared about me in America."

"You're going to make me cry," she said.

They placed their drink order with the waiter.

"That man gives me the heebi jeebies," Nila said, returning Mark Zalinsky's stare from behind the counter.

Bruce raised his hand and waved at Mark, who turned away. "A friendly man."

"He lost Eva. He has to live with that knowledge everyday."

Mark knew that he was innocent. He had been minding his own business and it wasn't his fault.

"It's an emergency," Caroline Lindley had told Rosa, Mark's gum chewing receptionist with big hair, fake eyelashes that made her look like Bambi, and long manicured talons with fake rhinestones on the tips.

"I'll let the Doctor know," Rosa picked up the phone from its cradle and hit the buttons with a pencil head. "He'll be right with you."

"Can I help you?" Mark appeared at the door behind Rosa. He was wearing surgical scrubs; a mask pulled down under his chin. Caroline followed him into the examination room and told him she had been sipping on an iced drink while driving past his office when she felt a pain shoot through her tooth and electrify her brain. She said she had gasped from it and when she inhaled, a jolt of air hit the tooth, richocheted in her mouth, and flew up and pinched her optic nerves. "I thought I was going to crash. I couldn't see."

"Let's take a look," he said as he pulled on rubber gloves.

Dentin hypersensitivity, he told her after examining her front tooth. "I'll give you something to block the pain and a temporary sealant until you see your regular dentist which you should do right away," he said.

He walked her out. When she stopped in front of the receptionist to settle the bill, he said, "Please, no."

He was surprised then to see her three days later. She wasn't as pretty as Eva, she had enough filler in her face to swell up a balloon, but he had liked her perky demeanor. She held out a long and narrow jute bag towards him.

"For being a good Samaritan."

"Please," he said, waving the bag away.

"It's a very special Bordeaux . St. Julien Beychevelle." Caroline was insulted.

"It was nothing," he said.

"It wasn't nothing," she said, and backed out the door.

At the end of the week, as he was sitting in Rosa's chair studying a sales brochure about the holy grail in dentistry, eliminating bad breath, the phone rang.

"Dr. Zalinsky," he said.

"Drill me," Caroline said.

He had a good woman waiting for him at home, but what could he do? It wasn't his fault.

Nila and Bruce fell silent as the waiter set their drinks in front of them. Nila looked at Mark and shuddered. She thought of Eva and wondered who she could introduce Eva to, who Eva's twin flame might be, who would be good enough for a woman like that, a saint who helped torture victims. She would mull over this problem later, she decided.

"How are the kids?" Bruce asked.

"Doing well. You're their favorite uncle."

"I get them. Is Rae any happier with them?

"I don't think they'll ever measure up in his eyes."

"Rae is a systems thinker. He doesn't understand how their brains work is the problem," Bruce said.

"Yes, they're wired differently. He just doesn't get them. I worry that he'll never know how kind and loving they are as long as he judges them. They can see how disappointed he is with them," Nila said.

"He's a good man. He'll learn."

"And you? You okay with your life?"

"Geography is everything, right? Once I got to Azyl Park, I felt a sort of recognition that this was to be my home. It took a while to figure out how to be relevant, how to climb into your fusion chamber. But the last five years have been great."

"You're a real estate mogul now," Nila smiled.

"Nothing like that. Who can compete with Gabe and Rae? But I get by. It keeps me busy. I feel connected. I belong."

"I'm glad everything worked out for you, Bruce."

"Well, not everything. I was watching Robert D'Niro in this movie I watch a lot, and he talked about major chord. When everything works out perfectly, when you have the work you love, the money you need, the woman you love. I don't have her yet."

"But you're going with all the wrong people!" she said.

"What do you mean?"

"I see you with two kinds of women, babies and bimbos. The last one was a whack job."

"True that."

"There's a woman who's crazy about you. Who's been in love with you for as long as you've been here," Nila said.

"Nila!" He looked at her shocked, a pained expression on his face. "Please don't tell me this! I love Rae and the kids."

"Not me, you idiot!" Nila threw her head back and laughed. "Tina. She loves you. You should be with each other."

"Tina? No way. Uh uh, no way."

"She's dying in that marriage waiting for you to rescue her."

"Tina!! Are you sure?"

"You belong together. She's your twin flame." Nila glanced at her phone. "Oh, look at the time, I have to go to the travel clinic for my shots." She stood up.

"Wait. You said you had something for me. Was that it? Tina?"

"Oh, I completely forgot." Nila fished an envelope out of her bag and handed it to him. She leaned over the table, placed a hand on Bruce's shoulder to draw him forward, and kissed him on both cheeks. She straightened herself and placed a hand on his cheek. "Take this the right way. I want to see you happy. Promise me you'll talk to Tina."

"I'll think about it," he looked up at her.

"Promise me." she insisted.

"Yes, Maharani," Bruce drew her hand from his cheek and kissed it. "I will." He watched her walk out of the restaurant. When she was in front of the windows, she waved and blew him a kiss, a radiant smile on her face. He raised his glass to her, smiling, and watched her until she disappeared from view. He put the glass down, opened the envelope, and pulled out a folder with flaps. It held articles ripped out from newspapers and entertainment rags. Brew Meister Flips Out. Brew Meister Goes Wagga Wagga. The Rise and Fall of Bruce Halliday.

A few days later, Nila walked from the Crescent to the beach, made a left turn on Iris, and looped back south to City Realty on the Square.

"Nila!" Trang said as she locked the door.

"Are you on your way for a showing or lunch?"

"My stomach is growling. I need to eat," Trang said.

"May I join you?"

"Of course."

"What do you feel like?" Nila asked.

"I'm feeling shawarma."

"Perfect."

"You think this place will make it?" Tina asked after the host seated them.

"Remember when it used to be Mint Leaf then Bay Leaf?" Nila said.

"Yes and then Reza's. Then was it Tamarind?"

"Turmeric," Nila corrected her.

"Right, and then it was Cairo," Tina said.

"Don't forget Osama's."

"That was ridiculous branding," Tina said.

"Absurd," Nila agreed.

"So, how are you? Excited about the trip?" Tina folded her arms above the table.

"Yes and no. Traveling is a hassle. The thought of India makes me panic. It's so in your face. Rae likes order. I want him to be comfortable and not complain, so it's been a military operation coordinating luxury travel."

"Yeah, you don't want beggars handing Rae their babies."

"He'll freak out." Nila said.

"Why did you decide to go then?"

"It seemed like a pilgrimage I had to make. I've gone to see relatives a few times but I don't really feel I know it, which is a disgrace. My mother says I have a fetish for India because of my ignorance. I think going will cure me. I think going may help Zara and Hari too."

"In what way?"

"Ground them in their racial identity. It may fortify them for an America outside Azyl Park."

"You don't have to worry about that. All of America will be like Azyl Park. Give it twenty years," Tina said.

"Well, that depends on who wins in November. Doesn't it?"

"He won't win."

"I still think he may," Nila said.

"He must not win. Once you give a con man power, you never get it back. That's been true everywhere."

"He's turned America against all of us. It hurts me," Nila said.

"Reason will prevail. In the end, we won't reject the American Experiment. I go to Vietnam and everybody is the same. I'm sure it's the same in India and China and Japan. But here, you just bump up against the whole world. I love it."

"Except when it's a Serb named Maja Novic?" Nila teased.

"She's a piece of work. I don't know how Ivan puts up with her."

"You know my theory. Mating when done wrong is two people finding God in a shared neurosis," Nila said.

"And when done right?" Tina asked.

"When done right, it can't be explained. Only felt. You know?"

"No. I don't know. How would I know? What you've got is the full monty. A beautiful husband who adores you, two wonderful kids, all the money you could want. Why couldn't I have that?"

"Did you want it?" Nila asked.

"I certainly did, but I was with the wrong man. Under all that Buddha serenity Roger is a very selfish, cruel man. Sitting in that house painting very bad Monet impressions, not working, going to Buddhism conferences."

"I'm really sorry for bringing you together, Tina."

"I don't think it was a mistake. I knew diddlysquat when I got here and when I realized what a failure he was, I knew I had to make my own way in the world. I just had to. My ghastly marriage made me the person I am today," Tina said.

"Will you leave?" Nila asked.

"Well, I think he should leave. But he wont. He sits there day after day like he's getting it all worked out in the here and now, so that he'll have the ground rules down to live perfectly in the next life. It's really pathetic."

"Why don't you divorce him?"

"I could, but I'm a loyal person. I could have been doing pedicures in St. Paul. He saved me."

"Tina, do you know why I called my business Twin Flames?" Nila told Tina about Plato's Symposium, and Aristophanes, and Zeus splitting humans in half, and Apollo sewing them back together, and split humans living in utter misery until they found each other and achieved full understanding through unity. "When you meet your twin soul, your twin flame, you will be forced to face your self."

"That is so incredibly beautiful," Tina sat back in her chair. "And so utterly depressing. Others have Twin Flames and I have Roger? Let me just go and slit my wrists now."

"Well, you do have a Twin Flame who's been longing for you as much as you've been longing for him." Nila replied.

"Who? Where?"

"Right here in Azyl Park. He's crazy about you. He's been in love with you for as long as you've been here," Nila said.

"Who? Zalinsky, the psycho dentist, Mehta the misogynist, Ivan the war criminal. This is soul crushing."

"Bruce," Nila said.

"Stop! Don't make fun of me like that!" Tina giggled.

"Bruce is the one you should be with."

"Bruce? Oh, I don't see it at all, Nila. He's so Australian. He's double my size. I'd fit into his pocket!"

"He's a good man, Tina. Look beyond the outside."

"Seriously, he'd crush me with his weight."

"You're meant to be together." Nila said.

Chapter 25

EYES TO SEE

"I have a field assignment for you," Dean, Angeline's producer announced on their weekly Skype call.

"I thought you only needed me for digital and one on-air through spring," Angeline said. She was making headway with her manuscript. After a ninety-two hour tear festival—during which she played and replayed in her mind the night she spent with Gabriel, while she sat in pajamas, ate chocolates, drank wine, watched every American, European, and Australian tearjerker romance via livestream, and stared at the ceiling—she returned to Alexander Hamilton. She was pleased with the progress and did not want to break her stride to do reporting.

"Amnesty International just released a report on torture in Africa and the Middle East. I'd like a feature with a local angle. I'd like you to do a story on Kolbe House," Dean said.

"Oh, I can't," she said, remembering her first conversation with Gabriel when he had called her a moron.

"Why the fuck not?" Dean barked.

She thought about it. "Can't you assign it to somebody else?"

"Listen Lalande, I'll fire you in a New York minute if you don't pull your weight. What the fuck is wrong with you?"

"Can't Rita do it? I just don't feel I can."

"Do what I tell you or you can go blog on Huffington Post for free. I mean it," Dean said.

She wanted to finish her book. She needed the job. She couldn't afford to get fired or spend time looking for a new job. "You're right. My mistake. I wasn't thinking."

"That's more like it. I'll plug it on the slate. Maggie will call you after scheduling the interview and coordinating the crew."

WBYN's van pulled up at the end of Hyacinth on the following Tuesday. Angeline got out of the van and sized up the white bungalow. Her cameraman, audio engineer, and broadcast technician lifted equipment out of the back, while she made her way to the front door. A white cat sat on a ledge behind a window and stared at her. She rang the bell and waited.

A young woman led Angeline to Eva's office.

"I've followed your career, respect the serious work you've done, which is the only reason I'm allowing this interview," Eva said, as she rose from her desk.

"I understand. I'll be very careful," Angeline said.

"You can't divulge our address or mention Kolbe House by name. I won't permit it. I won't make any clients available to you. And you will not film anywhere but in this office with me. I'm the only one whose name may be revealed."

"I understand," Angeline said. She handed Eva a release agreement to review and sign, explained how the interview would proceed, and eased Eva into prep.

The doorbell rang. The volunteer left the room and returned with the crew. The team set up the equipment and lights in the area where Eva held her session with clients. The audio engineer pinned microphones on the two women. Caravaggio and Cleo watched the proceedings. The hour long interview went well. Eva was poised, serious, on point. She was able to humanize the data in the Amnesty report with stories about individuals who had endured torture—the complexities of culturally appropriate therapeutic healing, and the ways in which her clients had transcended their experiences. She was professional and compassionate without being sentimental or apologetic. She rejected the word, victim, calling her clients survivors instead.

"That was great. Thank you. The guys are going to review the tape for sound and lighting. It'll be a few minutes," Angeline told Eva, and stood up.

Eva stood up too and adjusted her shawl round her shoulders.

Angeline stepped over the electric cables running from the crew's apparatus towards a side table. She picked up a crayon drawing.

"That was my morning client," Eva said.

"It's horrendous," Angeline placed a hand over her mouth as she looked at the details in the drawing.

"Yes, she was only fourteen. There were thirty six men who had their way with her in one night," Eva said.

"Will she make it?"

"It's touch and go," Eva said.

"You must dream of a day when Kolbe House is no longer needed."

"That would be delusional. The fact is we're very small, and the need is getting more urgent every day. We only have capacity for forty clients, a tiny fraction of the people who need our care. We'll open a second facility in Fall. It will serve two hundred clients," Eva said.

"Two hundred. Where does the money come from?"

"We have donors."

"How do you raise money for a secret operation? That must be complicated," Angeline said.

"It's very simple actually. We have one donor," Eva said.

"One donor?"

"Yes, he made a major gift which will allow us to continue this work for several generations."

"Who is this?"

"I'm not at liberty to say."

The crew shuffled out of the room with their equipment.

"It's wonderful that you have support and resources."

"Yes. It's a miracle."

"Can you tell me who it is?

"Only off the record. In confidence. Not for reporting. I can't tell you otherwise. He swore me to confidentiality"

"Alright."

"Gabe Khoury of IBI Worldwide."

"Gabriel?" Angeline was stunned.

"Yes. We were running out of money fast. I couldn't find anybody to give us what we needed to stay open. Our fundraising was costing more than it was bringing in. He made an endowment of $10 million to Kolbe House. If he hadn't stepped in, we would have gone under."

"I guess he needed the tax write-off," Angeline shrugged. If he was giving money away, there had to be a benefit for his bottomline.

"Oh no! He could have given to anybody. He cares about our work."

"I don't buy that."

"I shouldn't have told you," Eva said. "I'm not sure why I did."

Chapter 26

RECKONING

Gabe had been with Angeline in early April and it was now summer. He'd sent her flowers, written emails, left voicemail, and still hadn't heard back.

Perhaps she was deep inside her book, he thought. He respected other people's privacy but he missed her. He wanted to be with her. The possibility occurred to him that she was offended he'd left while she was sleeping. But he'd already explained to her that he needed time, that he needed her to be patient with him.

It had been a beautiful night. "What?" he'd asked, when she looked at him so deeply, disarming him. They were turned on their sides facing each other.

"I'm trying to fix your face in my mind. I want to recover the memory of it at will," she said running a finger down his nose.

"Do you ever stop thinking?"

"I find it hard to switch off," she laughed.

"What do you think about?"

"Outside of my son and Hamilton?"

"And the slaves and pirates and Nevis and Louisiana," Gabe said.

"You've bedded a very studious librarian," she conceded.

He slipped a finger into the ring of a curl that fell against her cheek.

"I think about death a lot."

"Why am I not surprised?"

She wrapped a leg around his hip. "What do you think will happen to us when we die?" Do you think our souls will live on?"

"I hope some part of us lives on. It would be such a waste if all the knowledge we accumulate over a lifetime is lost," he said.

"I know. It would be so sad for it to just evaporate."

"All that information about Alexander Hamilton needs to be in the ether."

"Ha ha."

She had a curious mind that wouldn't rest, that needed to be consoled with words, ideas, conversation. It was contrary to his taciturn nature, but full expression was something he was willing to learn to give her.

"You're so far away all the time, Gabriel. How will I ever get to know you if you don't let me in?"

Too much of this would undo him, turn him to liquid. He turned onto his back and stared at the ceiling.

"I hope you'll learn to tell me everything one day."

"Like what?"

"Like how did you get these marks on your neck. Your skin is so perfect otherwise."

"Never." Some things he buried to save his sanity.

"What kind of stunted love is this?" Angeline raised herself on an elbow. "I want to comfort you. I want comfort from you."

"It's all I've got."

"Give it to me," she said, as she straddled him.

"Don't you get lonely, Gabriel?" she asked, afterwards.

He was not used to articulating every thought. So much of him was unspoken. He worried about surrendering his interior self to her, the one of premeditation, the sharp knife lodged inside him that cut cleanly the way in front of him.

She clamped her leg high around him so he could feel the heat of her sex. Her eyelashes grazed his jaw. "I sometimes stand on a busy intersection and feel utterly alone, desolate. I have to remind myself that I am plugged into people I love. That there's a strong cord attached to my son, my mother, my sister. What about you? Do you have people who love you?

"I'm alone but not lonely. Work saves me."

"What do you do when you can't stand being alone?"

"The last time it happened, I called you."

Don't close your eyes, he had told her. He'd never said that to anyone after Farah. The gold streaks in her irises flared and receded, receded and flared. What struck him was her ferocious softness. She was quiet, laid back like a morning breeze, yet steely and intense.

He dialed her number. "Angeline?"

"Gabriel."

"Happy Birthday."

"I never told you about my birthday."

"It's on your Wikipedia."

"Thank you," she said, and slipped back into silence.

"I've missed you. I hoped that you'd return at least one of my calls."

"That's great revisionist history. You bolted first, like a thief in the night. I dove into the rabbit hole with my book after you left."

"I'm sorry."

"You should be. I was angry with you."

"Was means there's hope for me. Is your dance card full or can I see you tonight?"

"My dance card is non-existent," she sulked.

"My luck then. Be ready at seven. I'll send a carriage."

She accepted the invitation but then wondered if she was doing the right thing. She had been angry with him for the way he had left her the last time. But Eva's revelation had made her think of him differently. There were other notes to him, other complexities, and she just had to wait. Besides she was very lonely. She'd spent the whole month with a man, a brilliant man, who had taken everything from her and given nothing back. Alexander Hamilton was all consuming. But he couldn't keep her warm at night. She was excited about the date with Gabriel. She started getting ready at four.

She changed into a sleeveless white chiffon dress with a scoop neckline. The curls in her hair had tightened into spirals and corkscrews from the steam in the shower. Her face was gaunt. She had circles around her eyes from keeping late nights to get the already late manuscript to her publisher, and she had lost five pounds, all from her face, it seemed.

A few minutes before seven, Albert buzzed to say Angeline's ride was downstairs. Gabe had sent a town car for her. She wondered why he hadn't come himself. The driver turned the dial to a smooth jazz station as the car glided along Shoreland Drive. He drove to Azyl Square, turned right on the beach, and pulled up in front of a house on the Crescent. The driver led her up the stairs to the front door and rang the bell. Gabe himself opened it.

Thank you Mickal, he dismissed the driver and drew Angeline through the door. He was dressed in a teal shirt and black pants. He had an aftershave glow. He looked beautiful to her eyes.

"This is where you live?" Angeline allowed him to help her shed her silk coat.

"This is the house I bought to grow into," he hung the coat in a closet by the entryway.

The house was a spectacular shell.

"Wow, these floors are beautiful. And you don't believe in furniture?" she said looking around the room. There was a bean-shaped sofa, a coffee table, a plush rug in front of the fire, and a piano by the French doors leading out to a balcony overlooking the lake.

The coffee table held a cooler with a bottle of champagne, and a tray with petite quiche, crudités, and berries. She settled on one end of the sofa.

"Happy Birthday, Angeline," Gabe said, handing her a glass of the champagne, before taking the other end of the couch.

"I haven't forgiven you for running away from me."

"Don't give up on me. I need time."

"How long should I wait? How long will it take you to be with me?"

"I'm a fast learner. An autodidact."

"I won't wait forever, you know. So hurry up."

"I have something for you." He retrieved a gift bag sitting on the floor near him. He presented it to her, and sat down again.

"That's so thoughtful," she said retrieving the smaller of the packages from the bag. "What's this?" She opened the package. "Eu de Hadrian," she mulled the name.

"The perfumer was inspired by Youcenar's Memoirs."

"Ah! You saw the book!" she said.

"Open the other one," Gabriel said.

"Two presents. You're too lavish." She opened the second package. A book. The front cover was blank. She flipped it to look at the back cover, also blank. She was perplexed; she opened the book to locate a title. "What is this, Gabriel?"

"Alexander Hamilton's letters to Elizabeth Schuyler, and her responses. Do you have this compilation? " Gabe asked.

"Where did you get this!? How did you get this?" Angeline flipped through the pages and ran her fingers over the dates. "I thought that she burned all her letters! This is incredible Gabriel."

"The letters were in a private collection. They were willing to give me copies in return for a donation to Mrs. Hamilton's orphanage."

"The Graham Home?"

"Yes. I had two copies of the book pressed, one for you and one for the collector. "

"I can't imagine how much it cost."

"Stop talking about money."

"Such a beautiful gift, Gabriel." Angeline looked up at him.

Gabe watched her as she turned the pages and skimmed paragraphs. "Thank you for being so thoughtful," she looked up and closed the book. "If I don't stop now, you'll have to watch me read all night."

"Save it for tomorrow."

"I will." She set the book on the coffee table. "Do you play?" she nodded at the piano.

"No, but when I was a bum without a penny to my name, I just had this vision that I wanted a piano and that it would be positioned just so against French doors. It's the oddest thing since it's not anything that was culturally relevant to me. But it embodied everything I wanted in my life at eighteen when I was penniless. I don't know where I got this vision. Certainly not at the camp."

"Where was the camp? What was it called?" Angeline went into reporter mode. Her journalism training compelled her to probe, to press a finger against old scabs, scratch them.

Gabe wasn't sure he wanted to take the conversation back to the past. This was a part of his life nobody knew about. But he wanted to try to explain to her who he really was. "It was a UN refugee camp in Lebanon. Dbayeh," Gabe finally said.

"How old were you when you got there? When did you leave?"

"I was born there. I escaped when I was eighteen."

"What happened to your family?"

"My grandfather lost his mind. He sat with the other elders in the camp drinking arak. And when he came back to our concrete box, he drew maps on the floor and walls and ceilings with chalk and paint."

"What kind of maps?"

"Of Iqrit and Kafr Birim and all the other villages in Galilee that the Israelis took in '48. As if drawing maps would make the villages real again. The maps were detailed. My mother said he drew the houses as they stood before the Israelis leveled Iqrit."

"Your grandfather wasn't mad. He was a cartographer. A historian. He did the right thing. He was sealing memories like in those Paleolithic cave paintings. He was documenting those lost villages for the future. For posterity," she said. "Where's your family now?"

"Dead. My mother, aunts, and grandfather. I buried them in Iqrit."

"You took them home."

"Yes."

"What about your father?"

"I can't say too much about him. Only that he joined the resistance."

"Is he alive?"

"He's one of the leaders. If he dies, it will be major news."

"He's with Hezbollah? Or Fatah?"

"No, he smuggled himself into Gaza through Rafah."

"Hamas then?"

"I've already told you too much. Don't ask me anything more."

"I don't blame him. He has nothing to lose."

"He has his life to lose. He's a high value target for Mossad. He's on their playing card deck. I read recently that they blew up his second lieutenant with a cellphone. They told him his son was on the phone and when he picked up they detonated it. His head exploded. I'm hoping they won't do that with my father. Tell him I'm on the phone and blow him up."

"Gabriel. My God! How do you stay sane?"

"Who said I'm sane?"

Prejudice is a safe default position, Angeline thought. Judging someone is easy, effortless. But how do you deal with someone who has dimensions, secrets, fears, a withheld self, a self that grows and expands and shifts and changes and surprises. She had so much to learn.

Chapter 27

GOING HOME

August 31, 2016. Gate 6, Dabolim Airport, Goa. Nila couldn't wait to go home. India was incredible. India was impossible. Nila was ready to go home. She thought about her house on the Crescent. She imagined walking through the antique wood door, casting her eyes over her favorite pieces of furniture, checking the blooms on her orchids. She imagined sinking back into her life, waking up with Rae in their bed under the skylight, doing sun salutations on the deck, replenishing the bird feeders, scheduling Twin Flames interviews, meeting Rae for lunch, visiting her children at work, walking the grounds of the Baha'i Temple to admire the stone masonry, shopping, picking herbs from her garden, cooking elaborate meals for her family, stewarding them towards conversation, talking to her parents and Arun. And she thought of the work ahead of her. Both Zara and Hari had told Rae they were ready to go back to school either in Fall or Spring. She'd have to help them. She was eager to find out if Tina and Bruce's relationship had blossomed into a romance. She'd organize a double date as soon as she and Rae rebounded from jetlag. She wanted to bring Roger and Eva, the mystic and the healer, together. They would be a perfect couple—twin flames.

Nila studied her husband and her children. They were sitting next to her at the Air India gate, empty seats between them. After two weeks near the Equator, Rae, Zara, and Hari had turned a deep shade of almond. They looked utterly delicious and somehow unfamiliar. She wanted to taste them, hold them in her mouth like Eucharist. Hari undid his carryon to retrieve his electronics. Zara pulled out three Booker Prize-winning novels by Indian writers. A girl's reach must exceed her grasp or else what's heaven for? Both kids plugged their ears with noise cancelling headphones and stared into space. Rae reached over for a kiss.

The Oberois had begun their train journey through India, two weeks earlier, from Goa's Curchorem Railway Station. A crew of men wearing gold and saffron *kurtas* and Nehru jackets with gold epaulets greeted them as they entered the Moving Palace. The special railcar was hitched to the Konkan commuter train that made the two day trek from Goa to Kanyakumari, the southern most tip of India. The train was a surfliner, it ran parallel to the Arabian Sea. They saw coconuts bobbing in the water, children in tattered clothes playing with deflated balls and boats made of coconut husks, elephants with elaborately painted faces and trunks standing like high priests outside temples, stooped old women, men everywhere. In Karwar, they alighted the train at night to watch a Kathkali dance show. In Mangalore, they toured the old port and took pictures. They stopped at Murudeshwar to visit a sari palace and a spice plantation. In Cochin, they went to Chinatown, and in Thiruvananthapuram, they visited the burial site of the Apostle Thomas and took a short cruise on a houseboat. They arrived in Kanyakumari, land's end where the Arabian Sea, the Bay of Bengal, and the Indian Ocean flowed into each other.

They flew back from Trivandrum to Goa to spend four days there before their flight home via Frankfurt. They stayed in a colonial style heritage hotel with walls painted in mustard gold and brown plantation shutters. They visited Old Town to see its Portuguese architecture and the grounds once stomped by Vasco da Gama. A guide gave them a private tour of Bom Jesus Basilica that housed the remains of St. Francis Xavier. They looked up at the mausoleum, a gift from Cosimo Medici, carved by Florentine sculptor, Giovanni Foggini. It was made of jasper and brown marble and set in three tiers, a base, the mausoleum, and a casket hand-tooled by Goan silversmiths. The Oberois looked at each other with expressionless faces as the guide told them how the Church hacked off Xavier's body parts, more than two hundred pieces, fingers, toes, arms, organs, slices of limbs and torso to distribute to Catholic churches all over the world.

"I can't believe what Catholics do to dead bodies" Nila said afterwards, as they dined on curried crab and shrimp, brought to shore from a boat, and cooked over an open fire.

"So gross," said Zara, sucking on a crab leg.

"Wonder where his penis is." Hari said.

"Eeew!" Zara said.

"Probably in the pedophile wing of the Vatican," Nila said.

"He was a criminal. The Goa Inquisition was heinous.," Rae said.

"Yet Indians venerate him. How can they not know history?" Nila said, wiping her mouth with a napkin.

Rae and Nila made love that night, under the mosquito nets, over the rose petals.

You are my church, he said.

You are my religion, she said.

It was close to seven in the evening, the sky began to change colors. Zara looked down from the second floor balcony of her room at tourists. Westerners lounged like royalty thanks to the exchange rate in their favor. She saw young waiters, slim brownies like her, delicate boned, handsome men dressed in maroon bush jackets and matching pants, dancing attendance to obese Europeans exposing without shame, beer paunches, sagging breasts, butt cheeks in thongs.

The world isn't fair, she thought. The brown person gets screwed both ways. They're pressed into servitude wherever they are, both at home and abroad. She looked at the young men bending, bowing, kowtowing to new adventurers from Plovdiv and Varna, Moscow and Leningrad, St. Petersburg and Novosibirsk. They're expatriates wherever they go, we're always immigrants. Not fair.

She ordered room service of chicken cafreal with saffron rice and mango ice-cream even though she wasn't hungry. She and her parents and Hari had eaten a hefty lunch on the beach and decided to skip dinner.

"Room service, Ma—" the waiter caught himself. She wasn't a madam by any definition. He placed the tray on the coffee table, handed her a leather folio with the tab, stood with his fingers clasped in front of him, looked through downturned eyes and the frill of his eyelashes at her gorgeous legs. After a long shift of looking at blotchy pink sunburned skin and cellulite, he found her spellbinding. She was Indian like him, in her twenties like him, same coffee color skin like him.

"They're making you run around," she said, nodding towards the window. "Rishi," she read his name tag.

"It's my job," he said. Resignation was an essential part of sanity. He being Indian knew what it took to brace the self, accept things, expect nothing. It was Americans like her who had a problem, who wanted too much.

"What does Rishi mean?"

He looked down at his name tag. "Something stupid."

"It's a beautiful name."

She signed for the order and added a ridiculously large tip on the tab.

"Don't you want to get away from everything? Tell them what to do with themselves?" she asked, holding the folio to her chest in the x of her crossed arms.

"This is the best hotel in Goa. We get five star racists instead of two star racists, so I take it," he said. He needed that folio in order to receive his tip. He reached for it. She drew it behind her, drew his hand holding the folio behind her, wrapped his arm around her.

"Don't go." She touched his face, felt the hollow under his cheek, touched his lips, thick and pouty, that pleased her so. "Stay. Lay your hands on me."

The sky behind him, over his shoulders, turned orange, then blood red. She felt brave enough to do anything.

"The world is upside down," he whispered, stepping closer, cupping a breast.

"No. It's upright and perfect," she said, leaning into him. Something important needed to happen. She found him under his clothes.

"Slow down." he said.

But she couldn't. She wanted what she wanted. Quickly, before things changed. The dying sun dipped and hovered, hovered and dipped, over the Arabian Sea beyond him. They moved to a raga only they could hear. They fell inside her desire, they dove inside his want, ascending, descending, rising, falling. He shuddered. *Aww tuzo mog kortha*, he said. She cried.

Hari met four IDF soldiers on R&R, dispatched from Gaza to Goa to recover from Operation Protective Edge. They were no older than he was. They invited him to Ravers Club on Tito Street. "We can shoot up." "I don't do heroin or cystal but I'll try something else." They paid the door fee, bought a round of beer and listened to a middling band play a terrible rendition of Radiohead's *Creep*. They drifted to a row of video game machines and played Mortal Kombat and Chiller. They asked the bartender for tokens for the machines, ignoring a bevy of pretty blonde Australian girls hanging out at the bar.

"What the fuck is wrong with you guys? Those girls are prizes. Get over there and do me proud," the bartender said.

"Eh, Meh. Not impressed," one of the soldiers said.

"We're looking for what's good," another said.

"Look for the Tamil Rasta." The bartender made a hitchhiker's thumb and pointed at the back.

They walked out the backdoor and into the alley. A man wearing dreadlocks, garish tie-dye shirt, and tattered jeans ripped at the knees and thighs, beckoned them with a sideways tilt of his head. The soldiers and Hari followed the man. He ducked behind a high brick wall. They followed. The wall provided cover for a row of outdoor urinals. After a five minute negotiation in two accents, the soldiers asked for the works—heroin, syringes, swabs, spoons. Hari requested two MDMA pills. The man left and returned five minutes later with the goods and distributed them. The soldiers sat down in a circle and shot up. Hari stood next to the Rasta and swallowed the tablets. Hari went back into the bar and waited for the giant wave. When it came, he surfed it. He felt all of him disappear except for his heart which felt like an organ of love. Warmth and kindness washed over him. He felt love, for the girls at the bar, for the soldiers, for the bartender, for his family, for all humanity. He gave a beatific smile to the girls. I, You, We, God. LOVE. He felt his heart would explode with pure, unadulterated joy.

When he roused from the altered state hours later, he found himself lying face down near the outdoor urinal. He retched into a vessel and stumbled to the bar to find the soldiers. The band was playing a second show and *Creep* sounded even worse. He gave up looking for the soldiers and walked back to the hotel. He remembered all the times he'd come out of a drug high and found himself alone, his homies, bros, dawgs, crew, posse long gone. "You need to give this shit up loser," he thought.

Nila had chosen first class both ways. For the thirteen hour flight from Goa to Frankfurt via Mumbai, she selected lounge seats that converted into full length beds. The seats were three feet wide, upholstered in supple leather with mahogany wood accents. The backs of the seats rose a foot above the head into gently sloping wings for a measure of privacy. At seven thousand dollars a seat, there were few takers and the rest of the cabin was empty. But instead of spreading out to the rest of the cabin and sitting separately, the Oberois remained where they were, since the first row had unencumbered legroom. She took the window seat on the left next to Rae. Hari sat across the wide aisle from Rae, Zara next to him..

"You happy with the trip, Raja?" Nila asked. Vacation is a kind of work, she felt very tired, achy.

"Yes, I'm very happy you made us do this. You did a great job as impresario. Everything ran like clockwork. I got to be with you without work in front of me. And I got to know my kids."

"What do you think of them, Rae?"

"They're good kids. They're beginning to please me. Zara. What a piece of work she is. The apple doesn't fall far from a tree. So much of you in her. She's very smart. Has great business instincts. I think we've got a tech entrepreneur on our hands. I'm going to enjoy helping her develop."

"Don't let Zara get everything of you. Hari needs you more," Nila said.

"I know. He's lost. Frightened of how to be. I need to figure out how to give him confidence, how to help him claim his space, to stop being hesitant."

“Will they make it?”

“They’ll both make it, with some guidance,” Rae assured her.

Rae would soon be pulled back into his business empire. Where would he find the time for the children? “From Bruce, you mean?” she said, as she shifted in her seat and adjusted the angle of her torso.

“From me, Nila. They need a father.”

“This is all I wanted to hear,” she clutched his hand, then retracted her arm to recline her seat.

Nila knew that it would be the last time Zara and Hari would allow themselves to be children. They’d go back to school, they’d find their lives, and they’d be gone. Life churned like a water wheel, and soon there would be another generation. She couldn’t wait to meet her grandchildren. She wanted a gaggle of Hari’s and Zara’s kids running around her kitchen, clutching the paloo of her sari, burying their heads in the sari pleats, straddling her while holding her shoulders as if they owned her body. She’d be a perfect grandmother, she decided. Her grandsons would always remember the kisses she placed on their foreheads that would make them know tenderness, her granddaughters would never forget the spunk she ingrained in them. She’d teach the girls to be American, bust the balls of any man who tried to control them. **Nila Waz ‘Ere, Yo!** These are her descendants. Don’t mess with them.

Four hours out of Mumbai, Nila opened her eyes, turned to Rae, and said, “I feel so tired.”

“You should be tired. All that planning took it out of you. Go back to sleep. Do you want the bed turned down? When you wake up we’ll be halfway home,” Rae patted her hand, as he stared at the screen showing the plane’s forward thrust to Frankfurt. He decided that instead of reading or watching a movie or listening to music, he'd do nothing. He had everyone he loved next to him. He couldn't think of anything else he needed.

Nila turned her body towards his and lay her head on the slope of his arm. She started breathing heavily. Rae stroked her cheek with his hand to calm her and kissed her on the top of her head. "You're okay. Just go to sleep."

"Baby, I'm in trouble," she moaned and sat up. Her eyes were wide, frightened, she clutched her chest. She groaned. Her heart was doing thunderclaps. It was not a localized pain near the heart but in her whole chest. She could feel a hum in her ears that matched the drone of the plane's engines. She felt sluggish. When she tried to lift an arm, it felt heavy like a hundred pound weight.

"Nila," he cried. "What's wrong?" he put an arm around her, reached for the button to recline her seat, touched her forehead to check for fever.

"What's wrong with Mom?" Zara cried from the opposite aisle seat. She shook Hari who was watching a Bollywood action film. "Mom!" Hari yanked the buds off his ears and jumped out of his seat.

Nila's eyes were closed, a tendril of hair over her right cheek quivered from the belt of air from the overhead fan. Her body was a calm lake.

Rae pushed the bell on his armrest. An attendant came forward, a tall, thin woman with long lashes—ambling. Rae couldn't find the words to explain. "My wife," he said.

Hari and Zara stood next to the attendant. "I'm the purser," a uniformed crewmember joined them.

"It's a medical emergency. Can we turn back?" Rae asked.

"We're halfway between Mumbai and Frankfurt. Half a dozen of one, six of the other," the purser said. "We're trained in CPR. Please make room."

"Get the defibrillator," Hari told the attendant. "There are four hundred Indians on this plane, there must be at least one doctor on board. Can you make an announcement?" he called after her.

Rae and the purser unfolded the tray tables between Nila's and Rae's seats, turned down the armrests, and stretched Nila's body across the width of the makeshift bed, her head at the window, her feet near the aisle. A flight attendant announced the call for a doctor several times. No doctor appeared.

"What's wrong with Mom?" Zara was in tears.

"She needs to be on the floor," Hari said, getting on his knees between the purser by the window and his father near the aisle, and slipping his arms under his mother's lower back

Rae and the purser lifted her from the seats and placed her on the floor. Hari held her body in the bow of his hands until it touched the floor. Nila's lips were purple. He held his fingers under her nose and felt her pulse. She was unconscious but breathing.

The purser knelt next to Hari and started chest compressions on Nila.

"You've got to tilt her chin and head back to unblock the airways." Hari raised his mother's chin, opened her mouth and swept a finger across her tongue to make sure it hadn't folded.

"Are you certified?" the purser asked, pressing down on Nila's chest.

"Yes, hands only and mouth to mouth."

"When did you do it?" the purser kept pushing down on Nila's chest.

"Last year." Hari had taken the course because he and his friends were deep in the drug scene, trying every chemical, heroin, crystal meth, and cocaine, and he wanted to be prepared in case somebody OD'd.

"Take over. My methods are dated," the purser said.

Hari placed his laced hands over the purser's. Both of them pumped before the purser withdrew his hands for Hari to continue the compressions on his own. His father had shut down; he was in shock. His kneeling body was there, but his brain wasn't. He held Nila's feet. The night before, Nila had placed a foot on Rae's crotch. She was showing off her newly pedicured toenails: fuchsia with rhinestone decorations radiating from the center, set off by silver rings on the middle toes, the feet from toes to ankles painted in henna in an intricate lacework . "I feel like a royal concubine," she said seductively. "Come here my favored courtesan, my harlot," he had replied and pulled her on top of him. She was ravenous.

"Mom, it's going to be okay. Dad, Zara, come closer. See, Mom, we're all here." Hari kept pumping. Sweat and tears, oily and thick, ran down his face and stung his eyes. His back was soaked, the thin shirt he was wearing heavy with protein and lipids.

Nila's eyelids fluttered, her breathing winding down like the end of a long day. "Defibrillator! Now!" he screamed.

The attendant handed Hari a yellow kit with a handle that looked like a child's toy. His mother's lips were blue. He had to hurry. He opened the AED and a friendly male voice he recognized issued familiar instructions. He pulled out a plastic pouch from a sleeve in the cover, tore it open, and lay its contents on the seat in front of him. Gloves, scissors, razor, towel. He pulled on a pair of surgical gloves, grabbed a pair of blunt scissors, and cut Nila's jersey top off her. He wiped the sweat off his face with his sleeve and cut his mother's bra at the center front gore. The two cups separated to reveal his mother's breasts, the areolae light purple and beaded with perspiration. He wiped her chest with the towel to make sure the surface was free from sweat, and peeled the plastic seals away from the shock pads. He placed one pad above Nila's left breast and the other below her right breast bone. He waited for the AED to assess his mother's heartbeat and to prepare to administer a shock. "Dad, take your hands off Mom. Pull back." Nila's body heaved off the floor from the shock. The voice issued a command to administer CPR and mouth to mouth.

Hari pressed down, over and over. He alternated with mouth to mouth. Tears ran down his cheeks. "Stay with me, Mom," he tried to will his mother back to consciousness. Nila's breathing flat lined. The AED administered another shock and Hari continued alternating between hands and mouth-to-mouth CPR. "Mom, don't go. Stay."

Rae put his hand on his Hari's shoulder. "Stop, son."

Zara sobbed, as she stood next to Rae.

The attendant returned from the crew area, a few minutes later, with an unzipped body bag and lay it on Nila's seat. "Help me, Dad," Hari instructed his father. Together, they lifted Nila back onto the seat and worked the bag around her legs, her torso, her arms, as if they were dressing her. Hari zipped up the bag up to her neck and pulled the oxygen mask down from its holder and placed it over her mouth. Hari fastened the safety belt around his mother's waist and pressed the recline button of the seat until it was set at the same angle as Nila's favorite Eames lounger. He stretched his mother's legs out in front of her.

"Do you wish to move to the rows behind you?" the purser asked the family. "She can remain where she is." Sitting next to the dead was not a rare phenomenon. But they were lucky there were so many empty seats.

Rae and Hari declined. Zara remained where she was, because what would her father and brother have thought of her if she had vacated her seat? They sat in stunned silence, enclosed in their seats. Hari stared at the blank video screen in front of him. Zara wailed.

"You should both take this," Rae offered a sleeping pill each to Hari and Zara. Hari declined. Zara took hers and allowed Rae to recline her seat into a bed. He covered her with a blanket and watched her drop into a slumber.

"Son."

"No," Hari turned his head into the wing of the chair.

Rae returned to his seat. He reclined it and spread a blanket over himself and Nila. Her body folded itself into Rae as naturally as it had done all the years he had been with her. Please make it so that she's just tired, Rae prayed for the first time in his life, even as he saw an unfamiliar stone begin to settle under her luminous skin. He brushed a dribble of saliva from the corner of her mouth with the palm of his hand and a tear on her cheek with a finger. Her face already set like marble looked pained at the leaving. She wouldn't have left him and the children willingly.

Chapter 28

ADIEU

July 4, 1804

This letter, my very dear Eliza, will not be delivered to you, unless I shall first Have terminated my earthly career; to begin, as I humbly hope from redeeming grace and divine mercy, a happy immortality.

If it had been possible for me to have avoided the interview, my love for you and my precious children would have been alone a decisive motive. But it was not possible, without sacrifices, which would have rendered me unworthy of your esteem. I need not tell you of these pangs I feel, from the idea of quitting you and exposing you to the anguish, which I know you would feel. Nor could I dwell on the topic lest it should unman me.

The consolations of Religion, my beloved, can alone support you; and these you have the right to enjoy. Fly to the bosom of your God and be comforted. With my last idea; I shall cherish the sweet hope of meeting you in a better world.

Adieu best of wives and best of Women. Embrace all my darling Children for me,

Ever yours

AH

March 29, 1802

Dear Sir

I felt all the weight of the obligation, which I owed to you and to your amiable family, for the tender concern they manifested in an event, beyond comparison, the most afflicting of my life. But I was obliged to wait for a moment of greater calm, to express my sense of the kindness.

My loss is indeed great. The highest as well as the eldest hope of my family has been taken from me. You estimated him rightly—He was truly a fine youth. But why should I repine? It was the will of heaven; and he is now out of reach of the seductions and calamities of a world, full of folly, full of vice, full of danger—of least value in proportion as it is best known. I firmly trust also that he has safely reached the haven of eternal repose and felicity.

You will easily imagine that every memorial of the goodness of his heart must be precious to me. You allude to one recorded in a letter to your son. If no special reasons forbid it, I should be very glad to have a copy of that letter.

Mrs. Hamilton, who has drunk deeply of the cup of sorrow, joins me in affectionate thanks to Mrs. Rush and yourself, Our wishes for your happiness will be unceasing.

Very sincerely & cordially Yrs.

A. Hamilton

July 10, 1804

My beloved Eliza

... This is my second letter. The Scruples of a Christian have determined me to expose my own life to any extent rather than subject my self to the guilt of taking the life of another. This must increase my hazards & redoubles my pangs for you. But you had rather I should die innocent than live guilty. Heaven can preserve me and I humbly hope will but in the contrary event, I charge you to remember that you are a Christian. God's Will be done. The will of a merciful God must be good.

Once more, Adieu My Darling darling Wife

`A H

Chapter 29

BREAKABLE

Nila's funeral and the internment of her ashes took place at the Baha'i Temple. A registered member and generous donor to the temple for more than a decade, Nila, who rarely attended services, was well known to members of both the local and national Spiritual Assembly. But the Baha'i faith required a body to be buried within one hour of the place of death—to discourage the soul from being attached to one geographic place. Nila's brother, Arun, implored leaders of the assemblies to waive the requirement for burial on technical grounds. He asked them to consider aeronautics and the speed at which she was traveling. He argued that since Nila was flying across the earth at 700 miles per hour, her soul could not have attached itself to any particular place. The members of the two assemblies, in consultation with the international governing council of their Universal House of Justice, agreed to make an exception in her case. They gave their approval for the funeral rites to be performed at the temple and for her ashes to be buried in the cemetery grounds.

According to Nila's will, set in a codicil a fortnight before the flight to India, she expressed her wish that upon her death, she be cremated and that her ashes be mixed with the seeds of a tree and placed in the ground. Once the tree had grown to its full stature, she asked that a wooden bench be positioned under it. She stated that she found death unreasonable and funerals insufferable, and that her funeral should be a celebration of her life rather than a lamentation.

She expressed her strong aversion to black, navy blue, and gray, and asked that everyone attending her funeral come dressed in bright, colorful clothes—that they come dressed as if to an Indian wedding. She selected a reading from Kierkegaard to be read by the circle around her grave, as she was lowered to her final resting place.

Nadia, David, Sophie, and Cris, dressed in confectionary colors, escorted people to their pews. Jeanie, Jehan, and Roger wore *kameez* and *kurtas* from Whole World Style. Tina wearing a pink *ao di* burst into tears when she spotted Rae and the children. Cris held Tina around the shoulders and led her to a seat next to Gabe, Eva, and Bruce. A dozen of Nila's clients arrived at the temple with their twin flames and children, all dressed in bright colors. The Baha'i congregation of fifty were dressed similarly. Rae's parents were absent. His mother had called from a holiday resort in St. Lucia two days earlier, after Arun had sent her the news. Should I come back? she had asked Rae. Don't trouble yourself, Rae had said, and slammed the phone down. His father had asked if he could come the following week as he was on a cigar factory tour in Cuba. Don't bother, Rae said.

Decked out in jewel-toned traditional Indian garments, Arun and his family, Nila's parents, and various relatives, sat in the front pews with Rae and the children. Hari wore an electric blue kurta with white pants and Zara wore one of Nila's favorite saris, a sea foam green chiffon with embroidered silver sea horses and shells. Rae wore a *sherwani,* the embroidered gold long frock coat, garnet red pants, shawl, and turban that he had worn two decades earlier to marry Nila. She was eighteen. Her parents had wanted her to complete her education first; they had pressed her to wait. "Why should I wait? I already know what I want." The wedding had been a simple affair by Indian standards. It took place on a farm in Madison. Rae and Nila recited in unison the words to complete the seven steps of the Saptapadi as they walked slowly around dancing flames in a sunken firepit.

Now let us make a vow together. We shall share love, share the same food, share our strengths, share the same tastes. We shall be of one mind, we shall observe the vows together. I shall be the Samaveda, you the Rigveda; I shall be the Upper World, you the Earth; I shall be the Sukhilam, you the Holder - together we shall live and beget children, and other riches; come thou to me! We have taken the Seven Steps. You have become mine forever. Yes, we have become partners. I have become yours. Hereafter, I cannot live without you. Do not live without me. Let us share the joys. We are word and meaning, united. You are thought and I am sound. May the night be honey-sweet for us. May the morning be honey-sweet for us. May the earth be honey-sweet for us. May the heavens be honey-sweet for us. May the plants be honey-sweet for us. May the sun be all honey for us. May the cows yield us honey-sweet milk. As the heavens are stable, as the earth is stable, as the mountains are stable, as the whole universe is stable, so may our union be permanently settled."

The funeral rites were simple with a member of the Spiritual Assembly reciting the Baha'i Prayer for the Dead.

O my God! This is Thy handmaiden and the daughter of Thy handmaiden who hath believed in Thee and in Thy signs, and set her face towards Thee, wholly detached from all except Thee. Thou art, verily, of those who show mercy the most merciful. Deal with her, as beseemeth the heaven of Thy bounty and the ocean of Thy grace. Grant her admission within the precincts of Thy transcendent mercy that was before the foundation of earth and heaven. There is no God but Thee, the Ever-Forgiving, the Most Generous.

Flanked by four leaders of the Spiritual Assembly, Roger and Jehan, carried the wooden box bearing the ashes, small as a child's casket, to the gated cemetery behind the temple. Rae, Zara,

Hari, Arun and his parents walked behind the pallbearers. Bruce, Tina, Gabe, and the rest of the funeral procession fell into step behind them.

For his sister who had never settled for drab, Arun chose the seeds of a new strain of Japanese maple that would reach fifteen feet. In Spring, reddish purple flowers would bloom in umbels with lime green stems. In Fall, samaras would ripen and the tree's deeply cut leaves would turn yellow, red, purple, bright crimson, and bronze, like so many degrees of a sunrise.

They gathered around the plot, a dug out circle in the ground, four feet in diameter and two feet deep, with mounds of earth piled around it. Zara and Hari flanked Rae and held his hands. The others stood further back. Roger held the chest open as Jehan lifted the urn out of it and handed it to Arun. A groundsman wearing overalls held up a large biodegrable vase that held the maple seeds. Arun poured the ashes into the vase and held his hands out to receive the vase. The groundsman stepped into the hole, took the vase from Arun, and placed it in the center of the circle. After the groundsman hoisted himself out of the hole, he picked up his shovel. Everyone gathered around the hole and closed the loop around the Oberois. Arun signaled Tina to begin the reading as everyone picked up fistfuls of earth and began to drop it into the hole.

Tina opened a book to a page marked by a ribbon. "What is it that makes a person strong, stronger than the whole world, or so weak as to be weaker than a child? What is it that makes a person firm, firmer than a cliff, or yet so soft as to be softer than wax? It is love," Tina read and passed the book to Bruce.

"What is older than everything? What is it that outlives everything? What is it that cannot be taken away but itself takes it all? What is it that cannot be given but itself gives everything? It is love," Bruce read and passed the book to Eva.

"What is it that stands fast when everything falters? What is it that comforts when other comforts fail? What is it that remains when everything is changed? What is it that abides when what is imperfect is done away with? It is love," Eva read and passed the book to Gabe.

Rae allowed his children to hold on to him, didn't flinch when Zara lay her head on his shoulder. Didn't inch away when Hari wrapped an arm around his back. But he wanted to jump into that hole, curl up like a baby in a womb, his knees up to his chest, and stop breathing.

"What is it that does not cease when visions come to an end? What is it that makes everything clear when the dark saying has been spoken? What is it that bestows blessing on the excess of the gift? What is it that never alters even if all things alter? It is love." Gabe read and passed the book to Sophie. Sophie, Cris, Jeanie, Jehan and the others continued reading until the groundsman had shoveled the mounds of earth to refill the hole.

July 14, 1804, New York, New York. Guns fired from the Battery, church bells rang with a doleful sound, and ships in the harbor flew their colors at half-mast. Around noon, to the somber thud of military drums, New York militia units set out at the head of the funeral procession, bearing their arms in reversed position, their muzzles pointed downward. Numerous clergymen and members of the Society of Cincinnati trooped behind them. Preceded by two small black boys in white turbans, eight pallbearers shouldered Hamilton's corpse, set in a rich mahogany casket with his hat and his sword perched on top. Hamilton's gray horse trailed behind with the boots and spurs of its former rider reversed in the stirrups. Then the cortage followed. Collectively, they symbolized the richly diversified ... mosaic that Hamilton had envisaged for America. So huge was the throng of mourners that the procession streamed on for two hours before the last marchers arrived at Trinity Church. Not a smile was visible, and hardly a whisper was to be heard, but tears were seen rolling down the cheeks of the affected multitudes.

Two months after the funeral, Rae had still not returned to work. He left management of Raj Cabs to his senior team, his CFO, and his personal assistant. He communicated with them via email. He didn't want to speak, as if the simple act of uttering words would reveal his existence in a world without Nila. He didn't know how long his heart would hold out. He cried a lot when he was alone, so he didn't have to in front of his children.

He woke up each morning and instinctively put out his hand to feel the flesh of his wife. Sometimes, he took the decorative bolster that lay across the width of the bed and placed it vertically next to him, so that he could pretend that she was lying next to him. He kept his morning beach routine. Even though he woke up with raw grief, the daily walks through the dunes, the sunrise over the lake, the birds, the marram grass, the water—still as glass sometimes and then wild like galloping horses—helped rinse his bleeding heart. He didn't feel stable in the world. Nila had explained him, had given his life a size and a shape and a meaning. He no longer felt lucky. Nila had been his home, his hearth. He had lived inside her rooms. He felt homeless once more.

After he returned from his walks, he prepared breakfast for himself and his children. Zara was fragile, she had stopped going to Silicon Curry. After breakfast, she went upstairs and locked herself in her room until lunchtime. Hari went to Geek Patel everyday because he couldn't bear to look at his broken family. He called Rae and Zara several times during the day to check in, and returned from the shop at midday to have lunch with Zara or Rae, or both of them.

Rae drove to the temple cemetery every day after lunch to lay flowers or set tea lights at Nila's grave. The tree was five feet tall by November. In December, he saw a hard sheet of ice in the tree bed and wept. He walked over to the groundskeeper's utility cart and returned with a shovel. He cleared the snow off the rectangular bed and wiped the grave stone plaque with the sleeve of his coat. He dug the snow out of the decorative urns on each side of the tree with his gloved hands and arranged the garnet gerber daisies inside each vase. He breathed clouds of vapor and licked the salt of tears and sweat from his upper lip. On his way out of the cemetery, he instructed the groundskeeper to keep Nila's grave clear of snow and ice. "I don't want her to be cold."

Gabe stopped by at the house to see Rae after multiple emails, texts, and phone calls went unanswered.

"I just wanted to check in," Gabe said, as soon as Rae opened the door.

"I'm fine."

"Can I come in?"

"I'm fine Gabe. I'll call you if I need anything," he shut the door.

Gabe called Eva. "Rae is drowning. You'll know what to do."

Eva, in yoga clothes and wrapped in a prayer shawl, appeared at Rae's front door early the next day, carrying an open wicker basket of fruit in one hand and a tote hung over her shoulder.

"Rae?" she searched his face.

"I was just going for my walk," he looked down at his shoes. There is an ugliness and jealousy entwined with grief that only the grieving know. When they see someone unaffiliated to their grief, a repulsive thought rises to the surface of their minds. "Why are you alive?" "Why do you get to live?" "What makes you so special?" "What right do you have to breathe?"

"May I set this in your kitchen and walk with you?" she raised the basket. "It's for the kids."

Rae took the hamper from her and placed it on the kitchen counter. He shut the door behind them and walked in front of her, down the stone stairway to the beach and lake. Eva held the tails of her shawl and walked behind him. He walked faster to put distance between them. The pebbles crunched under his feet. She didn't try to match her pace with his. She held back. She would let him lead, she would accompany him. She trailed behind him as he did a loop around the pier's lighthouse and walked north on the beach. He walked all the way to the end of the lake where sand ended and a barricade of boulders began. When he turned to head back south, Eva kept walking north to the boulders. She turned back and trailed him. Their feet ground and crunched sand, pebble, and gravel. He entered the bird landing strip where the marram grew, staggered, dropped to his knees and doubled over.

Eva ran towards Rae and sank to the ground beside him.

"I don't want to take this anymore," he groaned. She braced his shoulders with her hands. She held him and rocked him. She knew she could offer him no words to transmute his sorrow, no medicine to still his pain. All she could do was give him her presence and retreat when he gave her a sign. It would be a long winter. He raised himself from the ground, kneeled on his haunches, and looked up at the sky.

"I can't go on." Tears ran down his cheeks.

Eva closed her arms and the two ends of shawl around him. It was how she would get him through it.

Chapter 30

DEDICATION

The Elders Council received formal approvals for the name change from the city authorities in February. The Council, minus Rae who was still in seclusion, decided that the street light pole banners emblazoned with the new name should be rushed to the printers and hung as soon as possible. Since most of the merchants on the Square shortened their hours or remained closed on Tuesdays, the Council organized the banner hanging for a Tuesday afternoon, when business mostly ground to a halt.

Bruce and his crew assumed the task of hanging the printed banners. Bruce lifted a box of banners from the back of his SUV and placed them on the pavement next to City Realty. He unfurled a banner with the new name and handed it to Lev, his head janitor. Lev's brother, Zve, held on to an aluminum ladder leaning against the lamp pole. Bruce watched Lev's slow arthritic crawl up the ladder. The routine morning shots of Bloody Mary did not equip Lev with the necessary speed and dexterity. Each time Lev placed a foot on a ladder rung, he flailed about, and exclaimed "Oy Oy," and "Manish Tanah." A constellation of red tilaks on foreheads, the Dot Heads, gathered around Bruce. Malik and Kumar greeted Bruce with a fist bump and a dap. The rest of the boys looked up at Lev with concern.

"Lev, come on down before you break a bone," Bruce shouted. To the boys, he said more softly, "He's going to break his bloomin' arse." The boys cackled.

"You kids get up there and show me your stuff." He pulled banner scrolls out of the box, two at a time, and handed them to each of the Dot Heads. He tasked Lev and Zvi with rounding up more ladders from the merchants. The boys worked in pairs, one positioning the ladder and stabilizing it, while the other climbed it to hang the flags. Bruce walked up and down the block to supervise the boys, handing them more banners to hang. "I'm putting some money on this. First one who hangs ten banners gets a twenty."

"You're a pushover, you should have lowballed with a fiver," Tina Trang came out of City Realty to watch the production.

"I wanted to incentify them," Bruce acknowledged Tina with a nod.

"How are you?" Tina looked up at the Dot Heads.

"Still reeling. I loved that woman. You?"

"Same. I lost my friend, my sister, the director of my life."

Bruce dispensed motivational advise to the boys. Kumar, if you pull your pants up, you'll win the race. Anil stop showing compassion, it slows you down.

"You're good with kids," Tina said.

"I get them. That age, man-boys, tough on the outside, shuddering on the inside."

When all the signs were duly hung, Bruce thanked them, handed each of them crisp twenty dollar bills from his wallet, and invited them to lunch. "What do you guys feel like?" Tina?"

"Bibimbap," they shouted in a chorus.

"That's a great idea," Tina said.

"What the fuck is that?" Bruce asked.

The Dot Heads walked ahead of Bruce and Tina, leading the way to the Korean diner.

"How do you like the name? As a realtor?" Bruce asked.

"I love it. It's so perfect," she said.

They walked on the Square past Mehta's, past Whole World Style. Bruce stopped. "What?" Tina looked at Bruce and then at the store.

"I met Nila here for the first time."

"So sad. I don't understand God. She shed light wherever she went. They loved each other and the kids. It's not fair!"

"There's no God. It's all random. She was one of the most beautiful people put on this earth."

"Yes she was," Trang said.

"You looking in on Rae? I'm tending to the kids but I'm not who Rae needs right now," Bruce said.

"He's shut me out. The only person he lets in is Eva."

The boys were already at the counter of the diner when Bruce and Tina entered. Bruce took charge of the order, while Tina claimed two tables side by side with benches. Vin, Anil, and Kumar ferried the food from the counter to the table, as Malik, Chung Ho, and Phan dragged four chairs from other tables to accommodate all six of them at one table, leaving Bruce and Tina at the other.

"How are the kids?" Tina asked.

"Zara is a mess. She's on meds, seeing a therapist, talking to me. Sitting like a zombie and staring into space mostly. She's not sleeping. I take her to all her doctors' appointments. I'm just trying to make sure she doesn't top herself. It's going to take her a couple of years to put herself back together."

"How about Hari?"

"Hari is the only one I'm not worried about. It's touch and go with Zara. But Hari has changed. Rae though. I don't know what will happen to him."

"Eva will get him through it. She knows trauma," Tina said.

"You kids up for more banners after lunch?" Bruce asked the Dot Heads.

"Yeah!!!" the boys replied in unison.

"How's Roger?" Bruce turned back to Tina.

"Roger is Roger. He's seeking enlightenment and everybody else can go fuck themselves."

"Why do you stay?"

"I don't have enough family in my life to get rid of the only one I have." Tina poured tea into two cups and handed one to Bruce.

"That's not a reason to stay, Tina." Bruce spooned gravy over his plate and hers.

"If in your entire life, only one person ever waited for you, ever wanted you, you stay."

"I'll wait for you."

Tina held her chopsticks in midair, eyes wide, heart pounding. "Bruce! What are you saying?"

"I want you."

"Please don't say it if you don't mean it."

"I was told you're my twin flame."

"Nila!" Tina threw her head back, smiling, before her face crumpled and tears ran down her cheeks. "Sweet Nila."

"I'm warning you," he stared at her. "I'm no bargain."

"I'm no prize either."

Chapter 31

LIBERTY LANDING

The Elders Council agreed that formal celebrations to mark the renaming would take place in April, after the first songbirds began returning from South America. Shoreland Drive was cordoned off at the Square between Anemone and Trillium, with north south traffic rerouted to side roads and parallel streets. White canopy tents lined both sides of the Square. A dozen restaurants on the verge of financial collapse sold food from the tents to serve the crowds attending the daylong celebrations. The vendors had never looked happier. Money in the hand is honey in the lap, Mr. Mehta told the vendors as he wandered past the tents tasting all manner of food and complimenting the cooks.

Other tents were occupied by a petting zoo, a reading room for children, and merchants on the Square, including a psychic, an astrologer, a massage therapist, a numerologist, and an Ayurvedic healer. A handful of residents from the nursing home sold prayer shawls and samosas in support of Kolbe House. A choir and a band from the grade and high school performed throughout the day. A comedy act, Lev and Zve, The Depressed Russians, performed skits. "How are you?" "Not so good."

At dusk, the town's people led by the Elders Council walked in a procession to the nameless pier, which the Council had decided would no longer remain nameless.

A flute choir from Kolbe House marched behind the Elders playing a wistful raga. The Elders gathered around the lighthouse. The townspeople stood hundreds deep from the beginning of the pier to the lighthouse, and on the beach and dunes.

The Mayor arrived promptly at seven, as light drained from the sky and twilight rolled in. Accompanied by a contingent from the City Council and a large crew of media, the Mayor made his way through the crowd to the lighthouse beacon.

At Bruce's nod, the Dot Heads walked through the crowd handing out white candles with drip protectors. The Mayor stood behind a podium and microphone at the base of the lighthouse, his back turned to the lake, facing the crowd on the pier. Gabe, Bruce, Tina, Ivan and Maja flanked the Mayor on each side. Behind them a large white canvas drop cloth was draped around a tall object, on a high podium next to the lighthouse. The Dot Heads, Malik and Kumar, stood on cantilever ladders on each side of the drop cloth.

The Mayor offered his remarks about the most immigrant friendly city in the world and the most immigrant friendly town in the world. He cited the demographics of the town, the number of languages spoken there, the more than hundred nationalities who lived there, and praised their contribution to the life of the city and to the economy.

The Dot Heads, Vin and Anil, walked through the crowd with brass butane candle lighters and lit the candles held up by the gathered. The dark night lit up with tear drops of light.

The Mayor read from a scroll handed to him by a staffer. "We today honor the Founding Father who embodies the immigrant experience in America, who this immigrant community has been moved to identify as the embodiment of the American Experiment."

I therefore submit this Mayoral Proclamation for the records. "Whereas, this town first populated by immigrants was called Azyl Park, Azyl Square, and Azyl Crescent, and whereas the immigrants and their descendants affirm the principals of freedom, equality, and inclusion, and whereas the negative connotations of the word Azyl contradict the expectations of respect and dignity regardless of race or religion, and whereas the people through ballot have chosen to reject racism and prejudice, now therefore I, Mayor of this Great American City do hereby proclaim this 13th day of April 2017, that the town will henceforth and forthwith be named Hamilton Park, its Square shall henceforth and forthwith be named Hamilton Square, and its crescent shall henceforth and forthwith be named Hamilton Crescent. The section of Azyl Park now loosely referred to as the Landing shall henceforth and forthwith be officially named Liberty Landing."

Malik and Kumar whipped the cloth away to reveal a bronze statue of Alexander Hamilton, inspired by the cast in front of the U.S. Treasury. The statue was larger than life, six feet two, although the Founding Father was five feet seven in real life. History flattered him. His ruffled shirt, waist and dress coat, and close fitting leggings gave him the air of a flaneur. But his eyes blazed with intelligence. He was in the prime of his life, a fully actualized American, his hunger and ambition satiated. He didn't look at the lake or the horizon, but inland—at Liberty Landing, at the heartland, at the slice of a continent, at a set of laws, at the speech of a people.

The crowd applauded, whistled, cat called.

Angeline stood in the front row, in a phalanx of media, beaming.

A tabla band and flute choir from Kolbe House played *America the Beautiful*.

The Mayor walked the length of the pier, shaking hands, before he was driven away in a black sedan, his security detail trailing in black SUVs behind him.

Gabe made his way through the press corps gathered near the lighthouse to Angeline.

"You got your way," he said. "You got your man from Nevis his due."

"I'm so thrilled Gabriel," she smiled.

Gabe hadn't seen her for more than four months. It had become harder and harder for him to do without her. In the course of a day, he found himself feeling impoverished, like the kid he had been in Dbayeh. He had to remind himself that he was wealthy beyond measure, but he felt poor, penniless.

"You didn't take my calls. I stopped counting after fifty," Angeline said. "I wanted to comfort you."

"I know. Nothing would've helped."

His father's assassination two months earlier had been momentous. While major US media had given Jairus Khoury's death primetime coverage, with a roster of Israel and pro-Israel experts celebrating "the kill" with rhapsodic praise, he had grappled with his loss alone, in silence. An appeal to his state senator, who remembered Gabe's donation to his first election campaign, led to a fortnight of negotiations between the State Department and the Israeli Ministry of Interior to allow Gabe to claim his father's body for burial in Iqrit. A second donation to the senator's reelection, yielded a seven-day humanitarian visa for Gabe to travel.

The morgue at Kamal Adwan hospital in Beit Lahiya was a cramped room, wide enough to hold a long metal table for shrouding corpses for burial and six body refrigerators flush against three walls. Gabe stood with his back against a refrigerator, a mask over his face, the sweat running down the neck of his shirt and turning into a chilled glaze on his back from the cold and metal. An attendant wearing plastic scrubs and a mask opened a refrigerator and pulled out a rack on wheels. He nodded to Gabe. "Abuk—your father, a martyr," he lifted and peeled back the white sheet covering the body, making a flap near the waist. His father was naked, a fighter's body. A mat of black hair on his chest and arms bristled like astroturf. Frost and a thin dusting of cement coated his cheeks and hair. Mossad had been thorough. His mouth was open and his tongue hung out. Around his neck, an avulsion from the piano wire that had been used to strangle him. A chain of dried blood, pink fat and white connective tissue leered at Gabe. On his father's chest, three bullet wounds, gaping like Christ's stigmata. Gabe wanted to retch. He was livid with his father.

"Blessed be his memory," the attendant said in Arabic.

"He was a fool," Gabe thought.

"You will take him to Iqrit?"

Yes, Gabe nodded and turned to walk towards the door. "Get him ready, I'll come back with a van."

"I am alone. I need help to prepare him," the attendant said.

Gabe drew out his wallet from his shirt pocket and opened it. "Hire somebody. What do you want? Dinar? Dollar, Shekel?"

"You could help me."

Gabe pulled out a sheaf of dollar bills. "Here's two hundred dollars. Get him ready. I'll give you the rest when I come back."

Gabe hired two security guards recommended by the American consulate in Jerusalem and drove his father to Iqrit, 104 miles of efficient Israeli highway that put him in mind of the Autobahn. It was a Monday and the hilltop cemetery of the Church of Our Lady was desolate. A trio of young Palestinian men, squatters in the church exercising their right to return to their ancestral home, greeted them.

"I need a priest," Gabe told the men about his father.

"Father Elias will be here on Sunday," one of them said.

"I don't have that kind of time," Gabe said, and opened his wallet.

"Khallas!" "Your father was our hero."

They went inside the church and returned with two shovels, a pickaxe, and a trowel. The men helped Gabe and the guards dig a hole. They worked silently until one of the men jumped in the hole and said, Kafia. Enough. They lowered Jairus' pine casket into the ground. As the young men prayed for his father, *It is not a struggle to go back home because we all go back home in the end*, Gabe said, "The devil take you."

"How are you?" Gabe asked Angeline. In a mere seventeen weeks, he had been splintered, and oriented for a different future. He wanted to tell her everything that had happened to him. His story. Only to her.

"I've been busy. In Nevis for my final rewrite. It was good to be with my kid." "I'm done, right?" she turned to a line producer. He gave her a thumbs up. She handed her microphone to a grip.

While she had been rewriting, the spirit of Alexander Hamilton had been invoked by legions of Americans and several members of the Electoral College to stop a dangerous demagogue from assuming the Presidency.

The Federalist Papers: No. 68

The Mode of Electing the President

From the New York Packet.

Friday, March 14, 1788.

HAMILTON

To the People of the State of New York:

THE mode of appointment of the Chief Magistrate of the United States is almost the only part of the system, of any consequence, which has escaped without severe censure, or which has received the slightest mark of approbation from its opponents. The most plausible of these, who has appeared in print, has even deigned to admit that the election of the President is pretty well guarded.1 I venture somewhat further, and hesitate not to affirm, that if the manner of it be not perfect, it is at least excellent. It unites in an eminent degree all the advantages, the union of which was to be wished for.

It was desirable that the sense of the people should operate in the choice of the person to whom so important a trust was to be confided. This end will be answered by committing the right of making it, not to any preestablished body, but to men chosen by the people for the special purpose, and at the particular conjuncture.

It was equally desirable, that the immediate election should be made by men most capable of analyzing the qualities adapted to the station, and acting under circumstances favorable to deliberation, and to a judicious combination of all the reasons and inducements which were proper to govern their choice. A small number of persons, selected by their fellow-citizens from the general mass, will be most likely to possess the information and discernment requisite to such complicated investigations.

It was also peculiarly desirable to afford as little opportunity as possible to tumult and disorder. This evil was not least to be dreaded in the election of a magistrate, who was to have so important an agency in the administration of the government as the President of the United States. But the precautions which have been so happily concerted in the system under consideration, promise an effectual security against this mischief. The choice of SEVERAL, to form an intermediate body of electors, will be much less apt to convulse the community with any extraordinary or violent movements, than the choice of ONE who was himself to be the final object of the public wishes. And as the electors, chosen in each State, are to assemble and vote in the State in which they are chosen, this detached and divided situation will expose them much less to heats and ferments, which might be communicated from them to the people, than if they were all to be convened at one time, in one place.

Nothing was more to be desired than that every practicable obstacle should be opposed to cabal, intrigue, and corruption. These most deadly adversaries of republican government might naturally have been expected to make their approaches from more than one querter, but chiefly from the desire in foreign powers to gain an improper ascendant in our councils. How could they better gratify this, than by raising a creature of their own to the chief magistracy of the Union? But the convention have guarded against all danger of this sort, with the most provident and judicious attention. They have not made the appointment of the President to depend on any preexisting bodies of men, who might be tampered with beforehand to prostitute their votes; but they have referred it in the first instance to an immediate act of the people of America, to be exerted in the choice of persons for the temporary and sole purpose of making the appointment. And they have excluded from eligibility to this trust, all those who from situation might be suspected of too great devotion to the President in office. No senator, representative, or other person holding a place of trust or profit under the United States, can be of the numbers of the electors. Thus without corrupting the body of the people, the immediate agents in the election will at least enter upon the task free from any sinister bias. Their transient existence, and their detached situation, already taken notice of, afford a satisfactory prospect of their continuing so, to the conclusion of it. The business of corruption, when it is to embrace so considerable a number of men, requires time as well as means. Nor would it be found easy suddenly to embark them, dispersed as they would be over thirteen States, in any combinations founded upon motives, which though they could not properly be denominated corrupt, might yet be of a nature to mislead them from their duty.

Another and no less important desideratum was, that the Executive should be independent for his continuance in office on all but the people themselves. He might otherwise be tempted to sacrifice his duty to his complaisance for those whose favor was necessary to the duration of his official consequence. This advantage will also be secured, by making his re-election to depend on a special body of representatives, deputed by the society for the single purpose of making the important choice.

All these advantages will happily combine in the plan devised by the convention; which is, that the people of each State shall choose a number of persons as electors, equal to the number of senators and representatives of such State in the national government, who shall assemble within the State, and vote for some fit person as President. Their votes, thus given, are to be transmitted to the seat of the national government, and the person who may happen to have a majority of the whole number of votes will be the President. But as a majority of the votes might not always happen to centre in one man, and as it might be unsafe to permit less than a majority to be conclusive, it is provided that, in such a contingency, the House of Representatives shall select out of the candidates who shall have the five highest number of votes, the man who in their opinion may be best qualified for the office.

The process of election affords a moral certainty, that the office of President will never fall to the lot of any man who is not in an eminent degree endowed with the requisite qualifications. Talents for low intrigue, and the little arts of popularity, may alone suffice to elevate a man to the first honors in a single State; but it will require other talents, and a different kind of merit, to establish him in the esteem and confidence of the whole Union, or of so considerable a portion of it as would be necessary to make him a successful candidate for the distinguished office of President of the United States. It will not be too strong to say, that there will be a constant probability of seeing the station filled by characters pre-eminent for ability and virtue. And this will be thought no inconsiderable recommendation of the Constitution, by those who are able to estimate the share which the executive in every government must necessarily have in its good or ill administration. Though we cannot acquiesce in the political heresy of the poet who says: "For forms of government let fools contest That which is best administered is best," yet we may safely pronounce, that the true test of a good government is its aptitude and tendency to produce a good administration.

PUBLIUS.

Angeline and Gabriel walked away from the lighthouse. Angeline trailed her hand above the top guardrail hemming the walkway that stretched from the lighthouse to the mouth of the pier.

"Angeline," Gabriel stopped and faced her. "I need to know if you care about me or not. If not, please tell me now." He knew how to deal with pain. He'd get over her as he got over Farah.

"I more than care about you. I love you. But how can it work? I love my son. I miss him so much. He's still young. I want to be with him," "How can I have you both?" she looked up at Gabe.

"You don't have to choose. Be with me and bring him back here."

"I can't. I won't!" Her face was set in a burn, her eyes hard, her jaw clenched, a fury ready to erupt.

"Bring him home, Angeline."

"Don't talk to me about home! There is no home for my son here!" her voice trembled with anger. She stared at the water behind him.

"You're taking anecdotal evidence and drawing wrong conclusions from it."

"Black men getting killed for nothing is not anecdotal evidence. It is a fact. Incontrovertible!" she shouted. She kept the evidence in a folder marked "Never" on her laptop. Whenever she read news online of a police killing of a black man, she saved the document as a pdf and dragged it into the folder—309 just this year.

"Waking up every morning and stepping out in the world is a risk. According to your logic, we should never go out," Gabe said.

"Not we. You're fine. You'll always be fine. I'll be okay because I can pass. But the black male has to wake up daily with the odds stacked against him," she said.

"Like President Obama, you mean?"

"He's different."

"No he's not. He just decided to stake a claim and take possession despite the long odds." Gabe looked at the statue and then at her. "Stand by your principles. You're breaking faith with Alexander Hamilton if you don't. Bring him back, Angeline."

"I want him safe. Is that too much to ask?" a sob caught in her throat.

"He'll be okay here. I can't say that about someplace else, but he'll be safe here."

"You say that. But can you promise me that?" her voice quivered. "Can you promise me that Andre will be safe here in this America?"

The rise of the rabid right, the KKK, the white supremacists, the Alt-Right frightened her. Where before she worried for her son's safety, now she worried about her own as well.

"The chances are good that he'll be as safe here as I am. As you are. As the Dot Heads are," he pointed at the boys with their red tilaks. "Look at me," he circled his arms around her waist.

Angeline arched her back and looked up, forehead furrowed, heart weighted down with the lead of worry. She knew too much. A fearless, relentless researcher and obsessive archivist, she hoarded information—in her head, in her soul, in her hard drive. Her memory was never full. There was always more to archive. Just when she thought she'd read everything there was to know about slavery, a new article freshly enraged her. "Celebrated father of gynecology experimented on slave women without their permission and without anesthesia." She saved the article into a new folder—Keeping The Accounts. Her "Never" folder was a crypt and a registry. Dontre Hamilton, 31, a paranoid schizophrenic, for disturbing the peace of coffee drinkers at Starbucks; Trayvon Martin, 17, for wearing a hoodie; Eric Garner, 43, for selling loose cigarettes; John Crawford, 22, for holding a toy BB gun at Walmart; Michael Brown, 18 while walking; Ezell Ford, 25, a mentally ill man for reasons unknown; Akai Gurley, 28, while walking down a stairwell; Tamir Rice, 12, for holding a toy gun; Rumain Brisbon, 34, for holding a pill bottle; Jerame Reid, 36, for stepping out of a car with his hands in front of his chest; Tony Robinson, 19, for reasons unknown; Phillip White, 32, while in medical distress; Eric Harris, 44, killed by reserve officer who mistook his own gun for a Taser; Walter Scott, 50, shot in the back for running away from a traffic stop; Freddie Gray, 25, after being stopped without cause.

"You cannot live in fear. You have to trust life. Trust me. Alright?" Gabe said. "Alright?" he lifted her chin. "I'll take care of you both."

"Don't lie to me. Be real with me. Do you know how to love us? Do you have it in you to take care of me and Andre?"

"Yes."

"I don't believe you."

"I didn't before. Now I do." His had been a journey of exorcism, of ridding himself of phantoms and specters, wounds and fury. He wanted now only to win her heart, to cleave to her, to abide in her.

What would she do? She loved him. She wanted Andre with her. She was tired of her anger, tired of her fear. She wanted to trust life, trust Gabriel, begin a dream with him.

The months since his father's death had compelled Gabe, inexplicably, to search for his father in the media coverage. He didn't understand why he cared. He had hated his father, loathed him, excised him from his psyche, yet he shuddered awake in bed, haunted by the necklace of blood and gore around his father's neck, The Lion, Mossad had called him. "I could see the whites of the target's eyes. I could smell the fear on the target's breath. I plunged a knife into the target, then I used my silencer. The target was still alive, still fighting, enraged. I finished the target off with the piano wire, 18 gauge. Clean as a whistle."

Gabe knew what he had to do. He would invest in his father's mission with his resources, without his father's violence. He would see what he could do for what remained of a people, what remained of a nation. "What Palestinians want, what Palestinians ever wanted, is your American Dream," Jairus Khoury had written in his last letter to Gabe.

They walked towards Bruce and Tina, Rae and Eva, and Hari and Zara, gathered near the statue. Gabe introduced Angeline to Bruce, Eva, and the children.

"How are you?" Gabe shook Rae's hand.

Rae shrugged and looked down at his shoes.

"We're fine." Eva looked at Rae and smiled back at Gabe.

It had been almost nine months since Nila's death but Rae was still floundering. That morning, Eva had woken up to the sound of grinding metal outside the window of the guest bedroom that opened onto the Oberois deck.

"Treat this like your home, it's more comfortable than the bunker you're in," Rae had said, when he had first invited her to stay the night several months earlier. Eva was mystified by the offer of the guestroom, but accepted. She needed a daily respite from Kolbe House. And she needed clarity from Rae. She'd find out living with him, sharing his home. What was she to him other than his walking companion on the dunes, his grief and trauma counselor, his friend, his dinner partner in a broken foursome?

"What do you need from me?" she had asked.

"If you love me, don't leave," he'd said. He promised her that he would learn to love her as she deserved to be loved, once his shattered heart had forgiven God.

She'd climbed out of bed that morning, slipped into her robe, walked through the living room, and opened the sliding door to the terrace. The solarium's roof was retracted and she could hear birds and waves. "Good morning," she said, as she walked towards the wrought iron table. Rae tilted his chin up and then down. "Pour me one too?" he said. She prepared two mugs, placed one near him, sat down, and watched as he filled one of the feeder flasks with birdseed mix. When he finished replacing the flask in its suspended frame, he turned around and looked up at the sky. A small flock of sparrows descended on the feeder, the sound of their wing beats creating a meta sound. "Oh! Wow! Look at that one," Rae rocked back on his heels. A startlingly radiant songbird with a blood red body and jet black feathers and beak, a Scarlet Tanager, circled the terrace in a wide loop. If Nila had an avatar, that resplendent beauty would be it. Eva was pleased to see him care about such a small wonder. He'll be okay, she thought. An hour later, however, while sitting down to lunch with Zara and Hari, she could sense Rae withdraw, his body in front of them, his soul leaving it for a sweeter, more perfect homeland.

"Who came up with Liberty Landing?" Eva slipped her hand around Rae's arm and asked the group.

"Angeline was on a roll," Tina teased Angeline. "And you, kiddo," she turned to Hari. "You got into all the right schools. Where will you go?"

"Haven't decided yet. I may stay here and go to U of C."

"Whatever you decide will be okay with your Dad I'm sure," Tina said, looking at Rae. "We're so proud of you Hari."

Hari thanked the group and drifted off to the lighthouse. His mother's death had given him his future. Where everything before her death seemed gauzy, lived behind folds of white voile in an innocent forgetting, what lay ahead had definite edges, blunt solidity. He would spend the next three decades studying the human heart, the first developing organ, the immigrant of organs, the slave of workers, that beats a hundred thousand times a day, thirty-five million times a year, two and a half billion times in a lifetime. The organ of love. The organ of devotion. The organ of intense sorrow. He would work to solve the biggest mystery in cardiology, sudden cardiac arrest in healthy people. His mother's death had birthed him, made him once-dead, twice-born. An essential part of him never disembarked from that plane. He would try for the rest of his life to resurrect his mother.

"I don't want him to stay. He needs to go forge his life." Rae said.

"Let him stay, Rae. There's time enough to go. He needs to be with his family right now. He'll leave when he's ready," Bruce said.

"You both look good," Tina smiled at Eva and Rae. "Don't they babe?" she turned to Bruce.

"Indeed." Bruce agreed.

"Eva keeps me alive," Rae drew Eva by the waist, closer to him. They docked like a plug into a socket. It was a pale, delicate, quiet thing, his feelings for Eva, but it would be enough. He carried Nila inside him, contained her in the reliquary of his heart, in the ossuary of his soul, in the sepulcher of his mind, in the mausoleum of his veins. It would never be enough.

"Zara, you look like you swallowed the moon." Tina said, admiring Zara's belly.

"When are you due?" Angeline asked.

"Any day now," Zara held her hands under her belly. Her night with Rishi was significant, though she hadn't expected a baby. When she'd told her father, he had been surprised. "But when? I watched you like a hawk while we were in India."

"In Goa, at the hotel."

"Are you planning to inform him?"

"I'm not sure. He was an innocent party. It was all me."

"He has a right to know."

"Maybe. I'll think about it."

"You should keep the baby, Zara. Mom would want you to," Rae had said.

"I mean to," Zara had said.

In her grief over her mother's death, Zara had turned to the Bhagavad Gita for consolation. Never a religious person, she found comfort in Hinduism's convictions about life and death and reincarnation. On the battlefield, Krishna tells Arjuna, "As the embodied soul continually passes, in this body from boyhood to youth to old age, the soul likewise passes into another body at death. The self-realized soul is not bewildered by such a change." Zara wanted to believe that her mother's soul had reincarnated in the baby in her womb.

In the years that followed, as Rae and Zara and Hari learned to live without Nila, the saving grace would be Zara's baby, a girl named after her grandmother. She would give them a sense of meaning and purpose, that they were not a family cast adrift in a cruel and hostile universe marked by unspeakable trauma and grief, but a family of blood and bone and love and memory. And Eva would draw her prayer shawl around the family she had found midway to midway.

Gabe and Angeline, Bruce and Tina, Rae and Eva, Hari and Zara, David and Nadia, Nila, and Alexander Hamilton. All of them. All of us. This is how we journey, cross borders, risk our hearts, give our lives, find home and heaven in people. A foot fall at a time, in faith, in hope, in love. Our stories inside us, inside each other.

"We die containing a richness of lovers and tribes, tastes we have swallowed, bodies we have plunged into and swum up as if rivers of wisdom, characters we have climbed into as if trees, fears we have hidden in as if caves. I wish for all this to be marked on my body when I am dead. I believe in such cartography - to be marked by nature. We are communal histories, communal books. We are not owned or monogamous in our taste or experience."

Michael Ondaatje
The English Patient

"… I will never regret that I chose to remember."

Ibtisam Barakat
Tasting the Sky

ACKNOWLEDGMENTS

My gratitude to the Great American Novelist, Bob Shacochis for encouraging me and teaching me about story as I began this book. I bow to you, Teacher.

Many thanks to the gifted writers who read my drafts: Vanina Marsot, Thaila Ramanujam, and Tom Silva; and to Dr. Stephanie Han, writer and literature scholar, for contextualizing *Liberty Landing* within the literature of exile, migrancy, and cultural translation.

Namaste to my special angel, Dan Tyrrell.

Many thanks to LaVonne Kosmen for cover art design, and Nick Caya and team for book art and science.

During the writing of this book from 2010 to 2017, I read widely and obsessively, and did extensive research of primary, secondary, and tertiary sources to construct my fictional universe and animate my characters. When I fell in love with a sentence that I wished to share with readers, I deployed it in service of the story. I list all my sources below. If there are any omissions of references or improper citations and use, please contact Mirare Press at ariapr@sbcglobal.net for inclusion or correction in the next edition of this book.

"In the heartland, on a slice of the continent, in a set of laws, in the speech of a people," is from John Dos Passos' *USA*.

"How nice it must be to feel nothing and still get full credit for being alive," is from Kurt Vonnegut's *Slaughterhouse-Five*.

"Sooner or later one must choose a side if one is to remain human," is from Graham Greene's *The Quiet American*.

"Living in Japan … is like an asthmatic on an inhaler for the first time," is recalled from memory from a New York Times article quote from the 1990s that I've been unable to locate.

The Federalist Papers: No 68 is from Alexander Hamilton's collected writings.

With the exception of "The Ant's Belly" letter from Alexander Hamilton, his letter of 1774 quoting "The Didascalicon of Hugh of Saint Victor," the chapter Histoire, and purported letters of Elizabeth Schuyler Hamilton which are all fictions imagined by this author, the Hamilton references in *Liberty Landing* are a result of researching, interpreting, or quoting from Library of Congress and public domain information and from Ron Chernow's splendid biography of *Alexander Hamilton*.

The letters of the Founding Fathers are quoted from their diaries and writings or from public domain information.

Some torture victims' testimonials in the Kolbe House chapter were sourced and fictionalized from real torture survivors' testimonials.

La Jaula de Oro (Golden Cage) is a song about Mexican immigrants in the US written by Enrico Franco, performed by Los Tigres del Norte.

S. Yizhar's village name, Khirbet Khizeh, is resurrected as a literary device.

The true story of Fadil Fejzic of Bosnia was reported in media worldwide.

"Midway to Midway" is a riff from "In the midway of this mortal life" from Dante's *Inferno*.

The story of Native American burial mounds is from news reporting in Illinois media.

The concept of America as fusion chamber was first introduced by the writer, Bharati Mukherjee.

The Twin Flame theory is sourced from public domain information and a blog by Antera on soulevolution.org

The Saptapadi is the Vedic rite in Hindu marriage ceremonies.

The history of Iqrit is sourced from chroniclers of Iqrit history.

The history of Israel and Palestine are sourced from various media including film, diaries, books, essays, and articles.

Grace Halsell's *Journey to Jerusalem* offered keen observations about refugee life.

References to Israeli nighttime raids are sourced from the film, Gatekeepers.

"I've been sitting on my suitcase ..." was inspired by the poem, "Diary of a Palestinian Wound" by Mahmoud Darwish.

"Mount Carmel is in me and on my eyelashes the grass of Galilee" is paraphrased from the poem "Diary of a Palestinian Wound" by Mahmoud Darwish.

The Baha'i *Prayer for the Dead* is set in italics.

Graveside prayers are from Soren Kierkegaard's writings on love from *"Works of Love," and "Upbuilding Discourses."*

"My feet are lacerated, homelessness has exhausted me," is by Palestinian poet, Taufiq Sayigh

Alexander Hamilton